Love Still Stands

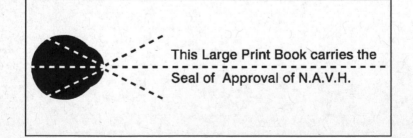

This Large Print Book carries the
Seal of Approval of N.A.V.H.

LOVE STILL STANDS

KELLY IRVIN

THORNDIKE PRESS
A part of Gale, Cengage Learning

LP

 GALE
CENGAGE Learning·

Detroit • New York • San Francisco • New Haven, Conn • Waterville, Maine • London

GALE
CENGAGE Learning®

LIBRARY OF CONGRESS CATALOGING-IN-PUBLICATION DATA

Irvin, Kelly.
    Love still stands / by Kelly Irvin. — Large print edition.
       pages ; cm. — (The new hope Amish series ; #1)
    ISBN-13: 978-1-4104-6178-0 (hardcover)
    ISBN-10: 1-4104-6178-5 (hardcover)
    1. Women teachers—Fiction. 2. People with disabilities—Fiction. 3. Amish—Missouri—Fiction. 4. Large type books. I. Title.
    PS3609.R82L67 2013b
    813'.6—dc23   2013035140

Published in 2014 by arrangement with Harvest House Publishers

Printed in the United States of America
1 2 3 4 5 6 7 18 17 16 15 14

To Tim, Erin, and Nicholas
Love always

Be joyful in hope, patient in affliction,
faithful in prayer.
ROMANS 12:12 (NIV)

My grace is sufficient for you, for my
power is made perfect in weakness.
2 CORINTHIANS 12:9 (NIV)

THE NEW HOPE FAMILIES

Luke & Leah
Shirack
William
Joseph
Esther & Martha
(twins)
Jebediah
Bethel Graber
(Leah's sister)

Aaron & Mary
Troyer
Matthew
Molly
Reuben
Abraham & Alexander
(twins)
Ella
Laura

Silas & Katie
Christner
Jesse
Simon
Martin
Phoebe
Elam
Hannah
Lydia
Sarah
Elijah Christner
(Silas's brother)
Ida Weaver
(Katie's sister)

Benjamin & Irene
Knepp
Hiram
Daniel
Adah
Melinda
Abram
Joanna
Jonathan

Thomas & Emma
Brennaman
Eli
Rebecca
Caleb
Lilah
Mary & Lillie
  Shirack
(Emma's sisters)

Peter & Cynthia
Daugherty
Rufus
Enos
Deborah
Rachel
John

Mark
Phillip
Ruth
Naomi

Tobias & Edna
Daugherty
Jacob
Michael
Ephraim
Nathaniel
Margaret
Isabel

PREFACE

An author's imagination grows in fertile ground. The New Hope, Missouri, of *Love Still Stands* is a fictitious town that sprang from my imagination. The idea that a town would reject a group of Amish families blossomed from a simple "what if?" What if they weren't met with open arms? Let's be perfectly clear, however. I don't know of any real town in Missouri where this has happened. I do know there have been cases of "Amish bashing" in other places, which led me to the premise of this story. This storyline gave me the opportunity to explore what bigotry does to its victims, but also what love, kindness, forgiveness, and Christlike turning of the other cheek do for bigots. While I was writing this story, my husband and I rented a car and drove 1,500 miles on the highways and back roads of Missouri. Everywhere we were met with the lovely hospitality of the great Show-Me State. My thanks to the kind folks in Jamesport who shared their observations and experiences with us. The same in Bolivar, Stockton Lake State Park, and Branson. My husband is really sorry he scared the Park Ranger with his Fox 29 TV cap. We truly enjoyed our stay.

Also a word of thanks to Cathy Richmond, who kindly shared tips about physical therapy with me. Any mistakes in this arena are mine and mine alone. That also holds true for the descriptions of the Amish way of life. Please remember that every Amish district has its own set of rules, the New Hope Amish included.

I hope you enjoy this story as much as I enjoyed writing it. As always, my thanks to Harvest House Publishers, Kathleen Kerr, Mary Sue Seymour, and the multitude who have helped me on this writing journey. Tim, thank you for being my driver, traveling companion, best friend, and the guy willing to do the talking when the introvert in me chickens out.

Let all the glory be to our Lord and Savior Jesus Christ.

CHAPTER 1

Bethel Graber longed for the fresh air of a buggy ride. She craned her aching neck from side to side, trying to ignore the pain that radiated from her leg after hours of watching the white lines on the asphalt whip toward her and then vanish underneath the van. Pain accompanied her daily now. Crammed between her nieces' car seats, she had no room to evade it. Instead, she breathed through it, inhaling stale air scented with diapers and little-boy sweat. The girls' chubby cheeks and sleepy smiles made her want to pat their rosy faces, but she didn't dare for fear they'd wake and the squalling would begin again.

The drive across southern Kansas to a tiny town in Missouri called New Hope should've taken under five hours, but the children weren't used to traveling in a car. Poor William suffered from car sickness and Joseph needed to stop for the restroom at every gas station along the way. Fortunately, their driver seemed to have a limitless supply of patience. Bethel, on the other hand, had plumbed the depths of hers.

"Are we getting close?" She leaned forward to make herself heard over the rumble of the van's engine. She didn't want to wake Jebediah either. The youngest of Leah and Luke's brood had cried a good part of the first two hours of the drive. Blessed silence, indeed. "Shouldn't we be getting close?"

"You're as bad as the *kinner.*" Leah rubbed her eyes. Her older sister had managed to keep her apron spotless and her chestnut hair smooth around her crisp prayer *kapp,* but dark smudges under her eyes made her look bruised and weary. "We'll be there when we get there."

"Your sister's right." Luke adjusted his arms around Joseph and William, who slept burrowed against their *daed*'s chest, one seated on either side of him. "But having made this trip a few times now, I can tell you we're about to go around a bend in the road, turn right, and make our way down a long, bumpy dirt road. At the end, you'll see our new home."

Our new home. Our new start.

Leah's nose wrinkled, and her lips turned down in a thin line. She faced the window as if interested in the landscape, more and more different from the flat plains they'd left behind. Bethel did the same, anxious for a glimpse of this new home. Towering oak, hickory, and sturdy spruce trees vied for space along the road, which seemed to rise and fall as the terrain became more hilly. The trees were dressed in autumn colors, their orange and red leaves brilliant against a radiant blue sky overhead. The spaces between the trees had their own decorations, mostly in yellows, purples, and pinks — brown-eyed susans, sunflowers, sweet clover, morning glories, and tall thistle that hadn't given up their colorful blooms to autumn weather just yet. In comparison, her memories of Bliss Creek already seemed drab.

"It's pretty, Daed. It's pretty, isn't it?" Yawning widely, Joseph wiggled from Luke's grasp and sat up. "I can't wait to see the house. Are the horses there? And the chickens and the pigs?"

"Hush, son, you'll wake your *bruders* and *schweschders.*" Luke tipped Joseph's straw hat forward on his head. "The livestock will be there, as I told you before — three times — and your clothes and the furniture. It'll all be waiting for us to unpack and start working."

13

His gentle tone and good-natured smile endeared her brother-in-law to Bethel as it had many times in the past. Luke was a good man, a good husband, and a good father. Leah didn't seem to register her husband's words or her son's question. She returned to her knitting, the needles clacking, the blue and gray yarn sliding smoothly between them. God had showered the woman with blessings. Yet she seemed only to notice the half-empty glass.

Bethel tried to stymie her thoughts. They served no purpose. God made her a teacher; her sister, a mother. She tried, as always, to ignore the niggling thought that attempted to worm its way into her mind. *If only it were reversed.*

Stop it. She should be thankful for the short time she'd been honored to be in the classroom. Still, it hurt to think about her new circumstances. Now, with her injuries, she had neither children of her own nor scholars to teach and mold and shape.

God's plan?

What is it, Gott? *What is Your plan?* Bethel slapped a hand to her mouth, even though she hadn't spoken aloud. *Sorry, Gott, I'm sorry. I don't have to know Your plan for me. I have faith in You. You have a plan.*

Sitting up straighter, she smoothed her

14

apron, determined to be content with her lot. Better she should focus on helping Leah, easing her burden, with five children and only the boys old enough to be of any help. They could weed or gather eggs and pick vegetables in the garden, but the laundry, sewing, cooking, and cleaning? Leah had her hands full. Somehow, Bethel would help.

"When we get there, I can get the kitchen clean so we can start unpacking pots and pans." Bethel offered an olive branch in the unspoken fray. "That way you can make up the pallets of blankets. Tomorrow when the furniture is unloaded, we can start putting together the beds."

"It only looks pretty now, Joseph. The leaves will drop soon, and the snow will start." Her tone soft, almost resigned, Leah spoke as if she hadn't heard Bethel's offer. Her gaze didn't waver from her knitting. "We won't have time to plant a garden, much less harvest anything before it's too cold. We should've waited until spring to move."

"The bishop decided." Luke's patient tone mirrored the one he'd used with his seven-year-old son. "We're a little late, but we can still plant winter wheat and rye."

"You said yourself the later we plant, the

15

poorer the yield —"

"There. There's the turn." Luke cut his *fraa*'s sentence short. He leaned in front of her and pointed. "Turn right, Michael."

"I know. This isn't my first time, remember?" Michael Baldwin, Luke's favorite driver and a friend who would be missed when he returned to Bliss Creek, navigated onto the dirt road with ruts so deep the van bounced and rocked. "Whoa, easy does it."

They slowed to a crawl. To a speed more appropriate for a buggy. Bethel smiled at the thought. She wished again she *were* in a buggy. Then she could take the time to enjoy this new scenery, to smell the smells of her new home and hear the birds that surely perched in these trees. She needed this new beginning. She needed to leave behind the images of the furious storm that sent school desks flying through the air. She needed to forget the sounds of the screaming children on the day her career as a teacher had ended and her life on damaged legs had begun.

"For now, Joseph is right. It *is* pretty. And I like snow. We had plenty of that in Kansas too." She managed to keep defiance from her voice. "It's a good new start."

Her brother-in-law grinned at her. It made him appear much younger than his thirty

16

years. Under the brim of his straw hat tufts of his walnut-colored hair stuck out, making him look like Joseph, a boy enjoying an adventure. Bethel grinned back. She saw her hope and excitement mirrored in his face.

"You're right. A new start." He leaned toward Leah as if he would touch her, but he didn't. She didn't look up from her knitting, but her frown deepened. "Look out there, Leah. That's the land we'll farm in the spring. We'll have a bountiful crop and all will be well."

Still, Leah didn't look up. The van rounded another bend in the road. Bethel strained to see the house and the barn and the land that would be their new home, their new start.

"What's that?" Luke scooted forward on his seat. "What is that on the front of the house?"

Bethel saw the semi that held all their belongings first. She saw the animal trailers that held the horses and the buggies. Then she saw the house and the reason for Luke's dismay.

At first she couldn't understand. This house? For this place they'd driven almost four hundred miles? Someone had shattered the glass in every window, first and second floor. Neon orange spray paint marred the once white facade, the wide strokes winding their way between the shattered window-panes in wide, arching loops like a snake in search of its prey. The loops ended in words written in huge letters. The edges of the windows had been blackened by fire that appeared to have burst out from the inside. Trash littered the porch and the front door dangled from its hinges.

None of them spoke, the silence filled only with their ragged breathing.

Luke withdrew his arm from around William. The little boy rolled away, then sat up, his eyes wide at the abrupt awakening. "Daed?"

"We're here." Luke's tone had lost its gentleness. His jaw worked as he undid his seatbelt as if to get out. "Stay in the van — all of you."

Michael looked up at the rearview mirror. "Hang tight. We're almost there."

"I have to —"

"We're almost there, Luke."

"What's it say?" Bethel managed to breathe the words even though she had no air in her lungs. Their precious new start had gone up in flames, it seemed. "Those orange words. I can't tell what it says."

"It says *Go home.*" Leah's voice barely

rose above a whisper. "This is our new start?"

CHAPTER 2

Elijah Christner shifted from one foot to another. He breathed in and out. *Steady.* The moment had come. The dusty white van would arrive in minutes, chugging toward him over the pitted dirt road. Why he felt so responsible for the condition of his friend Luke's new home, he couldn't say. He'd only arrived himself. The damage to the façade had been shocking, but the inside contained far worse damage. Whether it could be salvaged or should be razed remained a question in his mind. The Shiracks, like the Christners, had come a long way for this new start. They might have to dig deeper for it, work harder, start from scratch. He pushed the thought away. A little spray paint and an indoor bonfire couldn't stop the likes of this load of Plain folks from doing what they set out to do.

"You want me to break the news?" Silas chewed on a blade of grass, his beard, more silver than blond now, bobbing. "I don't mind."

"I'll do it. Luke's my friend." Elijah forced himself to smile at his older brother. "You know Luke. He'll take it in stride, like he does everything else. It's Leah . . ."

Silas shook his head. "It's not our place to judge."

"I'm not judging —"

"Here they are."

In a cloud of dust and a spurt of gravel, the van rolled to a stop. Luke climbed out first. He leaned into the vehicle and exchanged muted words with Leah. After a moment, he turned, his face a mask of contained emotion, and strode toward Elijah and Silas. Leah got down on her own and then released the little ones, who were strapped into car seats. The older boys jumped out and raced about like foals set free from their stalls while the twins tottered on short legs, unsteady from the hours in the van.

"What happened here?" Luke stomped toward the house. "How did this happen?"

"We don't know." Silas spoke before Elijah had a chance. His big brother did that often. One of the challenges of being the youngest of ten siblings. Everyone spoke for him. "It was like this when Elijah arrived to check on the livestock. He came to find me right away."

Luke turned to Elijah. "Is it as bad inside?"

Elijah nodded. No sense sugarcoating it.

Kicking aside empty soda cans and beer bottles, Luke and Silas trudged up the steps. From the back they looked like twins with their blue cotton shirts, suspenders, broad backs, and black pants. Her tone stern, Leah admonished the boys to watch the girls and followed.

Elijah started to go with her, but movement in the van caught his gaze. He'd forgotten Bethel had made the journey with her sister. He pulled the sliding door wider. Bethel sat on the backseat, struggling to pull metal crutches from the cargo area behind the seat. He leaned in. "Let me help you."

"I can get them." Her smile, with its accompanying dimples, softened the brusqueness of her words. She'd always been quick with a smile. "But *danki*."

"Not from that angle, you can't."

Ignoring her protestations, he jogged around to the back and jerked open the double doors. Boxes of clothes, a cooler, and a large picnic basket crowded the small space. The crutches were wedged to one side. Bethel twisted, her arm over the back of the seat, her face contorted with pain. She continued to tug, but to no avail.

"I've got it." Elijah tugged from his end. Bethel let go. A crutch flew up and smacked him in the nose. "Ouch! *Ach.*"

"I'm so sorry!" Bethel's fair skin turned beet red. "I didn't mean to hit you. I'm sorry."

"It's not a fatal wound. It's just a little bump." Rubbing his nose with one hand, Elijah retrieved the crutches with the other and trotted back to the side door. "Let me help you out."

"That's nice of you, but I can manage." An undercurrent of stubborn insistence ran through the polite words. "I don't need help."

"It's too big a step."

Without thinking he put his hands on her waist and swung her gently from the van. Their faces were level for a brief second. He saw something in her expression he couldn't read at first, and then it squeezed his heart. A deep sadness resided in Bethel Graber's face.

He hesitated. Her blue eyes widened. Suddenly aware of her clean scent and her slender waist under his fingers, he set her on her feet on a shaggy carpet of grass that needed to be mowed.

He'd never been this close to her before. It surprised him to find she stood nearly as tall as he did. Not many women did. Her blonde hair shone at the edges of her kapp. The red dissipated from her face, leaving her fair skin even whiter than before. Lips pressed together, she ducked her head, grabbed the crutches he'd leaned against the van, and thrust them under her arms.

After a second or two, she met his gaze. "Danki." She swung the crutches forward in an awkward gait, her right leg dragging. "Don't do that again. Ever."

"I was only trying to help." Baffled by the emotion he'd seen in her face, Elijah struggled for words. "I didn't mean to offend you."

"I'm not an invalid."

It wasn't his touch that offended her — he couldn't take time to contemplate why that realization pleased him — it was the idea that he thought she needed his help. Everyone needed help sometimes. It wasn't a sign of weakness, only humanity. "That doesn't mean you don't need —"

The sound of sirens in the distance interrupted his response. Just as well. She obviously meant what she said. No helping. Elijah would find it hard to comply with that order. Having spent the last few years caring for his parents made helping second nature for him. Bethel's pretty face wouldn't make it any easier. Her disability didn't touch the loveliness of her eyes or her smile — even though she seemed so much sadder than when he'd seen her at prayer services and the singings. Just as he was.

"Is that an ambulance?" She pulled herself from the shadow of the van and peered at the car racing toward them. The uneven ground caused her to stumble. Elijah lifted his hand to help her, but then let it drop. No helping. "Is someone hurt?"

"No. The semi driver called the sheriff's office on his cell phone." Elijah put his hand to his forehead instead, cupping his fingers against the sun as he tried to see the car racing toward them. "There's more damage inside the house. The driver said it needed to be reported."

"What kind of damage?"

"It looks like someone tried to set fire to the place."

Her audible intake of breath made him wish he'd softened the words a little.

The car slammed to a stop. A grizzled-faced man in a brown uniform and shiny patent leather boots exited the driver's side. He left the car running, the sirens blaring, and the door open. Hand on the gun hang-

25

ing from his hip, he strode toward them. "Who are you people and what are you doing on the Johnson property?"

CHAPTER 3

The sound of a siren screaming pulled Luke from the depths of his disbelief. The destruction inside the house made the spray paint outside seem inconsequential. He couldn't believe this was the same house he'd stood in only two months earlier, envisioning himself sitting in a hickory rocker in front of the fireplace reading *The Budget,* Leah across from him darning the boys' socks, and the kinner playing games on the rug in the light of the pole lamp.

Someone, teenagers would be his guess, had used the living room for a party. A party that included a bonfire, apparently. They'd ripped apart old furniture left by the previous owners, torn out bookshelves and countertops, and then stacked them all on the living room floor for fuel. The walls and ceiling were seared black. The house reeked of burned wood, beer, and other things he didn't want to contemplate. An empty keg lay on its side in a tub with a few inches of water in the bottom. Broken beer bottles, red plastic cups, cheese curl bags, and crushed corn chips were strewn across the floor. The upstairs rooms were virtually untouched except for the occasional obscene drawing, but every window in the house would have to be replaced.

Someone had drawn pictures with purple, green, and blue markers on the one wall that still had discernible wallpaper, scenes that made Luke turn away. He chose not to imagine what activities had occurred in the downstairs bedroom. They'd found dirty blankets crumpled on the floor, more food and beer trash, a St. Louis Cardinals T-shirt, one blue sneaker, and one green rubber flip-flop.

The siren whopped and whistled, then died away.

"Did someone call the police?" He forced his gaze from the mess to Silas. "We don't need them."

"The semi driver called the sheriff's office." Silas lifted his straw hat and rubbed his bald head with blunt fingers. "He made the call while Elijah came to get me."

"Not your fault." Luke kept his gaze on his friend, not wanting to look at Leah's accusing face. Her repeated sighs hung in the air all around him, like question marks. Questioning his decision-making, questioning his leadership, questioning his love. "Did any of the others find this . . . this destruction at their places?"

"*Nee,* as far as I know, but I haven't heard from every family yet. Some, like you, are just arriving."

Luke squatted and peered at a brown blob on the charred floor. It smelled like rotten hamburger. "Let's talk with the policeman and then we'll get started cleaning up this mess."

"I'm not sure it's safe." Silas frowned, the skin of his forehead wrinkling. "It might not be structurally safe. We may need to raze it to the foundation and rebuild."

"The fire didn't penetrate to the load-bearing beams. The upstairs is still livable as it is. It can be salvaged."

"Let's wait until Thomas and Benjamin get here." Silas tapped the frame of the nearest window. The remaining glass broke free and showered his boots with a tinkling sound. "Benjamin's a carpenter. He'll know more about all this."

"The children have to sleep somewhere tonight. What about the barn? Is it damaged?"

"No, but it's filthy and filled with old

29

equipment. It will take a while to get it cleaned up. You could stay with us."

"I remember the equipment. We thought we'd sell it at the first school auction." Luke realized he was tugging at his beard and stopped. "You have a full house already. We'll make do here."

"I have our camping tents on the truck at our place."

Luke swallowed his anger. It burned his throat and made his belly hurt. They also had tents, purchased with the plan of taking the children camping in the nearby state parks later, when they were settled in, the work of creating a district done. *Gott, help me to forgive.* "They'll think it's great fun."

"I won't. It's clouding up out there. What if it rains? The nights are cool as it is." Leah pressed her lips together as if trying to corral her words. It didn't help. "I'll not spend the night outdoors when there's a perfectly good bedroom upstairs."

"Give us time to make sure the stairs are sound." Luke forced himself to soften his tone. "You don't want to put the kinner in danger."

"I'll get the cleaning supplies and trash bags from the semi." Leah marched from the room, Jebediah clinging to her neck. "William and Joseph can start picking up

30

the trash on the porch and in the yard."

"Give them work gloves. I don't want them cutting themselves on glass."

"I'll sweep it up." The words floated behind her as she let the screen door slam. "And anything else that might be . . . unhealthy out there."

"I sent Martin to get the others," Silas called after her. "My fraa and the girls will help you. Emma and Thomas will want to help. They're all on their way."

No answer.

"She's tired," Luke offered as he straightened. "We all are."

"No need to explain." Silas stood with legs spread and arms folded over his chest, his lined face stern. He reminded Luke of his own daed. "Did you spend any time in town when you came out here?"

"You mean did we talk to people to see how they felt about a load of Plain folks moving in next door?"

"Something like that."

Luke reran the memories of his two visits to this area with the other men selected by the bishop to lead the venture. The first time he'd been taken by the open tracts of farmland for sale and the lack of development nearby. The second time he'd talked with a real estate agent, a banker, and the folks who ran the restaurant next to the motel where they'd stayed. The first two had been anxious for their business. The cost of the farms had been in the price range needed based on what they expected to get from selling Thomas's farm with its oil reserves and the other properties in Bliss Creek. The folks at the restaurant had served good food and minded their manners. The most he'd garnered from them was that people in New Hope minded their own business and liked to keep to themselves. Since that described Plain people as well, he figured they'd fit right in. "The folks I talked to didn't seem to mind."

Silas looked like he would say something else, but the entrance of a man in uniform, followed by Elijah and Bethel, stemmed the flow of his words.

"This is Sheriff Virgil McCormack." Elijah's hands tugged at his suspenders, his usual easy-going smile missing. "He has some . . . questions . . . about the farm. And about us."

"Questions?" Luke took the hand the man offered. The sheriff had a firm grip and a cool hand. "I'm the new owner of this property."

"Who exactly *are* you?" Sheriff McCormack let his gaze wander from Luke to Silas to Bethel in obvious appraisal. He removed his hat and let it dangle at his side. "Some kind of cult or something? No offense, ma'am."

He directed the *ma'am* at Bethel, who looked exhausted as she leaned on her crutches. Luke took a second to school his tone. He wanted to start off on the right foot with their new neighbors. "Not a cult. Amish. I'm Luke Shirack. This is Silas Christner and his brother Elijah." He nodded toward the kitchen, left in shambles that matched the living room. "I'm sorry I can't ask the women to give you some tea or lemonade. We just drove up the road."

"You got proof of ownership then?"

"I have paperwork for the property if you need to see it."

Sheriff McCormack surveyed the scene and sucked on a toothpick perched between his front teeth. Finally, he removed the toothpick and stuck it his pocket. "That's what I figured. Too bad you didn't stop by to talk to me and some of the other folks in town before you decided to buy up the countryside here."

"Why is that?"

"The good folks of New Hope don't care much for strangers. Or religious zealots, for that matter." Without looking down, he

33

stepped on a bag of barbecued potato chips. They crunched under his heel. "We like to keep to ourselves. We've got no interest in the kind of Amish tourist trade they do up there at Jamesport. We don't need it. Most of our folks are farmers who make a decent enough living. We don't want a bunch of city slickers traipsing around trying to get pictures of you guys in your suspenders and straw hats and buggies that block traffic on the highway and cause accidents. Just so you know. Not to be unfriendly or anything."

Elijah made a move as if to break in. Silas shook his head.

"We like to keep to ourselves too. We don't invite tourists to gawk at us. We'd rather they didn't. We simply do nothing to stop them." Luke smiled in what he hoped was a friendly way. He didn't feel so friendly. Thanks to some of the good folks of New Hope they had a big cleanup ahead of them before he could put his kinner to sleep in their own beds. *Forgive them, Lord, and forgive me for being so surly today.* "We don't plan to be any trouble at all to the good folks of New Hope."

If the sheriff saw any irony in the repetition of description of the residents of his town, he gave no indication. "I'm just saying, we got plenty of campers coming through to go to the Ozarks and then we got the tourists headed to Branson. Our stores are doing fine. We don't need no more business. Not to be unfriendly or anything."

"I understand."

The sheriff looked as if he expected Luke to offer to pack up and head back to Kansas. When he didn't, the other man pursed his lips, the sun lines around them deepening. "You got a bunch of kids who'll be going to our schools? They're pretty full already."

"We build our own schools and teach our own children." Their kinner wouldn't go to school with children who did things like build fires in houses that didn't belong to them. "No need to concern yourself about that."

"I heard something like that. Be sure you get that school built right quick. Wouldn't want to send a truancy officer your way so soon after your arrival. Separate schools are for the best. With those outfits, your boys will be eaten alive by our boys."

"We'll homeschool them until the building is ready." He didn't plan to have a discussion with this man about the court case that gave Plain folks the right to educate their children as they thought fitting. "We want what's best for them."

"The winters can be harsh here."

"As they often are in Kansas."

"True enough." Sheriff McCormack poked at an empty brown beer bottle with the toe of his boot. It rolled across the floor and clanked against a green one. "Someone really did a number on your new place."

"It seems so." Luke forced himself to respond in the same even tone. "Our neighbors are on their way. We'll get it cleaned up and repaired in no time."

"You don't want to file a report then?" The sheriff touched a blackened wall and his finger came away dark with soot. "You'll need a police report to file for the insurance. I can get a guy out here tomorrow to take some pictures, see if he can lift a fingerprint or two."

There was no insurance to collect. They were self-insured, but the sheriff would never understand the Amish way of community care. Luke wouldn't mind seeing someone punished for this mess, but it seemed unlikely the sheriff would catch the culprits and their punishment wouldn't change the work that had to be done. Or give the newcomers goodwill in the community. "We don't need a report. Right now, I have five children who need places to lay

36

their heads tonight."

"It's your call." The sheriff slapped his hat back on his head. "I'll spread the word y'all are here so the teenagers will find another place to entertain themselves."

"This happens a lot?"

Luke wanted the question back the second he uttered it. He had spent only a few days in this part of the state, but it had seemed right for their needs. Reasonably priced land in large enough tracts that they could subdivide for their sons and stay close together. They could work hard and stay close to the earth and each other as God intended.

"There's not a lot to do in these parts, in case you haven't noticed." Sheriff McCormack looked grim. "The kids like to let off steam and sometimes they get carried away. I only have eight deputies for three shifts and it's a huge county. The best I can offer is to stop by the high school and give the whole bunch of them a talking-to about respecting private property."

Not that it would do any good, his tone indicated.

"Thank you for coming by, Sheriff. We're happy to meet you." Luke forced the words out. "We plan to be good neighbors. We don't make much noise."

37

"Not a problem." Again, his tone said otherwise.

"We'll be into town tomorrow for supplies. We'll need propane, paint, wallpaper, plywood, drywall, and cleaning supplies." In other words, the town might benefit in some small part from their business. "We'll be on our best behavior."

"Best behavior. You're a funny man, Mr. Shirack." Sheriff McCormack laughed outright. "I'll let my deputies know. The Amish folks are coming to town."

CHAPTER 4

Glancing at Emma Brennaman, who was sweeping the kitchen floor with great vigor, Bethel steadied herself against the one remaining kitchen counter. She didn't want Emma to see her struggle to balance and clean at the same time. She propped one crutch against the wall. That way she had at least one of her hands free to scrub the cabinets and countertop. Once the trash and debris had been cleared away, the kitchen didn't look so bad. Luke would need to replace one stretch of the countertop. The men had spent the previous evening examining the house room by room, boarding up the windows in case it decided to rain, and making lists of the supplies they would need to make the place livable. They all agreed it would take some doing, but it could be done. With time and money — money they could ill afford to spend. Still, it would be less expensive than tearing it down and

39

starting over. So they went to work.

A night in sleeping bags under tents had tickled William and Joseph, but for her it had been an agonizing experience. The pallet of blankets did little to soften the ground under her and her back ached with a throbbing ferocity that kept her eyes open most of the night. She could see why Leah had refused to do it, but not how she could take a baby into a house before it had been made safe. Long before dawn, Bethel arose to start work. No sense in tossing and turning any longer. Luke met her at the porch steps, looking like he'd slept about as well as she had.

Now, several hours later, she was beginning to see a little progress. The men had removed the old electric appliances in the kitchen to make way for the wood-burning oven, propane-fueled refrigerator, and a second propane stove. The kitchen remained a top priority so the women could cook for the men who swarmed the place, rebuilding the living room walls, replacing windows, and painting both the interior and the exterior. Dawn seemed days ago. She suppressed a sigh, not wanting Emma to notice her flagging strength. The medication her doctor prescribed for the pain seemed to be flagging as well.

If Emma noticed her white-knuckled grip on the lone crutch, she didn't say anything. She swept the floor so vigorously dust billowed up around her long dress. Bethel coughed, put her hand to her mouth, and immediately felt her leg buckle under her. Emma dropped the broom and grabbed her before she hit the floor.

"Sorry!" they exclaimed at the same time.

"What do you have to be sorry for?" Emma helped Bethel ease onto one of the four chairs the boys had carried into the kitchen after Thomas and Luke carted in a table. "It's not like you've done something wrong. Surely you know that."

"I'm sorry to be a burden, I guess."

"You're doing fine. Considering how badly you were hurt, it's amazing you're standing upright so soon after . . ." Emma's voice trailed away and her cheeks turned pink. "I mean the doctors said it would take months for you to get back on your feet and here you are only six weeks later. Thanks be to God."

"Patience has never been my strong suit."

"Yes, it is. You're a teacher." Emma had been one too before her marriage to Thomas. She knew about teaching twenty or more children ranging in age from six to fifteen in a single room. "A good one. Eli and Rebecca loved — love you."

"I *was* a teacher."

Emma picked up the broom again. "You will be again. I know you will."

"I pray I will. I don't know what I'll do if I can't teach."

"You'll do other things." Emma was nothing if not optimistic. "You'll be a fraa and a *mudder,* of course."

The words dropped around Bethel like a glass vase on a hardwood floor, the shards piercing her bare feet. Emma couldn't know how painful they were. Bethel tried to smooth her expression.

"The doctors . . ." Emma faltered as if looking for soft words. "What do they say?"

"They say I might regain the use of my legs, but they're not sure. What man would want a fraa who can't cook and clean and work in the garden and mow the yard and climb a flight of stairs to check on a sick child?"

Bethel stopped. Her breathing came hard. She'd kept the words bottled up for so long, they fairly poured out like a spigot turned full force.

Emma patted Bethel's hand. "I'll pray for God's will for you. You'll see. He has a wonderful plan for you. One way or another."

One way or another.

"You look tuckered out, teacher." Deborah Daugherty stood in the doorway, a box labeled *Pots* in her arms. "There's lots of us here and we'll have this place put together in a jiffy. We'll be cooking up a good supper before you know it. No more cold sandwiches for any of us."

"I'm fine." Bethel bit back the words. Deborah had no way of knowing. She was only eighteen, healthy, her cheeks pink, her back strong. She had no idea what it felt like to be a burden to anyone. "Thank you for helping. I know you have plenty of work to do at your own houses."

"Helping hands make everything go quicker." Emma picked up the broom. "And after that long drive yesterday, it feels good to move around. Circulate the blood. I sure got tired of sitting. All I did was eat. We ate all of Annie's brownies, so I'm looking forward to firing up the ovens and making a new batch. I'm sure you are too."

Bethel struggled to her feet and leaned her weight against the cabinet. She lowered her head and focused on scrubbing the countertop with a rag soaked in bleach water. Emma didn't need to know Leah had yet to let Bethel near an oven since her release from the hospital after nearly a month. She seemed to think Bethel would fall in or burn down the kitchen. "Put that box here, Deborah. I've already cleaned the cabinets along the bottom. We can put the pots there and save the top shelves for the plates and glasses."

Deborah plopped down the box. She slapped both hands on the counter as if she were holding herself up too. Her lips quivered. Bethel paused in her effort to rip the clear plastic packing tape from the top of the box. "What's the matter?"

"It's silly. I try so hard to be strong. Mudder says we all have to be strong."

"You miss home?"

"It's only been two days, but I can hardly bear it." Her shoulders heaved as she tried to stifle her sobs. "Don't you miss Annie and Miriam and Helen and Josiah? And all the others?"

"I do." Emma set her broom aside and joined them at the counter. "But we'll see them again when we go back for Helen and Gabriel's wedding. And at Christmas. They're less than a half day's drive away. It gives us something to look forward to."

For Emma the glass was always half full. Bethel loved that about her.

"I know. I know. But I can't stop crying." Deborah dabbed at her face with her apron.

44

"Mudder says I can't let the little ones see, but they don't care. To them it's a big adventure."

Bethel thought of Luke's grin in the van the previous day. She too saw adventure here. She saw possibilities. The things that hadn't worked out in Bliss Creek didn't matter. Deborah was too young to understand about missed opportunities and new beginnings.

Giving herself time to find the words to explain, Bethel struggled to lift a pitcher of lemonade at the far end of the counter. She knew from experience that a good swallow of cold liquid helped drown unwanted sobs and ease a throat that ached to let them out.

Emma tugged the pitcher from her grip and poured for all three of them.

"It's not a big adventure to you, I take it." Bethel focused on Deborah, who had been one of her students her first year as a teacher. She'd been a sweet, obedient girl with a knack for numbers. "Why didn't you want to move?"

"I don't mind. Really, I don't." Deborah scooped up her apron and held it to her face, mopping up the tears. "It's just . . . there's . . . well, there's . . . ."

"A man," Emma finished for her. "You have a beau."

45

"Had. I had a beau. Abel Wagler." The apron muffled the words. "He says he'll come here when he can, but his daed needs him on his farm and he won't let him come. Not yet, anyway. We were baptized in September and I thought we might get married, if not this November, the next."

"Abel's a handsome man." Emma smiled and Bethel knew she intended to cheer up Deborah. "All that curly red hair."

Deborah let the apron drop. "He is, isn't he?" She sniffed and managed a watery smile in return. "He's a hard worker too, and kind, and he listens to me when I talk."

"I taught Abel. He's a good young man." Bethel leaned against the counter so she could squeeze Deborah's shoulder. "It'll work out. It always does. Maybe not the way you thought it would, but it does work out."

Deborah nodded, but she looked dubious. It hadn't worked out for Bethel. At least that's what people in their community thought. That's what Leah thought. And their mudder and daed. She hadn't married. She didn't know why, but she'd been content teaching. Now that dream had been taken from her too.

"Doesn't look like much work is getting done in here."

Leah's entrance saved Bethel from having

46

to respond to Deborah's unasked question. Her sister carried another box, this one marked *Dishes*. There were dark circles under her red-rimmed eyes, and she looked exhausted. Her kapp had slid back a little. She might have cobwebs or dust in her hair. She set the box on the table with great care. "I don't know why I'm being so careful with this. I reckon the ride on that dirt road broke half the plates."

"I reckon we'll know when we get it open." Emma's smile took the edge from her words. She'd lived with Leah for a while before her marriage to Thomas. She knew how to handle her sister-in-law's moods. "I unpacked several of ours last night and they were fine."

"We'll see, won't we?" Leah's nose wrinkled like she'd bitten into a tart Granny Smith apple. "You wouldn't believe what I found in the cellar. I wanted to have the boys carry down our canned goods and it turns out most of the shelves are full."

"Full of what?" Bethel asked, surprised. They had a dozen boxes filled with fruits and vegetables canned with the intent of getting them through the winter to the growing season when they'd be able to plant their vegetable garden. "Do we need to clean it out first?"

"The family who lived here before left behind their canned goods. Perfectly fine jars of tomatoes and green beans and pickles. I think I saw peaches and strawberry preserves."

"Why would they do that?"

"They were older folks, Englischers. Going into a home, Luke said."

"That's sad." Bethel didn't mean to judge, but she liked their way of caring for older folks much better. That's what a *groossdaadi haus* was for. "They had no one who wanted their things?"

"Guess not. There are even boxes of Mason jars that have never been used."

"Well, we'll put them to good use then," said Bethel. Leah sniffed. Something about her expression said she wasn't so sure Bethel would be all that useful when it came to canning. She was wrong. Bethel could sit and chop up cucumbers and onions for pickles as well as the next person. She could snap green beans and pit cherries. She didn't need her legs for that. "Besides, we have plenty of canned goods to get us through —"

"It doesn't take three people to unpack dishes. You best get that downstairs bedroom cleaned up." Leah broke in as if she didn't hear Bethel talking. "They're almost

48

done painting it. You'll be sleeping there."

Of course she would, since it would take her too long to climb the stairs to the bedrooms on the second floor. Which meant she'd be little help with the babies at night. "I'll sweep the floor and wipe down the floorboards and windowsills. If the boys can carry in the frame and the mattress I can make up the bed."

Emma started across the room. "I'll get the bucket of water and the mop —"

"She can manage," Leah interrupted. "Lillie and Mary can help her. Your baby was fussing the last time I checked. She probably needs to be fed."

With that statement, she swept from the room. The implied criticism said Leah thought her sister-in-law was neglecting her baby. Bethel knew for a fact Emma had left her stepdaughter Rebecca in charge of watching baby Lilah and the smaller children in the grassy meadow that stretched between the house and the barn. They'd set up cribs and playpens and even a couple of rocking chairs so the middle girls could care for the little ones while the older girls cleaned. Bethel patted Deborah's back and shuffled along the counter until she could reach her other crutch.

"Everyone will feel better when they're

49

settled in." Despite Leah's orders, Emma grabbed a bucket, dunked it in the big tub of soapy water, and picked up the mop leaning against the far wall. At Bethel's raised eyebrows, she grinned. "I know she's your sister and all, but she does get a little bossy now and then."

"Now and then?" Bethel hid her own smile behind her hand. "Thank you for your help."

"Lead the way."

When she finally made it to the bedroom door, aware of Emma's attempts to slow her own pace, Bethel wished she'd stayed in the kitchen. Elijah tugged at a bed frame, trying to get the sides even and into their slots, his face and shirt wet with sweat. Despite two open windows that allowed the autumn breeze to sweep through the room, paint fumes permeated it. A box spring and mattress were stacked on the floor in one corner.

Bethel didn't know where to look. The bed frame? The mattress? Better to look out the windows behind him. Elijah straightened and wiped at his forehead with the back of his sleeve. His gaze collided with her. His ears turned red.

"I thought I'd . . . you know . . . the paint is pretty much dry so I thought . . . I didn't want you to spend another night sleeping on the ground, not you specifically, I mean, any of you, I mean, all of you."

His soft baritone sputtered to a stop, his gaze begging her to save him from himself.

"I . . . well . . ." Bethel cast about for something to ease the moment. "We . . . Emma and I —"

"We need to mop before you go bringing any more furniture in here." Emma side-stepped Bethel's crutch and set the bucket on the floor. "I think Thomas needs more drywall in the living room. Can you carry it in for him?"

"*Jah, jah.* No problem."

His skin the color of overripe tomatoes, he whipped around the end of the frame, tripped over the corner of the box spring, stumbled, righted himself, and squeezed past Bethel without looking at her.

"He sure knows how to make an exit." Emma held out the mop to Bethel. "I've never seen a man so smitten."

"Smitten?" Heat curled around Bethel's neck and brushed against her cheeks. "What are you talking about?"

"It's obvious." Grinning, Emma trotted to the door. "Elijah likes you. I'll bring some towels to dry the floor. The new windows look so nice and sparkling clean. You'll have fun making the curtains. We need a sewing frolic . . ."

Her words wafted in the air even as she disappeared from sight.

"Emma Brennaman." Bethel would've stomped her foot if she could. "Get back here and explain yourself."

But she didn't. Like all good matchmakers, Emma threw out the line and waited to see who would snatch the bait first. Bethel heaved her crutches to one side and leaned on the mop. It wouldn't be her. Emma wanted to see something that simply wasn't there.

He'd been embarrassed to be in her bedroom, that was all. Elijah saw a disabled woman who needed his help. He'd spent so many years taking care of his parents, he didn't know how to do anything else. Bethel didn't need his help or his pity.

Bethel didn't need him at all. She gave the mop a dispirited swish. She could make it on her own.

Taking a tighter hold on the mop, she cut a swath across the floor in a flourish, lost her balance, and went down in a heap on her behind.

CHAPTER 5

Luke inhaled and stifled the urge to wipe at his face. Ben's house felt crowded, even though they were a small district, only seven families. Their bodies wedged on the benches heated the room and made the air damp with sweat in spite of the cool autumn air. He raised his head to look at Micah Kelp. The bishop prayed, his thick beard bobbing as his head nodded. His eyes opened and their gazes met. He had arrived at Luke's farm the night before, ready to perform his duties and return to Bliss Creek as soon as possible. Micah's no-nonsense approach to their challenges had bolstered Luke's own sense that they were making progress, slowly but surely. The interior of the house was nearly done and everyone slept in their own beds now. The exterior shone with new paint and windows. Tomorrow, they would start planting the fields with winter wheat. Better late than never. All this met with Micah's approval, much to Luke's relief. They would be fine.

"Come now. I will hear your nominations for bishop." Micah's deep bass drew Luke out of his reverie. He started and looked around. No one seemed to notice. Micah lumbered toward the kitchen door. "This is an important decision you make today. I trust that you have prayed over it and meditated over it."

He stood then in the doorway as each man and woman filed past and whispered a name to him. Deacon Altman stood at his side, scribbling names on a piece of paper with a stubby pencil. Luke had prayed long and hard the previous evening, aware of Leah's furtive glances. She hadn't said so, but he knew. She didn't want it to be him. She'd done her own praying, silently, but somehow he found a sort of accusation in her bowed head. He understood. He didn't want it to be him either, but if it were God's will that he take up this burden, he would do so. He fervently hoped God gave the lot to another man.

At the door he leaned in and looked into Micah's face for one brief second, then whispered the name he'd chosen. It hadn't been difficult. Thomas was the wisest man in their group, the most even-keeled. He would handle matters of discipline, the *Ordnung,* and the community's spiritual life with fairness and honest supplication before God. He would make a fine bishop. Micah inclined his head. Luke moved on.

With such a small district, the voting didn't take long. Micah and Deacon Altman returned to their place in front of the rows of benches arranged in the living room. Without further discussion, Micah perused the names. "This is an unusual situation," he noted. "We must choose our minister and our deacon as well. All of you will be new to your duties. But as this is what the situation requires, so be it. The chosen must take up this yoke before God with the greatest commitment to this new community. You will bear the brunt of the decisions that must be made in order for this community to survive and to thrive. Come into the kitchen when your name is called."

He strode once again toward the kitchen where he paused in the doorway and without looking at the paper, began calling out the names. "Luke Shirack."

Luke sucked in air and stood, glad that he'd been spared the reading of the list. Better to get it over with than experience that sense of relief over and over as each name was called, only to have his be the last on the list. Some of the women cried. The seriousness of this moment was lost on none of them. The man who emerged from that kitchen as their bishop would also be their spiritual leader. Leah's face had gone white. He saw no trace of pride that his had been among the names their friends and family had nominated to lead the community. As well it should be. Pride served no one. Still, she shouldn't look so stricken either. If he were chosen, so be it. Gott's will. She knew that. She would adjust to the additional duties as did every other fraa whose husband served.

Their gazes met. Hers dropped. Then she turned and shushed Esther, who was giggling over a piece of paper and crayon she held in her chubby hands. Bethel pulled the little girl into her lap and gave her a cookie. The girl subsided. Leah didn't look back in his direction. He ducked past Micah and entered the kitchen, but his wife's face wouldn't fade from his mind's eye. She suffered, but he couldn't fathom why or how. She wouldn't tell him and her silence accused him night and day.

"Thomas Brennaman." The calling of the names continued.

Forcing himself to let Leah's image go,

Luke studied the row of *Ausbands* arranged on the table. Five of them. One of the hymnals held the slip of paper that would determine how the one chosen by lot would spend his remaining days. The designation of a bishop was for life . . . or for as long as the man could perform the duties of disciplining wayward members of the community — baptizing, performing marriages, and seeing to it that the community clung to the Ordnung.

He stood firm, arms crossed, waiting. *Come what may. Come what may.* Thomas entered the room, his expression somber. He nodded. Luke returned the nod. Benjamin entered next, followed by Aaron and Silas. The community had spoken. They had chosen well. Luke didn't know about himself, but he would be happy to have any of the men in the room as bishop. Each would bring their own way to the table, but they were all solid, careful, thoughtful men who lived by the Ordnung and brought their children up to do the same.

Micah entered the room followed by Altman. "We'll pray now."

Luke lowered himself to his knees, as did the other men. He closed his eyes. *Thy will be done, Lord. If it is your will that I take up this yoke, then I will do it cheerfully. Make me strong.*

The sound of shuffling forced his eyes open. Micah stood. "Now."

One by one, the men picked up the copies of the Ausbands in front of them.

Relief flooded Luke when his hands held steady and his legs didn't buckle under him. He didn't want to shame the people who had chosen him to come this far. He would hang on. He would do whatever he was called to do. He pulled the book to his chest and waited, his heart pounding. He tried to still his breathing. Purple dots danced in his vision. *Steady. Steady.*

"Hand me your book." Micah started at the other end of the row. One by one, he flipped through the pages of the hymnals. It wasn't until he came to Luke that he found what he sought. A look of satisfaction on his pudgy face, he slipped the piece of paper from between the pages and handed it to Luke.

On it were written the words, "The lot is cast into the lap; but the whole disposing thereof is of the LORD. Proverbs 16:33."

Luke licked dry lips. His throat felt as if it were on fire. He needed a drink of cool well water. He handed the paper back to Micah, his fingers still steady. "Godspeed." Micah's eyes were kind behind smudged spectacles. "You are chosen."

Luke could only nod.

"Come. Now we choose the minister, then the deacon."

Four Ausbands this time, already prepared and waiting on the table. A sense of stumbling in a dream inundated Luke. He followed Micah's lead, but he was sure any second he would awake and find himself in his bed next to his fraa. Not taking a songbook from his friend, his brother-in-law Thomas, and finding there a note with a verse on it that said this man of few words would be the community's new deacon. A man who would gather alms for their needy, investigate accusations of infractions against the Ordnung, and serve as a go-between before the publishing of marriage bans. A good man for this role. Very good.

Silas would take the role of minister. A man who handled words well and had been studious of the Bible. Once a good scholar, now a good husband and father. Silas would speak from his heart, giving long sermons without aid of notes. Again a good choice. God's hand moved over them. God made these choices. Luke could see that. There was no chance in this. God had spoken.

Without discussion, they returned to the

living room and stood before their community. The air crackled with expectation. Every face filled with a sort of awed trepidation. Micah stood silent for a few moments, than announced their names, starting with the minister, then deacon. Someone — maybe Emma — gave a little cry when Thomas's name was spoken. Luke couldn't be sure. He stood tall, staring straight ahead. When Micah gave his name to the community, silence reigned, then heads began to bob in affirmation. Men nodded, women whispered. He breathed and allowed himself a swift glance in Leah's direction.

She no longer sat on the bench between Esther and Martha. He caught sight of her bent head as she fled through the front door, Jebediah on her hip. She didn't look back.

CHAPTER 6

Bethel laid the knife aside and rose from the prep table where she'd placed a chair. She picked up the cutting board with one hand, using the other to balance herself so she could shuffle her way over to the stove. She had a system now. She could make it from the table to the counter to the washtub to the stove in a route that allowed her freedom from the crutches so long as she never tried to put her full weight on the bad leg. What did the doctors know? She'd be skipping before they knew it. She'd be jumping rope with Esther and Martha when they were a little older. The thought made her giggle.

Something about curtains fluttering in the open window, the pecan pie cooling on the sill, and the heady aroma of stew meat browning in the skillet made her feel content. Despite the heat of the ovens and the stove, she felt more comfortable than she had since the storm. Even her pain seemed less intense today. Leah had had no choice but to let her cook again. She had too much to do to get the household up and running and she didn't trust Bethel alone with the children yet. What if she dropped Jebediah or the twins ran off and she couldn't go after them? That half-empty glass again.

Bethel refused to let the thought spoil her mood. She'd made pecan pie. The sweet fragrance still lingered in the air, mingling with the stew. The scent of being blessed with abundance.

Careful to drop the potatoes in the hot beef stock without a splash, she turned to make her way back to the table to work on the carrots and celery. At this rate they'd have a nice vegetable beef stew for supper.

"Smells good in here." Luke stood in the doorway, his thumbs hooked on his suspenders. "What's for supper?"

Something about the tense set of his shoulders and his wary expression told Bethel he hadn't come to the kitchen to talk about beef stew. "Stew. I've only begun to brown the meat. It'll be a while before supper's on the table."

"I know. I came to tell you something."

Her good mood draining away, she dried her hands on a dish towel and folded it neatly, waiting.

He pushed into the kitchen and went to the refrigerator where they kept a pitcher of water. He took his time pouring a glass. After a long swallow, he wiped at his mouth with the back of his sleeve. His gaze met hers. "One of my duties as bishop is to oversee the building of the new school."

"Are you . . . glad to be the bishop?"

He looked surprised at the question, as well he should be, she supposed. Glad was beside the point. One was called to serve so that was what he did.

"Honored."

She nodded. He would be. Luke would never turn his back on service. He'd moved his growing family back home after his parents died in a buggy accident. He'd given up his blacksmith shop to go back to farming, which was how he'd ended up moving to Missouri when their farms began to fail in Kansas and oil was discovered on Thomas's farm. He simply forged ahead, confident in his faith.

She busied herself punching down the dough she had rising on the counter and began shaping it into rolls.

"We'll meet with the parents in a few days to set a date for building the school." He

63

cleared his throat. "We'll hire a new teacher then."

"A new teacher." She kept her back to him, deftly shaping the rolls and plopping them into a greased pan. "Not me, you mean."

"Not you."

"Not yet."

"Not now."

She propped herself carefully against the counter. She had no intention of falling in front of him. "Or ever?"

"Not as you are now."

"Then I must go to the physical therapy in town so I can get better." She admired the satiny elasticity of the dough as she broke it apart. Physical therapy would be her only chance to teach again. She would never get better on her own — Doctor Burns had made that much clear. He'd even made phone calls for her to pave the way in New Hope.

They'd spent almost a week repairing the house and making it livable. She hadn't dare ask about therapy before, when every hand was needed. Surely now she could do this. "I have the paperwork Doctor Burns gave me. He called it a referral. He gave me all the medical records they'll need."

Luke now had the authority to make deci-

64

sions about things like this. About her future. He leaned his back against the counter and stroked his beard. His hand trembled. This new responsibility shook him up. Words of encouragement welled in her. She stifled them. Luke didn't need her support. Leah's, perhaps, but not hers. It would sound condescending coming from a woman such as herself.

"Luke?"

"We'll see about the therapy."

"I have to go. It's my only chance of —"

"I know, and it is in all of our best interests if you go. We need you to be able to help with the chores and the babies and take care of the vegetable garden this spring. But how will you get there? I can't take time away from the farm, and the building of the phone shack and school and the prayer services —"

"All your new responsibilities." She swallowed disappointment that tasted bitter deep in her throat. "I understand."

"Leah needs you to get better. She needs your help. But she can't be taking you to town either, what with all these kinner, the cooking and cleaning and such."

"I can do it."

Both of them jumped at the sound of Elijah's soft baritone. So anxious to convince Luke, Bethel hadn't even noticed him at the back door she'd left standing open to create a draft from the open windows. He knocked as if he realized he'd been remiss in not doing so earlier. "I'm working here now anyway. Why don't I take you?"

"Nee."

"Jah."

Luke spoke at the same time as Bethel. She opened her mouth, then shut it. Beggars couldn't be choosers, her mother always said. She didn't want Elijah's help. It was enough that she kept running into him all over the farm and seeing him across the table at mealtime. Reminding her of his hands on her waist and the effortless way he picked her up and swung her from the van. She didn't want to spend that long hour in the buggy with him. She especially didn't want him lifting her in and out of it. Especially after what Emma had said. Heat singed her neck and cheeks. She hoped the men would think it was the heat of the cookstove and oven.

"How often are you supposed to go?" Luke asked. "Every day?"

"Three times a week."

"I can take you, then run errands for Luke and Leah, then come back around and pick you up." Elijah looked pleased with the idea.

66

"I want to learn my way around town anyway."

"As if that will take more than a few minutes in that little bit of a town." She spoke more sharply than she intended. "I mean, it's only a little bigger than Bliss Creek."

"But it's not Bliss Creek." His grin widened. "There's an interesting looking used bookstore and a store that carries all kinds of sewing stuff and material — you might like that one — and a farm implement store and a bakery. It won't be as good as Annie's, but . . ."

"I'm not going to shop —"

"Then it's settled." A look of irritation on his face, Luke broke in. "Elijah will drive you to town tomorrow."

"Tomorrow?"

"The sooner the better." Luke headed for the door to the living room. "I need to talk to my fraa. You could offer Elijah some lemonade. He's been working in the fields all morning. I imagine he's got a powerful thirst."

"Luke, wait." Bethel glanced at Elijah. He leaned against the doorjamb as if he had all the time in the world. "I think . . . there's . . ."

"What?" The look of irritation on her

brother-in-law's face deepened. "I have a propane tank enclosure and a phone shack to build and plans for the school to consider and fields to plant."

"Deborah Daugherty would make a good teacher. She's good at arithmetic and her English is good."

"Deborah Daugherty." His tone less brusque, he paused in the doorway. "She has no plans to . . ."

"Marry? Her beau is still in Bliss Creek. Looks like he'll be there a while."

"A recommendation from her former teacher will go a long way."

"Jah."

"I'll tell the others. I could use some lemonade later."

And he was gone, leaving Bethel not knowing where to look. Elijah seemed to fill up the kitchen with his height and his broad shoulders and his long arms and his eyes the color of summer sky.

"You heard the man." Elijah smiled. He had a cleft in his chin and a dimple on the left side. Bethel had never noticed that before. "I wouldn't say no to a glass of lemonade, if it's not too much trouble."

Too much trouble. Bethel saw plenty of trouble in his pleased smile.

CHAPTER 7

Luke entered the bedroom with even more trepidation than he'd felt upon entering the kitchen to talk to Bethel earlier. The thought irritated him further. A man shouldn't have to tiptoe around in his own home. When had he become so soft? Leah would understand. She would support him. That's what fraas did. He straightened his shoulders and clomped into the room. Jebediah moved restlessly on a baby quilt in the playpen near the window. His cheeks were rosy with sleep and his thick, dark curls formed ringlets around his face. He had Leah's upturned nose and high cheekbones. Luke forced his gaze from the sleeping baby to his wife. "Leah."

She didn't look up from her sewing, her legs pumping the treadle with a steady *thump, thump.* The tight white lines around her mouth and the red of her eyes said she'd been crying. No one ever saw the soft side of her — the side that cried. Just Luke. Once he'd considered it a place of honor, a place of trust. She trusted him like she trusted no other. She told him her feelings about being the oldest of three girls and three boys, of being the one who'd born the brunt of the strictest of upbringings — far stricter than his own had been. The Grabers weren't ones for laughing or lighthearted foolishness, as they called it. She'd been the one to take care of the others when her mudder was sick. She'd shouldered all the responsibility. She told him many things about her childhood when they were younger and had no children's cries to wake them after they'd fallen into bed at dusk.

Lately, she'd become more and more withdrawn from him. He understood the way she kept her distance from others. It was her way, but not with him. Never with him. Her husband. The more years they shared, surely the more closely they should be bound together. He crossed the room and stood in front of the sewing machine. The *thump, thump* continued.

"Leah."

She deftly removed a straight pin from the folded material, stuck it between her lips, and fed the material in a straight line under the metal feet and into the needle that

70

pumped up and down, faster and faster, as her feet drove the treadle underneath.

"Leah, stop. I want to talk to you."

The *thump, thump* ceased abruptly, but she didn't look up. Instead, she stuck the straight pin in a red pin cushion shaped like a fat tomato. She lifted the lever with a snap and pulled the material out, stopping to cut the thread against the sharp edge. Her hands shook. Luke wanted to grasp them and still their shaking. He knew better.

"Look at me, fraa."

She raised her head. Their gazes met. Luke saw no anger or defiance, only a bewildered confusion bordering on resignation. "Keep your voice down," she whispered. "Jeb finally succumbed to sleep. That child takes fewer naps than Annie's Noah."

"We need to talk."

"There's nothing to talk about. You make the decisions. I live with them."

"We live with them. What would you have me do?" He eased onto the edge of bed they shared and patted the spot next to him. "Sit here."

Leah frowned. Her jaw worked. Only because he knew her better than anyone else on earth could he see how hard she worked to hide her tears. "What is it? Why are you so unhappy?"

"I'm not unhappy." She stood and laid the curtain on a pile of others exactly like it. She picked up another swath of material. "I know my place."

"Sit with me." He let command creep into his voice. "I want to talk with you. I want this new start to work. For it to work, we have to be of one mind."

"Of your mind, you mean."

Despite the steel in her voice, she dropped the material and trudged to the bed. She sat far enough away that Joseph and William could've sat between them. Her clean, familiar smell of soap and vanilla engulfed him and he found himself leaning in to it, gulping it in like a drowning man. When was the last time they'd been close enough to touch? Only when she slept and her guard relaxed.

She clasped her hands in her lap and looked straight ahead. "Tell me what you want me to do and I'll do it, husband. I always have."

"But with such obvious dislike." He wanted her to *want* to do it. Like she had in the old days when they first married. She'd been so happy setting up their little house and counting the weeks until Joseph would come along. "Why can't you be happy here?"

"You want me to pretend to be joyous when all I feel is sad and lonely and homesick." Her voice broke. "I'm trying."

"You sound like a child." He gripped his hands together in his lap and forced himself to breathe. "I know it's a change, but you'll get used to it here. These are good families. People you know. You'll draw closer here. At least try to be cheerful."

"Whether it makes sense or not, I feel alone."

"You have Bethel and Emma and all the other womenfolk, not to mention five children." He cast about for words to erase the stricken expression on her face and replace it with the sense of excitement he felt at this new season in their lives. "I'll tell Emma the twins need to come home. They're older now. They can help more."

"Bethel and I . . . you know how it is between us. We're not close."

"Bethel is here to help you. She wants to help you."

"She looks at me and sees a person who has what she wants and can't have."

"I don't believe that. She was content as a teacher."

"Everyone was surprised and shocked when I married and she didn't." Leah's red, roughened fingers stroked the tiny stitches around blue and green blocks on the quilt underneath them. "Especially my parents. They were so sure she was the marriageable one. She's so much more . . . pleasant to be around."

"It didn't surprise me." Luke hated these conversations, but somehow they had to find a common ground before the distance between them became a chasm neither could cross. "I saw you at that first singing, and I knew."

"Stop it." She sniffed hard, looked around as if searching for something, and then resorted to patting her face dry with her apron. "You don't have to do this. You haven't the time to sit here trying to make me feel better. I'll make do with Bethel. Don't say anything to Emma. The twins are happy with her. They weren't happy living with me."

"Bethel will go to physical therapy. She's going to the doctor tomorrow."

"How's she getting there? You have much to do here. So do I."

"Elijah."

"Fine."

"She'll get better, and she'll be able to help you." He scooted closer and reached for her hand. The words stuck in his throat. He cleared it. "You also have me."

74

Pulling her hand from his, she snorted, a most unwomanly sound. "You're the bishop now. You'll officiate at weddings, communions, and funerals. You'll see to disciplinary matters and questions of the Ordnung. The school and the telephone and everything in between. You'll have no time for me or the children."

"Our families always come first."

"In word, if not deed."

"Have I not been a good husband to you?"

The long pause that followed made Luke's heart turn over. It pumped faster, then slower, banging in his chest so hard Leah surely heard it. "Leah?"

"You try."

"What did you expect when we married?"

"You were a blacksmith. We had a home. We started a family. We were happy."

"Then my parents died." To think of that awful day no longer left him breathless with the pain of the memories. "And everything changed."

"Jah, they died."

"Something I couldn't control." Why couldn't she see that? He didn't control God's plan. No one did. Why did she blame him? "It's not my fault."

"Nee. You couldn't and it's not."

"Yet you blame me."

"Nee."

"Then what?"

"I know I'm not an easy person to love." She plucked at her apron, her gaze averted. "Or even to like, but I expected you, of all people, to always . . ."

"To always what?"

She stood and went to Jebediah's playpen. She bent over and brushed the baby's hair from his face.

"To always what?"

"I never expected you to look at me like other people do." Her enormous brown eyes were filled with hurt and accusation. "Like I'm a horrible, difficult person no one would want to have as a friend, let alone a wife."

"What?"

"You look at me with disdain. You look at me through the eyes of your sisters, like all the others."

"I never —"

"I don't expect you to say flowery words. I don't expect you to show your feelings. Nee, I don't necessarily want you to do either." She stalked back to the sewing machine and picked up the material. She looked back at him, the emotion gone again. "But I never expected you to be ashamed to have me for your fraa."

CHAPTER 8

Elijah shifted on the wagon seat, careful not to get too close to Bethel. A cool autumn breeze lifted the ribbons of her kapp, then allowed them to settle. She looked crisp and clean and ready to meet her new neighbors. If she was nervous it didn't show. He forced his gaze back to the steady *bob, bob* of Daisy's head in time with the clippity-clop of her hooves. The familiar sound soothed Elijah. He sneaked another furtive gaze at his companion. Bethel seemed to be studying the countryside as if she'd never seen a tree or a bush before. His attempts at conversation had so far been met with polite one-word responses. *Beautiful day, isn't it? Jah. The air is cool now, but by afternoon, it'll be warm, don't you think? Jah. Are you excited about the doctor? Jah. Nervous? Jah. It'll be interesting to see the shops in New Hope. Jah.*

Fine. Two could walk that road. He forced

himself to focus on the task at hand and ignore how pretty she looked in her dark blue dress and how she smelled of fresh soap and how wisps of her wheat-colored hair curled on her neck.

The road, remember, the road. They were almost to the end of the dirt road that led to the highway and pavement. Which was a good thing. The dirt road needed work. The wagon, empty and ready for the load of lumber, drywall, and other supplies on Luke's list, swayed and jolted hard. Bethel drew a sharp breath.

"Are you all right?" His determination to speak no more flew away like a sparrow. "I'm sorry this is such a rough road. The ruts are so big we could lose a buggy in them. We'll have to grade it once we get the farms in order."

"No need to hurry on my account." Bethel gripped the seat railing with both hands. She bit her lip, her face white against the indigo of her dress. "I'm fine."

No help. No pity. Elijah understood that, but why did she have to be so prickly about it? He didn't pity her. He'd spent years taking care of his father after a stroke left him unable to use his right arm or leg. Daed struggled to feed himself, struggled to find words and make himself understood when he spoke. A strong, hardworking man re-duced to being lifted from the bed into a wheelchair. His father hadn't wanted pity and Elijah had never felt it. Only the love of a son for his father. In the end, his mudder hadn't known her own son, so deep did the dementia run. Still, he hadn't pitied her. Himself at times, but never his mudder. He missed her and thanked God she didn't remember enough to know what she was missing. The birth of her grandchildren, the love of her husband, her memories, and the ability to make new ones.

"Don't look so wounded." Bethel's words startled him from his reverie. "I don't mean to be mean. I just don't . . ."

"Want my pity."

"Anyone's pity."

"I don't pity you." Elijah tugged the reins and the horse halted at the stop sign. No cars in sight. Quickly, he moved the wagon onto the shoulder of the highway and urged Daisy to pick up speed. Still no traffic. He moved them into the right lane, then picked up the thread of their conversation. "I wasn't even thinking about you."

Her startled expression made him realize how abrupt those words sounded. "I mean —"

"Then why do you look at me like that?"

"Like what?"

"Like you want to carry me on your back over the next mountain that comes along."

"It's a habit, I guess." Five long years of caregiving. Daed had gone first after another stroke. Mudder, after wandering through the house at all hours of the night looking for someone, had followed quickly, painlessly, in her sleep. "I'll try to break it."

After that, Elijah didn't bother to fill the silence. Memories of his childhood with nine older brothers and sisters fit snug like a warm coat around his shoulders, giving him comfort as they always did. Every one of them, from Silas on down, had helped with their parents. His sisters had cooked and cleaned. His brothers worked the land. But only he had stayed at the groossdaadi haus, taking care of their daily needs. His opportunity to marry and start his own family passed without him acknowledging it. Mary Troyer had been her name. She married Duane Weaver. Elijah had attended their wedding.

Now that his parents were gone, he asked himself on long, silent nights if he'd missed any chance of having the life his parents had. He wanted it. Gott knew how much. He wanted a life with a fraa and children and backbreaking work in the field and coming home to a meal on the table and shining small faces smiling up at him at the end of the day.

Most likely the woman sitting next to him could not give him that. He knew little of her medical problems, but she could barely walk, let alone carry a child and cook and clean. So why was he so drawn to her? Better to bury the longing and look elsewhere.

Easier said than done.

"I know you took care of your parents for a long time." Bethel's tentative voice fluttered on the morning breeze. "Do you feel like you have to take care of everyone now? Because I don't need someone to take care of me."

She didn't say the words, but still, the implication hung between them. *Especially you.*

He shook his head. The woman liked to worry things, like a puppy that won't let go of a stick. "How about this? I won't look at you at all." To reinforce the words, he stared at the road ahead. "I'll keep my gaze on the ground whenever you're around."

Silence swelled between them again. Then she laughed, a giggle that made her sound younger. It made him want to laugh with her, but he didn't, in case she found fault with that too. "You don't have to go that far. Just treat me like everyone else."

"I'll do my best." He meant that — sincerely. He would treat her like everyone else. He snapped the reins and Daisy picked up her pace. Time to find a new topic of conversation. "I'm looking forward to learning my way around a new town. It's like a great —"

"Adventure." She laughed again. "I know. I've never been this far from home before. Things aren't really that different, but yet they are. Everything's greener and brighter for one thing. And it's not as flat. The houses have more colors too."

"It's strange to think we'll go into town and we won't know anyone." Elijah contemplated that thought. "There won't be any Plain folks. Just the ones from our new settlement."

"Strange."

They were both silent again. The first houses of New Hope came into view in the distance. Elijah's stomach did a strange flip-flop. He hadn't expected to be nervous, like a guest visiting a home for the first time.

The roar of an engine filled the air behind them. A horn blared, and then blared again. Elijah looked back. A green pickup truck was bearing down on them. The driver didn't slow. Why didn't he slow?

His heart hammering in his chest, Elijah jerked the reins and forced the wagon onto the shoulder. Time slowed. The wagon didn't move. Not fast enough. Not nearly fast enough. The truck would hit them. It would hit them and Bethel would be hurt. The thought made him snap the reins harder. "Go, go, go!"

The truck passed them.

The man behind the wheel yelled something at them through his open window. The words whipped in the wind made by the speeding truck and dissipated in the dust and belching exhaust fumes.

Daisy jerked forward, her powerful legs pumping. She whinnied and veered toward the ditch filled with overgrown grass and weeds. "Whoa. Easy, girl, easy." Elijah braced his feet against the floorboard and pulled back. "Settle down, Daisy. You're fine, girl!"

The wagon slammed from side to side. Bethel slid against him hard, then back the other direction. Elijah couldn't spare a hand to steady her. "Hang on!"

Finally, he stood and pulled back on the reins as hard as he dared. "Whoa! Whoa!"

"What did he say?" Bethel drew in a ragged breath as the wagon slowed and steadied, her arms wrapped around the railing. "He yelled something at us."

"Either hurry up or get out of my way, something to that effect." Elijah's own voice sounded hoarse and breathless in his ears. He contemplated stopping on the side of the road, but even that might be dangerous. They'd better get into town. "Something like that."

"Only you cleaned it up a whole lot." She wasn't laughing now. "He could've driven us into the ditch. He almost did."

"But he didn't. We're fine."

"Until the next truck comes along."

Bethel used her handkerchief to pat her damp face with a shaking hand. She drew a long breath. The last thing she wanted was to go into the clinic all shook up. She needed her wits about her to deal with the medical people who would want to see paperwork and ask her questions, lots of questions. She peeked sideways at Elijah. He looked cool as a chunk of ice. She had to admit he'd handled the horse well in the heat of the moment. A lesser man might have lost his grip and let them topple over into the ditch.

"You did well," she managed as they stopped at the first four-way-light intersection in their new town. "You kept us from flipping over."

"Just barely." He glanced both ways when the light turned green and started forward. "Everyone is sure taking a gander at us."

She'd been so shaken by the encounter with the truck that she hadn't been paying attention to the town. Or the people taking in the sight of their wagon and its occupants. New Hope had a fresh, clean look. The windows on the storefronts sparkled. The sidewalks were swept and the signs looked freshly painted. The bakery Elijah had mentioned came into view. And the farm implement store next to Wanda's Western Wear. A restaurant called Dizzy's Burger Joint. It struck her that this new town had no hitching posts. She saw no *Slow for buggy* signs or *No Hitching* signs or stores with familiar Plain names. More than one person stopped to watch them make their way through the town.

"Luke gave me a map he picked up when he was here the last time." Elijah pulled the wagon over to the curb and stopped. "Let me look at it again."

A lady wearing jeans and an embroidered work shirt paused, a broom in her hand. She stood in front of a long storefront with the words *Antique Mall and Flea Market* printed in gold letters across windows featuring displays of old rocking chairs, Raggedy Ann dolls, and Singer sewing machines. She approached the street. "You folks lost? Can I help you?"

"We need the medical center," Bethel said when Elijah didn't speak right away. "Can you give us directions?"

The expression on the woman's plump face changed under her tidy cap of silver hair. She hustled over to the side of the wagon. "Are you hurt or sick or what?" She tugged a tiny, flat phone from her pocket. "Should I call 911 for an ambulance? The medical center is on the other side of town."

In a town this size, that couldn't be too far. "No, but thank you, it's not an emergency. I should've been clearer. We're looking for the rehabilitation clinic that's near the medical center." Bethel managed to wedge the words in when the woman paused to take a breath. "We're new to town so we —"

"Don't I know it! Y'all have been the talk of the town for weeks now. We get lots of people on their way to camp in the Ozarks or tourists looking for Branson, but not folks like you. Aren't you as cute as all get-out in those outfits. Like pioneers on the prairie. I've read some of those Amish romance novels so I know what to expect.

86

These other folks are just ignorant. Don't mind them."

Pioneers. Romance novels. Don't mind them? Bethel was afraid to ask what the lady meant by her torrential onslaught of words. Elijah held up a hand and saved her from responding. "It looks like I take a left at the next corner and go about four blocks, then left again."

"That's exactly right. The rehab clinic is about six blocks from the medical center." The lady wiped her hand on her jeans and extended it to Bethel. "I'm Diana Doolittle, owner of the best junk store in town." She cocked her head toward the building behind her. "You need any dishes or kerosene lamps or such, stop by."

"Bethel Graber." Bethel allowed her hand to be enveloped in Diana's. "We brought most everything we need."

"You should get on down the road then." The comment came from a bent old man with a face like a bulldog who ambled past Diana's store, leaning on a cane and sucking on a reeking cigar. He pulled the cigar from his mouth and spat on the sidewalk. "And be sure you pick up after that horse. We don't want someone slipping in manure on our clean streets. It's a lawsuit waiting to happen."

"You just hush, Sam Black. You ain't the mayor no more. You're retired. If you can't say anything nice, don't say anything at all." Diana shook her finger at Sam. "*You* can just move on down the road, you grumpy old man."

Sam kept right on walking and Diana turned back to them. "Don't mind him. He's the grumpiest of the grumpy old men who think they run this town. My husband is an auctioneer. You ever need to do a sale, look us up. Doolittle and Doolittle Auctions and Farm Sales."

"We should be on our way." Bethel couldn't read Elijah's expression. It might be a smirk. "Elijah needs to pick up supplies at the hardware store, the grocery store, the lumber store, and the feed store while I'm at the doctor. Can you tell him how to get to those places as well?"

"Is this your husband or your boyfriend?" Diana bestowed a wide smile on Elijah, who smiled back. "He's a looker."

A looker. Bethel didn't know for sure what that meant, but she had an idea. The heat of a blush warmed her neck and cheeks. She tried valiantly to ignore it. Diana seemed nice. It was good to know one person in this new place, but now she needed to get this first visit to the clinic behind her. "The hardware store?"

Diana pointed it out on the map, then stepped back. "Stop by anytime." She waved as Elijah looked both ways and snapped the reins to get Daisy moving again. "Anytime, you hear!"

Since she was shouting, they couldn't help but hear. Elijah grinned from ear to ear. For some reason, that grin made Bethel want to smack him, something she'd never done to anyone in her entire life. She restrained herself. "What are you grinning at?"

"We've only been in town a few minutes and we already made a friend."

"That's all?"

"That and she thinks I'm a looker."

"What *is* a looker?"

He only grinned more widely. He had a nice smile. That dimple in his left cheek. Even teeth. Full lips. A nice nose too, not to mention those blue eyes and hair the color of hay. *Stop it!*

She made it a point to keep her gaze on the buildings that comprised the main street of New Hope until they arrived at the medical center campus. A kiosk at the intersection told them it was called the New Hope Regional Medical Center, which explained the size of the long, red brick building in the center of a series of smaller buildings. It served not only New Hope but the surrounding communities in this rural county. Elijah, who'd been humming an indistinguishable tune the entire time, pulled on the reins and slowed the wagon. "Where do you suppose the rehabilitation clinic is?"

Bethel studied the kiosk and surveyed their surroundings. "I think it's that way." She pointed to the left.

After another six blocks of medical-related businesses, they pulled into a parking lot in front of a small, wood-frame building that looked more like a house than a medical office, except for the glass double doors. "I think that's it."

"Yep." Elijah hopped down and wrapped the reins around the trunk of a spindly tree. He smiled up at her. "Down you go."

Bethel stared at his outstretched arms. Suddenly full of misgivings, she let her gaze travel to the building, painted white with a dark evergreen trim. It could've been someone's home, but it had no front porch, no steps, nothing to impede a person from entering, just a wide, flat cement ramp. So why did she feel the compelling urge to stay in the buggy?

"Come on. I promise not to drop you."

"It's not that." She faltered. "Maybe I should wait."

"Scared?" He leaned forward. She thought he would grasp her hands in his. Instead he wrapped his fingers around the arm of the seat, within inches of her own white-knuckled grip. "They'll be nice as can be, you'll see. They're medical folks. They like to help people."

"Like you."

His expression grew somber. "You're the only person I know who holds that against me."

"I don't hold it against you. I just don't want you to think of me like that."

"Why does it matter what I think of you?"

"Not just you." She struggled to explain herself. "Can we not talk about this right now?"

"Sure, but you have to let me help you down."

"Okay."

Elijah lifted her to the ground as if she weighed no more than Jebediah. "There you go." He handed her the crutches, waited for her to prop herself up, and then picked up the canvas bag that held her medical records. "Your papers."

Bethel held her arm out and he tucked the straps on her shoulder. His kind gaze studied her face. "You want me to go in with you?"

"I . . ."

"No need. I got this one."

Startled, Bethel twisted on the crutches and craned her head to see the owner of the hoarse, raspy voice. At first she didn't see anyone. She looked left and right, nothing. Then she glanced down. The speaker sat in a wheelchair, clad in camouflage pants and a black V-neck T-shirt. His copper-colored hair was cropped close to his head and one cheek marred by scars still pink in their newness. Bethel opened her mouth and then shut it, unsure what to say to this stranger who blocked her entrance to the rehab clinic.

"Come on, darlin'. Don't worry. I'm not crazy. I'm Private First Class Shawn McCormack. Also known as an Army grunt in training — past tense, of course." Grinning, he leaned over and stubbed a half-smoked cigarette into a container of sand filled with butts. He then proceeded to wheel his chair around her in a quick, neat circle, the muscles in his thick upper arms pumping. "Don't look so worried. Do you know what's waiting for you in there?"

"Nee — no."

He made a flourishing motion toward the door. "Freedom, darlin'. Freedom!"

CHAPTER 9

Bethel wavered. Her crutches dug into the cement sidewalk that led to the rehab clinic. Her palms felt sweaty and slick on the handles. Despite the early morning hour, the air seemed moist and heavy as if it were full of raindrops that refused to fall. The man in the wheelchair grinned up at her, his face expectant. Elijah frowned and took a step away from the wagon, his hand out. She swung out of his reach and started around Shawn McCormack. Her right leg, like a stubborn child, refused to cooperate. She gripped the crutches tighter. *Come on, come on, you can do this.* Bethel didn't look back, but she knew Elijah hadn't moved.

"Go on. Run your errands." She forced a cheerfulness she didn't feel. "I don't know how long this will take, so don't rush back."

"Yeah, take your time." Shawn whipped his chair around and rolled ahead of her. She stopped, balancing on the ramp leading to the double doors while he pushed a red button with the back of his left hand. He wore black leather gloves that didn't have fingers. His fingers were gnarled in a permanent curl. The doors began to slide open. "I've got this."

"Thank you," she managed to breathe. "But I don't need help."

"You might. Sometime. Come on. I'll catch you. I won't let you fall." Laughter danced in the words. She'd never heard anyone be quite so determinedly cheerful. It bordered on annoying. "You can sit on my lap and I'll wheel you in."

"I don't need help." Heat rolled through her, searing her cheeks and neck. She inhaled and caught the *schtinkich* of cigarette smoke lingering in the air around him. "I'm fine."

"I'm fine too." He rolled back, letting her go through first. Elijah still stood on the curb, not moving. Shawn followed her gaze. "That your boyfriend?"

"No."

"Good."

Unable to find a response to this stranger's bold cheekiness, she heaved herself through the doors and into the clinic's foyer with its light green walls and high ceiling. She stopped to look around. The slick black and white tiles shone in the natural light that bounced from a row of ceiling-to-floor windows. At the moment no one stood behind the low counter that divided the foyer from a long hallway.

"Hey, I'm sorry if I came on too strong." Shawn wheeled forward so he was even with her. "I do that sometimes."

"Have you been here before?"

"Sure."

"What do I do now?"

"You wait. People like us do a lot of that." He pulled up to the counter and pounded on it with both fists. "Hey, anybody home?"

A lady in pink hospital clothes that made her mahogany skin seem to glow trotted down the hallway toward the counter. "Shawn McCormack, you just hold your horses. I'm coming."

"Gorgeous Georgia, it's good to see you."

"Don't Gorgeous Georgia me. We use our inside voices around here."

"Yes, ma'am. I got a new customer for you." Shawn cocked his head toward Bethel. "What's your name, darlin'?"

Trying to ignore his use of the endearment in front of the nurse — she supposed Georgia was a nurse — Bethel cleared her throat and introduced herself.

"Bethel, that's a beautiful name." Shawn

twirled his chair around as if for punctuation. "Bethel. Bethel Graber. Nice."

"Shawn, behave yourself. Go read a magazine until Doctor Karen and Doctor Jasmine get here. This young lady needs some privacy to discuss her business. She doesn't need you sticking your nose where it don't belong. Get along."

Shawn grinned and wheeled back from the counter. "Yes, ma'am."

"Don't mind him. If anyone ever took him up on his outrageous offers, he'd faint and fall out of that chair." Georgia opened the envelope Bethel had laid on the counter and began to sift through the stack of paperwork. She nodded a few times, muttered "uh, huh" more than once, and then dropped the papers in a neat stack in front of her. She picked up a clipboard and shoved a new stack of papers under the clip with an efficient flick of her wrists.

"Okay, honey, what I need for you to do is to fill out these papers. You can have a seat right over there." She pointed to a bank of green upholstered chairs that lined the wall. "Take your time. Doctor Karen isn't here yet. She drives in three times a week to meet with the patients here for PT."

"PT?"

"Physical therapy. That's you."

96

Bethel couldn't help herself. She looked back at Shawn, who was thumbing through a magazine with the title *Prevention* emblazoned across the front. He looked up and smiled as if feeling her intent gaze.

"I'm telling you, honey, he's a case, but he's harmless. His daddy is the sheriff. He brought him up right." Georgia pointed to the chairs. "Besides, he's just so relieved to be alive, he can't help himself. Go on, honey, he won't bite."

Bethel couldn't believe the man sitting in the chair with the dusting of freckles so incongruous among the scars could belong to the gruff sheriff who'd done everything in his power to make her and her family feel unwelcome when they arrived in New Hope. "What happened to him?"

"I can't discuss other patients with you, Miss Graber."

"Just Bethel. Of course you can't. It's none of my business."

"Go on, have a seat. Like I said, he won't bite."

Maybe not bite, but he did look like he might clamp onto her and not let go. He seemed unaccountably happy for the son of a gruff man with a gun on his hip. What made him so happy while he sat in a wheelchair, his hands knotted, his face scarred?

Feeling as if she'd been given a question she should be able to answer without help, Bethel limped her way over to the chairs. She chose one well away from the spot Shawn occupied in front of a low coffee table covered with magazines ranging from *Sports Illustrated* to *Home and Garden*. She began filling in the blanks on the first sheet. *Name. Address. Referring Physician. Responsible Party. Nature of ailment. Insurance.* She plowed to a stop. None. She wrote *None* in her careful handwriting. She knew all sorts of bells and whistles would go off when Georgia saw that line.

Before she left the house earlier in the day, Luke had handed her an envelope and told her to give them a down payment or deposit — whatever they wanted to call it — for their services. She hadn't peeked inside. She knew by its weight it held a substantial amount of cash. Cash they could ill afford to spend on her health care, what with the land purchases and moving expenses and the remodeling of the house to erase the *Englisch* electrical lines and plumbing that depended on electricity to function. Luke told her not to worry about it. If she were to get better, it would benefit the entire community. She had his blessing, regardless of the cost of her treatment.

"You're not from around here, are you, darlin'?"

Shawn's voice sounded closer than it should. Bethel looked up to find him bearing down on her location. She pulled the clipboard close to her chest. "Nothing gets past you." She swallowed the rest of her retort and tried to smile. "I mean, no, I'm from Kansas."

"Like Dorothy? I don't think you and Toto are in Kansas anymore. I mean, you look like you're from a different time." He waved around his gnarled fingers. "Not that you don't look sweet in that outfit, darlin'."

"Why do you keep calling me darling?" This time she couldn't keep the tartness from her voice. "You don't even know me."

"It's a term of affection."

"You don't know me well enough — or even at all — to have affection for me."

"Ever heard of love at first sight?"

Heat billowed around her. She ducked her head, wishing she could run for the doors. But then, wasn't that why she was here? To get her legs back so she could run again if she ever needed to do it?

"Don't look like that. I'm just joshin' you." He settled back in the chair, arms resting on the padded rails. "I'll give you

99

time to adjust to the idea. Don't worry, darlin'."

"I wish you'd stop calling me that."

"There's something about you." The lighthearted humor disappeared from his voice. She looked up to see the first serious expression of the day on Shawn's face. "You should be someone's darling. Maybe not mine. Maybe that hayseed guy who brought you here. I don't know, but someone's."

Bethel's unease grew. She didn't belong in this place, talking to this man, even if he were in a wheelchair and posed not the least of a threat. She tottered to her feet. "I think I should go."

"Don't chicken out on account of me." A note of alarm in his voice, he held up one hand and rolled his chair back. "I'm sorry if I got ahead of myself. I'm always doing that these days. It just seems like there's no time to waste."

"Why? Why would you be in a hurry to know someone like me?"

"Easy. I saw a bunch of guys younger than we are fight and die in a war. I realized pretty fast that life is short."

"I don't worry about life being short. We're only passing through." She stopped. She had no idea what this Englisch man might think about God. "Our time here is a few grains of sand, that's all."

"Maybe so, but don't you want to enjoy life while you're here?" He cocked his head, his expression inquisitive, like a small child examining a lightning bug. "You want to get better, don't you? You want to walk and skip and hop and run through this life, don't you?"

"Yes, but how do you know what I want?"

"Because it's what I want. It's what everyone who comes through those doors wants."

Bethel contemplated his eyes. They were a deep chocolate brown and full of sadness she hadn't noticed before in all his bluster and chatter. It was as if an old man looked out at her from behind the face of a young man. "You don't think you'll get that?"

"I don't know, but if you go back through those doors, I know you won't."

He had a point. She sat.

"Good girl. I'll leave you alone now, I promise, and no more darlin'."

He wheeled the chair around. As he did, he glanced toward the long windows on either side of the sliding doors. "By the way, your farmer guy is still out there."

Bethel craned her head forward and followed his gaze. Elijah leaned against the wagon, arms crossed, staring at the building. What ailed him? Dropping her at the clinic had only been the first item on the list Luke had given him. *"Ach."*

She struggled to her feet again and swung to the door. There, she waved. Elijah straightened and started toward her. She shook her head and flapped her hands in a motion that surely said, *Go!*

He wavered, hands on his hips. Finally, he climbed into the wagon. She didn't move until he drove away. Her face warm with perspiration, hands slick on the crutches, she once again returned to her seat. She sank gratefully into the chair and picked up the clipboard. Embarrassed to imagine what he must think of all this, she peeked at Shawn.

He sat with a magazine in his lap, head down as if it were the most interesting article ever. An unlit cigarette dangled from two fingers. His lips moved as if he were reading silently.

Bethel had to clamp her mouth shut to keep from speaking to him. She'd only met him minutes earlier. So why did he suddenly seem like her closest friend?

He understood. That's why. This Englisch man might not know anything else about her life in a Plain world, but he understood the desire to run. To hop. To skip. To stand alone.

Shawn McCormack understood her.

CHAPTER 10

Bethel sat on the end of the tissue-covered examining room table, her cold, sweaty hands clasped in her lap, waiting. She'd been sitting there, in the skimpy cotton gown with its gaping back, for almost thirty minutes. Inhaling the astringent scent of cleanser, she contemplated sliding from the table and hiding behind the curtain where she'd been instructed by Georgia to change into this silly gown. Her bare feet didn't touch the floor, which made her feel like a child in a high chair. She wanted to put her clothes on and go home. She'd had enough of the crinkly noises of the tissue paper under her. She'd also had enough of the fluorescent lights glaring overhead and of the refrigerated air that made goose bumps pop up on her bare arms and legs. Not to mention the tinny music wafting from an unseen source with its lyrics that spoke of love lost and broken hearts and angry retorts. She longed for fresh air and sunlight and the chatter of the birds. *Lord, have mercy. Let me go home.*

No. If she ever wanted to teach again, she would stay. The thought held her on the table as tightly as a belted restraint. If she ever wanted to care for a home and children, she would stay. She could take it, embarrassing and shameful as it felt. She'd gotten this far. No turning back. She sighed and studied the enormous posters hanging on the green walls. A skeleton stared back at her, his bones and muscles exposed. An explanation of spinal cord injuries. The bones of the human skeleton. The muscles. A litany of strange terms that meant nothing to her. Big words that might as well have been in a foreign language. For all she knew, they were.

There was a knock on the door, and it swung open with a high-pitched squeak. Bethel jumped. Her hands flew to the back of her gown where she tried to close the gap with shaking fingers. Her heart pounded against her ribcage. She drew a deep breath. In strode a dark-haired woman in a white jacket that covered a bright purple pantsuit.

The doctor — Doctor Karen, Bethel presumed — looked at the manila folder she held in her plump hand. Her gaze warm behind rectangular, silver-rimmed glasses, she smiled and extended her other hand. "Miss Graber. Pleased to meet you. I'm Doctor Karen Chavez. Everyone around here calls me Doctor Karen. How are you today?"

"I'm Bethel and I'm fine." Well, not really fine. As she shook the other woman's hand, Bethel struggled with what she could truthfully say. "It's chilly in here and I really need to put my clothes back on. The gown is . . . well, it doesn't . . . I mean, I'm uncomfortable in it."

Doctor Karen laid the folder on a desk next to a computer. She plopped down on a wheeled stool and tapped on the keyboard. Words filled up the screen. "Hmmm, don't worry about the gown. Everyone feels that way, I promise. I'm sorry about the air conditioning, though. It seems to have a mind of its own. We'll get you out of here and into the PT room ASAP — don't you worry. You'll be plenty warm when you start your therapy."

PT room. ASAP. This wasn't her last stop? Bethel checked the clock on the wall over the doctor's head. She'd already been at the clinic for more than an hour. If Elijah took his time and stretched out his errands, he might not show up at the clinic doors for another half hour — at most.

"I really should be getting back to the farm." She tried to read the words on the screen. They were too far away. "We just moved here and we have much work to do to get settled in and a school to build and the house is a mess —"

"How's your pain level?" Doctor Karen wheeled around and faced Bethel. "I've reviewed Doctor Burns's records. He's very thorough. He indicates you suffer pain related to the incomplete spinal cord injury you suffered. I assume he's explained your injury to you. He also indicates you're a prime candidate for physical therapy. I agree with him that you have the potential to regain at least part of your mobility if you're willing to work at it."

More foreign language. "I'm willing to work at it. I just don't know what I'm supposed to be working at." Bethel skipped over the question of the pain. Some days it seemed unbearable. On those days, she resorted to the pills Doctor Burns had prescribed. But then she felt as if her arms and legs were overcooked noodles. Her head seemed stuffed with more noodles and her pillow beckoned to her. "Is this work something I can do at home? I need to watch the children and help with the cooking and the laundry."

"You have children? How many? Your record doesn't indicate that."

"No, no, they're my sister's children. She has five. Young ones. She needs my help."

"It's good that you're active. I'd like to start your physical therapy here at the clinic. You'll get a home program as well, but I want to supervise your movements, at least at the beginning." Doctor Karen returned to the computer and tapped the keys again. "The record indicates that your internal injuries healed rather nicely. They removed your spleen, repaired the damage to your uterus —"

"Yes, yes, I know." Bethel didn't need the recitation of her injuries and the words relating to her female parts only served to deepen her embarrassment. "Do we need to talk about this?"

Doctor Karen looked around, her thick brown eyebrows lifted, giving her a quizzical expression. "Do you want children?"

"Jah — yes."

"Then we need to talk about these things." She wheeled across the slick tiles within inches of the table. "There's a notation in your files about your faith. Your lifestyle, if you will. I don't know much about it, but trust me, everyone here is in the same boat as you. Georgia and I and the other staff members are the only ones who will see you in this gown. The PT is a different thing. Everyone uses the equipment. Do you own workout clothes?"

"Workout clothes?"

"A T-shirt. Sweatpants. Shorts. Sneakers."

Sneakers. She had sneakers. Feeling like a student trying to please her teacher, Bethel almost raised her hand. "I have sneakers. At home, I have sneakers. But no shorts. No sweatpants. We only wear dresses."

"The sneakers are a start. We'll work something out." Doctor Karen smiled as if pleased with her star pupil. "Now let me take a look at you."

"A look at me?" Bethel clutched the gown to her. "Is that necessary?"

"I'm a nationally certified physical therapist with a doctorate degree. It's what I do." She patted Bethel's arm. Her hand was cool and soft. "I need to see where you are so I can benchmark your improvement. Based on your records and exam, I can design a rehabilitation program for you. I'm not doing this to be intrusive or to embarrass you. I promise you that. Do you trust me?"

Bethel licked dry lips. She eyed the door. It was only a few feet away. She could escape. If she could get down, which she couldn't. If she could reach her crutches before she fell. Which she wouldn't. Wasn't that the whole point? "I do. I trust you."

Doctor Karen picked up a plastic circle that had two long arms on it. "Lie back. I need to get a baseline on your range of motion so we can track your improvement as we go along." She held up the plastic gizmo. "Don't worry. This is just like a ruler. It's called a goniometer. It won't hurt, I promise."

Bethel leaned back and stared at the ceiling. She followed Doctor Karen's orders. Lifting and bending, trying to ignore the spasms in her back. She breathed. *In and out. In and out.* It would be over soon. Wouldn't it?

"Good. Prop yourself up on your elbows." Doctor Karen laid down the gonio — the whatever the thing was called — and removed her glasses, letting them dangle from a chain around her neck. She put her hand on the sole of Bethel's bare foot. "Okay, I want you to push down like you're pushing on the gas."

"On the gas?" Bethel wanted to follow directions. She wanted to be a good patient. She wanted to walk again. "I don't . . . What do you mean?"

"Push. I want to see how much strength

you have in your leg." Doctor Karen looked as perplexed as Bethel felt. "Oh, oh, I forgot. You guys don't drive, do you? Okay, just push down as hard as you can."

Bethel did as she was told. Doctor Karen seemed to be watching her face as if trying to read her expression. Making a clucking noise in the back of her throat, she tried Bethel's other foot, then wrote something on the paper on a clipboard. "Does it cause you pain to do that?"

"A little." No more than trying to walk did. "Mostly in my back."

Nodding, her expression concerned, Doctor Karen brushed her fingers across the skin on Bethel's right leg. "Do you feel that?"

Suppressing a sudden giggle that had nothing to do with how she felt at that moment, Bethel nodded. "It tickles."

Doctor Karen repeated the action on the other leg. "How about this?"

Bethel couldn't help it. The giggle escaped. Doctor Karen must think she was a silly girl. "Sorry."

"Don't be. It's a good sign. Let's get you up." Doctor Karen held out a hand. "I want to see how you stand and walk."

The next fifteen minutes were excruciating. Not because of the pain she felt as she tried to stand straight for the doctor or walk without the crutches and then with them, but because of the agonizing embarrassment of being so exposed before a stranger, doctor or not.

Bethel gritted her teeth, acutely aware of the doctor's light breathing and scent of lilacs. *Gott, help me. I will not cry. I will not cry.*

"You're doing fine." Doctor Karen patted Bethel's shoulder. "Your range of motion has actually increased a bit from what Doctor Burns recorded. That's a good sign."

Bethel inhaled and blew out air, letting the pain seep away. She managed a nod.

"It doesn't look like the pain is any better, however." The skin creased on Doctor Karen's forehead as she lifted her eyebrows. "I can give you another prescription or we can try some injections."

"No. No, the pain isn't that bad." Bethel hated the catch in her voice. She cleared her throat. "If my range of motion has improved, why can't I put any weight on my right leg? Why can't I walk without the crutches?"

"We need to retrain your muscles. It takes time. And therapy. We need to get you on the bike. We can do some resistance band exercises, Pilates reformers, some warm water therapy. I also want you to do some strengthening exercises at home."

Resistance bands? Warm water therapy? Did that involve getting in a bathtub or a swimming pool? Bethel drew a shaky breath. "Water therapy?"

"We have a very small indoor swimming pool where you can do exercises in the water. It puts less strain on your muscles and back, but works the muscles in a therapeutic way. You'll see the pool in a minute." Doctor Karen pursed lips covered in pinkish-purple lipstick. "Do you have a swimming suit?"

"No." Physical therapy involved swimming. Who knew? Luke would never allow that, not here, not with Englisch folks. "Swimming will help me walk again, without the crutches?"

"That's the idea, but — no pun intended — it's one step at a time. At the very least, you could graduate to a cane. How are you sleeping? I noticed on the chart that you've lost five pounds. Are you eating well?"

"I sleep all right. Just more . . . dreams than before."

"Nightmares."

"Sometimes."

"Loss of appetite?"

"We've been moving. We've been busy."

"Moving is stressful on top of what you went through. You're not back in the classroom, are you?"

"No." Stressful? Bethel noticed Englischers tossed that word around a lot. Everything was stressful. "But I want to be."

"I'm sure you do, but first we need to build up your strength and that means eating right and getting plenty of rest. I'll send home some handouts with you. Lots of protein and carbs."

Protein and carbs? They ate the food they grew.

"I also think you'll benefit from our support group."

"Support group?" Her stomach swooped and she almost lost the few bites of bacon, eggs, and toast she'd eaten for breakfast. "Support like . . . what does that mean?"

"This is a full service wellness clinic. We treat both the mind and the body of folks with your kind of challenges. We have a staff person who facilitates group therapy sessions. It's a chance for you to sit down with some other folks who've been through what you've been through. Talk about it. Vent. Get it out of your system so you start to eat and sleep better. A lot of folks find it helpful."

School desks and a stove had fallen on

other people? Bethel had no desire to talk to people about her experience. Besides, the more commitments she had here, the longer she kept Elijah waiting. She checked the clock again. Another five minutes had passed. "It's my legs that need help. The rest of me is fine."

"Sometimes we tell ourselves that we're fine, but when our bodies are hurt and they won't do the things we've always been able to do — basic things, like walking — it affects our mind. The mind is a powerful tool in healing the body."

"I don't understand."

"If your mind thinks you can't do something, then you can't. If you believe you can do something, you'll be able to do it."

"To fix my mind, I have to talk to strangers about what happened?"

"Sometimes, it's easier to talk to strangers. They have no preconceived notions about who you are. They aren't judging you. They aren't asking you to be who or what you were before your accident."

Bethel wavered. Everything Doctor Karen said made sense. She couldn't talk to Leah. Leah had her own problems and she needed Bethel's help. All she saw was a sister on crutches who couldn't carry her own weight. Literally. And who else was there? All her friends were married and having babies. Her bruders were married with fraas who were having babies. Her mudder and daed. They couldn't understand why no one had wanted to marry their youngest daughter. Now, even less. If she fixed her legs, she might still have that chance to be a wife and a mother. To have her new start. Apparently that started with fixing her mind. "I'll do it." She hesitated. "I mean, I'll talk to my family to make sure it's okay."

"Talk fast." Her tone firm, Doctor Karen slapped her glasses back on her nose and gazed at Bethel over the top of them. "You start your first session tomorrow."

"I have to ask my brother-in-law if it's okay. We have rules."

"Your brother-in-law?" Her gaze sharpened. She reminded Bethel of Mudder with her no-nonsense approach to life. "I'm not sure what he has to do with your health care."

"He's not just my brother-in-law; he's the bishop. He interprets the Ordnung."

"The what? Never mind. If he gives you any trouble, you give me a call. I'll talk to him."

"We don't have a phone."

"No phone?" She contemplated Bethel as if trying to decide if she was serious. "I can deal with that. I sometimes wish I didn't have a phone. Especially late at night. Come get me and I'll drive out to see him."

"I don't think that's a good —"

"Right now, I want you to get dressed and meet me in the hallway. I'll show you around the PT room."

Despite her concern over Luke's reaction to sweatpants and therapy groups, Bethel didn't need a second invitation. Doctor Karen helped her down from the table and kindly left the room while Bethel huddled behind the curtain and dressed. A certain, surprising sense of relief and comfort flooded her when she grabbed her crutches and stuck them under arms. She could leave the room under her own steam.

That sense of relief drained away when she followed Doctor Karen into the physical therapy room. It was large and airy with overhead ceiling fans and long banks of strange-looking equipment. A bicycle that didn't go anywhere. Rows of weights. A woman wrestled with a red, stretchy rubber thing tied to a pole. A man in a blue outfit that looked similar to Georgia's sat on a bench across from a man in a wheelchair, throwing him a large striped beach ball. Every time the man caught it between hands with fingers that didn't straighten and

117

tossed it back, the man in blue clapped and whooped like a kid at a baseball game. "Way to go, Jay! Way to go!"

Doctor Karen closed the door behind Bethel. "Can you see why you'll need sweat-pants and a T-shirt or some other kind of workout clothes?"

Bethel surveyed the other patients. Mostly men, all dressed in sweat-stained T-shirts and shorts. Shawn McCormack pumped handheld weights, his face red with exertion, veins bulging in his temples and in his bare biceps. He wore dark blue shorts and a white T-shirt with the sleeves cut off. His legs seemed skinny and shriveled compared to his broad, massive chest.

He saw her a second after she saw him. He grinned and pumped the weight over his head. "Darlin' — I mean Bethel! Welcome to the torture chamber."

"I can't." Her stomach rocking and her heart pounding, Bethel slid around on her crutches and faced Doctor Karen. "I can't do this."

"You need to do this. It's the only chance you have of getting the full use of your legs again."

"I understand that. I want to do it. But not here. I can't do it here."

"I don't understand." Doctor Karen's

gaze did the once-over on Bethel's clothes again. "Is this related to your religion?"

"Sort of." Her skin burned white hot. She groped for words. "I need to keep myself covered. I can't do this." She waved her hand toward the equipment. "I can't do this in front of . . . other people."

"You mean men."

Bethel nodded so hard her head hurt. The doctor would understand, surely.

Doctor Karen wrinkled her nose. She scratched it and sniffed. "I'll tell you what. Can you be here at seven in the morning? Is that too early?"

"I'm usually up by five."

"No one will be here that early to unlock the door. But if you show up around seven tomorrow, I'll meet you here. You'll have the place to yourself for an hour before we open to the rest of the patients."

Relief made Bethel's limbs weak. For once, she was glad of the crutches under her arms, propping her up. She wanted to get better, but Luke, her new bishop, would never allow something like this. It seemed selfish to want the place to herself, but it wouldn't work otherwise. "I'll be here."

"Just make sure you wear workout clothes. Long sleeves, long pants, cover up all you want, but it has to be something you can move in. And plan to stay for the group therapy session afterwards. That's the compromise."

Bethel managed a nod.

Doctor Karen smiled. "Don't worry — no one has ever died of embarrassment in this room."

Not yet, anyway.

CHAPTER 11

Luke straightened and laid the hammer on top of the wooden shelter he and Thomas had constructed for the propane tank outside the kitchen. Leah had the windows open and the smell of cookies baking wafted around him. Much better then the acrid smell of the sweat that soaked his shirt. So much for fall weather. Clouds scudded across the sky and the air hung around him thick with humidity. The cool, crisp morning had evolved into a muggy afternoon. At least with the propane tank hooked up they could pump water into the kitchen. He could look forward to washing his hands and face in the sink without carrying in the water to do it.

He took off his hat and wiped his forehead with the back of his sleeve. Building the enclosure had taken longer than he expected. They had so much to do. Like constructing the phone shack, building a school, and planting winter rye. At least the wheat was in. He still needed lumber for the phone shack and they had yet to decide where to build the school. What was taking Elijah and Bethel so long? One thing at a time, he reminded himself. Building a community didn't happen in a day. He eyed his brother-in-law. Even though Thomas should be at his own farm planting his winter wheat, he looked the picture of contentment, hammer in one hand, nail in the other. He didn't seemed to mind the unseasonably warm weather or the imposition. He never did. Luke appreciated that. "You ready for something to drink?"

Thomas rocked back on his heels and shrugged. "I wouldn't say no to a glass of cold sweet tea." He sniffed the air, looking like a hunting dog. "Those cookies smell good, but Emma sent along some sticky buns she made last night. She couldn't sleep so she baked instead."

Luke hadn't slept much either. He'd lain awake listening to Leah toss and turn. He tried talking to her, but she feigned sleep. Her breathing didn't become soft and regular until well into the night. It would take a lot of sticky buns to sweeten his mood. "We can take a break if we don't sit around too long. We still need to get to the phone shack. And you have things to do on your property."

"There's no hurry. Silas's crew is planting his fields today, and they'll get to mine next. As far as the phone shack goes, Benjamin says we can always borrow his neighbor's phone. They let him call Micah before the ordination." Thomas stood and stretched, his long frame casting a shadow that shaded Luke from the heat of the sun for a few seconds. "He did say they seemed a little unsure as to whether they wanted the likes of him in their house."

"Folks around here are pretty skittish about strangers," Luke conceded. "Sort of like us."

"Anyway, we've had the ordination so I don't know why we need a phone right away. Except for emergencies." He gave Luke another sly grin. "Unless you're homesick and want to call someone."

Luke snorted and let that be his response to his friend's joke. He would see the rest of his family at Helen and Gabriel's wedding and for Thanksgiving.

"Besides, we won't have the lumber until Elijah returns." Thomas mopped his face with a faded bandana. "We need the paint and shingles too."

"The longer this takes, the longer it is

before we finish in the fields."

"Silas and Ben's boys will get to your fields by the end of the week. Everyone knows we have some chores to do that affect the whole community. We'll get them done."

Thomas was right. Luke gathered up his patience around him, like a well-worn blanket. "I can't imagine what's taking Elijah and Bethel so long. I would've gone myself if I'd known they were going to dillydally around."

"I doubt Elijah is doing any dillydallying. It's not his way." Thomas laid down his hammer and started toward the back steps. "It is the way with doctors, though. You do a lot of hurrying up and waiting. They're called waiting rooms for a reason."

Thomas would know. Luke read in his somber expression where his mind had gone. To the months he'd spent in and out of hospital waiting rooms after his first wife had been diagnosed with cancer. Some wounds never completely healed. "I guess you're right about that too." The endless to-do list in his head didn't seem to be shrinking. Instead it lengthened until he felt his head might explode. "It's worth it if they can do something to help Bethel."

"I'm amazed at what doctors can do these

days." Thomas clomped up the steps. "I'll see if I can impose on your fraa for that tea."

"She should've brought us some by now." He stopped. Leah had her hands full. Even with Rebecca and the twins, who'd made the ride over with Thomas, helping her with the yard work and the laundry. "I reckon she —"

The sound of horse hooves beating a rhythm on the dirt road made him turn to see the wagon coming around the bend and heading up the drive toward them. Elijah came at a good pace. Making up for lost time? Not so smart. If he didn't slow down, he'd lose the load of lumber.

The wagon slowed in a cloud of dust and then stopped a few feet from the back porch.

"It's about time." Luke strode toward them. "What did the doctor say? Did you get all the supplies we need?"

Neither Elijah nor Bethel answered. Bethel's face was red and her kapp askew, wisps of hair scraggly on her forehead from the windy ride.

Elijah hopped down and marched toward the back of the wagon. Luke started to follow, then trudged around to Bethel's side. "Did you learn anything?"

"A lot." She clutched a large plastic bag with the words *New Hope Discount Store* on the side along with her canvas bag. "Could you help me down?"

He did so. She thrust her crutches under her arms and swung away without looking directly at him. With a quick hello, she squeezed past Thomas on the porch and disappeared through the doorway.

"I'll help unload." Thomas wheeled around and pounded down the steps.

"Get the tea. Elijah and I have it."

"You sure?"

"Jah."

Luke trudged around to the back of the wagon where Elijah struggled to pull two twenty-pound bags of flour from between stacks of lumber and pallets of shingles and a dozen gallons of paint. Luke grabbed an enormous bottle of cooking oil and a second of vinegar. "Is something wrong with Bethel?"

"Nee."

"Did you get everything we need?"

"And then some."

"What do you mean?"

"Bethel didn't tell you?"

"She didn't tell me anything. Did you hear her talking to me?"

"She didn't tell you about the sweatpants and the exercise equipment?"

"What?"

Elijah tossed a bag of flour on his shoulder as if it weighed nothing, then grabbed a bag of sugar. "She didn't tell you about the therapy group? Or the *Englisch* soldier in a wheelchair who called her darling? I'm sorry, not darling, darlin'."

"What are you talking about?"

Elijah turned his back and marched toward the porch. "You're asking the wrong person."

Darlin'?

If something untoward had happened at the rehabilitation clinic, Bethel wouldn't be able to have her physical therapy. She needed that therapy. For her own sake, but also for Leah's. Luke wanted to groan, but he swallowed the desire. As bishop, he had to keep Bethel's best interests and her spiritual well-being first, along with the best interest of the community. His own needs as her brother-in-law — and those of his *fraa* — would come last.

Bethel wanted to go directly to her bedroom. She wanted to close the door and lock it and then throw herself on the bed and never get up. But she didn't. She had work to do. What a morning. As if the experience at the clinic hadn't been enough. She would never have told Elijah any of it if she'd known he would get so snippy about it. The silent condemnation in his face had been apparent when he picked her up and continued to grow as he agreed to stop at the discount store to buy the sweatpants and sweatshirt. He carried the items to the register for her after she decided she didn't dare take the time to try them on. He even insisted on paying for them. Only the obvious curiosity of the cashier kept her from arguing with him.

His increasingly angry silence had kept her from relaxing on the ride home. Her shoulders ached with tension and her head pounded. Or was it her guilty conscience? She hadn't done anything to encourage Shawn McCormack. Nothing. She squeezed past empty cardboard boxes stacked by the back door and wound her way through the kitchen. A pot of northern beans and ham hock simmered on the stove. The scent mingled with the sweet aroma of baking peanut butter cookies. A fresh batch of cornbread set on the counter, cooling.

Where *was* Leah? She hadn't been hanging clothes on the lines behind the house. Bethel moved toward the door that led to the laundry room. No Leah. Mounds of laundry dotted the scarred linoleum floor. The smell took her back to her childhood chores. Bleach and soap. The memories eased the tension between her shoulders.

The propane-run ringer wash machine made a nice *swish, swish* sound as it agitated the clothes back and forth in a white froth. It reminded her of the days when it had been her job to run the clothes from the soapy water through the ringer and into the huge tubs of cool rinse water. A simple job that took hours, what with a family of eight and endless piles of pants, dresses, and shirts. Three growing boys and three girls could turn laundry day into laundry days. She'd prided herself on never once getting her fingers caught in that ringer. Her sister Mattie had once and it hadn't been pretty.

A slamming screen door and a sharp cry from inside the house startled Bethel from her reverie. She swung her crutches back through the door and into the kitchen. The sound of sniffling came from the front room. Someone was in pain. "Leah?"

No answer. She rushed as fast as the unwieldy crutches allowed, nearly plowing into a couch shoved toward the middle of the living room. Everything remained covered with drop cloths as they slowly repaired each room in the house, with the front room saved for last. Thomas knelt before one of

129

the hickory rockers examining Lillie, whose small hands were clasped to her cheeks. Leah stood nearby, hands on her hips, glaring.

"It's about time you got back." At least Leah and Luke agreed on something. "Lillie has gone and gotten herself smacked in the eye with a rock."

Lillie's muffled sniffling told Bethel Leah's commentary wasn't helping. She swung over to Thomas. "Is she all right?"

"I was mowing the front yard and a big rock flew up and hit me right in the eye." Lillie sounded justifiably aggrieved. "The whole big yard out there and it had to smack me in the eye?"

"Accidents happen." Thomas's deep, steady voice soothed. "Bethel, can you wrap a chunk of ice in a washcloth? We need to keep the swelling down. You're going to have quite the shiner, little one."

Bethel started back toward the door, but Leah brushed past her. "I'll do it. It'll take you a week. By the time you get back, the ice will be melted."

A quick breath didn't take the sting from Leah's comment. Sometimes the level of her sister's meanness astounded even Bethel, who'd lived with her most of her life. She swung back around to see Thomas looking up at her. She shook her head. "She's got her hands full."

"Seems like we all do." Thomas stood, the joints in his knees cracking. "She's your sister. Might be a good idea to find out what the problem is."

"I will." She'd been so wrapped up in her own problems that it had been a long time since she tried to talk to Leah about anything other than the many daily tasks that had to be accomplished. Bethel moved so she could get a better look at Lillie's injury. "Can you see all right, Lillie?"

"I could if it would stop watering so much." Lillie rubbed at her eye with the back of her plump hand. "I want to finish the yard. If I don't get back out there Mary will do it first."

Apparently the twins had decided they enjoyed mowing. Bethel hadn't minded the chore either. Compared to cleaning the chicken coop, it could be considered quite fun.

"She'd see just fine if you were out there mowing the lawn instead of her, Bethel." Leah bustled into the room, ice and towel in hand. "She's really not tall enough to be handling that push mower."

"I like mowing," Lillie protested. "I mow for Emma, don't I, Thomas?"

131

"You do, and a fine job you do too."

"Don't back talk." Leah thrust the towel at her. "Keep this on your eye. Mary can finish the job while I get the laundry on the line. Can you at least take care of the ham and beans and the cookies, Bethel? All you have to do is make sure neither of them burn."

"I can." The words stung like a slap to the face. Bethel tried to ignore the burning heat that spread across her neck and cheeks. "I will. Can I watch the babies for you?"

"Rebecca is putting them down for a nap. She can run up and down the stairs. You can't. When she's done, tell her to go to the cellar and bring up some canned peaches. You can't handle those stairs either."

No need to rub it in. Bethel bit back the words. Even the sound of Leah's skirt swishing back and forth sounded angry as she disappeared into the kitchen.

"It's not my place to interfere." Thomas pushed his hat back on his head and offered Bethel a small smile. "It's just an observation. Whatever it is, it's getting worse."

"I know."

"Was the doctor's appointment helpful to you?"

"What's this about a soldier calling you darling?" Luke's frame filled the doorway.

His stern gaze held hers. "What's this about some sort of group therapy thing? And sweatpants?"

"What did Elijah tell you?"

"He told me I should ask you."

"I'll drive the wagon out to the road and unload the lumber." Thomas made it to the front door in two easy strides. Apparently he thought that would be safer than passing Luke to go to the back door. "Lillie, come with me. Bring your ice pack. You can help Leah hang the clothes."

"Leah doesn't like the way I do it. I'm too short."

"Then you can take down the dry clothes, fold them, and put them away. Let's go."

A second later Bethel stood alone in the room with her brother-in-law, who also served as her new bishop. Which would he be first?

Luke sank onto the drop-cloth covered couch and leaned back, his face lined with exhaustion. He looked older than his thirty years. "Tell me what happened."

She settled into a chair across from him and recounted the morning's events, leaving nothing out. Luke didn't interrupt, but his expression darkened. He leaned forward. His hands gripped his knees when she arrived at the part about Shawn calling her *darling.* She didn't mention his declaration of love at first sight. Why enflame the situation? Shawn didn't mean it. He couldn't have meant it. Love at first sight didn't exist. Certainly not between a Plain woman and an Englisch soldier.

Luke tapped the sofa's arm, an absent look on his face. He sniffed. "You will do the therapy. I trust you to make good choices." He frowned. "But no swimming suit. Nothing in the pool. We have a bathtub and a pond. Make do."

"I will."

"Just get better."

"I will." For the look on his face, her brother-in-law needed that reassurance. "As soon as I can. I promise."

CHAPTER 12

Elijah thrust his spoon into the bowl of ham and beans and tried to look content to be seated at the Shirack table, enjoying good food. In all honesty, if he could've found a way to politely refuse Luke's invitation to eat supper with his family, Elijah would've done it. He stuck the heaping spoon of beans in his mouth. It burned. Hot. Very hot. He opened his mouth wide and tried to suck air in and out. "Ouch, ouch!" he dropped the spoon into the beans and waved his hand in front of his face. Finally, he had no choice but to swallow. The beans burned all the way down his throat. "Hot!"

"Do you like cold beans better?" Joseph giggled. William immediately aped his older brother. The little girls, Esther and Martha, banged their spoons on the table. In their booster seats they barely reached it. "Ham and beans should be hot, shouldn't they, Daed?"

135

"It's not nice to make fun of other people," Luke admonished his sons. "Be quiet and eat your supper."

"It's okay. Joseph's right." Elijah smiled at the children to let them know he didn't hold a grudge. "I got in a big hurry because it smelled so good. Your mudder makes a good bowl of ham and beans."

Leah, busy buckling Jebediah into his high chair, actually smiled. He tried to remember if he'd ever seen her smile before. Not in recent memory. It transformed her rather plain face, softening its sharp edges and lightening her dark eyes. She slid into her seat, the last to do so. "It's nice to have someone notice. Have some more cornbread. It's fresh."

She handed the basket to Bethel. "Pass this to Elijah."

Bethel barely looked his way as she shoved the basket at him and let go before he could get a firm grasp on it. The basket toppled onto the table, spilling its contents.

"What's wrong with you?" Leah stood and leaned over the table. She swept the contents back into the basket, mangling some of the squares. "I know your legs don't work, but there's nothing wrong with your hands, is there?"

Bethel's face went white and her eyes red-

136

dened. She lifted her napkin to her lips as if to hide her face. "It's my fault." Fingers shaking with his embarrassment, Elijah took the basket from Leah. "I have terrible table manners. My mudder always said so."

"No need to defend me." Bethel dropped the napkin in her lap. She was the only one he knew who could mix that kind of defiance with a quivering voice. "I don't need your help."

"You've mentioned that." He managed to keep his discomfort from his voice. "I'm not trying to help you. A Plain woman who can go into a discount store and pick out a pair of sweatpants that fit without trying them on is a woman to be reckoned with."

"Sweatpants?" Leah's lips twisted in distaste. "What's this about?"

"Nothing." Bethel glared at Elijah. "Nothing that a person should bring up at the supper table."

"Are you gonna wear pants?" William elbowed his brother. "Bethel's gonna wear pants."

"Can I see you in them, *Aenti*?" Joseph aimed a spoonful of beans at his mouth and missed. The juice spattered on his chin. "You'd look funny."

"Hush and eat your supper." Leah slapped her glass of water on the table harder than

137

necessary. "And wipe your chin. Little boys should be seen and not heard."

That brought another round of giggles from the boys. They certainly had their father's sense of humor.

"What do sweatpants have to do with making your legs better?" Leah asked, her gaze on her sister's face. "You haven't told me anything about what the doctor said. It sounds like you need to find a different doctor, one who understands our ways."

"Bethel had an interesting session with her new doctor today." Luke looked unperturbed. He spooned more beans into his bowl and crumbled cornbread into them. "Right now, I'd like to eat in peace. Quietly."

Amen. Elijah remembered just in time to blow on the beans before he stuck the spoon in his mouth. Better he keep it full than get himself in trouble again.

"Jah." Bethel pushed her bowl away. She'd hardly touched her food. "It's no one else's business. No one else should be spreading rumors about it."

So that's what this was about. She was mad that he'd said something to Luke. "It's not a rumor when it's true and it's for the person's own good."

"You're not my brother. Or my father."

For that he was thankful. "I don't want to

138

be either." The words came out without thought of how they would sound. Heat burned his ears and neck. He fumbled for a way to smooth away the words. "But I'm not just your driver. I'm a friend."

"He's right." Luke chewed and swallowed. "What he told me needed to be said."

"Told you what?" Leah threw both her hands in the air. "What are you talking about?"

"I would have told you." Bethel paused, her gaze fixed on the table. "Not that you're my father, either. I have a father. Begging your pardon, Luke."

"He's not here and you live in my house." Luke's easygoing tone had disappeared. He threw his napkin on top of his bowl. "I'm also your bishop."

"I didn't do anything wrong. I didn't invite the attention."

"What attention?" Leah stood. "Someone tell me what's going on here."

"Nothing's going on. Nothing happened."

Bethel rose also, grabbed her crutches, and hopped from the room. Leah picked up her bowl and glass and followed her sister into the kitchen.

"Can I have sweatpants too?" William asked. Joseph burped and giggled. "We both want them."

Luke fixed them with a stern stare. They went back to stuffing cornbread in their mouths.

"You know, if you wait too long, you'll miss your chance." Luke sighed and leaned back in his chair. "Especially if you keep making her mad like this."

Elijah squirmed in his chair. Courting involved only two people. More constituted a crowd. Bethel had been right about one thing. The caregiver in him needed a rest. He'd done his share of taking care of folks. The question of children also hung out there. He watched the two boys feed pieces of cornbread to the twins while Jebediah smeared chopped peaches all over his high chair tray. Elijah wanted it all — fraa, kinner, a complete life. "I did what I thought was right."

"You were right to tell me." Luke picked up Jebediah's plastic bowl and set it on the table beyond the boy's reach. "She's right too. She would've told me. That's the way she is. She's a strong believer. She doesn't waver from the Ordnung. She wants to get better, but not at the expense of doing what's right or proper."

"I'm just her driver." Bethel had made that abundantly clear. "I'm happy to do that much for her."

"You're not just her driver. But you need to keep driving her."

"I plan to."

"I need you to watch over her."

"Because of the Englisch man?"

"I trust Bethel to make the right decisions, but the Englischers around here don't know our ways. She's a kind person. She might not know how to handle his attention."

"I won't have a problem doing that."

"Remember, we're new here. We'd like to get off on the right foot."

Luke's sentiment reminded Elijah of the incident on the road into town and the old man on the street who'd been so rude. He told Luke about the truck nearly running their wagon off the highway.

"They'll get used to our slow-moving wagons and buggies." Luke picked at crumbs on the table and tossed them into his bowl. "It's best to let those things go. Like I said, we need to get off on the right foot."

"Had the wagon tipped over into the ditch, Bethel could've been hurt or killed."

"But she wasn't, I imagine because of your driving." Luke met Elijah's gaze. "I appreciate that."

"I did the best I could."

"I know. Do the best you can with Bethel

and these visits to the clinic too."

"So she's to do the physical therapy, then?"

"And the other therapy too. The support group thing."

"Is that for the best?" He didn't mean to question Luke's authority as the head of his household or as the new bishop. "I mean . . ."

"She has to get better. Leah needs her help."

"It's that bad?"

Luke didn't respond. Again, Elijah regretted putting the fear to words. Luke wouldn't want to admit he couldn't get his own wife to settle into her new situation.

"She said something about being there by seven in the morning. I'll be here at dawn to help with the chores before I take her in."

"Good." Luke stood. "Speaking of chores."

Elijah slid back his chair. At least chores he knew how to do. Handling a woman remained a mystery.

Bethel leaned against the counter and plunged her hands into the dish tub as Leah added more hot water from the stove. "I'll wash if you want to dry."

142

"That's fine." Leah's voice was tight. She set the pot on the stove with more force than necessary. "I'll bring in the dishes from the table."

"Leah, wait." Thinking of Thomas's words earlier in the day, Bethel grabbed a towel and dried her hands. She faced her sister. "Are you all right?"

"I'm fine. It bothers me that you would tell Luke things before you tell me, your sister, but other than that, I'm fine." Leah twisted a dish towel between hands that looked chapped and red. "Why?"

"Nothing bad happened today. A man talked to me in a way that was unexpected. Nothing came of it. I don't want to talk about that. I want to talk about you. You seem unhappy." More than usual, Bethel wanted to add, but didn't. Doctor Karen seemed to think talking about things helped heal hurts. Maybe Leah had a hurt that needed to heal. "Is it being away from home?"

Leah's lips quivered. She swallowed. Her hand went to her cheeks and brushed away a tear. To Bethel's horror, she realized her older sister, who had raised her younger brothers and sisters through Mudder's two bouts with cancer, was crying. "What is it? Tell me, please."

"I can't. I don't know what it is."

"You don't know?"

"Since Jebediah was born, I've felt . . ." She eased into a chair, her face lined with guilt. What could this woman, who worked hard morning, noon, and night, have to feel guilty about? "Having babies was all I've ever wanted. Now, since Jeb, I'm so tired. And it sounds ridiculous . . . I'm sad. So sad I don't want to get up in the morning. I don't want to feed him. I don't want to change his diaper. How can I tell anyone that? I can't tell Luke. He'd think I've lost my mind. I have lost my mind. I shouldn't even be telling you."

She drew a deep breath and sank back in the chair, shoulders bowed, head down, as if this pouring out of words had emptied her. Her hands tied the towel into knots. After a second, her expression fearful, she looked up at Bethel as if waiting for her to pass judgment. Bethel didn't know what to say. Her sister was born to be a mother. Leah's lips twisted. "Say it. I'm a terrible mother, a terrible fraa. Aren't I?"

"Nee! You're a good mudder."

"Then why do I feel this way? I always bounced back after every baby, even the twins."

"When the twins were born, Emma and

Annie helped you. Now you have five children under the age of ten and me for help. Me with my crutches."

"All the women in our community have several small children. That's the way we want it. That's the way it's meant to be." Her voice dropped to a painful whisper. "What's wrong with me?"

"You've moved to a new place. Doctor Karen says moving is stressful."

"Stressful?"

Not a word in their vocabulary. Bethel scrambled to explain. "It makes you tired, not just physically tired, but in your mind."

"I want to lay my head on the table right now and go to sleep."

It wasn't only the words that broke Bethel's heart, but the look on her sister's face. She looked lost and scared and confused, like a woman who'd opened her eyes from a long sleep and found herself in a foreign land. Scared and confused were two things Bethel had never associated with her sister. Leah had always borne the brunt of that burden and she'd never complained. "I'm so sorry I haven't been more help to you."

"You do what you can."

To have her sister acknowledge that meant a great deal to Bethel. "It will be more, when I get better."

"It has to be more." Tears trickled down Leah's face. "I don't mean to burden you, but it has to be more. I can't do this by myself."

"I understand."

"You don't."

"I'll work harder. I'll get better, I promise."

"I'm expecting again."

The words struck Bethel with the force of a shovel slammed against her chest. Another baby. A blessing. God rained blessings down on her sister and Luke. She chased away fleeting envy. "Does Luke know?"

"I haven't told him."

"Why?"

"Because he will be so happy, and I can't let him see the truth in my face."

"What truth?"

"Haven't you been listening?" Leah wiped her face with the knotted towel. "I can't bear the thought."

"It'll be all right. We'll get through it together." She grabbed her crutches and hopped closer. "Let's write to Mattie. She would love to come for a visit. You know she would. Together she and I can give you a chance to rest. You'll feel good as new."

"Mattie has her own family. You should be

146

having your own life too. It's selfish of me to ask for your help when there's a man . . ." She stopped and dropped the mangled towel on the prep table. "I should get the dishes before all the food hardens on them. Makes more work for you."

"What do you mean, a man?"

"Open your eyes, schweschder." All the anxiety and sadness and fear drained from her face, leaving a mask. "You have a chance for a life of your own."

Wishful thinking on Leah's part. Bethel refused to be sidetracked. "You have to tell Luke."

"Nee."

"Why?"

"When he married me, he expected me to be his fraa." She sounded so defeated. "To have his children and care for them. That's my job."

"He'll understand."

"I don't even understand."

"Go to a doctor." She thought of Doctor Karen's kindness. "Doctors can help."

"And tell them what? I find after having five children that I'm a terrible mother?"

"You're not."

"Elijah didn't get dessert."

It took Bethel a second to realize Leah had changed the subject again. "What?"

147

"Take Elijah one of the cinnamon rolls I made yesterday. They're still fresh." Leah waved her hand at the dish tub, her tone back to the usual no-nonsense bossiness that had been her hallmark as long as Bethel could remember. "The dishes will be here when you get back. They need to soak, anyway."

The Leah she knew would never let the chores go, even for a few minutes. "What are you doing?" asked Bethel.

"Just because I'm miserable doesn't mean I want you to be." Her voice trembled, but her gaze didn't waver. "I want you to be happy."

If lightning had struck Bethel at that moment, she wouldn't have been more surprised. "Please talk to a doctor. Talk to someone."

"I talked to you. Now go."

A wave of inadequacy rolled over Bethel. "At least tell Luke about the new baby. It'll help."

"Cut the cinnamon roll."

Leah disappeared through the door.

Bethel stared at the spot where her sister had stood. The weight of Leah's words pinned her against the counter. Another baby. Somehow, she had to help Leah get through this. Her sister needed to know she could depend on Bethel. And Bethel needed to get better. Fast. Which meant trips to town. It meant spending time with Elijah. She went to the table and cut a huge cinnamon roll from the pan and put it on a saucer. A peace offering.

At the screen door, she held her breath and peered out. He hadn't gone yet. "Wait!" She pushed against the screen door with her shoulder. The cinnamon roll slid across the plate and teetered on the edge. Her crutch caught on the threshold. She started to go down, caught herself, and the door swung away. She breathed a silent prayer of thanks. "Elijah, wait."

He looked up from the horse he was untying from the new hitching post in front of the house. His expression didn't look inviting. In fact, he looked as if he might leap on to the horse and flee.

"Wait, you didn't get dessert. Have a cinnamon roll before you go."

His hand on the horse's long mane, he still didn't look convinced.

"Leah made them yesterday. They're almost as good as Annie's and Annie runs a bakery."

Slowly, he moved to retie the reins to the post. His stride toward the porch bordered on laborious. She held the plate out.

His warm fingers touched hers when he took the saucer from her hand. "I suppose it can't hurt."

"Can you sit for a moment?"

"It's getting late. It'll be dark soon." He took a big bite of the sweet pastry, flakes of icing catching at the corners of his mouth. She stifled the urge to wipe them away. For a minute he looked like William and Joseph, eyes rolled back in pure delight. "We have to be off to town early in the morning."

"That's what I wanted to talk to you about." She sank into the hickory rocking chair positioned behind Leah's favorite blue and green piece rug. "I wanted to say I'm sorry for being so grumpy today."

"Grumpy." He eased into the chair next to her. "I don't think grumpy is the word. Strong headed. Stubborn. Mulish."

"You can stop now." His comical expression made her laugh for the first time all day. "I'm not that bad."

"It was an uncomfortable situation for both of us. I handled it badly." He wiped his hand on his pants and held it out. "Forgive and forget. Friends?"

She could use a friend. The weight of Leah's confession made her shoulders ache. To her surprise, sudden tears welled up. She blinked them away and grasped his hand in a quick shake. "Friends."

"I don't plan to let that man bother you."

"You don't understand." She wished she had her basket of sewing. It soothed her to keep her fingers busy. "You say you want to be my friend. Then you have to realize something."

The saucer in his hand remained suspended in the air. "What?"

"The man's name is Shawn McCormack."

"I know. I remember."

"All the girls who were my friends when I was growing up are married now." Would he understand what she was saying? His expression said no. "They're married. All my sisters and brothers are married. I'm the only single one. No husband, no kinner."

"So you think this Shawn, this *Englischer,* is somehow going to change that?"

"Nee! He wants to be my friend." She pointed to her legs, hidden by her long skirt. She raised her head to meet his gaze. "He understands about this. I need a friend who understands."

Elijah stared out at the lengthening shadows cast by the house. The sun dropped behind a cloud on the horizon and the world darkened. Finally, his gaze came back to her. "*I* understand. The cinnamon roll was good."

He set the plate on the table, stood, and stomped across the porch, his boots thudding on the wood. At the bottom of the steps he turned, his head haloed as the sun drifted out from behind the clouds. "I figure you never stopped to think I might understand too."

"I don't —"

"I'm not just your driver." He swung onto the horse with the ease of long practice and sat tall and straight in the saddle. "See you in the morning."

Bethel sat there a long time, watching as the horse's gentle trot became an easy canter and then a full-fledged gallop. Regardless of what Elijah had said, he seemed to be doing a good job of putting as much distance between them as possible as quickly as possible.

CHAPTER 13

Elijah urged Ned forward. He'd waited too long to leave the Shirack farm. Dusk gathered quickly and it was past his bedtime. He shouldn't be angry with Bethel's declaration that she needed friends who understood her situation, but he couldn't help it. She'd chosen this soldier she'd met once to be a friend over a Plain man standing right in front of her. A man she'd known since childhood. He would have to accept that. He didn't want to be the one to take care of her, anyway. He'd had enough of that. Hadn't he? He heaved a sigh and tried to relax into the saddle. The familiar rise and fall of the horse under him soothed his physical tension, but his determination did nothing to fill the empty void in his chest. He had willingly taken care of his parents while others chose their fraas and married. Now his parents were gone and he lived with his brother, watching Silas's family grow and helping him start a new farm and a new life. Elijah had a good life. A blessed life.

Gott, if it's Your will that I remain alone, so be it. I accept Your will for me. But if it's not, Lord, help me find the right woman to be my fraa. Set her directly in my path because I seem to be too dense to know her when I see her.

On the highway overhead lights popped on, startling him from his prayers. At least the highway would be well lighted. The dark dirt road that led to his brother's house once he left the highway would be another story. Despite every attempt to let it go, he continued to mull over his conversation with Bethel. The woman made no sense to him whatsoever. He snapped the reins. *Let it go. Let it be. What will happen, will happen.* The horse picked up his pace as if he too longed for his stall and a night's rest. "Let's go home, Ned. We'll both feel better at the other end of a good night's sleep."

At least not many cars traversed the road at this time of the evening. Not on a week-day. Most folks were already home doing their evening chores and settling down to read the paper or sew or play games — or if they were Englisch, watch TV. He let his mind wander to that contraption and the made-up stories they watched on it. Was it really that different from reading a book? He didn't care enough to belabor the thought. He sighed and settled into the saddle, wishing for his bed and his pillow.

A horn blared, its shriek making him jump. Ned leapt ahead. The Morgan strained against the reins, nearly ripping them from Elijah's hands. *Here we go again.* He fought to keep control of the power-house of horseflesh beneath him. "Easy, boy, easy!"

The headlights flashed around him. The car bore down on him. Elijah swerved to the shoulder and hazarded a glance back. The lights engulfed him, blinded him. He threw his hand to his forehead, trying to block the glare.

Why didn't they slow? Couldn't they see the mammoth horse striding along the side of the road? Surely the driver saw him. How could he not? This wasn't a darkened dirt road off the beaten track. "Hey!"

The car, its color and style lost in the brilliant lights blinding Elijah, hurtled toward him. A swoosh of wind caught his breath and took it away.

Ned screamed in a high, fierce whinny that went on and on. The front bumper glanced off the horse's side in a powerful blow. The force of the jolt knocked Ned into the embankment. No longer able to maintain his grip on the flailing horse, Elijah sailed airborne. He somersaulted in a dizzying trajectory that seemed to last for days. He fought to see. The lights overhead tilted wildly around him. Ned reared up on his hind legs, his front legs beating the air.

Elijah had no time to prepare for impact. His body collided with the ground in an all-out, bruising assault that knocked any remaining air from his lungs. He instinctively curled into a ball and allowed himself to roll. Pain shot through his body. Eyes closed, he came to rest, weeds tickling his face. He tried to comprehend what had happened. He waited, thinking he would hear a door slam and footsteps. None came. The car hadn't stopped.

So be it. Time to get up. He didn't want to move, but he couldn't stay here forever. Elijah tasted salty blood. He'd bit his tongue and his lip. He swallowed against nausea. The ham and beans and cinnamon roll rose in his throat. He breathed through it. He moved his arms and legs and immediately regretted it. His breathing sounded ragged in the sudden, blaring silence.

Adrenaline faded, leaving behind a deep weariness. He had to get up or he would simply spend the night beside the road. He forced himself to open his eyes and sucked in cool night air, once, twice, three times, then moved his head to look around. Pain rippled between his eyes and along the back side of his head. He stifled a groan. A soft nicker answered. Ned had returned. The sound of the horse's labored breathing joined his own.

"Ned." Elijah struggled to sit up. Purple and black dots danced in his vision. His head pounded. "Ned, are you all right?"

The horse nickered again. Elijah tested his arms and found both would take his weight, so he pushed off the ground to pull himself upright. His legs held. He slapped both hands on his knees and stayed bent over a few seconds, waiting for the dizziness to pass.

"You can do it." He spoke aloud, more to himself than the horse. He straightened. The road in front of him tipped side to side, then righted itself. "That's better."

A few more shallow breaths and he trusted his legs to carry him toward the horse. "Hey you, Ned, come here, boy. It's okay."

The horse didn't move toward him, but didn't skitter away, either. The whites of his eyes shone in the overhead lights. The horse's smell of sweat and fear wafted from him. Whispering soft nothings, Elijah tramped through the overgrown weeds and grass until he reached the horse. He smoothed his hand down the animal's sleek neck. "It's okay," he murmured as he moved toward the animal's back. "Driver needs to be more careful, I reckon, don't you?"

He ran a hand down each leg. The front right one was swollen. "That hurts, doesn't it, boy?"

Ned tossed his head and nickered, more loudly this time. He shied away from Elijah's touch. A dark wetness coated his fingers. The horse had a gash the length of his left front leg. "I'm sorry, boy." Elijah wiped away the blood on the weeds that reached nearly to his waist. "I'm so sorry."

He bit his lip against the bruising pain. It felt like a baseball smacking against the back of his head over and over again with no discernable rhythm. "Well, we can't stay here, can we, boy?"

He gathered the reins and tugged. The horse followed, but with a profound limp. Elijah longed to strike out at someone, anyone. *No.* He cringed at his own disobedience. *Forgive me.* Doing wrong when wronged only led down a dark, violent road, a place he never wanted to go. As his mother often told him, two wrongs did not make a right. "It was an accident," he said instead, as if Ned could understand. "And even if it wasn't, it's my job to forgive this person who doesn't know me and probably doesn't realize what a problem he's caused."

Enough talking aloud to himself. Better to save his breath for the long walk. After they turned on to the dirt road that led to Silas's house, it became harder and harder to lift his feet. He stumbled in the deep ruts. Ned slowed so much Elijah resorted to tugging on the reins. As much as he didn't want to hurt the animal, he had to keep him moving forward.

Time passed in fits and starts. He might still be stumbling along at daybreak. Maybe days from now. He concentrated on putting one foot in front of the other. He counted the steps.

Lights flashed ahead of him, up and down, in the ruts of the road. He jerked from the dazed reverie of someone who needed desperately to sleep. After a second, he realized he was seeing the battery-operated lights of a buggy coming toward him.

"Elijah, is that you?" Silas's voice boomed behind the blinding lights. "What are you doing? What's wrong with the horse?"

Elijah staggered to a stop. He bowed his head. *Thank You, Jesus, thank You.*

"It's me."

"Where have you been? You're always home by dark. I was beginning to think you lost yourself in this new countryside."

"Nee."

Silas stopped the buggy in the middle of the road. He clamored down. "What happened to you?" The humor in his voice had disappeared. "Is that blood on your forehead?"

CHAPTER 14

Bethel took a side-swipe glance at Elijah. He held the reins with a white-knuckled grip. The patch of bandage on his forehead peeked out from under his hair and his hat. The scratches and bruises on the side of his face were made all the more noticeable by the paleness of his skin. A man normally as neat as a Plain living room, he looked as if he'd slept in his clothes. Scratches covered the back of his hands, red and raw looking. When he arrived well before the appointed hour to take her into town, he'd refused her offer of a cup of *kaffi* and declined to come in the house. He tried to hide the grimace when he helped her climb in the buggy, but she saw it and heard the stifled grunt. Still, he hadn't said a word. She clutched her bag with its sweats and sneakers close to her chest and waited for him to tell her what happened.

Nothing. He hadn't said two words the

entire time they traveled on the dirt road or when they turned onto the highway. "What's the matter?" It couldn't hurt to ask, could it? "You seem awful jumpy."

"Nothing. I'm not jumpy. I just want to get you into town quick as possible."

"At this rate, we'll be early." The sun hadn't risen yet, and cars were few and far between. "We practically have the road to ourselves."

"I like it that way." His face reddened. "I mean, I don't like a lot of traffic."

"So that's why we left earlier than need be."

"Jah."

"Are you going to tell me what happened to you, or do you want me to guess?"

"It's not that interesting." He glanced over his shoulder as if checking to see if they were being followed. White lines tightened around his mouth. "You don't need to know."

"You're hurt. That interests me. I want to know."

"I don't want you to be scared or worry. I think it was an accident. Just an accident." For the first time he looked at her directly. The cut across his nose gave him a battered look, like someone who'd been in a fight. She hadn't seen that on a Plain man before.

162

"A car ran me and Ned off the road last night. But I'm fine."

"Fine? You look like you've been beat up." She contemplated his words. "You're sure it was an accident? Yesterday that truck —"

"Just coincidence. People drive too fast on this highway. They're not used to buggies and horseback riders. We need to be more careful." He sounded as if he were trying to convince himself as well as her. "I took a tumble, but I landed in the weeds. Silas's fraa doctored me. I'm fine."

"Did the car stop? Was it intentional?"

"The car didn't stop. I don't know if it was intentional. I suspect it was an accident, but then the driver was scared of getting into trouble, so he moved on."

"And left you on the side of the road."

"Jah."

"So you just got up, dusted yourself off, and rode on home?"

"I got up, dusted myself off, but then I walked Ned home. His leg is hurt pretty bad."

"Can it be fixed?" Bethel knew how much horses meant to the farming operation, and they were very expensive to replace. They were held in high regard. "Did Silas doctor it?"

"He tried, but we figure we need to get a

163

vet out there to look at him." He sighed. "I think we'll have to put him down."

"I'm sorry."

"Me too."

"Do you hurt?" She ventured the words, not sure how he'd react to such a question. Men didn't like to admit to pain or weakness.

Again, he glanced at her, then back at the road. "Jah."

"Do you need a doctor? We'll be near the medical center. The emergency room will be open."

"Nee. I'll drop you, then go by the vet to see when he can come out."

"The veterinary hospital won't be open this early. You could go to the emergency room. Are you sure —"

"Could we not talk?"

Surprised and a little bewildered by his brusqueness, she nodded. Elijah had always been so quick at conversation. She didn't like what this had done to him. She thought of the horn blaring on their first trip into town. What if that truck had gotten too close to them? She sneaked another peek at Elijah. His jaw was set, his expression grim. What sort of new beginning was this? First the house vandalized and nearly burned down. Then the incidents on the road. Did the Englischers dislike them that much? How could they? They didn't even know her family and friends.

These thoughts occupied her as they drove into New Hope. The closer they got to the rehab clinic the more tense she felt. Soon she'd be in a room filled with these very people. People who didn't want her or her kind around. Maybe she should tell the doctor she'd changed her mind. But she couldn't avoid therapy and help Leah. She had to help Leah.

Elijah pulled the buggy up to the curb in front of the clinic. "Whoa." He didn't move to get down immediately. Neither did she.

Finally, he turned to her. "I'm sorry."

"For what?"

"For taking it out on you."

"You didn't."

His gaze went beyond her to the building and then back to her. "You must be a little nervous about this, and I'm sorry if I made it worse."

"You didn't."

"Do you have to be so nice?"

He jumped down from the buggy with a grunt. His back to her, he bent over for a second, hands on his knees. His breathing sounded too loud to her. "Elijah, please."

He strode around the buggy and looked

165

up at her. The purple-green bruises and angry scratches stood out against the whiteness of his skin. He held out both hands. "Down you go."

"You need to go to the doctor."

"I don't."

"You're stubborn as an old man."

"Jah."

She allowed him to help her down. He handed her the crutches and then started toward the double doors. "What are you doing?"

"Luke said I was to deliver you to the doctor."

"That's not necessary."

"I'm not leaving you standing out here. Let's go."

She had no choice but to follow him. He tried the red button Shawn had used the previous day. Nothing. He peered through the glass. "Looks dark in there. Nobody's here yet."

A red car sat in the parking lot in a slot marked *Staff.* "Someone's here. Try knocking."

He knocked and a few seconds later the doors opened. Doctor Karen waved and smiled. "Right on time. Are you Bethel's boyfriend? Come on in. I can give you a little tour if you like."

"Not her boyfriend." His face red as a radish, Elijah backed up, making room for Bethel to enter. "Just her driver."

Bethel started to protest, then stopped. "He's Elijah. He'll run errands while I do this."

"Nothing's open this early except the diner on Main Street. They serve outstanding pancakes and even better steak and eggs for breakfast." Doctor Karen smacked her lips as if she could taste the pancakes. "You look like you could use a cup of coffee, Elijah."

"I could," he conceded. He turned to Bethel. "You all set?"

She wanted to grab his hand and hang on. She wanted to run away. But of course she couldn't, which was the whole point of being here.

"Bethel?" Doctor Karen patted her arm. "Not to worry. This won't hurt. I promise."

Maybe not physically. Sweat ran between her shoulder blades. At seven in the morning. She blew out air and nodded.

"Come back in about two hours or so, Eli. Can I call you Eli? That'll give us time for the PT and the group stuff." Doctor Karen made it sound like they were planning a wonderful frolic. "It might take a little longer this first time around, but you're

167

welcome to wait in the lobby. There's coffee and water and doughnuts and magazines —"

"It's Elijah. Thank you." Elijah fled as if trying to escape the deluge of words.

Doctor Karen led Bethel down the long hallway to the same rooms she'd visited the previous day. "The other guy must've been a lot bigger." She held a door open. "Your boyfriend got walloped."

"He's not my boyfriend. And it was a car."

"He's good-looking. He should be your boyfriend. And what do you mean, a car?"

"A car hit him."

"What kind of car? What was he driving? Did you report it to the police?"

The litany of questions flooded around Bethel. She couldn't breathe, but that might be the nerves that clanged with anticipation. She'd been awake most of the night, staring into the dark, thinking of the sweatpants and the enormous rubber bands and the bicycles she'd seen in the physical therapy room. A swimming pool with warm water. Would she see Shawn today? Her lungs couldn't seem to get enough air.

"I don't know. He was on a horse." Her voice sounded high and breathless in her ears. "No police. We don't need the police."

"You need to calm down. You sound like

168

you're about to self-combust." Doctor Karen cocked her head toward the door. "This isn't a torture chamber. We'll start easy and work our way up. You'll like it. Especially when you get to throw away those crutches. I promise. Now get in there and change so we can get started."

Bethel clutched her crutches. Her feet were frozen to the spot.

"It's okay. We're the only ones here. I promise." Doctor Karen gave her a sympathetic smile. "I understand. You're very modest. I promise I won't say a word to anyone. Everything in here is between you and me."

Inside, Bethel slid from her dress and pulled on the sweatpants with shaking fingers. She felt like a small child learning to dress herself. She pulled the sweatshirt over her shoulders. The neck caught on her kapp in a painful jerk. "Ouch." She tugged it free and stuck her arms through the sleeves. Her gaze caught the image of herself in the mirror that hung on the wall in the tiny dressing room. Why? Who needed to see themselves dress?

Still, she couldn't look away. She didn't own a mirror and she had never seen herself in a full-length one before, only the little pocket mirrors her childhood friends occasionally kept in their bedrooms. She looked scared. And silly. In her lumpy, shapeless gray outfit with its elastic waist and baggy legs and black Converse sneakers she looked like someone else. An entirely different woman from what she imagined herself to be. Her bun had loosened in the fight to don these Englisch clothes. She took a step toward the mirror. So this was what she would look like if she'd taken a different road. If her *rumpspringa* had taken her to a different place. Unlike some of her friends, she'd never explored this path by wearing Englisch clothes. The woman looking back at her was a stranger.

Her cheeks reddened. She put her hands to her face, fascinated by the transformation. *Stop it. Stop looking. Gott, forgive my vanity.*

She turned her back on the mirror, removed the kapp, and carefully redid her hair. Years of practice allowed her to do it with her eyes closed. The kapp was placed firmly back on her head and affixed with pins. She was ready.

Still, her throat dry, hands sweaty, she hesitated.

"Are you about done in there?" Doctor Karen's disembodied voice floated through the door. "We don't have all day. Let's go. I won't look. I promise."

But she did. Bethel saw the woman's lips curve into a small smile when she slinked into the hallway on her crutches. "There you are. See, it's not so bad."

Famous last words. After a long series of stretching exercises, Doctor Karen coaxed, cajoled, encouraged, and bullied Bethel into using muscles she hadn't used in several months, maybe in her entire life-time. The weight machine wasn't so bad because she could sit and use her arms, which had grown stronger as she relied on them for everything, even as her legs grew weaker. The therabands were unfathomable. Doctor Karen started her with the yellow one, but she couldn't make her legs stretch it. "Nothing's happening."

"It's all right. You start small and work up. You'll move up to the green band before you know it. Let's move to the stationary bicycle."

No better. Her efforts to make the pedals turn were fruitless.

"I can't do this." Sweat dripped in her eyes, but she didn't dare raise her hand to wipe it away. She might fall off. "Nothing's happening."

Doctor Karen adjusted the straps that held Bethel's feet in the pedals. "Come on!

Push! Push, try harder!"

"I'm trying."

"Not hard enough, obviously!" Doctor Karen clapped her hands. "Do it, do it! Push!"

Bethel leaned into it. Her back ached, her muscles screamed. Every part of her wanted to give up. The pedals moved. Her legs pumped up and down. "I did it! I did it!" She laughed with relief and gasped for air. "I'm riding a bicycle!"

Doctor Karen stood back, arms crossed over her chest, a grin on her face. "You sure are. Now keep it up."

Bethel managed to do just that for two minutes before her legs gave out.

"That's good. We don't want to overdo it." Doctor Karen unbuckled the straps and held out a hand. "Come on. Let's get you changed. You've got a group session to attend."

"Already?" Bethel took the woman's hand. She'd rather endure this grueling physical assault on her body than talk to a group of strangers about her life since the storm. "I can do more."

"Not today. This is a marathon, not a sprint." Doctor Karen squeezed her hand. "I'm proud of you, Bethel. You did well. It's all about attitude. You've got a good one and that's half the battle."

Buoyed by the woman's kind words, Bethel tried to take a step without her crutches. She could do it. She could. Her right leg buckled. Doctor Karen grabbed her with both hands. Not today. "Like I said, it's a marathon, not a sprint."

"Sorry."

"Don't apologize. You have spunk, young lady."

Spunk. Just what a Plain woman wanted.

CHAPTER 15

Back in the dressing room, Bethel contemplated the door with the sign that said *Shower Room.* Her clothes were soaked with sweat. She probably smelled. How could she sit in a room with a bunch of strangers smelling like this? Still, she couldn't imagine taking a shower in this place with its open stalls and flimsy shower curtains. She'd never taken a shower in her life. She longed for the quiet washroom and its roomy tub where she had all the privacy she needed. Stink or clean? Her head ached with the choices. What would Leah do? What would Mudder and Daed tell her?

After a few seconds of contemplating her choices, Bethel stuck her dress and apron over one arm and pushed through the door using her shoulder. A long bank of shower stalls with skimpy blue curtains lined one wall with a series of sinks along the other. That would do. She leaned her crutches against the counter and used it to prop herself up. Every muscle in her body ached, but it felt good. She might pay tonight or tomorrow, but for now, it felt good.

She snatched paper towels from the dispenser, ran cold water, and began washing herself. She added pink, flowery smelling soap from the dispenser and rubbed it against the paper towel until it became sudsy and washed her face, neck, and underarms. She removed the sneakers and sweats and wiped down as best she could. Then she struggled into her dress, her damp body making it a battle that took her last ounce of strength and most of her remaining patience.

"There."

Bethel heaved a sigh and looked for the first time at the long mirror that covered the wall over the sinks. Mirrors everywhere. Why? The woman looking back at her had color in her face that hadn't been there before, but otherwise, it was her. The Plain woman she'd always been. The sweats and the exercise machines hadn't changed that. They would simply allow her to be the person she'd been before and do the things she needed to do to be a helpful member of her family and her community. The ends justified the means. What would her Daed say about that? He'd say it was a slippery slope. He'd say she needed to understand how a wrong step might send her tumbling into the arms of a world that would separate her from her family and her community, and most importantly, from God. She walked a thin line. Bethel managed a soft laugh to herself. As if she could walk any line. She smoothed her hair one last time and patted her face dry. She smelled fine.

Doctor Karen stood outside the room, waiting, just as she had earlier. "I thought you might want some company walking to the group session." The woman had an inexhaustible supply of smiles. Bethel decided she liked that about Doctor Karen. "The first time can be a little intimidating."

"I'm very tired. Maybe I should do this next time."

"Nice try. Don't worry. It's very relaxed. No running involved." Doctor Karen started down the hallway, adjusting her efficient stride to Bethel's crutch-assisted hop. "You don't even have to say anything this time. Sometimes listening to what the other folks have to say can be as helpful as talking. What they're going through might sound familiar. It can be surprisingly enlightening."

Enlightening? Unless there were some

Plain folks in the group, Bethel doubted any of them faced quite the same set of circumstances. Englischers had so many conveniences in their homes. And fewer children to raise, which meant less cooking, cleaning, and sewing.

Doctor Karen gave her back one last pat and trotted toward her office. Bethel slid into one of only two remaining empty chairs in the circle of padded green chairs that filled the small room. Posters with smiling people and encouraging quotations lined the walls. She tried not to look directly at anyone, but she couldn't miss Shawn's welcoming grin. He'd pulled his wheelchair into a spot next to a woman in an identical one. She looked young too, with black hair cropped close to her head and streaked with purple and pink color, a silver stud in her nose, and a lot of black goop around her blue eyes. One hand twisted a lock of purple hair. She didn't look up from studying the floor when Bethel came in.

"Hey, it's nice to see you again, Miss Bethel." Shawn's smile came and went suddenly, like a flash of light. "Are you doing your first workout today?"

"Already did." She managed to get the words out. They sounded cool in her ears, but wasn't that what she wanted? Luke's instructions had been clear. *Do what the doctor tells you to do, but keep to yourself. It's for the best.* "Nice to see you."

"Wow, you must be an early bird." He frowned, looking like a little boy denied a fry pie. "I didn't know you could work out that early or I would do it. I'm always up before the rooster crows."

Bethel took a closer look at him. He had dark circles under his eyes. He was such a bundle of energy, she'd missed it. Another person with bad dreams.

Another thing they had in common.

Forcing herself to ignore that thought, she gazed at her damp hands lying limp in her lap.

A hand touched her shoulder. She jumped.

"You must be Bethel. We're so glad to have you. I'm Doctor Jasmine Leaning Tree, the group facilitator." The young woman — she couldn't be much older than Bethel — had olive skin and wore her long black hair in a braid twisted around her head. Clad in khaki slacks, a blue pullover, and a purple jacket with the name of the clinic embroidered on the pocket, she looked too young to be a doctor. "Let's have introductions first for the benefit of our new member, then I'll ask Bethel to tell you about herself."

178

Around the room they went. Bethel tried to grasp and hold on to each name. Leaning Tree would be easy because it was so different. But the other six . . . why did it seem hard to remember them? Her palms were sweaty and her dress damp. Maybe she smelled after all. The girl with the multicolored hair: Crystal Macon. She'd been in a car accident nine months earlier, she informed Bethel, and no miracle would allow her to use her legs again. Mark Stover, a young guy, maybe sixteen, dove into the river while partying with a bunch of his friends from high school. He broke his neck. Before the accident he played basketball, baseball, and football, and hunted with his dad. Now he was paralyzed from the neck down and needed a respirator to help him breathe. He spent his spare time playing video games.

Ed, an elderly man with a walker, was recovering from a stroke. His wife had died only a few months earlier, he informed her, his face morose, his voice quivering with barely contained emotion. A chubby lady named Janice Lytle had crutches at her side that looked just like Bethel's. She turned out to be the victim of a hit-and-run driver. She'd been trying to lose weight by riding her bike on the road near her house. "They never found the guy who did it. It happened so fast I really couldn't give them much to go on." She plucked at a thread on her snug denim pants. "To be fair, I'm not even sure what kind of car it was."

When Shawn's turn came, he shrugged. "You know about me."

"Just your name." She squirmed in her chair, wishing she had let it go. "Not your story."

"My story?" His light tone seemed forced this morning. "I graduated from high school and I decided to serve my country, see the world, and get an education at the same time. I wanted to get away from this town. Instead, I ended up back here for good. I thought . . ."

Bethel waited, wanting to know what he thought, but he didn't finish. Doctor Jasmine nodded to the remaining member of their group. A tall, pretty woman in a lacy green dress with a white collar that was too fancy for the meeting. The color made her hazel eyes stand out against beautiful white skin. She also sat in a wheelchair, her hands, with their long, elegant fingers and diamond rings lying limp in her lap. "My name is Elaine Haag." She had a low, melodious voice that made everyone lean forward slightly as if she had something very important to say. "I have MS. I'm a homemaker. I have three children."

Bethel scrambled to remember. MS. Multiple sclerosis. She nodded.

"A homemaker," Crystal snorted. "She used to be a model in New York City. She was an actress."

"Crystal, you had your turn. This is Elaine's turn. Remember the rules." Doctor Jasmine held up one finger, its neatly trimmed nail painted a pale pink. "No interrupting and let others have their turn. Were you done, Elaine?"

Elaine nodded.

"Come on. At least let her know who she's dealing with. Full disclosure." Crystal jerked a thumb at Elaine. Her nails were painted black. "Her husband is on City Council and he runs the bank. She's very important people here in little New Hope. A VIP."

Elaine gave Bethel a small smile. "Don't mind her, she's allowed her anger over her accident to stunt her emotional growth."

"Hey —"

"Enough. Bethel's turn." Doctor Jasmine's tone brooked no argument. "Go ahead, Bethel."

Bethel nodded. She wanted to get off on the right foot with these people. All of them had a story to tell. All of them had challenges similar to hers, each in their own way.

"I'm Bethel. I used to be a schoolteacher —"

"I can't hear you." That from Ed. He cupped a hand to his ear, which sported a tiny hearing aid. "Speak up."

She tried again. "I used to be a schoolteacher. Then there was a storm."

"A tornado?" Crystal interrupted. She apparently didn't understand the rules or liked to ignore them. "Like Dorothy in *The Wizard of Oz*. Where are your ruby red slippers? Do you know you're not in Kansas anymore?"

Mark guffawed, but Shawn glared at Crystal. Bethel hadn't seen the movie, but she knew the story. She could tell from the girl's tone that she meant to make fun of Bethel, but she smiled anyway. "Not a tornado. Just high, straight winds that took the building apart." She smoothed her apron, remembering. "Anyway, I hurt my back and it affected my legs so here I am."

"Why do you dress like that?" Mark asked. He gasped a little for air whenever he spoke. A brace held him in his wheelchair and kept his head held back so he had to peek at her from the corner of his eye. "I mean, you look like a pioneer or something."

"She's Amish." Shawn broke in.

"Like those people in Utah who used to have more than one wife?" Crystal smirked. "That's totally gross. People around here won't put up with that kind of stuff."

"No, no, we don't —"

"Or that cult in Texas where the guys marry little girls?" Mark threw in the question. "We especially don't put up with that. The men around here will ride your kind out of town on a rail. They're real good with their rifles."

Bethel worked to remain calm. She grasped for words but they skittered away.

"You're such an idiot. Leave it to the high school principal's son to be ignorant and start talking about rifles and running people out of town." Shawn roared to her defense before she could manage to do it herself. "You're as stupid as your jock friends. The Amish are Christians. They just don't use electricity or drive cars. They don't have phones. They like to keep to themselves so they don't get all caught up in the bad things happening in this world. That's it. They're farmers, like most people around here."

Mark's face turned a deep purple and he sputtered, but before he could retort, Doctor Jasmine held up both of her hands in a stop signal.

183

"We don't tolerate name-calling, Shawn. You know better. It's nice that you've done your homework, but there's no need to attack other members of this group. We support each other. We don't tear people down." Doctor Jasmine's voice remained soft, but Shawn hung his head, a mottled red creeping across his cheeks and overtaking the scars. "You seem a little out of whack this morning. Why don't you tell us what's going on with you?"

He squirmed in his chair, glowering at the floor. Bethel appreciated his explanation of her community, but she didn't need his help. She could defend herself. She felt hot and then cold with the aftermath of the unexpected attack from two people who looked not much older than her scholars. How did people get these strange ideas? From television?

"Shawn, what's going on?" Doctor Jasmine's gently insistent voice broke through Bethel's reverie. "Remember, that's what we're here for, to help each other through our daily challenges."

"I went in to see my military doc yesterday in Springfield." Shawn cleared his throat and looked over Bethel's shoulder at the windows on the far wall. "Same story. No improvement. He says this is it. This is as good as it gets."

His expression bleak, he beat a rhythm on the wheelchair arms with both gnarled hands.

"You knew that. You've expected it." Doctor Jasmine's voice softened some more. "Something else is bothering you."

The rhythmic *slap slap* of his hands stilled. "My parents are getting a divorce."

"I'm sorry."

No wonder Sheriff McCormack had been so cantankerous. Like her mudder said, walk a mile in the other person's boots. The conviction that she had been uncharitable toward the man who'd strolled through their new home shamed Bethel. No matter his behavior, hers should've been better. She wanted to say something to Shawn, something comforting but the thought that she might draw attention to herself made her heart pound. *Go on. Go, say something.* She opened her mouth. Nothing came out.

Mark's oxygen machine slurped. "I'm sorry, dude," he wheezed. "I know how that is. Mine only made it six months after my accident."

So simple. Simple words. Why couldn't she say them? Bethel's cheeks warmed. She'd spoken in front of her scholars hundreds of times, maybe thousands. Yet she couldn't offer simple words of support to this one man in front of seven other people. *Gott, forgive me.*

Shawn nodded at Mark, but he didn't make eye contact with the other group members. His gaze roved toward the windows again.

"It's not your fault," Crystal added, her surly attitude gone. She dropped the lock of hair she'd been twisting between her thumb and forefinger and dug around in a denim purse, finally producing a bedraggled tissue which she proceeded to offer to Shawn. He shook his head and muttered his thanks. She shrugged and used it herself with a loud honking sound. "We all know that's what happens. The stress and money stuff — it gets to them. My dad sleeps on the couch a lot, and he drinks more than he used to do."

"Crystal's right. It's not your fault," Doctor Jasmine added. "Do you feel like it's your fault?"

Shawn's jaw worked. A pulse pounded in his temple. "The military pays for my medical care, but my parents had to make the house accessible, but that's not what they fight about. They think I'm never going to have a life now. I have no future. They think they won't have grandkids. I'll live at home forever and be a burden to them in their old age." Even as the words picked up steam, his voice broke and then faltered. He cleared his throat again. "They fight about what to do, how to help me, whose fault it was that I joined the army. I hear them through the walls when they think I'm asleep. Finally, he comes in and tells me he's moving out, that it's for the best, that all this fighting isn't good for me. For me? When I tried to talk to my mom, she said it was over. She said it had nothing to do with me, but that's not true. I'd have to be deaf to think it wasn't."

The Shirack and Graber families didn't fight about money or whose fault Bethel's injuries were. She was family. How blessed she was to have her family and her community of faith. The thought hit her with renewed joy. Her parents, sad though they might be at her diminished capacity as a woman, would see it as God's will and welcome her home at any time. Family meant everything in her community. She couldn't imagine not having that.

"I'm sorry," she whispered. Emotion caught at her voice. She ignored it. "I'm sorry."

"Not your fault, darlin'." His crooked grin took her back to the previous day. It was all an act, she realized. Shawn didn't want people to see his pain. The swagger in his voice and the cocky upward tilt of his chin were simply show. "I know how you can make me feel better, though."

"Shawn, stay on point here." Doctor Jasmine stood and went to his side. She laid a hand on his shoulder. "Look at me."

He ducked his head.

"Look at me, please."

He raised his head. His gaze landed on Bethel first and she saw the hurt there and the question as if he begged her for something. What, she couldn't be sure.

"Shawn."

His Adam's apple bobbed and he looked up at the doctor.

"You know it's not your fault, right? You're not responsible for the actions of the people around you or their inability to handle what's happened to you." The kindness in her voice made Bethel's throat tighten. "Do you think they're right? That you have no future?"

He sniffed. This time his gaze met Bethel's head-on. "No. They're dead wrong. Just because I'm in a chair doesn't mean I can't have a life. Or a family. I'm gonna have it all."

"Good. That's good." Doctor Jasmine sounded brisk now. She returned to her

188

seat. "Bethel, you said there was a storm. Tell us what happened."

Back to her again. Bethel managed to stifle a groan. Her story didn't compare to war wounds or diving accidents or a hit-and-run driver. "There's not much to tell. I was teaching and a storm came up. That happens a lot in Kansas. I didn't think much of it. I kept teaching." She closed her eyes, seeing the faces of her scholars. They trusted her. When she told them to keep working on their sums, they kept working. "I kept teaching until the wind tore the building apart."

"Were the children hurt too?" Elaine, the one among them who had young children of her own. She would understand. "How badly?"

"Yes, they were hurt, some of them badly. The wind picked up the desks and dropped them on us. The windows shattered and tree branches fell on top of us. The roof was ripped off."

"Didn't you have a basement? How come you didn't go in the basement?" Her face avid with curiosity, Crystal leaned forward in her chair. "Do you feel guilty?"

Guilty? Yes, she felt guilty every time she thought of Lettie with her broken legs and Seth with his concussion and Ruth Ann,

189

who was in the hospital almost a month. "It happened so suddenly. I thought it was just a storm. We have lots of storms. I thought it would pass."

"So you think their injuries and your injuries are your fault?" Shawn shook his head. "I know all about that. If I had done something different in Paktika, maybe the humvee wouldn't have blown up when it ran over the IED. Maybe my buddies would still be alive. That's the thing about hindsight. It's twenty-twenty."

Yes, hindsight. The terrified faces of the children reeled through her head, one after the other. Their screams swirled around her. She swallowed against the bitter taste in the back of her throat. "It *was* my fault. As the teacher, I had the responsibility to keep them safe, but they've forgiven me."

"So you only have to forgive yourself." Doctor Jasmine smiled. "We'll work on that. Mark, how about you? How was your week?"

To Bethel's immense relief, Jasmine moved on and the conversation flowed around her. She looked at her hands in her lap. Her fingers were white in the intensity of her grip. Her fingernails had left red half moon imprints on her skin. She loosened them and forced herself to take a long breath. The children and their parents had forgiven her.

Figuring out how to forgive herself, well, that was a horse of an entirely different color.

CHAPTER 16

Elijah tied the buggy reins to the corral railing not far from where a dark blue, dusty pickup truck was parked. The vet's truck, he supposed. He hoped. He shielded the sun from his eyes with one hand so he could see Bethel more clearly. The strain around her mouth and eyes apparent when he picked her up from the rehab clinic hadn't eased during the ride to his brother's farm. Whatever had gone on at her physical therapy session and the support group, she didn't want to talk about it. Neither of them had been in the mood to talk. His thoughts were on what the veterinarian would say about Ned. The vet, an older man with thick glasses and a thicker salt and pepper beard, hadn't hesitated after Elijah explained the situation. He'd left a younger doctor in charge of what sounded like a whole mess of barking dogs behind the front counter and told Elijah he'd head to the farm immediately. Not to worry. It used to be the Jensen farm. He'd visited there plenty, what with their horses, cattle, and sheep.

Not to worry. Hard not to what with Ned's listless stare, his whinny when he tried to move in his stall, and the swollen leg with its angry, bloody gash. Ned was not only a living creature, but one who made big contributions to the work they needed to accomplish on this new farm, especially come spring. No point in worrying. Worrying accomplished nothing. The doc would take care of it.

Elijah focused on Bethel. "You sure you don't mind? I could've taken you home first."

"Then you'd just have to turn around and drive back to our farm again after you came here." She waved away a bee that buzzed in her face. She had long, slender fingers. Nimble with a needle. They would be gentle with babies. "I know you're worried about the horse. Go see what the vet said."

Surprised at where his thoughts had gone, Elijah jerked his gaze from her hands. "Let me help you down first. Katie will give you some lemonade and cookies. You look worn out."

"I'm fine. I'd rather go with you to see about Ned." Her expression troubled, she

193

held out her arms. "If you hadn't stayed so late at the house last night, if I hadn't brought you the cinnamon roll, maybe you wouldn't have been on the road after dark —"

"Nee. Don't be daft. Accidents just happen." He said this to convince himself as much as her. He didn't want to believe anyone would intentionally run a man and his horse off the road. He lifted her from the buggy and handed her the crutches. "The vet said he would come directly here. He's probably already taken a look at Ned."

"Then let's see what he has to say."

Elijah would rather she not see the results of the accident. She already knew the extent of his own injuries. But she looked resolute and he didn't see any point in arguing with her. They started toward the barn. Silas and Doctor Womack came through the doors. From the look on Silas's face, the news wasn't to his liking. Elijah stopped walking. He heard rather than saw that Bethel had done the same. "How is the horse?"

"Had to put it down." Silas's somber face matched the gruffness of his voice. "Nothing to be done about it."

Birds squawked and flapped from the oak trees that lined the drive. A cat shot across the grass and disappeared into the meadow

194

across the road. Bethel gave a small cry, like a kitten's pitiful meow. "Why?"

"Fractures in two places in one of his front legs, ma'am." The vet transferred a leather bag from one hand to the other and smoothed his ragged beard. "Horse was in pain. It was the humane thing to do."

"You couldn't put a cast on his leg?"

"Missy, horses put sixty percent of their weight on their front legs. It's not like he can lay down until it heals. It's not like we can put slings on 'em. He was in terrible pain. Like I said, humane."

Elijah sucked in air and worked to keep emotion from molding his features. "I suspected as much." He cleared his throat, embarrassed at the slight crack in his voice. "I better get Bethel home then. I'll come back and help with the burial. Doctor Womack, I'll take the bill."

"I done got the bill." Silas glowered at him. "My horse, my bill."

"I was riding him when it happened."

"Through no fault of your own."

"Silas told me what happened." Doctor Womack broke in. "I have to tell you, I don't think you belong on the highway. It's meant for fast-moving traffic. Not a man on a horse. This isn't the nineteenth century."

"You think what happened to the horse is

Elijah's fault?" Silas put his hands on his hips and planted his boots in the dirt, oblivious to the chickens that had taken an interest in the visitor. "He wasn't riding down the middle of the road."

"I think riding a horse on the highway at dusk with no reflectors is asking for trouble. I think the horse paid the price."

"I meant to start back earlier . . ." Elijah pondered the man's face. He looked sincere. He looked like his job took its toll on days like today. "We value our animals. We need them to do our work. I wouldn't intentionally endanger an animal."

"You all could do with some reflectors like you have on the back of your buggies." Doctor Womack hesitated, his lips a thin line over his beard. "Give the people here time."

"Time for what?" Silas looked puzzled. Elijah's brother was a staid man who spent most of his time in the field. He didn't see grays. Only blacks and whites. "We're not in any hurry for anything."

"I'm just saying it takes them a while to warm up to strangers, but eventually they do. If you're decent folks. And you seem like decent folks."

Bethel hadn't said a word. Her face was white and her eyes red-rimmed. She had such a soft heart. His throat constricted.

Stop it. "Let's go, Bethel. Time to get you home. Luke will wonder where we are."

"I'm sorry." She slid a step back from him, her crutches sinking into the gravel. "It's just one more thing, isn't it?"

He wasn't sure if the words were directed to him or to Silas. His brother didn't answer. He was a pragmatic soul. He would replace Ned come the next horse auction. Until then, they'd make do.

"Jah." Elijah moved past her, still grappling with the disappointment. "We'll make do."

"There's a car coming." Silas's tone held a hint of concern. "It's a police car."

"That would be the sheriff." Doctor Womack cleared his throat. "I called him before I came out."

"Why?" Elijah kept his tone neutral. The vet had a reason. What, he couldn't imagine, but still a reason. "We don't want to press charges against anyone. Even if we could say who caused this."

"I called him because you were involved in an accident. There were injuries. I'm concerned about your treatment of animals."

"Treatment of animals?" Elijah remembered the sensation when he hit the ground with such force it rattled his bones and his

197

teeth. "Both the horse and I were injured. An accident occurred, but we didn't cause it."

"Not intentionally. I know that now. But when you told me the story at my office, I felt an obligation to let the sheriff know."

"An obligation?"

"Yes, an obligation."

Elijah faced the car that rolled into the drive in front of the corral, dust billowing behind it. He'd hoped never to talk to Sheriff McCormack again. From the look on the sheriff's face when he stepped from his car, he'd hoped the same thing.

Bethel swayed on her crutches. Her legs ached from the unaccustomed exercise earlier in the day. It cost her to continue to stand, but she wanted to be here for this conversation. If Elijah had his way, he'd shoo her into the house with Silas's fraa, but Bethel wanted to hear what the sheriff said. Surely he wouldn't blame Elijah for what a speeding car had done. This was a rural area. Surely people rode horses on the highway all the time. Sifting through her memories of Bliss Creek she thought of the Englischers who frequently brought their slow-moving farm equipment onto the highway to move from field to field or farm

198

to farm, but they never rode horses on the highway. They had no need to do so. The horses weren't transportation. They were used on the farm for moving cattle or getting into the fields, but not often on the highway.

The memory of Shawn and his sad face when he talked about his parents' divorce danced in her mind's eye. Sheriff McCormack might not be easy to deal with right now, but he had reason to be cranky. She'd try to give him the benefit of the doubt. She should've told Elijah about it, but Doctor Jasmine had made it clear that the conversations in the group were to be kept among only the participants. Confidential, she called it. Bethel mentally buttoned her lips and prepared to be kind.

Sheriff McCormack slammed his car door and started toward them, dark shiny sunglasses hiding most of his face under his ball cap. He tipped the hat to her as if to acknowledge her presence first, and then he moved on to Doctor Womack without speaking to Silas and Elijah. No friendly greetings.

"What did you find?" Snapping the gum he chewed with vigor, he pulled a narrow notebook from his hip pocket and a pen from his shirt pocket. "How's the horse?"

He didn't ask how Elijah had fared.

"Had to put him down." The vet's regretful tone matched his mournful expression. "Fractures to the left front leg. He was a fine piece of horseflesh, but I had no choice."

The sheriff's gaze fixed on Elijah. "How did it happen?"

Elijah recounted the events without decorating them.

"You realize there's a minimum speed limit on the highway."

"Pardon me?"

"A minimum speed limit. You need to keep moving."

"I wasn't dillydallying. And there was plenty of room to pass me without hitting me."

"Neither here nor there. The highway is meant for cars. If you're going to impede traffic, stay off it. I'd hate to see you lose another horse. Do you have a driver's license?"

"A license?" Elijah looked momentarily confused. They didn't have licenses. They didn't drive motor vehicles. Bethel could feel his anxiety as if it were her own. This wasn't his fault, yet the sheriff seemed bent on making it an issue. "No. We don't have licenses. We don't take photos and we don't drive cars. No need for a license."

"Have you ever studied the rules of the road?"

Elijah's face turned beet red, but he didn't lower his gaze. "I know the rules of the road."

"If you weren't at fault, why didn't you report it?"

"No need."

"No need. You lost an expensive piece of horseflesh. You got insurance on him?"

"We don't have —"

"Insurance. I remember. From the house. Your friend, what's his name?" The sheriff flipped through his notebook. "Luke. Luke Shirack."

"No. No insurance. And we wouldn't press charges, anyway."

"I'm sensing a pattern here." The sheriff adjusted the sunglasses on his long, sunburned nose. Bethel didn't like not being able to see his eyes. "I'm giving you fair warning. Keep your animals off the road if you're going to create a hazard with them. It's not fair to the animals. We don't think highly of people who mistreat their animals."

"We don't mistreat animals." Bethel couldn't help herself. The gross exaggeration of his charge filled her with an outrage she didn't know she was capable of feeling. Silas frowned and shook his head. Women were to be seen and not heard in these situations. "Nobody treats animals better than Elijah."

The sheriff's sunglasses pointed her direction, but she couldn't see if his gaze met hers. A slow smile spread over his grizzled features. "For people who seem awful polite, y'all are not much for introducing your womenfolk. Who might you be?"

Now she'd done it. She'd called attention to herself. "Bethel."

"Were you present at this incident?"

He said *incident* like he meant to say *crime*. "No."

"Well, that's a shame. We could use an eyewitness." He waved his notebook toward Elijah. "Consider yourself warned. Let the others know. I've read up on the issues caused in other settlements. Use reflectors. Stay on the shoulder when cars pass. Don't plant yourself in front of cars, and you won't have a problem."

He tucked the notebook in his back pocket and pulled out another book in which he proceeded to scribble with big flourishes. No one spoke. Doctor Womack coughed, a hacking cough that didn't sound good.

"Here you go, sir." He tore off a piece of

paper and handed it to Elijah.

"What is this?" Elijah stared at the paper, his expression puzzled. He shook his head. "You're giving me a ticket."

"It's just a warning. Don't worry. No fine or anything."

"A warning for what?"

"For obstructing traffic and endangering an animal in the process."

"I . . ." Elijah stopped. "Understood."

Bethel opened her mouth. Silas shook his head again. She closed it. She tried to see an inkling of Shawn in this man. Nothing. The sheriff had dark hair, weathered skin, and, if she remembered correctly, brown eyes. Shawn must take after his mother in everything, including his good nature. *Walk in his shoes. Jah, Gott, I'm trying.*

"Good talking to you all. You done here, doc?"

"Done."

"I'm heading out. What about you?"

"Heading out."

The two Englischers started toward their cars. "How 'bout them Chiefs, think they got a chance at the Super Bowl this year?"

The vet laughed, a deep belly laugh that turned into a cough. "About as much chance as I have."

The sheriff laughed, a gruffer, less amused sound.

"Sheriff, wait." Bethel swung after them on her crutches.

Elijah made a noise behind her. "Bethel, no."

The sheriff swiveled to face her, his expression a cross between curiosity and annoyance.

"I met your son."

Slowly, he removed his sunglasses and stared down at her. His eyes were indeed brown. He looked much older than he had the day they'd arrived in New Hope. "Where?"

"At the rehab clinic for physical therapy."

"Yep. That's where he spends most of his time now." He seemed to hesitate, his gaze dancing over Bethel's shoulder to the horizon, then back to her face. "He doing all right?"

Besides being devastated over his parents' divorce? "He seems all right."

"For a twenty-two-year-old boy stuck in a chair for the rest of his life, you mean?"

He wasn't a boy. He was a man who had fought for his country and nearly died for his efforts. Bethel didn't understand about wars and military things, but she understood courage and bravery. She also understood

204

how a young man might feel about his father abandoning his family. "He seems like a nice person."

"I never wanted him to go into the army." Sheriff McCormack returned his sunglasses to his nose, hiding his eyes, but his gruff tone couldn't hide his anger. "I got calls to make. You take care, ma'am. I'd hate to see you dumped on the side of the road. You could end up like my boy. Stuck in a chair instead of running around on crutches."

"I'll be careful."

"You do that. Don't be stupid."

The unspoken words hung in the air. *Don't be stupid like my boy.*

Bethel's heart wrenched in her chest. Her daed might not shower his children openly with affection. It wasn't his way. But she never once doubted his love for her. A sadness for Shawn enveloped her, but it didn't end there. It engulfed the man who stood before her doing his best to act as if he felt nothing. How he must hurt to see his son trapped in that chair, unable to move. But standing tall didn't always involve standing on two feet. She knew that as well as anyone. "Goodbye, Sheriff."

He didn't answer. Instead, he spun on his heels and marched away. He picked up speed, his long stride eating up the ground between him and the car with its lights on top.

He looked for all the world like a man being chased.

CHAPTER 17

Bethel leaned against the back of the wagon and tugged at the box. It held several dozen cookies she and Leah had baked the previous day. Surprisingly heavy for cookies. She inhaled the crisp, cool morning air. Autumn had arrived and it nipped at her cheeks. She welcomed her favorite season, always so refreshing after the heat of summer. The sun would pop up over that horizon any second and the pounding of the nails would start. She inhaled the scent of fresh-cut lumber mixed with mowed grass and earth. Earlier in the week, the men had set the foundation in this little nook and cranny of land nestled near a stand of spruces not far from the road. What a perfect day for building a school on that foundation. She batted away the thought that immediately followed. She might not be the teacher when this school opened, but she could do her part to give the scholars a simple place to come each day to learn. God had given her this role to play on this day.

"I'll get that for you." Elijah had slipped up to the wagon without her noticing. He raised his head and sniffed like a hound dog, a look of ecstasy on his face. "Snicker-doodles. Fry pies. Gingersnaps. I see peanut butter cookies. They all smell good. I want to carry that box."

"You have a good nose."

"Given its size, how could I not?"

His nose looked quite nice to her. Not that she would tell him that. Bethel backed away and let him get at the wagon. She had learned to set aside her pride and not to argue about these things. She couldn't handle her crutches and carry a box. After three weeks of physical therapy she thought she saw some improvement in her muscles. On the other hand, it might be wishful thinking. She continued to do the exercises before she went to bed each night as well. Her left leg lifted slightly on command, but the right one refused to respond. Doctor Karen said it could be months before that changed. But it would change. Of that, she was determined.

"You should be at your therapy today." Elijah moved a box filled with loaves of freshly made bread and tugged on a cooler that held ham and roast beef sandwiches, cold fried chicken, pickles, and cheese in his direction. His bland expression belied the accusation in the words. "How do you expect to make progress if you miss sessions?"

"Everyone is expected to help when we have a frolic. That includes you and me. How could I go without someone to drive me?" She didn't need him inside her head, reading her thoughts. Even though his words echoed the very argument she'd had when she realized the school build would conflict with her next session. It would be selfish to put her progress ahead of this important work. "My progress is not as important as our new community and building a school so our scholars can get back to learning."

"They're getting plenty of learning." He set the box of cookies on top of the cooler and tugged it to the edge of the wagon. "They're learning how to create a new district. They're learning how to be a new community. They learned about ordination. They're learning from their parents. That's just as important as book learning."

Spoken like a man who'd had no interest in school. He'd been a fair scholar, if Bethel's memory served, but, like so many of her friends, had relished the day he'd been set free from the schoolhouse. "Of course it is, but their book learning only lasts a few short years. They have many years — their whole lives — to learn the things you speak of."

"Spoken like a true teacher." He stopped, his face reddening from his jawline to his hairline. His gaze dropped to the cooler. He'd only spoken the truth, but his consternation at reminding her of her loss showed in his face. With ease he lifted the cooler and the box and started toward the tables they'd arranged in long rows several yards from the worksite. "The folks from Webster County are already arriving. With their help this should go quickly."

"It'll be nice to meet our neighbors even if they are a good distance away." Relieved at the change of subject, she stuck the handle of a basket filled with napkins and silverware over her shoulder and grabbed her crutches. He didn't mean to be insensitive. Everyone had avoided the subject of her replacement as teacher. No matter. She understood Luke's decision. "Luke says they've done real well up there."

"Their Englisch neighbors have welcomed them . . . or at least left them in peace."

He didn't elaborate and it was better he

210

didn't. The encounter with the sheriff and the vet had left them both uneasy. Elijah had spoken with Luke about it, but her brother-in-law insisted they must settle in, work hard, and mind their own business. The folks in New Hope would get used to their presence and leave them alone if they weren't a burden to the town. They had no need for an open-armed welcome. Only simple acceptance.

A burden. How could they be a burden? She shook her head.

"Talking to yourself?"

"What?"

"You shook your head." He looked at her over the box that reached just below his chin. "You look like you're carrying on a conversation only you can hear. What are you thinking about? Not about what I said, I hope. I didn't mean to pour salt in an open wound."

"You didn't. Luke made the right decision. It's not that."

"What then? You look concerned."

She worried her lower lip with her teeth. She didn't want to lie to Elijah, but she didn't see how she could share these thoughts with him. He had enough on his plate. He and Silas had attended a horse auction the previous week, but the horses had sold at prices beyond their means. In the meantime, Silas's daughter Hannah had fallen from the trampoline and broken her arm — again. Silas had dismantled the thing and vowed to sell it at their next school fund-raiser. It had meant their first encounter with the New Hope Medical Center emergency room and medical bills.

"Nothing important. Just thinking about what the winter will bring."

"You talk to yourself, don't you?"

"Do not."

"I've seen you." His voice took on a teasing quality that reminded her of their schoolyard days. "Do you have imaginary friends too?"

"Don't be silly." She tried to sound disapproving, but the effort was spoiled by her giggle. "They're not imaginary just because *you* can't see them."

His smile broadened. That nice smile that brought out the dimple in his left cheek. What would he look like with a beard? Contemplating his face, she forgot to watch the ground in front of her, stumbled over something hard, and lost her grip on one crutch.

"Whoa!" Elijah dropped the cooler and the box. The bags of cookies tumbled out in all directions. He lunged forward with both hands outstretched, trampling them. "Bethel!"

Her feet skidded on the damp grass. Down she went, legs askew, skirt twisted, landing with a painful thump. She closed her eyes, the heat coursing her neck and cheeks. Her eyes burned with unshed tears. She would not cry. She would not cry.

"Are you all right?" She could feel Elijah's breath on her cheek. He was close to her, too close. She didn't want to open her eyes. Not yet. Fingers closed around her arm in a tight, warm grip. Elijah's sure grip. "Did you hurt yourself? Can you get up? Let me help you."

"I can get myself up." She jerked from his grasp and opened her eyes to see his concerned face hovering inches over hers. He smelled like soap, clean and fresh. Fine lines were starting to form at the corners of his eyes and mouth. Smile lines. "I don't need help."

"I forgot." The look of concern fled, replaced by a fierceness that startled her almost as much as the fall. "You don't need *my* help."

"I didn't say —"

"Is everything all right?"

Still sprawled on her back side, Bethel looked up into the dawning day's light to see a woman she'd never met standing over them. She wore a lavender dress and crisp apron, but it was her face that drew Bethel's stare. The woman had dark blue eyes that seemed enormous against her white skin. She was petite and slender in a way that made Bethel feel immediately enormous and clumsy. Of course, she had the advantage of standing upright, while Bethel sprawled on the ground — a fact Bethel tried with every ounce of her being not to resent.

"I fell." Her face hot, hands cold with sweat, she saw no reason to elaborate.

"Are you hurt?" The woman shifted the casserole pan she carried to one arm. "Can I help? My sister is good at doctoring. I can go get her."

"I'm not hurt."

"I've got her." Elijah scrambled to his feet. Despite his words, he didn't attempt to help Bethel get up. His gaze remained on their visitor. "Are you from Webster County?"

"I'm Viola Byler and yes, I'm from out by Seymour."

Bethel positioned her crutch to one side and attempted to pull herself up. Her efforts proved fruitless, but neither Elijah nor Viola seemed to notice. They stared at each other with unabashed interest.

"Elijah?" To Bethel's mortification, her voice sounded weak. "Never mind."

Determined, she rolled to one side, ignoring the grass stains and mud on her skirt. Mustering all her strength, she planted herself on her knees, used a crutch as a wedge, and swung herself upright until she stood.

"I'll just . . . if you'll just . . ."

Elijah's gaze finally moved in her direction. He looked as if he didn't recognize her at first. Then his face flamed crimson. "Right. I'm sorry." He knelt and scooped up the bags of cookies and tossed them back in the basket with such force they'd surely be even more broken. Viola joined him, her long skirt folding around her in a graceful display. Their heads came precariously close to bumping. They laughed.

Bethel might as well have been in another country. In fact, she wished more than anything that she were.

"I'll take the cookies." Viola set her casserole on top of the box. "Elijah can get the cooler. Lead the way, Bethel."

As if they were best of friends. Bethel swatted away her resentment. This woman, along with the other folks in Webster County, had come to help. She should welcome Viola with open arms. A friendly face in a place where she'd met few.

"This way." She sought a topic of conversation that moved away from her fall. "The casserole smells good."

"It's called taco surprise. My sister made it. It has layers of tortillas and hamburger and shredded cheese and hot sauce in it. It's really delicious."

"Sounds tasty. We set up some Coleman stoves. You can keep it warm on one of them." Bethel swung under the canopy where tables had been set up for the food preparation and serving. She nodded at the long row of coolers under the tables. "Elijah, you can put the cooler there with the others. I'm sure Luke is looking for you. He's chomping at the bit to get started."

If the words didn't dismiss him, her tone surely did. Elijah's lips formed a thin line. No dimple visible now. His gaze seemed to bore a hole in her forehead. He tipped his hat and left the tent without another word.

Gut. She didn't want to talk to him anyway.

CHAPTER 18

Luke laid the hammer on the planks positioned across two saw horses and shoved his hat back on his head. So far so good. He inhaled the scent of cut wood. Clean, full of promise, mingled with the smell of paint, sharp and fresh. If blacksmithing had been his first choice for vocation, carpentry would've been a close second. Creating with his hands. But God had had other plans for him. Growing food for his family and other families. He was content. The school would be complete by late afternoon and the outhouses soon after, thanks to the crew from Webster County. The crew working on the new well had struck water ahead of schedule. God's hand lay upon them.

"I'll get the windows started," Elijah called from the newly constructed porch. He tucked his hammer into a toolbox on the floor. "Simon and Martin can help place the glass."

"Fine. Let Tobias's boys help." Luke rummaged through his toolbox looking for the right screwdriver to install the door hinges. "But don't leave them alone with the glass."

"It's looking good." Elijah surveyed the front of the building. "We're right on schedule."

"Jah, we should be able to get the desks from Tobias's barn tomorrow and bring them in."

"What about the stove?"

"We'll have to install it soon. Winter will be here before we know it." Some of his earlier optimism faded. Starting a new school from scratch cost money. Their funds were dwindling. "We need to plan for a school fund-raiser."

"Silas's fraa says they made good progress at the sewing frolic last week. They'll have plenty of goods to sell. Plus we have all that equipment left in the barns and outbuildings. And the appliances from the kitchens." Elijah moved a pane of glass so it leaned more steadily against the outside wall. "I met a lady in town who can help us with a place to sell the goods."

Luke nodded as Elijah proceeded to describe a lady named Diana Doolittle who owned a flea market and auction house in town. A good contact. They needed friendly faces in New Hope. They'd bought many supplies there now, but most of his conversations with the folks had been short and polite.

"One thing at a time. Best get Tobias's boys and get those windows installed now."

The boys were eager to work but hadn't yet learned the importance of slow and steady for most tasks. Elijah would serve as a good teacher. He did slow and steady with the best. Too bad he didn't have his own boys to teach. Maybe he still had a chance if he would stop dragging his feet with Bethel. None of Luke's business, of course, but sometimes slow and steady needed a nudge from behind. Of course he would never say that. He'd already said more than he should.

Setting the situation aside, Luke surveyed the neat one-room building built by many helping hands. Their first community project. As bishop, he could take no credit for it. He smiled, thinking of the day when his youngsters would be old enough to do more than carry nails and act as gophers on barn raisings. Three boys and two girls. All would attend the school. A good start. Boys to teach to work the land. Girls who would learn the importance of house and home from their mother. He looked forward to more. Many more with God's blessing.

As if to punctuate his thoughts, a baby's squalling broke through the sound of hammers pounding nails as a group of men led by Thomas shingled the roof. The cry had a familiar sound to it. People who didn't have children might not believe it, but Luke knew the distinct sound of each of his children's cries. Even the twins'. The squalling grew in fervor until it became a high-pitched scream. Half irritated and more concerned than he wanted to admit, Luke looked toward the canopy they'd erected between two enormous poplars. There the women cleaned up the remains of lunch and prepared for supper while the older girls cared for the babies and kept an eye on the children who weren't old enough to work yet.

He didn't see Leah among the women. Bethel cast a look in his direction. He tried to decipher it. He couldn't read her any more than he could read his fraa. While their personalities were at the opposite ends of the spectrum, as were their looks, they both had a stubborn private streak. He had no idea what brought it on and no time or patience for the introspection needed to figure them out. He stomped across the yard, ignoring the looks thrown his way by his sister Emma and several women from Webster County who stood chatting among themselves. "What ails the child?" He had to raise his voice to be heard over the caterwauling. "Where's Leah?"

Bethel held Jebediah against her chest and rubbed his back in a steady circular pattern. His chubby legs kicked and his arms flailed against her, but she didn't flinch. In fact, she began to rock back and forth as if to soothe him. "I don't know."

"You don't know what's wrong with him, or you don't know where my fraa is?"

"I don't know where Leah is."

"Poor baby's teething." A woman he didn't know laid a stack of napkins on the table and strolled over to Bethel. "Can I take him for a bit? Maybe an unfamiliar face will take his mind off his poor gums."

Bethel drew back. Something in her expression caught at Luke. She didn't like this woman, whom she surely had just met. That wasn't like Bethel, a sweet-natured woman who seemed to like everyone she met. Curious, he introduced himself.

"I'm Viola Byler." The woman gave him a smile that lit up her face. She had mighty nice eyes. Sort of blue like cornflowers, the color brought out by her dress. "I don't have any children of my own just yet, but I teach

221

up at one of the schools in Webster County."

Bethel's expression darkened. Her arms tightened around the baby, who continued to wail.

"You have your hands full slicing the roast for sandwiches, Viola. I'll take my little nephew. He knows me." Emma, her face full of calm efficiency, didn't give Viola or Bethel a chance to argue. His sister had grown confident and self-assured in her role as wife and mother. She slipped the crying baby into her arms. "I'll put some ointment on his gums and give him a nice cold teething ring. I put one in the ice chest. You two can look for Leah. I think she was feeling poorly."

Her face a myriad of emotions that Luke couldn't begin to read, Bethel grabbed her crutches and swung from the tent. Viola shrugged and returned to the table. Luke followed his sister-in-law.

"Why would we need to look for Leah? Hasn't she been helping?" He thought back to lunch. Leah had been there serving sandwiches. She looked tired, but he didn't find that surprising. She'd been up most of the night with a teething baby. "What's going on?"

Bethel didn't look up. She doggedly worked her crutches across the uneven ground, her gaze glued to the ruts, rocky soil, and weeds.

"Bethel, I asked you a question." He had been careful not to use the position of bishop to order his own family members into compliance. They recognized his role as head of the household; nothing more was required. "Answer me."

"Leah's tired. She doesn't feel well. Jebediah didn't let her sleep much."

"He's teething." Of course she was up. Babies kept their mudders up during the night. Bethel, although not a mother, knew this. "She's done this many times."

"I'm surprised you noticed." Her tart tone stung. "You might want to pay more attention to that."

"You don't have babies, but you'll learn that it comes with the territory." He didn't need his sister-in-law telling him how to lead his family. He knew his responsibilities well, better than she who had no husband or children. He almost stopped moving, so struck was he by the meanness of his own spirit. *Gott forgive me.* He drew a breath and softened his tone. "Leah doesn't mind. She knows that. She's a good mudder."

Bethel plowed to a stop. "How could you be so . . . she's expecting again!"

"Expecting?"

"Expecting."

Her breathing ragged, Bethel planted herself in his path. "Your fraa is expecting another baby." Bright red spots spread on both her cheeks. Red blotches mottled her neck. "Haven't you noticed?"

Luke could never have imagined having this conversation with his sister-in-law or any woman not his wife. Why hadn't Leah told him? They were to have another child. How could she not share that blessing? So little time they'd spent together, what with his travels and the preparations for the move, the setting-up of the new household. It hardly seemed possible. God had truly blessed them.

"Stop looking like that. She's not seeing the blessing in it at the moment. Later she will, but not now." Bethel's sharp tone brought him back to the here and now, to the reality of her words. "She's somewhere out there throwing up. She's been throwing up all day. She's been throwing up for days. She doesn't get any sleep, she can't eat, and she has five children who need her attention."

"Ach."

"Ach? All you can say is *ach?*"

"She didn't tell me."

"And you didn't notice." The red blotches

spread. She bowed her head, her breathing audible, quick and short as if she'd been running. "I may never have been married or with child, but I recognize the symptoms. I know what's wrong with Jebediah, and I know what's wrong with Leah because I pay attention."

Luke swallowed a retort. Bethel only spoke the truth. He didn't know why his fraa hadn't confided in him. It shamed him to the bone that she hadn't. He needed to talk to her. Not Bethel. This wasn't a conversation he would have with her. "I'll speak with Leah."

"That's all you have to say?"

"You have no place to criticize me. This is between my fraa and me."

"You're right. I'm sorry." She stared at him, her eyes red. Her lips quivered. "I find it . . . mean that you would throw my lack of children in my face."

And with that she swung past him on her crutches, her face averted.

"About that, you are right," he called after her, shame coursing through him. As a bishop, he'd failed her. As a member of her family, he'd done worse. He'd hurt her. "I'm sorry."

She stopped, but she didn't turn around. "Find Leah. You need to talk to her."

He'd rather dig seventy outhouses, but he wasn't a coward. "Which direction?"

"Toward the creek."

A few minutes later he trudged through pine and birch trees to the edge of a creek that meandered through their property. A wet autumn had filled it to a rolling stream that gurgled as it rushed past. The sound of the water alone was enough to make him feel cooler, even calmer. The shade of the trees and the rustle of the leaves on laden boughs made him want to stretch out on the grass and take a nap. How much more must Leah feel the need? The question struck him across the face. So wrapped up in his new duties and his new farm, he hadn't bothered to take notice of his fraa's condition. Nor had she told him. That wasn't like Leah. She told him everything, often more than he wanted to hear, often in a shrill voice that irritated his ears and caused him to tune her out.

You're not a good husband. The words cut like a finely honed butcher knife. *Not a good husband.*

"What are you doing here?"

Leah's voice, not shrill now, but soft and weary, floated toward him from the other side of the creek. She sat on a flat rock, her knees pulled up under her chin, her skirt covering shoes he knew to be as sturdy and reliable as she had always been. Her arms were crossed over her knees, her head down. She didn't raise it.

"I came for you." What else could he say? He'd come because Jebediah had been crying. Because he heard his son's wailing, but not his fraa's silent cries for help.

"Why didn't Emma send one of the girls? You have work to do."

"Bethel would've come, but I told her I —"

"On her crutches? What's wrong with Emma? She could send Rebecca. That girl gets away with far too much. Emma spoils her."

"Emma shouldn't have to send anyone." He hadn't meant to sound so harsh, but the words were out there, hanging between them, accusing her. He scrambled to sound more conciliatory. "She's putting ointment on Jebediah's gums and giving him a teething ring. She said not to worry."

"No, she didn't. She sent you to find out what's wrong with me and bring me back. Your sister is a bossy one."

"What *is* wrong? Why are you sitting out here?" He knew, but he wanted her to tell him. He wanted to know why she hadn't shared such blessed news with him. He

227

should've been the first to know. He tried to ignore Bethel's words ringing in his ears. *Pay attention.* "Are you feeling poorly?"

"Nee."

"What is it?"

"I'm overly tired, what with the teething and the girls having ear infections."

"Bethel told me . . . she said . . . well, she told me you're . . . you're expecting."

At that, Leah's head snapped up. Color rushed into her white face. "She had no right."

"That's beside the point. Why didn't you tell me?"

"I would've. I couldn't."

"You couldn't tell me that we're to have another child? That God has blessed us once again? I don't understand you. I'm your husband. You're my fraa."

"I couldn't bear to hear you spew all those words about blessings and babies. I didn't want to talk about it. Or think about it."

"How can you say that?"

"Because I'm tired and I'm homesick."

Tired could be fixed. A good night's sleep. Homesickness, well, that Luke couldn't fix. Only time would make it better. "Go home. Emma will watch the children. Go home and rest."

"There's work to be done." She put her

hand to her mouth. Her throat moved convulsively. She breathed. "I will, as soon as I'm sure I won't vomit again."

"The sickness will pass." Easy for him to say, but after five children, he knew it to be a true statement. "So will the homesickness."

He wasn't so sure about that, but he needed to believe it. For his family's sake. His wife had to embrace this new beginning. Soon.

"Go away."

"Nee."

She stretched forward and retched on the ground. "Please, go away."

He found the rocks she'd used to cross the water and went over to her. On the other side, he approached her with care, wishing he had a handkerchief or a bandana to wipe her face. "Leah, let me help you back to the buggy." He touched her heaving shoulders, brushing back a tendril of hair that lay on her cheek. "I'll drive you home."

"Nee. I have work to do." She coughed and cleared her throat. "So do you."

"Others will pick up the slack."

"I don't slack." She jerked from his touch and curled into herself, her knees tight against her chin again. "Go."

"You need to rest and get better. The

babies need you."

She didn't answer.

"Leah?"

Nothing.

"I need you."

"You need a fraa who cleans your house and does the laundry and has babies and takes care of them."

Luke had always thought of all these as good things. He thought Leah did too. It was what women did. Now, the world tilted on its side. Now, in the face of her unrelenting sadness, he felt a sense of guilt. He had done something wrong. He simply couldn't be sure of what. "You act like you . . . you act like you don't want another baby."

Her head came up. Her gaze met his. She looked far older than her years with her pale, drawn face, reddened eyes, and chapped lips. "I don't. God forgive me, I don't."

Her tone, miserable and filled with defiance tempered by guilt, tore at him. He swallowed words of anger. She didn't mean it. She couldn't mean it.

Her face said differently. He read something else there. Fear. She didn't understand what was happening to her. Neither did he. But she wouldn't cling to him, her husband. Why? "You don't want another baby, or you don't want another baby with me?"

She stared at him with those huge, dark eyes that had held him from the first time he'd noticed her sitting across from him at school in the eighth grade. She'd been there before, of course, but he'd never noticed those eyes. Enormous eyes that devoured him, questioning him, even though she didn't speak to him, not once. She'd been tired then too. He hadn't known why until much later.

This time she didn't hesitate.

"Both."

CHAPTER 19

Elijah followed Silas, Viola Byler, and her father, Menno, across the gravel road, past the corral, and into an expanse of dirt that was fenced with wire and wood posts. The pen covered a good half acre. The stench of ammonia hit him first. And then the noise. The sound of the orangey-red hens' cackling rose in a steady crescendo mixed with the answering cacophony of goats bleating. The fowl scattered at their approach while the goats crowded the fence as if expecting a treat. Elijah inspected them. He'd never given much thought to raising goats, but the chicken farm was another matter. Silas had read that organic eggs were popular at farmers' markets now. Englischers wanted pasture-fed chickens and cattle. They were buying what Silas called organic produce and something called free-range cattle. Then he'd talked to Menno Byler at the school raising and discovered here was a Plain farmer who had firsthand experience with this so-called organic farming. At Luke's bidding, Elijah and his brother had come to investigate. Luke wanted to explore all options for farming that would help them successfully plant their new district.

It didn't hurt that Viola Byler was Menno's daughter. Elijah swept the thought aside, as he had done on the entire ride to Webster County. Guilt pinched him right between the eyes. What did he have to feel guilty about? Bethel acted nothing but snippy with him. She didn't want his help and he wasn't getting any younger. He needed a fraa. He wanted children. And he wasn't going to wait for an ornery, stubborn woman on crutches to wake up and get the message that people who loved each other helped each other, relied on each other, and trusted each other, even when it meant opening themselves up to the possibility of being weak.

Deep thoughts for a beautiful fall day with such a nice breeze.

And a nasty smell. He coughed and covered his nose and mouth with his hand.

"They stink, don't they?" Viola crinkled her nose. She had a pretty nose. Everything about her was pretty. *Pretty is as pretty does.* His mother's words rang in his head. "But the eggs are very good. We sell to restaurants and bakeries and at the farmers' markets. They bring top dollar because we let them run around."

The chickens strutted across the dirt, pecking at the ground. One of the larger birds squawked and flapped its wings as if it might fly away. "How expensive is the start-up?"

"Not too bad." Menno lifted his hat and scratched his bald head. "Viola is my book-keeper. A smart one, this girl."

"Do you use a calculator?" Elijah raised his eyebrows at her. "Or do you do addition and subtraction in your head?"

"I'm allowed to use a battery operated calculator, but I'm a schoolteacher." She took the challenge in the laughing manner in which it was offered. "I'm quite capable of doing the sums in my head."

He chuckled. "Better you than me."

"Not a good student?"

"He was lazy," Silas butted in. "He'd rather count the stars than do his multiplication tables."

"A dreamer." Viola's eyes glowed with laughter. "If I had been your teacher, I would've kept you in line."

"You're far too young to have been my teacher."

Menno scratched his head again, his sun-lined face perplexed. He glanced from his daughter to Elijah. His whiskered countenance took on a pleased expression. "Y'all can stay for the noon meal, can't you? My fraa is frying up some chicken. Mighty fine eats. Fried potatoes. Gravy. Green beans. Lemon meringue pie."

It sounded mighty fine.

They started back across the field, Silas deep in conversation with Menno about equipment, feed costs, feeding schedules, and a litany of other details. Elijah tried to concentrate, but he found himself acutely aware of the woman who strolled next to him at a proper distance. She had a firm, easy stride, and she kept up with him without obvious effort despite being at least a foot shorter. "So you're the teacher."

"Jah. I enjoy my scholars very much."

What he really wanted to know was whether she had a beau. And if not, why not? Smart, pretty, a hard worker with two jobs.

Or maybe that was why not. Two jobs.

"And you keep the books."

"I like math too." She lifted her face to the sun streaming down on them. The air had the nip of early winter in it and the sun felt good to Elijah. Viola seemed to enjoy it as well. "I like to bake and sew. I love babies. I help my sisters with theirs — they have eight now between the three of them. I'm the youngest."

A Plain woman's life. Laid out there for him. And it still didn't answer his question. "Is there anything you don't like?"

"Gossip. Vanity. Waste. People who don't earn their keep."

"A good list." He glanced at her father's back. He was deep into the pros and cons of certain kinds of feed, his hands gesturing, face a grimace. "I wondered if you . . . I wondered why . . ."

"I like teaching." She chuckled, a sound like the tinkling of wind chimes. "For now. I'm certain God has a plan for me. I only have to wait for it to unfold."

A firm believer. Another good quality in a fraa. "I see."

She ducked her head. She looked young and sweet and simple. Sniffing with an upturned nose, she smiled, revealing two distinct dimples. "Smell that?"

He followed her example and sniffed. The smell of chicken droppings had been replaced by the smell of chicken frying. "I do."

"I'd better help Mudder put the food on the table."

"Can we talk later?"

She smiled. "I'd like that."

"I just want to prove to you that you aren't the know-it-all you seem to be."

She grinned at that, looking even younger than she had a moment before, and slipped past her dad into the house. Elijah watched her go. She was pretty. And smart.

So why did he look at her and see a woman who would work hard and make life simple for her husband, but not very interesting.

It seemed that Bethel had something Viola, with her smarts and her beauty and her pleasing nature, did not.

Elijah feared it might be his heart.

CHAPTER 20

His nose practically touching the glass, Luke studied the sign propped in the display case inside the window at Doolittle's Antique Mall and Flea Market. In fancy script, it advertised a consignment sale and auction for the following week. He peered closer. It seemed likely Leah had been right when she observed a few months ago that he needed reading glasses. Now she wouldn't bother to remark on it. She didn't remark on anything. She barely spoke to him at all. He brushed away the thought. One thing at a time. The auctioneer listed was Bob Doolittle and according to the sign, he was the best auctioneer in the state. Luke hoped Bob Doolittle also offered his services at a reasonable rate. If they were back in Bliss Creek, old Jim Carter and his sons would call the auction for free, each taking a section of the fairgrounds for their own. Luke had no illusions about the possibility of that happening here in New Hope.

With time, they would come around. He hoped.

He touched the door handle and then stopped. Every muscle in his body wanted to return to the farm and get back to work. Plunge his hands into dirt. Wield a hammer or a saw. This being bishop wasn't his bowl of soup. He'd rather shoe thirty-five horses in a day than talk to these folks about needing something from them. God didn't make mistakes, that Luke knew, but how could choosing Luke to be bishop make sense? The second the thought bolted through his mind, he breathed a prayer of repentance. God's choice. God's plan. Luke's obedience.

Still, he stifled a groan. He didn't want to talk to these folks. He didn't want to be responsible for making sure the school had the supplies, books, and furnishings needed to provide a proper education. He didn't even put a lot of store in book learning. Didn't matter. The lot had been cast. How could he expect Leah to accept it, if he didn't himself? He thrust the door open. It banged against the display on the other side. A bell jangled overhead and half a dozen sets of wind chimes shimmied and tinkled in a confusing variety of notes. Above all that noise, music with lots of whining instruments he couldn't identify played over loudspeakers.

Who could stand all this noise?

Two steps later he slowed. The smell of old paper and dust welcomed him, along with a sight to behold. The store went on and on, acres of rows of . . . stuff. Old sewing machines, quilts, clothes on hangers stuck on a rope tied between bookshelves, kerosene lanterns, books with yellowed paper and worn covers, jars of buttons, jars of marbles, jars of snaps and safety pins, rocking chairs, jewelry, belts, old shoes, denim jackets, high chairs, bassinets, tricycles, bicycles, tea sets, watering cans, milk cans, coffee tables, paintings of flowers, paintings of landscapes and cowboys and the Last Supper and bulldogs that seemed to be playing cards on black velvet. Stuff occupied every inch of space, every nook and cranny, high and low. Hung close to the ceiling were stop signs and street signs and license plates from dozens of states. All the homes in his new community combined did not contain as much stuff as did this store.

"What can I do you for?" A chubby lady dressed in jeans and a pink T-shirt that read *Sweet as Cotton Candy — Missouri State Fair* trilled the question in an exaggerated Southern drawl as she trotted from between an aisle of pottery and an aisle of skillets, pots, and pans. She swished a dish towel between her hands. Dust billowed from it. She sneezed one tiny, almost polite sneeze. "Oh, it's one of you."

Luke wasn't sure what she meant by that, so he kept quiet.

She tucked the towel under her arm and produced a wrinkled, white handkerchief from the back pocket of her jeans, wiped her nose, and stuffed the hankie back from whence it had come. "Sorry about that. Can't keep up with the dust in here and it aggravates my allergies something fierce."

She held out a hand. "Diana Doolittle."

"Ah." Elijah had done a good job describing her, with her silver cap of hair and chubby cheeks. "Luke Shirack, one of them."

She chuckled. "Sorry. One of these days, you'll be one of us."

Not something he necessarily aspired to be, but he understood the sentiment. "How long does that usually take?"

"The folks who bought the old Reilly place fifteen years ago are still newcomers around here."

"Figured as much."

"You need something for your new

241

kitchen? I've got complete sets of dishes. Beautiful china. Picked 'em up at an estate sale in Clark last week. Got plenty of kerosene lanterns too. I figured since you don't have electricity, you need plenty of lanterns."

Elijah had been right about the avalanche of words too. "I'm interested in having an auction to raise money for our school."

"An auction?" Her bushy white eyebrows popped up, giving her the wide-eyed look of someone not quite right in her noggin. "What do you have to sell?"

"Our womenfolk make quilts —"

"Oh, yes, I've heard about that. You know they could sell them on consignment here in my store, if it's a way to make money you're looking for."

"It's not just quilts. We have home canned fruits, vegetables, jams and jellies, knitted baby blankets, baby clothes, embroidered table clothes. The men are handcrafting chairs, tables, wood furniture of all kinds. There was a lot of old equipment and appliances still in working order that were left on the farms we bought. Lots of stuff we don't need." Luke explained the purpose of the auction. "Everyone contributes. In Bliss Creek, a lot of the Englisch folks donated items too. I thought if we had it here in town

242

at the auction yard, more people would come . . . it being more convenient and all."

"The auction yard. What a great idea. My husband's the auctioneer, you know. He's really good at it too." Her plump cheeks pinked up. "You don't think it's getting to be too cold to have it outside? Our schedule is pretty tight. We have dates open in early December. Of course, that's good timing for people looking to buy Christmas presents. Those quilts make fabulous Christmas presents. Course, I can never give them up. I have one on every bed in our house. Bought a couple up in La Plata and another one in Jamesport."

She paused to take a breath. Luke leaped in.

"We need to raise the money now. Is your husband here?" Luke longed to be back at the farm. He longed for spring and planting time. Digging fence post holes would be easier than this. "I'd like to ask about his services."

"Bob's in the back." She mumbled the words as if she couldn't quite spit them out. "He's in a . . . meeting."

"Who's in a meeting?"

Out strolled a man tall enough to make Luke look up, and Luke was no shorty. The man's hair was longer than his wife's and

243

the color of pewter. Behind him trotted a bent, wizened man leaning on a cane. He was made short by virtue of his bent shoulders and bowed legs. The air immediately reeked of cigar smoke.

"I thought you were in a meeting with some of the city council folks and the sheriff." Diana's hands fluttered in the air. "This man here is looking to have an auction. Quilts, furniture, homemade goods, maybe some livestock. A fund-raiser for their school."

The pink on her cheeks had deepened to the color of cherries. Not a good sign. Luke studied the man who crossed his arms against a western-style checkered shirt. He made an obvious appraisal of Luke, head to toe, and then turned to the man sucking on the stinking cigar. "You hear that, Mayor? They want to have an auction to raise money for their school."

"Now, dear, Sam is retired. He's not the mayor."

"That's right, I'm the mayor, thank you very much, Diana, for reminding me of that." Bob rolled his eyes. "Sam is mayor emeritus. I consult with him on matters of importance."

"Like you have all these huge issues to resolve in this little town." Apparently this

244

lady didn't feel the need to agree with her husband, even in front of other men. "Really, Bob."

"We're booked through the end of the year."

"But we have dates —"

"Diana, you know as well as I do the schedule's full right up until January."

Her mouth opened and shut.

"What do you need your own school for anyway?" Sam had the gravelly voice of a smoker. "We got fine schools here in New Hope."

"Our schools got plenty of students." Sheriff McCormack strode from the same direction as the other two men had a few minutes earlier. He had his own cigar held between thumb and forefinger. Luke covered his mouth and coughed. The sheriff grinned. "I already had this conversation with Mr. Shirack."

"Just Luke."

"Just Luke, the folks around here don't want your crafts." Bob attempted a smile, but it had more the look of a sneer. "They get plenty of those down in Webster County around Christmastime."

"It seemed one way of introducing ourselves to the folks here."

"Folks here keep to themselves."

"So you said, Sheriff." Luke drew a breath. *Tread softly.* "If you have no openings in your schedule, that's fine. We'll work something out. The school is fine in the meantime."

"So they're in school."

"Jah. It opened earlier this week."

"Good to know." The sheriff rested his hand on the butt of his gun. "Can't have them running around the countryside."

"When they're not in school, they're working. No running around." Why did he feel the need to say that? He tipped his hat. "Thank you for your time."

"No problem."

"Remember, if the ladies want to sell their quilts on consignment here, it's no problem." Diana ignored her husband's frown. "Forty percent fee."

No problem for her. She'd would receive almost half of the proceeds for sales meant to benefit the school and the scholars. The quilts were highly sought after and would bring a healthy price at the fundraiser. "I'll let them know."

He'd let his folks know they would be coming up with their own location. Maybe Webster County had a Plain auctioneer. They might want to travel here for a sale out in front of the school. The New Hope

246

Plain families could return the favor come time for fund-raisers out their way.

Keeping themselves apart from the world wouldn't prove to be difficult here in New Hope. He should consider that a blessing. Instead, he felt unwelcome. And homesick.

Don't be such a little boy. Buck up. What would his daed have done? He'd buy some candies for the kinner, go home, and get to work. So that's what Luke did.

CHAPTER 21

Panting, Bethel pumped the stationary bicycle pedals. She closed her eyes and pretended she was riding the bike on the dirt road that curved its way through the farm and along the path that would take her to the creek that divided their property from the Daughterties'. That would never happen. Her district didn't allow bicycles. Some did, she'd heard, but Bishop Kelp had said no to the rubber tires. She'd never really given any thought as to why. The Ordnung was the Ordnung. Sweat dripped down her forehead and she swiped at it with the sleeve of her sweatshirt. Missing two physical therapy sessions had set her back. The muscles in her legs trembled and the ones in her back seemed to be caught in perpetual spasms. She inhaled, intent on breathing through the pain. What did Doctor Karen keep telling her? No pain, no gain.

Easy for her to say with her sturdy legs

and quick stride that carried her around the room *snap-snap.*

Bethel opened her eyes and peeked. Maybe her time was up. The PT smiled at her and gave her two thumbs up. At that moment, Bethel hated those thumbs. "You're doing great. Keep going. You have to make up for lost time."

She smiled back, glad Doctor Karen had stopped chewing her out. She had not been happy about the two missed sessions. She fussed on and on about losing muscle tone faster than she acquired it. Bethel hadn't told her about the upcoming trip to Bliss Creek for the wedding. She'd miss a few more sessions — soon. And she couldn't wait to see her folks and her brothers and sisters and her friends. God forgive her, she couldn't wait to get away from the morose silence at the supper table each night as Leah slapped dishes on the table and Luke stuffed food in his mouth so fast it was obvious he simply wanted to finish and leave the table. Neither had spoken about the day of the school build. Bethel pedaled harder. Leah had everything she wanted and yet she was unhappy. *Gott, how could that be? You've given her everything.*

She pedaled still harder. She had no right to question God's wisdom. His plan. *I only want to understand. I suppose I have no right to ask. No right.* Her muscles ached and her arms trembled. No right to ask why Elijah had gone to Webster County twice since the school build. Once with Silas to see the chicken farm run by Viola Byler's father. Viola, the schoolteacher. Once to look at a horse Silas had decided to buy to replace Ned. Why did she care? Elijah could do whatever he wanted. It wasn't like they were courting.

Her face burned at the thought. Of course they weren't. She didn't look at Elijah that way. He certainly didn't look at her that way, as evidenced by his interest in Viola. He was a helper. Nothing more.

Still, sometimes it felt like more. She could admit that to herself. Even though the thought made her heart do a strange one-two, one-two beat and her skin feel hot with embarrassment. That night with the cinnamon roll. The way he'd looked at her when he said those words. *You don't think I can understand?* And each time she rode in the buggy with him to these sessions. Maybe she was guilty of letting herself imagine that they were doing more than sharing a ride into town. Nee. Pain gripped her heart in a sickening embrace. She caught her breath and swallowed against it. Her legs slowed.

Her hands felt slick on the handle grips.

Just a driver. Just a driver. It wasn't like he'd ever shone a flashlight in her window. No one had done that since Abraham Hartman when she was seventeen. Abraham who'd changed his mind and married Ruth Hostetler that next November.

"You're slowing down. Get a move on, girl. Pump those legs."

The voice she'd thought so lovely and sweet at the beginning of their sessions now grated on Bethel. It sounded more like her mother on laundry day. Still, she picked up the pace and tried to keep her mind off Elijah and his oh-so helpful ways that didn't extend beyond giving her a ride. Or his strong hands, callused and tanned, with the scar that ran along his knuckles where he'd caught it on barbed wire. His eyes the color of a brilliant blue sky. The dimple in his left cheek when he smiled.

Stop it.

She closed her eyes and put herself back on the bike in the woods by the creek. She might not ride a bike there, but someday she would run. She would run, arms pumping, legs stretching. And then she would play volleyball and baseball with her scholars in the field by the new school. She tried to imagine the creek with its rushing water and the birds calling to each other in the trees. Scolding each other, chattering. They always sounded like nosy women gossiping about this and that, nothing important.

The path smelled like damp moss and decomposing leaves. The water smelled fresh. It reminded her of swimming in the stream back home in Bliss Creek with her sisters and her friends when they were twelve years old and summer nights lasted forever. Chores were done. Stars sparkled in the sky. Mosquitoes buzzed. They swam and splashed each other and then grabbed their towels and ran home when the boys showed up for their swim.

Elijah had been one of those boys. His skin tanned, hair bleached from the sun, laughing as the girls tore past them and ran barefooted on their dirt road, leaving wet tracks behind them.

The memories made her throat ache and tears well up behind her closed eyelids. *Stay at the creek.* Now the ride wasn't as pleasant. She gritted her teeth and imagined the wind rustling the trees. Frogs croaked, sounding like bullhorns. Cicadas chirped.

Music broke the silence. Tinny notes with lots of drums. Reluctantly, Bethel opened her eyes. She was still in the PT room with its odor of stale sweat and cleanser. Doctor

Karen grabbed her phone from a nearby chair and put it to her ear. Immediately her expression turned grim. "Just a minute, Mom." She held her hand over the little rectangle. "I need to take this call. It's very important or I wouldn't. If I step into the hallway for one minute, will you be all right? I'll be right there so holler if you need me."

Bethel nodded. She could sit and push pedals round and round without supervision.

Her expression a cross between fearful and hopeful, the woman stepped out, already talking into the miniature phone. Bethel wondered what that must be like. Doctor Karen not only talked into it all the time, but she typed on it and slid her fingers across it, staring at it like it was the most interesting, mesmerizing thing she'd ever seen. How much of the world around her did she miss while she fixed her gaze on that phone?

"Hey, there you are."

Bethel froze at the sound of the low, sandpaper rough voice. She forgot to push on the pedals and the bike ground to a halt.

"Don't stop working out on my account. Dragon lady will get after you." Shawn rolled his chair across the floor from the far entrance on the other side of the hand

253

weights. "I don't want to get you in trouble."

"You can't be in here right now." White heat crackled around Bethel like lightning rippling across the sky on a July night. She had no towel. Nothing with which to cover herself in her English clothes. "I have this room to myself until eight o'clock."

"What's the matter? Are you afraid of me?" Mock horror drenched the words. He waved his arm in a flourish that showed off a bulging bicep. He wore a black T-shirt with the sleeves cut off, gray shorts, and black sneakers shiny in their newness. Never walked on. Ready to work out. "Seriously? I'm paralyzed from the waist down, darlin'. I'm no threat."

"It's not that. No, of course not." She stuttered. She wanted to wipe sweat from her face, but she was afraid to let go of the bike handles. If she fell off the bike in front of him she'd never forgive herself. He wouldn't be able to help her up. And he would feel bad about it. The little she knew of him told her that. Another helper. "I . . . it's just that I'm . . . it's these clothes. I don't want you to see me in these clothes."

"Well, they ain't a prom dress, but you don't look any worse than the next girl in sweats. Fact is you're too pretty to look bad in anything."

Prom dress? "No, no. I don't want you looking at all." The more she talked, the worse it got. She wasn't trying to get compliments. "I mean, it's . . . I come at this time because we don't wear these kinds of clothes, and we don't do things like exercise with men."

"I noticed the clothes thing. Dress and apron. Must make getting dressed in the morning easy. You look nice in them." He backed the chair up a few paces. "I didn't mean to embarrass you. I'm just trying to figure out what's okay and what's not. I knew you'd be here, and I wanted to talk to you."

"Why?"

"I like you."

Three simple words. Why did Plain men find them so hard to say to her? Her legs began to move, her feet pushed the pedals. She was here to get better. Nothing more. "I'm sorry, but you need to leave."

"Come on, don't be that way."

"I mean it. I asked for this time so I could do this alone." Luke's stern face appeared in her mind's eye. Elijah's irritated features followed. Not that Elijah's opinion counted. Not at all. "If I don't do it alone, my family won't let me come anymore."

Concern washed over his face. "I don't

want to get you in trouble."

"Then leave. Please."

His hands went to the wheels and he shoved hard. The chair zoomed toward the door. He looked like a little boy sent to bed without his supper. Bethel ducked her head. How could a few words of conversation hurt? She understood him. He understood her. This was about their shared experiences of not being able to make their legs do what they needed them to do. Nothing else. It was mean to send him away. She could consider it an extension of the therapy group. Luke had approved that. They were out in the open. Doctor Karen was nearby. The workout clothes covered her from her neck to her toes. What more could he ask?

"Wait."

His head came up and the chair whirled around and zipped back. "I knew you couldn't resist me." His broad grin made the scars on his cheek crinkle in a mass of angry red welts. "You like me."

"If you talk like that you can't stay." Better to establish ground rules now. "And you can't look at me."

"Seriously?"

"I'm very serious."

"Yeah, you are." He tilted his head and examined her like a doctor examining a patient. "How about I go over there and straighten up the hand weights? Put them in order by weight? They're always getting messed up because people are too lazy to put them back right." He pointed — or tried to point — at the other side of the room. His fingers didn't cooperate. "We can still talk, but you won't be uncomfortable. I won't look at you and technically, I won't be working out with you."

The spirit of the law and the letter of the law. Bishop Kelp had talked about that more than once. They shouldn't be tempted to circumvent the Ordnung in little ways any more than in big ways. What did the Ordnung say about two disabled people giving each other support? She didn't know, but she could guess when it came to one of them being a man — an Englisch man at that. Why was she finding it so hard to do the right thing?

She stared at his face with its light dusting of little boy freckles that contradicted the angry scars. It wasn't his looks or the fact that he was a man. She saw herself in his face. His held the same wistfulness she saw in the mirror. The same longing. Shawn didn't want to be alone anymore. Neither did she. He didn't want to be different. Neither did she. He wanted to run. So did she. She swallowed hard. "Okay."

"Are you sure? I don't want to get you in trouble."

She nodded, still pedaling, and waited until he positioned himself with his back to her before she spoke again. "Why are you trying to figure out what's okay and what's not?"

With a grunt, he picked up a huge weight that probably weighed as much as the twins combined. "I told you that first day. Love at first sight."

"Don't. I'm being serious. If you can't be serious, we can't talk."

"You never kid around?"

"You mean like tease?"

"Yeah, tease."

She thought of Elijah and his assertion that she talked to herself and had imaginary friends. "Yes, we tease." She hid the memory under a pile of bittersweet memories of conversations and singings and buggy rides that had led to nothing but the realization that she might never marry. Back in the days when she'd been happy for the opportunity to teach. She pumped harder. Now she didn't have that either.

"Why do you look so sad, darlin'?"

She looked up to see that he had swiveled in his chair, the weight still lifted chest high.

"You're cheating."

"Sorry." He settled into the chair, his back to her. "Doesn't mean you can't answer the question."

"You didn't answer mine. Not seriously."

"You're different from any woman I've ever known. You don't try to get the attention of men. You don't wear makeup or jewelry or clothes that show off your figure. You don't care what people think of you."

That wasn't entirely true, but she knew what Shawn meant. "We don't draw attention to ourselves. Men or women."

"Why?"

"Because it's vanity. We want to remain humble, without pride. We can't take credit for anything we have or do. It's all because of God."

"I get that."

"You do?"

"Yeah. I try to remember when I'm feeling sorry for myself that God got me home from that war. A lot of guys didn't come home. I should be thankful."

"But you're not."

"Some days."

"And other days?"

"I wish I were dead. I wish I died over there in battle with my buddies. It would be better than sitting in this chair for the rest of my life."

His matter-of-fact tone chilled her despite the sweaty heat of her exertion on the bike.

"Don't worry."

She looked up to see him swiveled in the chair again. "Don't look at me, Shawn."

"I can't help it. You're so pretty, especially with your cheeks all red like that."

"Stop."

"I just meant to say don't worry — I won't kill myself. I would never do that to my mother. She's been through enough."

"What about your father?" She contemplated the back of his head. "I met him — twice."

"Lucky you."

"That's disrespectful."

He dumped the weight back on the rack and selected the next larger sizer. "He doesn't respect me."

"He asked me how you were doing." She pictured the sheriff's face. She did see some of Shawn there, the part trying to find his way through the pain. "He seemed sad."

"He's pathetic. He knows where I live. He doesn't want to run into Mom." Shawn shoved the weights over his head and then out, up and out, repeat. He wasn't even breathing hard. "He could call me. Did he lose my number or something?"

"No. No. I don't know. But he seemed very sad."

"He's a pathetic, sad excuse for a dad."

"Shawn!"

"Tell me about what it's like to be Amish. Plain you call it, right?"

So he wanted to change the subject. She understood that. She didn't want to talk about living with her sister and brother-in-law when she should be married and taking care of her own children. "We believe we have to keep ourselves apart from the world so we don't end up worldly. We believe in putting Jesus first, others second, and ourselves last. We believe God has a plan for us."

"So no cars, no electricity, no telephones, no computers, no TVs, no movies."

"No."

"How's it working out for you?"

She tested the words, trying to decide if he were making fun of her. She heard only a sincere desire to know. "If I could learn to walk again, it would work out fine."

"Why aren't you married then?"

"I don't know. Why aren't you married?" She couldn't believe she'd asked that question. It must be the sweatpants. "I'm sorry. Don't answer that."

"I don't know either." His smirk didn't

261

cover the sadness than ran through his tone. "Couldn't be the chair, could it?"

"The chair? The chair is nothing. It doesn't change who you are."

"Any more than your crutches do, right?"

"Jah, I mean right."

"Which is why you're in here, busting your behind to fix your legs so you can throw away the crutches."

"You don't understand. In our community, women, like men, work hard. There's laundry and canning and cooking and growing gardens and mowing the yard. It's hard physical labor because —"

"Because you don't believe in making it any easier on yourselves with electricity and rubber tires. I got all that when I searched you online."

"Searched me? Online?"

"Not you. Amish folks." His voice held a note of laughter. "Online. You know, Google search."

"No. I don't know."

"So you think Englisch folks don't work hard just because they have electricity and microwaves and tractors and cars and such?"

"I'm sure they — you — work very had."

"Well, I don't. I sit around on my kiester playing video games and watching soap operas with my mom."

"Get a job."

"Doing what?"

"What did you want to do before you went . . . over there?"

"I was gonna be a cop like my pop."

The sheer desolation in his voice combined with the great effort he made in order to hide it broke Bethel's heart. She gritted her teeth, knowing no man wanted a woman to cry for him. "What was second on the list?"

"Huh?"

"Aren't there other things you like to do?"

He wheeled his chair around. "I like talking to you."

Bethel ducked his gaze. "You're not supposed to look at me. That was the rule."

"Get a pop with me after the group session. There's a coffee shop next to the clinic. It's close enough for you to walk."

"I can't."

"Is that a rule too?"

She squirmed on the uncomfortable bike seat. "Yes."

"You always follow the rules?"

Until today, she would've answered yes to that question. Until she met this man in a wheelchair with his way of getting under her skin. "It's what we are called to do."

"Shawn, what are you doing in here?"

Bethel jumped and nearly lost her hold on the bike. Shawn's expression grew morose. Doctor Karen charged into the room, looking like a momma cat that had discovered a pit bull threatening her kitten. "I thought I heard voices. I'm sorry, Bethel. You should've called for me. I shouldn't have taken the phone call. It was my mother and she's been sick and I hadn't heard from her about some test results we were waiting on. Shawn McCormack, you don't have permission to be in here. This is a closed session."

"I invited him in." Bethel had to raise her voice to be heard over Doctor Karen's outrage. "It's all right. He asked and I accepted the invitation to work out together."

Gott, forgive me.

"Because you're too polite to say no." Doctor Karen glared at Shawn. "Out. Now."

How Bethel wished that was the reason. Politeness had nothing to do with it. Selfishness, everything.

"I'm going. I'm going." Shawn rolled across the room, his biceps pumping. Just when Bethel thought she'd dodged the bullet he'd fired a few seconds before, he paused at the doorway. "Have a pop with me. After."

Aware of Doctor Karen's curious look,

264

Bethel shook her head.

"It's just a pop."

Not trusting her voice, she shook her head again.

"Okay. But I'm going to keep asking. It'll be a standing invitation."

A standing temptation.

CHAPTER 22

Bethel swung toward Doctor Jasmine's office, careful not to meet Shawn's gaze as he wheeled himself into the group therapy room. She should never have agreed to let him stay in the workout room. The minute Doctor Karen broke the connection between them with her shriek of disapproval, Bethel had known. She'd known before, but had tried to sweep it under a rug of excuses woven together with her own need to talk to someone: He needed her help, he needed to talk to someone who understood, they weren't really alone, Doctor Karen was there in the hallway, he wasn't looking at her, on and on. Still, at the heart of her excuses, she recognized a truth. Their conversation had meant everything to her. It had been the kind of conversation she couldn't have with anyone else. The kind of conversation she wanted to have with a man. Not just any man. But a man who cared about her.

She swallowed the ache in her throat and picked up speed on the crutches. Her legs didn't want to cooperate. They weren't getting better. As long as they didn't improve, she would continue to come here. Continue to be in the same room as Shawn. She needed to work harder. Get better. And get on with her life at home. That's what she wanted. She'd keep telling herself that until she believed it.

For now, she needed to stop thinking of herself and think of others. Think of how her actions would affect them. Going against the Ordnung would hurt Luke, the new bishop, and Leah, her own sister. Both had enough problems already.

"Doctor Jasmine, could I ask you a question?" She managed to get the words out before she lost her courage. "In private?"

Doctor Jasmine lowered a file she'd been trying to read while she trotted down the hallway. Her braid had come undone and hung down her back to her waist. "Sure, what's up? You missed a few sessions. You know what we talked about. No missing."

"I have . . . things I have to do at home." She wavered at the door to Doctor Jasmine's tiny office. The therapist shooed her in with a flapping motion. "And I have to go back to Kansas in a few days for a wedding. I won't be here next week."

"That's not good. We're not meeting on Thanksgiving as it is." Jasmine tossed the folder on her desk where it was immediately swallowed up by dozens more that looked just like it. She eased into her chair and fixed Bethel with a stern stare. "I'm sure Doctor Karen has told you that you have to make your physical therapy a priority. The same goes for your group sessions."

"I know. I will." If she came back. The situation with Shawn had her wondering if she could trust herself to do that. There was a reason they were told to keep themselves apart from the world. "That's not what I came to talk to you about, though. It's something else."

Doctor Jasmine must have heard the hesitation in her voice. She pointed to the chair squeezed in on the other side of the desk that filled most of the cramped office. "Have a seat. You can talk to me about anything. Everything said in this room stays in this room." She chuckled. "Like Las Vegas."

"Las Vegas?"

"Never mind." Her face became serious again. "What's up?"

"It's . . ." Everything said in this room

268

stayed in this room. Bethel breathed. What was she thinking? She reached for the crutches. "I'm sorry, I shouldn't have bothered you. The others are waiting."

"Bethel, tell me. It will stay between you and me. That's a promise. Whatever it is, you've come this far."

Yes, she had. For Leah's sake, she had to ask. She dropped the crutches against the chair next to hers. "I think there's something wrong with my sister."

Her eyebrows raised over dark, serious eyes, Doctor Jasmine leaned back in her chair and steepled her fingers. "Medically wrong?"

"Like the kind of wrong we talk about in therapy groups. Like in her head."

"What makes you say that?"

"She cries a lot."

"And she didn't before?"

"Well, she has five children and I'm all the help she has and we just moved here and she really didn't want to come." Bethel waved a hand over her lap. "And I'm really not that much help."

"Don't feel guilty. You didn't cause the storm that led to your injuries. And you're doing everything you can to get better — except skipping sessions, of course."

"No, I know. This isn't about me."

"Five children is a lot. Where is her husband? Can't he help her?"

Bethel struggled to explain the division of labor. It worked. It always worked. "That's the thing. Nothing has changed. Luke works hard in the fields every day. It's Leah's job to take care of the children, just like it's always been. Now she doesn't want to."

"Which is hard for you to understand because you would love to have those babies."

Why did Jasmine keep bringing this back around to Bethel? And how could she know exactly how Bethel felt? "It's not about me."

"You keep saying that, but I see something different."

"Leah is expecting another baby and all she does is cry. I don't think she wants the baby."

"You sound shocked and disapproving. Your sister already has five children. By most people's standards, that's plenty."

"Not by ours. Babies are gifts from God. The more the better. Family is everything to us. Our children share in the work and together we support each other."

"How old are Leah's children?"

Bethel counted them off. "Jebediah is eighteen months old. The twins are three. William is seven and Joseph is eight. William and Joseph help with the chores already. They mow and they spread manure and feed the livestock and help Luke with the hay, but still, Leah has to do all the laundry and cooking and cleaning."

"Five children under the age of ten, including three-year-old twins. Your sister is exhausted. She cooks, she cleans, and she takes care of children all day long. No wonder she cries."

"That's what all Plain women do. We like it. We enjoy our work."

Doctor Jasmine's dark eyebrows did push-ups. "All Plain women like it. Plain women never complain?"

"Well, not never, but we grow up knowing this is what our life will be. We long for it. We pray for it."

"You mean you pray for it."

"Yes. I did pray for it."

"But not now."

"I pray for God's plan to be revealed to me in His time."

Doctor Jasmine sighed. She began stacking the folders on her desk. It didn't matter. It remained a mess. "I can't tell much for certain without actually seeing your sister. What you're describing does bring to mind a particular diagnosis, however. Have you ever heard of postpartum depression?"

"Postpartum?"

"It means after birth."

Bethel rolled the words around. After birth depression.

"We don't get depressed. And after babies are born, we're happy because babies are blessings."

"I understand. That is what you believe. And beliefs are powerful. But so are hormones. So powerful that a woman who desperately wants a child and is so happy and excited the day that baby is born can go home and find herself suicidal when she's there all alone taking care of that baby on her own while hubby works. She can want to kill herself. She can even want to harm her own child."

"No."

"Yes. It happens. More than most people want to admit."

"Not to Plain women."

"Are you sure about that? Go home. Talk to your sister. Then tell me that."

"What do you do about it?"

"Number one, you don't leave a depressed mother alone with her children. Number two, you get her to see a doctor. Well, if she's pregnant, she's seeing a doctor. Right?"

Bethel didn't answer, but she knew her expression gave her away.

"No prenatal care?"

"She's had five healthy children with the help of midwives."

"Doctors can prescribe medicine to help her after the baby comes."

"Medicine?"

"Yes, antidepressants."

Bethel tried to imagine Luke's reaction to such a conversation. She didn't even know where to begin to present such an argument. Even if Leah would let her, which of course she wouldn't. "Thank you for your help."

"Look, I understand things are different for you folks. Get your sister to come see me. I'd be happy to talk to her."

"Thank you." Leah would never do that. Still, putting a name to Leah's troubles helped Bethel. It wasn't Leah's fault. It was something in her body. Her sister wasn't rejecting their way of life, even if her body was. "I'll try."

Doctor Jasmine nodded. Her cell phone rang, a sing-song jumble of notes that sounded like a merry-go-round at the county fair. Her smile broadened. "I have to take this. It's my husband."

She hadn't thought of Doctor Jasmine as having a husband. She worked many hours as a therapist. Bethel studied the photos on the shelves behind the desk. A smiling man in a uniform had his arm around her. Another military man. She wondered, as she had many times before, what called them to this service. She stood and swung toward the door.

"But I thought you didn't deploy until after the holidays."

Jasmine's voice lost its usual smile. Bethel kept moving. She didn't want to hear conversations not meant for her ears. Her crutches dug into the carpet and she swung into the therapy room where the others were already assembled. The only chairs left were next to Shawn. She left a seat between them and plopped into the plush padding.

"Where's Doc?" Crystal snapped her gum and twirled a lock of purple hair between two fingers. "I got things to do."

"Shut up, Crystal." Mark sucked in oxygen. "She'll be here when she gets here."

"Easy for you to say. All you do all day is play games."

"Like you got a job to go to?" Shawn interjected. "Or maybe you have a date?"

"Let's be nice." Bethel knew they were playing with each other. They liked to bicker. And they did it a lot when Doctor Jasmine wasn't in the room to mediate. Bethel liked getting there a little early when they were sitting around teasing each other. They were so at ease with each other and themselves. "She's on the phone. She'll be here."

At that moment the therapist hustled into the room. A tissue in one hand, she had the usual smile fixed on her face, but her eyes were red. "Sorry I'm late, folks. Got behind."

Guilt assailed Bethel. Late because of her need to talk.

"What's the matter, Doc?" Shawn leaned forward in his chair. "You look like you got some bad news."

He wasn't as self-absorbed as he seemed. Another point in his favor. *Stop it!* Nobody was keeping points, least of all Bethel.

"No, no, I'm fine." Her smile trembled. "Besides, this is about you, not me."

"Come on, Doc, we sit here and spill our guts to you all the time." Crystal shook her head so her purple and pink hair flailed around her head. "We're here for you."

"That's not the way therapy works." Doctor Jasmine eased into the chair between Shawn and Bethel. "It's not about me."

"Is it your husband?" Ed spoke up in his stroke-slurred voice, much to Bethel's surprise. The elderly man rarely said anything. She caught him watching her a few times, as if mildly interested, but mostly he wiped his nose with a handkerchief, his faded blue eyes filled with sadness. "Did something happen to him?"

"Okay, if y'all feel the need to know, I'll tell you this much. Lou is being deployed overseas early." She smoothed her purple jacket even though it was perfectly crisp and wrinkle-free, as always. "But it's fine. We knew he was going. We just didn't know it would be so early."

"Where is he going?" Bethel hoped it was all right to ask. Doctor Jasmine knew everything about her life. "What does he do?"

"He's an army doctor. He's going overseas to take care of our troops. For twelve months."

"It's okay, Doc. We'll take care of you." Shawn jerked his head toward the others. "Isn't that right?"

"Absolutely." Crystal wiggled in her chair, her voice full of enthusiasm. "You can come to my house for Christmas Eve. We make popcorn and string it on the trees in the yard. At least we used to. If my dad stays sober long enough, he might remember."

"We're having some folks over for a little get-together on New Year's Eve," Elaine offered. "You're welcome to join us."

"Oh, that'll be fun," Crystal sneered. "All

those wine drinkers with their pinkies in the air."

Elaine colored. "Actually, we don't drink."

"Now there's a recommendation," Shawn chortled. "Teetotalers."

"What's wrong with that?" Bethel fixed him with her schoolteacher stare. "Some people could do with less of it."

"That's enough, children, enough." Doctor Jasmine took a deep breath and smiled her usual bright smile. "I have family here, lest you forget. I'll be fine. Let's talk about you guys." Her gaze roved, then settled on Bethel. "Bethel, let's start with you since you'll be gone all of next week. How do you feel about going back to Kansas? Are you looking forward to it?"

Bethel interlaced her fingers in her lap and contemplated the question. She tried her best to be truthful in these sessions, but she'd come to the conclusion that being the center of attention and speaking of personal things in front of these folks caused her more stress than her disobedient legs.

"It's not a trick question. I only want you to share your feelings. Talking about them helps. I promise."

Bethel raised her head but still avoided making eye contact with the others. "I'm happy to go home. I'm happy to see my mudder and my sisters and brothers. Thanksgiving is a wonderful time of visiting and sharing our blessings."

"How come you didn't mention your pops?" Shawn shifted in his chair. "Aren't you glad to see him?"

"I mentioned him. I'm glad to see him." Bethel cast around in her memory. She had mentioned Daed, hadn't she? "Of course I'm glad to see him."

"Not everyone gets along with their parents. You don't have to feel guilty." Doctor Jasmine shrugged. "We don't get to choose our parents. It's important to recognize that."

"Amen," Crystal crowed. "You got that right."

"My daed — father — is a fair, honest, hardworking man."

"Sounds cold," said Mark. "Not much fun."

"It's not about being fun. He had to provide for six children. My mudder — mother — had cancer when I was little. He worked hard — harder than most."

"But you don't like him."

"Yeah, you don't like him, admit it."

That Mark and Crystal were ganging up on Bethel came as a surprise to her. She always tried to be helpful and nice when

278

they talked in group.

"I think what Mark and Crystal are saying is that you were probably a little scared and sad when your mom was sick." Doctor Jasmine's warm, sweet tone eased the agony of embarrassment that had a stranglehold around Bethel's throat. "Maybe you wished your father would've taken the time to comfort you or show you his own emotions."

"No. No!" Bethel shook her head, not wanting to entertain for a second the idea that Daed had any obligation to do such a thing for a scared ten-year-old. He expected her and the other children to have faith in God no matter what happened. It wasn't theirs to question God's plan. "Daed did what he was supposed to do. He worked hard and put food on the table. He made sure we said our prayers and learned the things we needed to learn. Everything else was up to God."

"Do you really believe that?" Shawn scoffed. "You believe all that God-has-a-plan stuff."

"I do."

"How can you? You thought it was God's plan for you to move to New Hope and look how people have treated you here. What's up with that?"

She chewed her lip and forced herself to meet his gaze. He looked as if he really needed to know. Her answer mattered. "God never promised life would be easy. You were the one who said you learned to appreciate life because of what happened to you in Afghanistan. You said God brought you back alive and you were thankful. Have you changed your mind about that?"

"Wouldn't it have been a lot better if he brought me back with my legs working?" Bitterness sprang from the words like arrows, pointed and painful. "Then my parents would still be together and I'd be at the police academy in St. Louis by now. I might be . . ."

"You might be what, Shawn?" Doctor Jasmine's tone was so soft and gentle Bethel wanted to cloak herself in its warmth. "Go on."

"I might be married by now. I might be a dad."

He wanted all the same things Bethel did. The thought hurt her down to the marrow in her bones. He wasn't so different. Clothes and cars didn't make the Englischers so different from her. "God didn't throw that stove on me," she said. "I've been reminded by this experience that I can rely on Him when I can rely on nothing else. So can you.

He might not give you your heart's desire, but He will give you what you need according to His will and in His time. He is with us and will always be with us, no matter what happens. That's what gets me through."

She drew a breath, astounded at the words that had flowed from her mouth. She'd never had to defend her beliefs to others before. She'd never been so struck by how important it was that Shawn and the others find comfort in faith.

"Beautifully said. Thank you, Bethel, for putting up with these critters. And for sharing so openly and honestly with us. I know it's not easy for you." Doctor Jasmine nodded at Bethel, the twinkle back in her eyes. "It's somebody else's turn on the hot seat. Ed, how are you doing today?"

"Today would've been my sweet Marian's seventieth birthday." Ed's wispy voice teetered on the brink of disappearing. "We always ate strawberries and pound cake on her birthday."

Weak with relief that the attention had been drawn to another, Bethel thought ahead to making a cake for Ed after she returned from Bliss Creek.

"Hey, Ed, we could take you out to the cemetery to visit Marian, if you like." Shawn cocked his head at Elaine. "Elaine's got a big Cadillac, don't you Elaine?"

Elaine straightened. "Yes, but . . ."

"Do you have a chauffeur?" Crystal chimed in. "That would be cool."

"No chauffeur. My sister drives me."

"Then it's a date." Shawn grinned. "I'll bring the flowers. We'll go this afternoon, after lunch. You coming, Bethel?"

"I'm sorry, I can't. I have work to do at home for my sister. She's . . . it's . . ."

"It's all right." Even as he smiled, Ed wiped at tears that didn't seem to embarrass him in the least. "Family is important. You don't realize how important until you don't have any around."

It might be pushy on Shawn's part, but the smile on the side of Ed's face that didn't droop made it worth it. Shawn had an unwavering need to help others. That made him like Elijah. Why did she keep pushing Elijah's help away when she found Shawn's willingness to help others a fine quality? What caused her to be so unfair to Elijah? Bethel stared at her hands to keep from looking at Shawn. No matter how kind he was, Shawn didn't have a place in her life. The faith she'd mentioned earlier precluded it. Faith could move mountains, but it would not change the fact that her life ran in a road parallel to Shawn's, never touching.

Maybe that's what made him so appealing. The thought stung. She wanted what she couldn't have. The fact she couldn't have it made her want it more. For shame.

CHAPTER 23

The words of the other people in her group flowed around Bethel as Doctor Jasmine made sure to gently nudge each one. Ashamed that she'd let her attention wander, Bethel tried to focus on the conversation. It was the polite thing to do, but she badly wanted out of this room. She wanted away from Shawn and the questioning expression on his face every time he looked at her. Temptation sitting in a wheelchair within arm's reach. She was a grown woman, strong in her faith, sure in what was right. Still, she couldn't look at him. Finally the clock on the wall hit nine and they were released. Bethel waited while the wheelchair users lined up and left the room first. It seemed only fair to give them a head start.

"Have a good trip, Bethel." Doctor Jasmine touched her arm. "Do your exercises. Doctor Karen will get after you if you lose what ground you've gained."

"I will." Bethel twisted on her crutches, feeling awkward. "And thanks for the advice about my sister."

"Walk with me to my office. I have a couple of brochures I want to give you."

Bethel followed her down the hallway and waited while she rummaged through stacks of paper on a bookshelf squeezed into one corner of the office.

"Here's some information for you as a family member to read." Doctor Jasmine handed her a trifold with a picture of a woman holding a baby on the front of it. "Get your sister to come see me. Or if she'd rather see someone more private — someone not already assisting a family member — I can get you the name of a good psychotherapist in Jefferson City. It's a bit of a drive in a buggy —"

"Don't worry about it. I'll see how it goes." Tucking the brochure in the canvas bag hanging from her shoulder, she cast about for the right words to express her feelings. "I'm sorry about your husband being gone for the holidays."

"It's okay. We'll Skype and get on Facebook."

Neither meant anything to Bethel. Her confusion must've shown on her face. Doctor Jasmine chuckled. "We'll talk."

"Oh, okay."

Relieved to be out of the room, she swung down the hallway and pushed through the double doors with her shoulder and swung onto the sidewalk. Elijah sat on the buggy seat, licking a double-scoop ice cream cone. He looked up at her and grinned. "You're late." He grabbed a white bag from the seat and dangled it in the air. "I brought you an ice cream sandwich, the kind you like with the Neapolitan ice cream in it. I figure you could use it after all that therapy stuff. I know it's the wrong time of year for ice cream, but I couldn't help myself."

He looked like a little boy with the vanilla ice cream dripping on his hand and a smudge of it on his upper lip. She had to smile back. Forget Webster County. Forget all that man and woman stuff. It took the fun out of life. She loved ice cream. If he'd brought a few slices of pizza to go with it, she would've considered it a complete treat. "It's never the wrong time of year for ice cream. Help me up."

He nodded, his face full of something Bethel couldn't identify at first. Then it hit her. His face shone with hope. She'd made his day by asking for his help. His desire to help her was not born of pity; it was born

286

of an innate goodness. Helping her gave him pleasure. She shouldn't deprive him of that pleasure. Elijah hopped down from the buggy and sprinted toward her, the cone bobbing precariously.

"Bethel, there you are." Only one person said her name like that, with such an invitation in his gravelly voice. "I thought I'd missed you. I figured if you wouldn't come with me, I'd bring the pop to you."

She swiveled. Shawn sat on the sidewalk that led from the rehab center to the coffee shop next door. He had a cardboard cup holder in his lap filled with two cans of pop and an assortment of candy bars and chips. "I didn't know what you liked so I got a little of everything."

Bethel faced Elijah. He skidded to a stop just short of touching her with his free hand. The top scoop of ice cream toppled from his cone and landed at her feet. Bethel shook her head. "You know I wouldn't do this."

Elijah backed away. His gaze slid toward Shawn. Bethel couldn't read his expression, but his back was rigid, his movements jerky. He dumped his cone in the trash. "Let's go."

"I turned down his invitation."

"Darlin' —"

"Go away, Shawn."

Disappointment flashed on Shawn's face. He wheeled around, arms pumping. Elijah grabbed Bethel's crutches and stuck them in the back of the buggy with a bang.

"Easy on the crutches." She forced herself to keep her tone light. "They'd be expensive to replace."

Elijah lifted her into the buggy without replying. His hands didn't feel gentle around her waist today. They were tight, too tight. He paused, his gaze lifted to hers. "You give me no choice, you know?"

"No choice?"

"I have to tell Luke."

"Tell him what? An Englisch man offered me a pop?"

"An Englisch man is in love with you."

"Shawn's not —"

"Believe me, I recognize it when I see it."

With that outrageous statement, Elijah hoisted himself into the buggy and took off.

"What are you getting so mad about?" Bethel grabbed the arm-rest to keep from smacking against it as Elijah urged the horse into an abrupt trot. "How was Webster County?"

"What?" Elijah's face was set in fierce, angry lines. "What are you talking about?"

"Your trips to Webster County. Did you

see what you wanted to see?"

The second the words passed her lips Bethel regretted them. She had no business sticking her nose in Elijah's affairs.

"Webster County was fine."

"Webster County was fine or Viola was fine?" She clapped her hands to her mouth and swiveled her head so she looked at the passing stores. How could she be so forward? She had no right. "I'm sorry. Ignore me. I've had . . . it's been a bad morning."

The pulse jumped in Elijah's jaw. He gritted his teeth and stared straight ahead.

The silence stretched, filled only with the clip-clop of the horse's hooves and the racket of cars that swerved to go around them. The longer it stretched, the more time Bethel had to study her regrets. They went on and on. This was why she would never marry, never have children. She was too pigheaded.

They were almost to the farm before Elijah spoke. He didn't smile and his gruff tone told her he was still angry. "If I shone a flashlight in your window, what would you do?"

It was the last thing she'd expected him to say. Her pulse pounded in her ears and her mouth was so dry she didn't know if she could form the words. "I don't know."

"You'd best figure it out and soon."

"I will." The words came out in an embarrassing croak. "I promise."

He snapped the reins and urged the horse forward. "I still have to tell Luke."

"I know."

Would it be her brother-in-law she faced or her bishop? She preferred the bishop. He would be wise and fair. The brother-in-law would be angry first, then wise and fair.

But at the moment, she was far more worried about the flashlight.

CHAPTER 24

Elijah had never felt more silly in his life. Why say something stupid like that to Bethel? Why not just show up one night and take her for a ride? He hadn't meant to bring it up. He'd been fighting the idea since the first time he'd lifted her from the van that brought her to Missouri. Then Shawn McCormack's invitation in the form of pop and candy had been a wake-up call. Speak up now or forever hold your peace. He snapped the reins, hoping the new horse would show a little more giddy-up and go. No such luck. This horse was no Ned. "Come on, giddy-up!"

"Don't take it out on the horse." Bethel's first words since the question. Accusatory and not a little snippy. "It's not his fault."

"I would never . . ." He started to argue, then drew a breath. She wanted to draw him into a debate. He wouldn't fall for that. "He's a nice horse. Silas made a good . . .

Who is that? Is that William? William and Joseph?"

Bethel sat forward and raised her hand to her forehead to shield her eyes from the sun. "It is. What are they doing? And why aren't they in school?"

Joseph sat on the grassy bank of the ditch that ran alongside the road. His brother William knelt next to him. With their dark pants, blue shirts, and matching brown heads they could have been twins, little miniatures of Luke. They seemed to be examining Joseph's arm. William's hat lay at his feet and brilliant red stains covered the front of both boy's shirts.

"Is that . . ." Bethel's horrified voice trailed away. Her face blanched. "Elijah."

"I know." He pulled hard on the reins. "Whoa, whoa!"

Bethel tried to climb from the buggy before it came to a complete stop. Elijah slapped his arm out in front of her. "Not yet."

She drew back and grasped the buggy arm. He tightened the reins some more and the buggy jerked to a halt, dust billowing around them as they hit the shoulder of the road. "Now you can get down. Or you could wait for me to help you."

To Elijah's surprise, she managed to lower

292

herself to the ground without falling. The sessions were helping. He hated to think what would happen when Luke found out about the latest encounter with the Englisch man. She might not be able to return. Would that be his fault for not handling it better? So be it. Her spiritual life was more important than her physical well-being. She might not see it that way at first, but she would forgive him. He hoped. He thrust the problem aside the better to deal with the one right in front of him.

Bethel sank to the ground in front of the two boys. "Are you all right? What happened? Why aren't you in school?" She touched her fingers to the sticky, wet mass on the front of Joseph's shirt. "Is this blood? Are you hurt? Joseph, are you hurt?"

"Nee. It's tomato." Joseph raised a tearstained face to his aunt. He looked so like his daed, but he had Leah's dark eyes. Right now they were red. He took a deep shuddering breath. "Teacher sent us home early. She said she didn't feel good. She was sad."

"Someone wrote nasty things on the outside of the school," William added when his brother ran down. "With orange paint."

Again with the orange paint. Elijah squatted and laid his hand on the boy's shoulder.

"How did you get the tomatoes on you?"

"We were walking home and some boys in a car came by." William sniffed, but he didn't cry. He was a big boy. "They threw the tomatoes at us. I think they were rotten. They stink."

They did indeed, but that was the least of their problems. "Why are you sitting here by the side of the road letting them dry on your shirt?"

"They kept creeping alongside us, calling to us." Joseph ducked his head. "They offered to give us a ride, but we said no, and we started running."

"And then Joseph fell down."

"And then they laughed and drove off."

"They said stuff like *weirdos* and *bowl heads* and said we should go home."

"That's what we were trying to do." Joseph's freckled face looked perplexed. "But I fell down and I think my arm is broken."

"Let me see." Bethel took his arm in both hands and pressed her fingers up and down it. She had a gentle touch, no doubt about it. Her fingers mesmerized Elijah. He jerked his gaze away, focusing on Joseph's face. The boy flinched when she touched his wrist. "I think it's probably only a sprain." She smiled at Joseph. "We'll wrap it when we get home. But first I think we should go see Deborah and make sure she's all right, don't you?"

Both boys nodded. Then the three of them turned their pleading gazes on Elijah. He bit his lip, looking at the boys' dirty, smelly clothes and wan faces. They were tough little guys. So was their aunt. "I think that's a good idea."

Twenty minutes later they pulled up in front of the school. Deborah sat on the porch step, a bucket of soapy water at her side, her head in her hands. She looked up when the boys called her name. "We're back, we came back to help you."

She burst into tears.

Bethel managed to slide from the buggy on her own again. Every time she did it, it surprised her. Joseph climbed down like a monkey and pulled out her crutches for her. She propelled herself forward, right behind Elijah even though he had a much longer stride. He covered the ground to the school-house steps in what seemed like leaps and bounds.

"Deborah, what happened?" A sick knot formed in the pit of Bethel's stomach. Would these boys, these men, whatever they were, pick on a young woman alone with a group of children? Would they wait until the children were gone and then harass her? "Did they come here? Did they hurt you?"

"They came and went. They threw stuff at the building and then took off, laughing. Who thinks such a thing is funny?" Deborah made an obvious effort to swallow a sob. "I'm no good as a teacher. You have to come back, Bethel, you have to!"

"Why didn't you send for help?" Doing her best to ignore Elijah hovering over them, Bethel lowered herself to the step so she could put her arm around Deborah. "Why didn't you have your scholars help you clean up this mess?"

"It's my fault. I didn't even try to make them stop. I didn't do anything. I froze." Deborah swiveled to look at the offending paint on the wall. "It doesn't come off, anyway, so it doesn't matter whether the children stayed."

"We'll paint over it." Elijah surveyed the mess. His disgusted expression didn't match the firm tone. Bethel could read it all in his face. All the time they spent cleaning up these messes was time the men didn't spend planting winter wheat and getting fields ready for spring crops. "Did you get a good look at them the second time?"

"I peeked out the window. All I saw was a gray pickup truck and some Englischers

296

who look like they were seventeen or eighteen, too old to be doing stuff like this. Why weren't they working?"

Bethel didn't bother to remind her that Englischers went to school until they were eighteen, longer if they went to college. She patted Deborah's back. "It's not your fault. Poor upbringing, I imagine."

Deborah cupped her hand over her forehead and peered at the boys. "What is that smell and what is that on your shirts?"

"Tomatoes." Joseph sounded gleeful now that he wasn't alone on the side of the road anymore. "And I fell and broke my arm."

"Joseph, you did not." Bethel shook her finger at him. "It's not acceptable to tell tall tales. You sprained your wrist and that's nothing to brag about. It just means you tripped over your own feet."

"Someone attacked you on the road?" Deborah looked as if she might lose her breakfast. "It's all my fault. I should've sent the older boys for help to let the parents know they should pick up the children."

"They can't pick them up every day," Bethel pointed out. "They need to walk home in groups, though. Safety in numbers."

"We never had problems like this in Bliss Creek." Deborah plucked at her apron, damp with her tears. "Of course, I wasn't the teacher in Bliss Creek. I don't think I'm cut out for this much responsibility."

"Sure you are." Bethel squeezed her shoulders again and then let her arm drop. "I didn't have these kinds of problems. People around here are still getting used to us."

"They broke two windows throwing rocks at the building." Deborah's tone was mournful. "And they left a dead skunk by the swing set. It stinks."

"They're just windows." Elijah hopped on the porch without using the steps. He grabbed the broom and started sweeping. "We'll replace them, good as new. We'll bury the skunk and air out the school. No harm done. I'll take the boys and go get Luke and the others. We'll have it cleaned up in no time."

"We'll stay here and clean up inside." Bethel stood and faced him. Time to lay their differences aside. They would forgive these hooligans and use the experience to strengthen the bonds of their new community. "Let Leah know for me."

Elijah nodded. His eyebrows wrinkled and he frowned. "Maybe you can help Deborah out with the classes, now that you're getting a little stronger. It might be better to have two adults here what with all this activity."

The thought bowled her over. Would Luke allow it? Would Leah? Bethel couldn't help herself. She smiled at him. "That's a very smart idea . . . but will Luke allow it?"

He smiled back. "When he hears all the facts, I think he will. He's a fair man."

Being a teacher's aide wasn't the same as being the teacher, but it was a step in the right direction. And it would take her mind off the therapy sessions.

And Shawn.

If Elijah had his way, she might not get to go to another session. She might not see Shawn again. The first bothered her more than the second. She was almost sure of that.

Almost.

CHAPTER 25

Bethel fought the urge to squirm in her chair. His sun-lined face grave, Thomas eased onto the sofa next to Emma. They had not come to the house for a social visit — of that Bethel was certain. The fact that Luke had stomped out the door to the barn as soon as supper ended and Leah had taken the children upstairs for a story and early bed told her as much. She surreptitiously wiped the palms of her hands on her apron, leaving damp spots. "Can I get you some cold tea? Leah made lemon meringue pie for dessert. I can rustle some up if you like."

"We just ate ourselves." Thomas clasped his big hands in his lap and propped his elbows on his knees as he leaned forward. "We'll make this quick so we can all get to bed on time tonight."

That was fine with Bethel. It had been a long day. Helping Deborah clean up the school the previous day had kept her mind off her own problems. But today, as she helped Leah with the cooking and the laundry, she hadn't been able to keep her mind off what was coming. Luke hadn't mentioned it at the supper table, even when she'd laid a place for Elijah that had remained empty. He didn't want to face her. That wasn't fair and she knew it. She struggled to keep her breathing even.

"You know it's the job of the deacon to investigate when concerns are brought to him regarding actions that might not be in keeping with the Ordnung." Thomas's level gaze pierced her to the bone. "Truth is, this is my first time doing this. You don't have your mudder and daed here or a brother. Luke is the bishop so it didn't seem right to have him here with you."

He didn't mention Leah, a fact for which Bethel was thankful. "Still, I felt it best that you have another woman present for this conversation. You'll feel more comfortable and truth be told, so will I."

She nodded, afraid to trust her voice. Emma gave an encouraging nod.

"That sounds good to me." Her voice quivered. She drew a breath, hoping to steady it. "Whatever you think is best."

"This is what I've been told." Thomas

301

outlined in short, broad strokes what Elijah had related to Luke, who in turn had reported to him. "I understand this young man in the wheelchair approached you each time. You have this group discussion and he's in it. He's taking an interest in you."

"Jah. You could say that."

"Does he make you uncomfortable?"

"Nee. He's a decent person with kind intentions."

"Kind intentions? How far do those intentions go? From what you know."

Bethel bit her lip. Her throat ached with the effort to hold back tears. She couldn't lie, but if she told the truth, they might not let her go back. She had to finish her therapy. She had to get better. So she could teach. So she could help Leah. So she could have a chance at marriage and children.

"Bethel?" Emma slid forward on the couch and patted Bethel's knee. "I know this is hard, but we only want what's best for you and for our families. This is a new community and we have to be careful how we treat our new neighbors. We want this to be a good fresh start."

"I know that." She sniffed and grabbed her hankie from the table next to her rocking chair. "Shawn is a nice man. He's kept an open mind about us from the start. He even did research so he'd know what we're about and try to not make me uncomfortable." She hesitated, trying to gauge how much she should say. Their conversations in the group were private — Doctor Jasmine called them confidential. No one was to talk about it outside the group. "He defended me — us."

"Why?"

"He likes me. And he knows what it's like to lose mobility."

"I'm more concerned with the first part of what you said. The real question is, did you do anything to encourage him? Did you go anywhere with him? Did you have a pop with him before yesterday when Elijah saw you together?" Thomas's tone sounded more stern now.

"He didn't see us together. I was going to the buggy to meet Elijah when Shawn came out with the cans of pop and the candy."

"I understand. What about before that? Did you go anywhere with him?"

"Nee." She hesitated. "But he did come to me."

The heat coursing up her neck to her cheeks told her in no uncertain terms that her face and neck were red.

Concern mixed with a kind of sadness softened Thomas's gaze. "He came to you where?"

"The PT room."

"You were supposed to be alone when you do your exercises. Luke said that was the agreement."

"Jah, but Shawn came in early yesterday morning."

"Because he knew you would be there?"

"Jah." Bethel couldn't contain herself. "Please don't take the workouts away. I need them to get better. I have to get better."

Thomas's expression didn't change. "Did you ask him to leave?"

"Jah."

"Did he?"

"Not right away. But we only talked and he faced the wall so he couldn't see me and nothing improper happened. We only talked."

"Why?"

"Because he understands."

Thomas studied his interlaced fingers as if he could find an answer there. "You asked him to leave and he didn't?"

"Not until Doctor Karen, my PT — my physical therapist — made him leave."

"If you'd asked him again to do it, would he have?"

"Jah."

"But you didn't."

"Nee."

"All right."

Thomas rose. Emma did the same. She smiled and offered Bethel a quick, tight hug without speaking.

Her palms sweaty, heart pounding, Bethel followed them to the screen door. "What will you tell Luke?"

"I'll go home and sleep on it and pray on it and then I'll decide. You should pray about it too. Pray for forgiveness. Pray you will make better choices in the future."

"I will." Her stomach flopped at his sad expression. Thomas looked so disappointed in her. "I'm sorry."

"Actions have consequences. Not only for you, but for this man Shawn. Think of his feelings. You encourage him and then he's disappointed. I believe you are strong in your faith and you will never leave it. Do you believe that?"

"Jah."

"Then why risk hurting another human being?"

The wisdom of his words washed over her in a drowning wave. "I don't know."

"You do know." He shoved his hat down on his forehead and pushed open the screen door. "I want to ask Luke about something else — I have a hog that seems to have a bellyache. Emma, can you wait here a minute while I talk to him about it?"

"Jah. It'll give me a chance to visit with Bethel on more pleasant topics."

The two were conspiring — Bethel could tell by the gaze they exchanged. A man and his fraa could communicate without speaking. She wanted that. She didn't, however, want to talk anymore. It wasn't her day for pleasant topics.

Emma didn't give her a choice. She settled into the rocker on the porch and waved at the other one. "I'm not in a big hurry to get home. Rebecca is watching the babies and the twins are doing the dishes. Take a load off and tell me something good."

"Something good." Bethel tried hard to change directions, but exhaustion weighed her down. "Let me get my darning. I try to keep up with the sewing. It's something I can help Leah with."

She grabbed her sewing basket and returned to the front porch. Taking her time to pull one of William's socks from it, she settled in with her needle and thread. Already she felt calmer. "I am sorry this is causing trouble for Thomas and taking your time away from home."

"Don't be. It's how it's supposed to be."

Emma leaned back and rocked for a second. "It's a beautiful evening."

Bethel hadn't even noticed. She let the sock fall to her lap for a moment and raised her face to the evening sky. An autumn breeze cooled her face. The air smelled of rain even though no drops had fallen yet. "Jah, it is."

"Thomas says Luke is considering letting you be a teacher's aide."

A more pleasant topic indeed. She plunged the needle into the heel of the sock and made quick work of the tear at the seam. "He says he's praying on it."

"He sets a good example."

Praying was good. She'd done her own praying. Now she wanted to be back in the classroom. Deborah needed her help. "He does."

"You say one thing, but your tone says another."

"I guess I'm . . . I want things to happen more quickly."

"You're impatient."

"Yes, but I've prayed for patience."

"So God is teaching you to have it."

Bethel laughed. "That's one way of looking at it."

"It's the only way when things are beyond your control, and all things are beyond our control."

Nothing could be more true.

"I need to go to physical therapy." She wrapped the sock up with its match and tossed the pair into her basket. A tear in Luke's shirt came next. She contemplated the rip. At least it was on a seam. He must've strained against it lifting something. "It's the only way I can get back into the classroom as a teacher."

"Do you like Shawn?"

The question startled her so much she stabbed the needle into her thumb.

"What kind of question is that?"

"A simple one."

She sucked at her thumb, not wanting to get blood on the shirt. Shawn had nothing to do with teaching, but she knew what Emma was trying to say. Shawn had everything to do with physical therapy and her journey into the Englisch world. She pictured his scarred face and gnarled hands. His sandpaper rough voice sounded in her head, calling her *darlin'* even as his pensive eyes stared into the distance over her shoulder.

"I think he's sad and he's looking for someone to talk to who understands, that's all."

"You didn't answer my question."

"I do like him, as another person." She avoided Emma's gaze, choosing instead to return to her sewing. Her hands shook, making it hard to keep the stitches even. They looked like something one of the twins had done. "As a person who has treated me kindly."

"Nothing more?"

"Nothing more."

"What about Elijah?" A smile played across Emma's face. "Not to be nosy or anything."

"He aggravates me." The words came easily even as she thought of his question in the buggy the day before. *If I shone a flashlight in your window, what would you do?* "A lot."

"That's a good sign."

"It is?"

"Jah, very good."

"That makes no sense."

Emma laughed, a light, breezy sound that cheered Bethel. "Thomas used to aggravate me all the time. Then I married him."

"We've already had this conversation. Who wants to marry a woman in my condition? And if they don't let me go back to the physical therapy I may never get off the crutches."

"If you can't go back to the sessions, then

you find another way." Emma's tone was tart. "You've already seen what you need to do. Just do it here."

"We don't have the equipment — the treadmill, the bicycle, the bands, the warm water therapy . . ." Bethel contemplated this idea. PT was more complicated than Emma could know. "Luke is the bishop, though. Maybe he can make an exception on riding bicycles. You're so smart and so wise. How did you get that way?"

"I'm not." Emma smoothed the arms of her chair with an absent movement. "There is the possibility that you won't ever walk freely again. Remember the disciple Paul's thorn in his flesh?"

Bethel stopped sewing. Emma stopped rocking. She sighed. "It's not what you want to hear. You might never walk freely again, but remember, God's grace is sufficient. His power is made perfect in our weaknesses."

The truth of those words stung Bethel. Or maybe it was the tears she refused to let fall. She bent over her sewing and Emma began to rock again. The silence stretched, filled only with the occasional barking of a dog in the distance.

"You remind me of your Aenti Louise." Bethel peeked at her friend's face to see how she would take this. It was meant to be a compliment. Emma and Luke's aunt had been loved by all for her long stories peppered with advice and wisdom garnered over almost nine decades of living.

"Always telling people what they didn't want to hear." Emma's expression turned wistful. "I would hope to be so wise. God rest her sweet soul."

"Can I ask you something?"

"I can't promise to have an answer, but jah, you can ask."

"Do you know anything about something called postpartum depression?"

Her eyebrows popped up and her smile disappeared altogether. "Why? Do you think that's what's wrong with Leah?"

Emma was quick. That didn't surprise Bethel. Her friend had been a good teacher before her marriage to Thomas. "You know of it?"

Emma took Luke's shirt from Bethel and folded it while Bethel pulled a pair of Joseph's pants from the basket. These needed the hem let out. The boys grew so quickly. Emma seemed to be contemplating the shirt in her lap. "I spent a lot of time with Aenti Louise. She delivered hundreds of babies. She talked to me about it some, when I got older. I helped her sometimes."

"I asked my doctor what to do about Leah."

"And she said it's might be this postpartum thing."

"She said it could be, but Leah needs to go to a doctor."

"Luke doesn't abide much with this kind of doctoring."

"I know, but she says it's bad. It could be real bad."

"It makes sense." Emma brushed a thread from the shirt with an absent look on her face. "Now that I think about it."

"What do you mean?"

"You know Luke and Leah moved back into the house after our parents died. I lived with Leah before I married Thomas."

"I remember."

"She was pregnant with the twins. She didn't seem . . . she wasn't . . ."

"Happy about it?"

"She was hard to get along with, but I thought she always had been difficult. She was always so stern, even as a girl at school."

"She practically raised us when my mudder got sick."

"She and Luke have been married about ten years. She's been pregnant or had a baby on her hip that entire time." Emma's smile was forlorn. Probably thinking of the baby she'd lost. Emma had waited a long time for babies. Like Bethel waited now. "Her grumpiness could be from the post-partum problems."

"We didn't know."

"We blamed it on her being an unpleasant person."

Guilt assailed Bethel. She had convicted her sister of something over which she had no control. "There's medication for it."

Emma sighed and shook her head. "For Englisch folks, maybe. I can't imagine Luke being willing to let Leah talk to a doctor about that sort of thing even if you could get her to do it, which seems pretty far-fetched."

"Wouldn't Luke want her to get better?"

"When my parents died, my sister Catherine — you remember her, the one who left the community — she suffered from what the doctor called post-traumatic stress. She was depressed. Luke thought . . . mind over matter. She should simply be able to get over it because it was the right thing to do. She couldn't."

"That's why she left?"

"One of the reasons, jah."

"Maybe he'd feel differently if he knew how bad this is. Doctor Karen says she shouldn't be left alone with the babies."

"Not to leave who alone with the babies?" Leah opened the screen door and peered out. "Are you talking about me?"

She looked from Bethel to Emma and back. "I can't believe you told her."

She let the screen door slam, then whirled and disappeared into the house.

Bethel dropped Joseph's pants into the basket and stood. Emma gave her an encouraging look and did the same. "Talk to her. If she's willing to get help, she can convince Luke that it's what she needs. I'd better go find Thomas. It's getting late and I want to kiss the babies goodnight before they go to sleep."

"It was nice talking to you." Bethel gave her a small wave. "Talk to you soon."

Emma picked up the basket and held the screen door for Bethel. She set the basket inside. "Remember, patience and kindness."

Patience and kindness.

Bethel found Leah in the kitchen, slamming pots into the tub of dishwater so hard the water sloshed over the sides and ran in rivulets to the floor.

"Leah, I didn't mean —"

"You told her about the baby." She took a deep shuddering breath. Bethel had seen Leah upset before, but never like this. "It's private. You had no right."

"I'm only trying to understand, and Emma knows so much about these things." Bethel picked up a towel and began to sop up the water. She sought the words. Kind words. "She can help. She wants to help."

"Why? Because she's had two babies? She knows how I feel and what I need? She has Rebecca and Eli and the twins to help her."

"Because she's kind and wise and she spent time with her Aenti Louise."

"It's private and you know it."

"I'm sorry. I only wanted to help."

"You want to help — do these dishes. You want to help — mop the floors. You want to help — hang the laundry on the line. Don't gossip."

"I would never gossip."

"You think I might hurt my own children."

"Nee, nee!"

"Then stop talking about me and start helping."

"Convince Luke to let me go back to physical therapy and I'll get better faster. I promise."

"Luke will do what Luke will do."

"He knows about the baby."

"Jah."

"He's happy?"

"With the baby, jah. With me, no."

"Leah, I talked to my doctor and she says

she can help you."

"You told your doctor about me?"

"Because I thought she could help. She says you have postpartum —"

"You tell Luke. You tell Emma. You tell a complete stranger. What kind of sister are you?"

Her face contorted with angry tears, Leah stormed from the room, a pot in her wet hands, completely forgotten.

Bethel stood in the middle of the room. Her behavior at the clinic upset Luke. Her contact with Shawn upset Elijah. Her discussion with Doctor Jasmine about Leah's strange symptoms upset her sister. Most likely, her failure to drink a pop with Shawn upset him. It seemed she'd managed to upset everyone. She'd let them all down. Worst of all, she'd let God down.

She sank to her knees and lowered her head. *Gott, forgive me.*

CHAPTER 26

Luke leaned forward in a chair and propped his elbows on his knees. His eyes burned with exhaustion. It seemed as if it had been years since he managed a good night's sleep. Between Leah's tossing and turning and his own tortured thoughts, he spent most of the night staring into the darkness at a ceiling he couldn't see. He cleared his throat and let his gaze rove over Thomas, Silas, and Elijah. Elijah, as the person who'd made the complaint, had been invited to the meeting where a decision had to be made about Bethel's behavior at the rehab clinic. The man crossed his arms over his chest, his lips a thin line in his stern face. He'd made it clear he didn't want to be here, but he knew his responsibility.

"Let's start with you, Thomas. What did you find out?"

"A couple of things." Thomas smoothed his beard. "First, nothing untoward happened between Bethel and this man Shawn McCormack."

"But she did allow him to be at the physical therapy session."

"In the same room, jah, but the therapist was outside in the hallway. She told him to face the wall and not look at her."

"So she knew it wasn't proper."

"She knew, yet she didn't insist he leave."

"You sister-in-law is a kind person. She has a soft heart." Thomas nodded at Elijah. "Wouldn't you agree, Elijah?"

His jaw worked. He stared at his hands. "I would."

"I think that's all this is. Bethel was a teacher because of her nurturing nature. She likes to help. This man has many challenges. She wants to help."

"She sure doesn't let anyone else help her." Elijah clamped his mouth shut. He inhaled noisily. "I mean, it depends on why she's helping him."

Thomas favored Elijah with a look that could only be described as fatherly. "For a man who spent five years helping his parents, you sure seem to object to Bethel helping out a stranger."

"He is a stranger, an Englisch stranger."

"The Good Samaritan helped a stranger on the side of the road," Thomas said. "Who are we to judge when our friend Bethel extends kindness to a man we don't know?"

"As long as that's all it is." Luke teetered in the middle, trying to balance the two points of view. This was his first disciplinary issue as bishop. He wanted to make the right decision, but Bethel was his sister-in-law. Leah needed her sister to regain the use of her legs. Bethel needed the full use of her legs even more so she could have a full life as the wife of a Plain man who would have certain expectations of his fraa. "There's the invitation to share food and drink. The man seemed to think she would take him up on it."

"Candy and soda." Thomas chuckled. "Not exactly romantic fare."

"What do you know about romance?" Silas snorted. "As much as I do, I'm thinking."

Both men chuckled.

"This isn't funny," Elijah glowered. "Your first decision in this community and you're making light of it."

"You need to get some perspective." Thomas's smile disappeared. "It is serious, I'll agree, but Bethel is a strong believer. She is a good person who's never intentionally parted ways from the Ordnung, not even during her rumspringa."

"Her life has changed since the storm." Elijah's hands tightened into a fist. A second later he spread his fingers out over his knees. "She thinks this man understands her and the rest of us don't. She's drawn to him because of that."

Luke understood Elijah's concern, but he also saw Thomas's point of view. They had to find a careful balance. Being rigid with rules as they tried to find their way in this new place would lead to an obsession with legalism and watching to make sure everyone else did the same. He wanted to lead these people to live in the spirit behind the rules. "She told you that?"

"Not in so many words. She said he understood what it was like not to have use of your legs. She feels a kinship with him. To be fair, with all the people in the group."

"Which I imagine is the point of the group."

"Jah."

"We need her to get better." Luke let his gaze drop. They couldn't know how much he needed for her to get better. "I want her to start helping Deborah at the school. My thought is Bethel should spend her mornings at the school three days a week. She will go to therapy once a week. Less time for trouble. She needs to be home on laundry day — Leah needs her."

His personal problems could not be the basis for any decision. The greater good of the community was more important. Leah knew that. She would deal with it.

"Is that going to be enough for Leah?" Thomas's gaze knew too much.

"She'll cope."

"I'll send Rebecca over to help."

"No need."

Thomas shook his head. "Don't let pride get in your way."

"We're getting far afield."

"Back to Bethel. Her spiritual well-being is at stake here." Elijah rubbed his clean-shaven face with both hands. "I know how much the physical therapy means to her, but . . ."

"You'd take it away from her? Her chance to get better?"

"To save her from herself? To keep her from stumbling in her faith?" Elijah's hands dropped and he looked Luke in the eye. "Wouldn't you?"

"I'm not sure you're being selfless in this."

Elijah's face darkened and his fists clenched again. When he saw Luke's gaze on them he loosened them. "What are you saying?"

"If you have an interest, get a move on."

"That's your direction as bishop?"

"Nee, as a friend."

Elijah's Adam's apple bobbed. "You've heard my thoughts on this issue. May I be excused?"

"Jah." Luke watched the man trudge to the door ahead of Thomas. He looked as if he had the weight of the world on his shoulders. "Elijah."

The man stopped, his hand on the screen door.

"Come for supper. You too, Thomas."

"Emma is waiting pulled pork sandwiches for me." Thomas brushed past Elijah, who backed off a pace, letting him through. "And macaroni and cheese casserole and a strawberry-rhubarb pie."

"Then you best hurry."

Elijah studied his boots until Thomas let the screen door slam behind him. "She won't be happy with me."

"She'll know you cared enough to be concerned for her."

He frowned and studied his boots some more. "I'll feed the pigs."

And stay for supper. That was good. "I'll take care of the horses. I want to check on Cinnamon. I think she might be expecting."

"It's a little early."

"I know. It's concerning."

322

Together they walked out of the house and went their separate ways. In these autumn-shortened days, dusk came early and the cold wind was enough to hurt his throat. The hint of dampness in the air made him look at the sky. Thick, dark clouds. He wouldn't be surprised if they got their first snow overnight. In the barn, William and Joseph wielded pitchforks and spread hay in the horses' stalls. They'd mucked all six already. They had their technique down. "How's Cinnamon tonight?"

"Off her feed," Joseph said, sounding like an eight-year-old horse expert. "She acts like she's too tired to eat."

"She'll eat when she gets hungry. In the meantime, don't forget the chickens."

"I'll do the chickens." William's tone was eager. "I'm gonna take a hoe. I saw a snake outside the shed, but it slithered off before I had a chance to get it."

"Careful you don't hit your toes."

Silas's boy Elam had done just such a thing last year. William hooted with all the confidence of a veteran snake wrangler. "We know the difference between our toes and a snake!"

Raucous laughter seeped into the barn. William stopped talking and the three of them stood still, listening. Loud shushing

323

sounds mingled with giggling. Luke held his finger to his lips and mouthed the words, *Get Elijah.* The boys nodded and scurried away. Luke slipped through the barn door and moved quietly along one wall. The dry, dead grass and weeds crunched under his boots. Whoever had decided to gather behind his barn didn't seem to notice. The volume of their whoops and hollers increased despite the exhortations of at least one person to hush.

At the corner, he paused and peeked. Half a dozen teenagers milled around, four boys and two girls. The girls wore tight jeans cut so low they exposed skin at their waists. The boys held cans of spray paint and one of them, a tall, skinny, dark-haired kid, sprayed a steady stream onto the barn.

Luke took a breath, then another. He tapped down the free-flowing stream of anger. Anger served no purpose. He gritted his teeth. They were children. Children who needed to be taken to their parents' woodshed, but children nevertheless. He stepped into the open. "What are you doing?"

The tall skinny boy jumped and whirled. The paint continued to flow from his can, spraying Luke's shirt and pants in a fine sprinkle of neon green that spread and deepened across his chest. It freckled his face and beard. He could taste it on his lips. He jerked up his arm to shield his face and stumbled back a step. "Stop it! Put the can down."

The girls laughed in high-pitched nervous giggles. They squeezed together and started to backpedal across the open space. Beyond them sat an old pickup truck, parked far enough away that William and Joseph wouldn't have heard its approach. "Come on, Doo, let's get out of here!" one of the girls said. "I told you we'd get caught. We should've waited until later. Let's go!"

The boy with the unlikely name, apparently the can-wielder, held his ground. "I'm not done with my painting."

The slur of his words and the silly grin on his face — not to mention the bravado of his unwillingness to see he'd been caught in the act of breaking the law — told Luke the boy was high on something. Maybe alcohol, maybe something more. The other boys adopted the same defiant stance as their cohort and lifted their cans of spray paint as if they were weapons. Luke supposed they were.

"This is private property. I'd like for you to leave."

"Or what? You're gonna stab us with a pitchfork?"

"I'm asking you nicely to leave." Luke perused his barn. The boys had painted a lewd picture in big, sweeping strokes. "This is my property and you're breaking the law."

"What are you gonna do? Call the cops?" Doo snickered. "Oh, that's right, you don't have phones."

He could report it to the sheriff, but that wouldn't give them the goodwill he sought for his new community. These kids were bullies, but not necessarily criminals. They needed a firm hand.

"Come on, Doo. They've got guns," said the second girl. "I saw him in my dad's store buying ammo in the sporting goods section."

"We hunt." Luke took a step forward. "We don't use guns on people."

"You were told to leave." Elijah spoke from behind him. "You leave now, no harm done."

Luke took a quick sideways gander. The boys huddled behind Elijah, their faces twin pictures of worry. Elijah held out a flashlight. Luke took it and pushed the switch so a stream of light shone on the trespassers. "I'm Luke Shirack. This is my friend Elijah and those are two of my boys, Joseph and William." He jerked his chin toward Doo.

"I know your name, what about the rest of you?"

"Get that thing out of my eyes." Doo put up his hand in protest. Luke lowered the beam but kept the light pooled on the boys' sneakers, now spattered in a rainbow of paint colors. "You know you don't need that light to get a good description of us for the cops."

"No cops. You come out here on my property, least you can do is introduce yourselves. It's the neighborly thing to do."

Doo shifted from one foot to the other, but the can of paint came down. "Like we're gonna tell you our names so you can ride into town in your little horse-drawn buggies and report us to the sheriff."

"I told you I won't report you."

Doo huffed a bark of a laugh. "Sure you will, fast as you can going five miles an hour."

"It's not our way."

The other boys started to back down the road to where the girls stood. Doo stuck his chest out and held his ground. "Why should I believe you?"

"I wouldn't lie to you."

"My daed never lies," William piped up, his voice eager. "It's a sin."

"You're crazy religious fanatics."

"No, just folks minding our own business."

Doo pursed his lips. Some of the defiance seeped from his face. He had the good grace to look uncomfortable.

"Come on, Doo, let's go, let's go." One of the other boys snatched at his friend's sleeve and gave it a jerk. "Let's get out of here."

"I'm Jake Doolittle. Mostly they call me Doo."

"Nice to meet you, Doo." Luke held out his paint-spattered hand. "I've met your parents. You look a lot like your father."

The boy stared at Luke's hand, then at his face. After a second he wiped his hand on his jeans and shook. "You gonna tell him?"

"No."

Doo's gaze traveled to the barn. "It was just in fun."

"For you."

"Doo, we're leaving."

Doo began to back away. "Sorry."

"Next time, knock on the door. My wife makes a great apple pie."

In the growing darkness Luke couldn't see the boy's face anymore, but he heard the tiny grunt of surprise. "Next time?"

"Come to the door. Best do it a little earlier, though. We're early risers and we go to bed early."

Doo tucked his can of paint into the long pocket of his sweatshirt and began to back away. "Sorry, dude."

"Give your mother my regards."

Luke had no doubt where these kids had learned their prejudices, but it seemed that Doo might have some of his mother's redeeming qualities. He might still have a chance to grow into a decent human being. Luke didn't know about the others. They piled into the pickup truck, the boys in back and one of the girls in the driver's seat. The engine sputtered, groaned, and finally turned over. The driver made a wide turn and managed to get the pickup on the dirt road headed the other direction.

"How do they get to the highway going that way?" Elijah came to stand next to him.

"I imagine the same way they got down here. Cutting fences and driving across fields." Luke studied the barn wall. The boys were doing the same. "Don't look at that. Get on up to the house and wash your hands for supper."

They averted their eyes but didn't move. "Why would kinner do something like this?" William squeezed up against Luke, his tone plaintive. "They drove all the way out here to paint on our barn. Don't they have their own barn to paint on?"

"I don't think so. They're city kids." Luke put his hand on William's shoulder. "It's not about the painting."

"What's it about then?" Joseph slid in next to his brother. "Don't they know we have to clean this up?"

He seemed more concerned about the extra work than the why, but Luke explained anyway. "It's about prejudice."

"What's that?"

"It's when people are afraid of folks who are different from them."

"Like if my hair is brown and a girl's hair is yellow?" William shook his head. "Who cares?"

"People don't know any better, I guess. They don't understand that what we look like is only skin-deep. Inside, God made us all the same." Luke struggled for words that young boys who still had open minds and hearts could understand. "We live our lives in ways that some folks can't understand. That scares them so they lash out and make fun."

"Maybe they aren't secure in their own beliefs," Elijah added. "They're uncomfortable and they don't like that, so they take it out on others."

"That's just not right." Joseph stuck his hands on his hips in an unconscious imitation of Leah when she was aggravated with him. "They shouldn't get away with it."

"We teach them they have nothing to fear from us by showing them love and kindness." Luke felt a sermon coming on. "Get a move on. It's time for supper. Your mudder doesn't like her food to get cold."

Prejudice had led his ancestors to come to this country to seek the freedom to worship as they saw fit. To be baptized as adults. It seemed a simple thing, but it had led to a journey into the unknown for his people. His boys had heard these stories, but Luke wasn't sure they really understood. He propelled them both forward with a small shove. "God expects you to be the salt and light of the earth." He could use a good reminder himself. "Never forget that."

A smile on his face, Elijah started toward the house. "With you around, they won't."

"We'll clean this up tomorrow after school."

Both boys groaned. "It's not fair."

"No, but it's life."

They would get many opportunities to learn that lesson, of that Luke was certain.

CHAPTER 27

Bethel slid the last batch of cookies from the oven and turned off the gas. She inhaled the scent of peanut butter and felt the muscles in her shoulders and back relax. Baking — that's what the folks in her therapy group needed. Not more talking. They needed to bake or sew or hang a load of laundry on the line and smell the fresh air while they did it. Not that she would be seeing much of the group in the future. Luke had been adamant. After the trip to Bliss Creek for Helen's wedding, Bethel would go to therapy one day a week. One day. To get better. She had Elijah to thank for that. No, that wasn't fair. She shut out the image of him sitting across the supper table from her, his expression somber, shoveling buttered noodles into his mouth and not speaking. After her disciplinary action and the trespassing and vandalism of the town teenagers, meals had been quiet.

The boys wanted to talk on and on about the spray paint and why people did things like that, but Leah had hushed them, exclaiming such things were not proper for mealtime conversation. His face lined with exhaustion each night, Luke shoveled food into his mouth with no indication he tasted it.

Elijah had said his goodbyes after supper tonight without meeting her gaze. She wouldn't see him again until they returned from Kansas, as he would be staying behind to take care of their farm.

It didn't matter. There was nothing between them. There couldn't be unless she got better. And he'd made sure she wouldn't by tattling on her to Luke. Again, unfair. He did what he thought was right. She shouldn't fault him for that. She would have to find a way to do the exercises at home. She would continue to improve until she could throw away the crutches.

She let one of the offending crutches fall against the counter. Supporting herself with the other, she quickly arranged the cookies on wax paper and washed the pan. Her back and legs ached with weariness, but somehow taking a batch of fresh baked cookies to her parents made the idea of the four-hour drive packed into a van with five children and two other adults seem easier to contemplate. They would leave before dawn and she would be ready.

Focusing on the here and now, she spot-checked the kitchen. No mess. No crumbs. It looked clean and orderly, just as Leah would expect it to be in the morning when she arose to cook a quick breakfast before they hopped in the van. A driver had been hired from La Plata after Luke had found none willing in New Hope. She didn't dwell on that. Not tonight. Time to sleep. The cookies had taken longer than she'd intended and the others had gone to bed much earlier.

After wiping her hands on her apron, she turned off the pole lantern and grabbed the second crutch. She trudged through the living room toward the hallway, wishing she could whip into her bedroom like a rock from a catapult. No heaving herself forward one swing of the crutches at a time.

A bright light flashed in the creases of the blinds that covered the windows. Bethel dug in her crutches and let her feet touch the floor. A flashlight?

Elijah.

Her heart began to pound and her mouth went dry. She touched her kapp with a shaking hand. It fit snugly, just so, right where it should be, but her apron was dirty and her face surely shone with perspiration from working around the oven.

The lights danced and then went out. It hit her. Lights. More than one. Not a flashlight.

Not Elijah.

To her surprise, a disappointment so profound welled in her that tears pooled in her eyes. *Get a grip.* Her hands tightened on the crutches and she moved forward. Then the sound of an engine registered in the moment that its rumble ceased. A car. Maybe the teenagers had come back. With no real repercussions for their actions, they might come back for the fun of it. Bethel swung herself to the front door and peered out the window. A car indeed, but not the pickup truck Luke had described. More like a jeep. Someone had parked it parallel to the hitching post. No one got out. In the gathering dusk, she couldn't tell who sat inside it.

Only one way to find out. She opened the door and forced herself out onto the porch. "Who is it?" she called in a semi-whisper, not wanting to wake the children.

"Darlin'!"

She stopped in the middle of the porch. Even in the weak light she could see that the man at the wheel was not Shawn, but the voice belonged to him. Glancing back at the door, she contemplated whether to run inside or stay long enough to tell him to go. The man at the wheel stuck a hand through the window and waved. "Sorry to bother you. Could you come out and talk to him? I'm afraid he isn't in any shape to come to you."

Her upbringing kicked in. Of course she would go to Shawn. He couldn't be expected to get his wheelchair out of the back of the Jeep, get himself in it, and then get up the four steps to the porch. She swung her crutches forward and took the steps with ease of practice. "Is something wrong?"

"He said he needed to talk to you." The man, whose white teeth shown in the dusk, offered a small, sharp salute. "I'm Rick, an Army buddy visiting from St. Louis. I'm afraid he's overindulged a little. Celebrating my visit, I guess."

"I'm Bethel."

"I know. You look just like he said you would. He's talked about nothing else all evening."

"The crutches give me away. I'm sure he mentioned those."

"Actually, he said you were beautiful."

Blood rushed to her face. She edged back toward the steps.

"I'm sorry. Don't go." Rick held up his hand. "He always said you were very modest. He just needs to talk to you for a second, and then I think I can convince him to go home and go to bed."

"Stop talking about me like I'm not here." Shawn's words slurred and then trailed off. "Please."

Rick cocked his shaved head toward the passenger seat, his expression begging her to understand.

Luke would take away her privilege of the remaining therapy session if he found out. Leah would be mortified at her sister's behavior. Talking to an Englischer after dark in front of the house while the rest of the family slept.

What would Jesus want her to do? It was a question her mudder often asked when Bethel came to her with a problem. Remember your joy? *Jesus first. Others second. You third.* How many times had she heard those words repeated? Never in a situation where one meant to flaunt a rule or an edict from the bishop.

Shawn McCormack needed a friend and she could be that friend. Like the Good Samaritan and the man on the side of the road. Others walked on by, but the Samaritan stopped.

Swallowing hard against the bitter taste in the back of her throat, she managed to work her way around the jeep. Her legs didn't want to cooperate. Her muscles shook and a spasm squeezed her back. "Shawn, what are you doing here? What do you need?"

He sucked on a cigarette and then let his hand rest on the open window. Smoke billowed around her, the smell making her stomach heave. His bloodshot eyes gazed out at her. "There you are."

"Here I am. What do you need?"

"You. I need you."

"Shawn, don't —"

"Why didn't you come to therapy?"

"I had to stay here."

"Because of me."

"Because I exercised poor judgment."

He straightened and pushed open the door as if to get out. "You mean because of me. They punished you because of me. Who? Tell me who and I'll go talk to him. I'll tell him it isn't your fault. I'll confess."

"Don't get out." She tried to push against the door, but he had all the muscles brought on by working the part of his body that still responded to his commands. His biceps bulged under his plaid shirt with its shiny snap buttons. The door didn't shut. "You can't get out."

"Tell me who I can talk to. How can I make it better?"

"You can't. You make it worse by being here."

"I love you, Bethel."

Rick stirred in the driver's seat. He cleared his throat. "Buddy, we should go."

"Shut up, Rick. You're only here because I can't drive yet." He wiped his face with his sleeve. "I'll be driving one of these days and I'll come for you, Bethel. I promise I will."

Bethel stopped pushing. She swayed on her crutches. For so long she'd wanted to hear those words. Three simple words that would change the course of her entire life. Now here they were, spoken by a man with whom she had one thing in common. The desire to overcome a seemingly insurmountable obstacle. They'd been thrown together in a place where neither had a point of reference. Even though they had never touched, she felt as if they had somehow become entwined.

"I can't."

Rich cleared his throat. It was bad enough she was having this conversation at all, let alone in front of a strange man. He turned off the car engine. Pocketing the key, he shoved open his door. "I'll take a little walk. Whistle when you're ready to go." He nod-

339

ded at Bethel. "Sorry about this."

Grasping at those few seconds to search for a response that wouldn't hurt Shawn, she waited until Rick had walked a good ways toward the corral before she spoke. "You've been drinking, haven't you?"

"I took a pain pill." He took another drag on the cigarette and then flipped the butt out into the dirt road. He slapped his hand against the car door, his tone belligerent. "Don't rag on me about it. Rick already did that."

"Good for him. You took a pain pill and that makes you act like this?"

"And washed it down with a beer. It's my own prescription for pain. Works wonders."

She bit her lip, searching for a way to ease his pain that didn't cause her further trouble. "Now you should go home and sleep. You'll feel better in the morning."

"I had to tell you to come back to therapy. I'll stay away if that's what it takes. I don't want to stand" — he laughed, a short bitter bark that sounded more like a cough — "I don't want to get in the way of you walking without those crutches."

"We can both go to therapy." She longed to touch the fingers curled around the lowered window. To give him comfort, nothing more. Her heart hurt for his pain as if it

340

were her own. "Just not together. And no pop. No candy. No gifts."

"But I love you."

"You don't even know me. You like the idea of someone from another world, someone who doesn't know how you used to be."

"You don't pity me, do you?"

"I didn't until right now."

"You pity me now?"

"Because you used drugs and alcohol to give you the courage to come here." She kept her voice soft, hoping to take the hard edges from her words. "That's not true courage. What happened to your faith in God? Why don't you turn to Him for courage?"

"How can you say that? He let this happen." Shawn's voice broke. He breathed noisily. "I use drugs and alcohol to numb the pain of knowing God let this happen."

"God didn't let it happen. Men make those wars. Not God. The drugs and alcohol do nothing to numb your pain. Ask God. He will help you."

"I have feelings for you."

"Mostly, you feel pain."

"Don't you?"

"Yes." She whispered the word. Having always been among family and friends her entire life, she rarely had the chance to share her faith. Maybe this was why God had put her in this uncomfortable, awkward place. "But I rely on God to ease it. You said God brought you back alive when others didn't make it. Why do you think He brought you home?"

"To meet you."

"No, His plan for you doesn't include me." Bethel grappled with the words. How could she know what God's plan was for Shawn? She didn't know what it was for herself. God would reveal His plan in His time. She had only to cling to that thought. "His plan for me doesn't include a man not of my community."

"You can't tell me you don't feel anything for me." His grip loosened on the window and he sank back in the seat. His head lolled to one side. Bethel had never seen anyone look so weary, so sad. A tear rolled down his cheek, followed by another. She'd never seen a man cry before. For some reason, it devastated her all the more. "Don't tell me that. Because that would be a lie."

"Please, Shawn, don't. It will get better. I know it will. It has for me."

"Go on, tell me the lie. Go ahead."

She chewed on her lip some more. She did feel something for him, but she couldn't be sure what it was and it didn't matter

342

because she lived her faith and she loved her Plain family more.

"See there." He laughed, a mangled half sob, half chuckle. "I can read you like a book."

"You don't know anything about me or you wouldn't be here in front of my family's home, trying to get me to tell you something that you know I shouldn't." She stopped. The effort to swallow her own sobs hurt her throat. "I care about you because you are another human being in pain." She swallowed again. Her throat closed. The ache hurt so much her hands went to her throat of their own accord as if to assuage it. "It hurts me to see you hurt because I understand how you feel."

"That's not love?"

"Not like you mean it."

"But if there were time, it could be."

Yes, if there were time and they were two different people living in a different world, but Bethel couldn't tell him that. She didn't want him to feel more pain. "Go home." She pushed against his door and he let her close it. "Go to sleep. You'll feel better tomorrow."

She waved at Rick, who leaned against the fence. The fiery red end of a cigarette bobbed in the dark. He straightened and started toward her.

"I'll see you tomorrow, right?" Shawn grabbed her hand before she could get beyond his reach. His fingers were cold and damp. "I'll see you tomorrow, right?"

"Tomorrow I go to Kansas for a wedding."

His grip loosened. Rick slid into the driver's side and started the engine. It kicked over with a loud rumble that Bethel figured could be heard in every room of the house.

"You're coming back, right?" Shawn hollered through the window as Rick pulled the jeep around and pointed it toward the road. "Tell me you're coming back."

"I'm coming back," she whispered. "Just not to you."

She stood there until the car disappeared from sight. Then she sighed and swiveled to face the house. Weariness embraced sadness. The two mingled and sat on her shoulders with such weight, she could barely stand. She wanted to sink to the ground and wail. She didn't. If she did, she'd never be able to get up again. Luke would find her sleeping in the grass when he came out to feed the livestock in the morning. She lifted her gaze to the sky. No clouds obscured her view. The stars twinkled down at her. They looked as if they were winking at her. Like they were enjoying a little joke together. Only she didn't get the joke. Not at all.

Why, Gott, why? The question shamed her. She had no right to question God's plan. An *Englisch* man had declared his love for her. In a drunken state, true, but still he expressed the feelings that she longed to hear. No other man had ever done that. No Plain man.

Give it time.

Never had the words been clearer. They echoed across the expanse of sky and through the fields barren in anticipation of a long, cold, dark winter. Patience had never been her virtue. Every day since the storm, God had taught her this agonizing lesson of patience. *Wait. Wait on Me. Wait.*

How long? She wanted to shout the question. Instead she slapped a hand to her mouth and swallowed her sobs. God didn't like a whiner either. She forced herself forward. A movement in the second floor window caught her gaze.

Luke looked down at her. After a long moment, he let the curtain drop.

CHAPTER 28

Bethel reveled in the warmth of her mudder's hug and her familiar lemony scent. After the long drive in the van, it felt so good to stretch and breathe fresh air. It felt good to be home. It felt good to be away from the loud silence in which Luke and Leah took turns staring out the windows, both so lost in their own worlds that the task of answering the boys' endless questions and shushing the twins and checking Jebediah's diaper fell to Bethel. Every time Bethel searched Luke's face, thinking he would say something to her about the previous evening, he simply looked out the window. Like he couldn't bear to contemplate her face. She'd done nothing wrong. She should tell him that. Or should she wait until he asked?

She hugged her mother tighter. She would live in this moment, back in the home of her childhood that smelled of gingersnaps and fry pies. It had been two months, but somehow Mudder seemed even sparser. Like there was less of her to hug. After her bouts with cancer, she'd never regained her former roundness and she always looked older than other children's mothers. But she had a sturdiness about her brought on by the fight she'd waged to stay alive until her children were grown. Bethel pulled back so she could see Mudder's lined face under the gray frizz that had escaped her kapp. "It's good to see you. Have you been well?"

"I'm fine. Your room is ready for you." Mudder picked up Bethel's beat-up leather suitcase. It had been in the family as long as Bethel could remember. "Mattie and the boys will be here shortly. Your brothers are coming too. Your daed is in town picking up a part for the spreader. After supper, we can all sit down together and enjoy each other's company. Well, everyone except Leah. I suppose she'll have supper with Annie and the Shirack clan. I saw Annie at the bakery yesterday and she was running about on pins and needles, she was so excited to see everyone."

The length of the speech told Bethel just how pleased Mudder was to have her flock home. "Give me that suitcase. You shouldn't be lifting that." Bethel tugged it from her mother's grasp. The driver had dropped her here after unloading Luke and his brood at the Shirack house. Leah hadn't mentioned coming to see Mudder and Daed, but surely she would. "I think it would be good if we could get Leah to spend some time here. You'll want to see your grandbabies."

"I'm surprised they didn't stop by before going to Annie's. I thought they would."

Bethel contemplated a response that wouldn't be a lie. "They're tired and the children are cranky. They wanted to wash up and unpack. I imagine they'll stop by for a visit after supper."

"I'm hoping we'll all be together for Thanksgiving too." Mudder's knees cracked as she trudged up the stairs in front of Bethel. She put a hand on the banister and pulled herself along. "With the wedding, time will go so fast. You'll be gone again before we know it."

Bethel hoped not. She wanted these days to stretch and stretch. Here, she could forget about therapy and Shawn and Elijah. Both of them. Equally. Just for a few days.

"You're sure moving much better. Your letters said the therapy was helping, but it's good to see it in person." Mudder opened the door to the room that had been Bethel, Mattie, and Leah's for their entire childhood. It held the same beds, the same wooden straight-back chair, and the same long line of clothes hooks as always. It looked like home. "Before you know it, you'll be throwing those crutches away."

Tears loomed. Bethel fought them back. "I hope you're right."

"What's the matter?" Mudder smoothed the white pillowcases and rearranged the pillows on the quilt. They were perfectly fine, but that was her way. Always making things neater. "You should be happy. God is good."

"I'm tired. Glad to be here, but tired."

"Unpack and come down." Mudder paused in the doorway, her wrinkled hand on the frame. "I have potatoes boiling on the stove for mashing and chicken to fry before I make the gravy, so I need to get back to the kitchen."

"I'll be right there to help."

"You can peel some carrots." Mudder uttered the words as if this were a great honor bestowed on her youngest daughter. "When Mattie gets here, we can send her girls down to the basement to bring up some canned corn and bread and butter pickles."

"And chow-chow. I have a hankering for relish." Bethel knew the recitation of this plan was Mudder's delicate way of acknowledging that her daughter could not handle the steep wooden steps that descended into the basement. With her achy hips and knees, neither could Mudder. Despite the difference in their ages they had common challenges. "It's good to see you."

"You too."

Bethel waited until Mudder left the room and then pulled her dresses from the suitcase and hung them on the hooks by the window. She stood for a moment in front of the long window that faced the west and the lukewarm autumn sun. Kansas didn't look all that different from Missouri on the eve of winter. Trees a little shorter and wirier, land a little flatter. Most of the trees had dropped their leaves and the grass had turned a sullen brown in the bright afternoon sun.

She'd missed this. She'd missed nice suppers with her family. Not that Leah and Luke weren't family. She sighed and shoved the thought away. Their tension spoiled the peace that should be mealtime at the Shirack house.

Shaking off the mood, she hobbled down the stairs and set her mind to the tasks at hand. She peeled dozens of carrots and cut them up and then set the table while Mudder dipped mounds of chicken pieces in flour and spices. She dropped the pieces into sizzling grease in two skillets on the gas burners and picked up tongs. "So what's the matter between you and Leah?"

"What makes you think there's something wrong?"

"You have a face like a chalkboard. You write everything there in big, fat print."

"I do not." Bethel laughed at the image so appropriate for a teacher — former teacher. "It's been rough in New Hope. The folks weren't so eager to have us move there."

"So you said in your letters. I've enjoyed every one of those letters. Keep them coming when you go home."

"I will."

"I haven't received but one from Leah." Her mother held up a piece of chicken and inspected it, frowned, then dropped it into the hot grease. It popped and crackled. The aroma made Bethel's mouth water. "She didn't say much, just mentioned the vandalism. Said something about Elijah driving you to and from your sessions."

"She's very busy with the children and the new house and trying to run the household with no help." Bethel ignored the mention of Elijah. "She has her hands full. Jebediah hasn't been sleeping through the night since we moved and the twins have ear infections every other week, it seems. She doesn't get enough sleep."

"She has you to help her."

"Mudder, look at me. How much help do you think I am, really?"

"Knowing your helpful nature, a lot."

Mudder began to lay pieces of crisp fried chicken on paper towels arranged on a large platter. "Leah grew up fast — even for a Plain child. She had more responsibility than most girls do at her age. I blame myself for that."

"There's no blame to be handed out. You had cancer. Daed needed her to step in. She doesn't regret it."

"She might, more than you know."

"She's never mentioned it."

Mudder started to say something and then stopped. She wiped her hands on a towel and cocked her head. "I think somebody is here. They're early, whoever they are."

She went to the door and pulled it open. Leah stood on the back steps, a suitcase in each hand. Jebediah and the twins toddled behind her. She stomped past Mudder into the kitchen where she dropped the suitcases with a *whap-whap* sound on the faded black-and-white checkerboard of the linoleum floor.

"Someone needs to return Josiah's horse

and buggy." Despite the bravado of her words, her face crumpled. "I've come home."

CHAPTER 29

Bethel squeezed into a chair between Mattie and Leah, trying not to make eye contact with her daed, who didn't seem to be unduly concerned with the presence of his six adult children, five of their spouses, and a mere seventeen grandchildren. As always, Uriah Graber ate with a bare minimum of conversation. It didn't matter that they'd been away. It didn't matter that it was the first time all his children had been under his roof at the same time in a good amount of time. People ate at supper time, pure and simple. He did, however, hazard a puzzled look at Leah over black-rimmed, rectangular glasses that had slid down his long, sun-beaten nose. The glasses were a new addition that didn't seem to fit him quite right. He pushed them up with a greasy finger and went back to sopping up gravy with a chunk of sourdough bread.

"Where're Joseph and William?" Diana,

Mattie's youngest girl, asked, a drumstick halfway to her mouth. "Didn't they come for the wedding too?"

"Hush and eat your food." Mattie held a napkin out to her oldest daughter, Rosie, seated at the far end of the children's table so the girl could hand it down the row. "And wipe your mouth. You have gravy on your lip."

"I want to play with them. You said I could play with them." Diana wiped at her face, smearing the gravy onto her plump cheek. "If I help Groossmammi clean up."

"Children should be seen and not heard at the supper table." Daed pushed his plate — clean except for the chicken bones — away from him and leaned back in his chair with a satisfied burp. "And everywhere else, for that matter. I wouldn't mind knowing, all the same, where the rest of your kinner are, Leah. Not to mention your husband."

Leah's knuckles went white on the fork she used to push food around on her plate. The amount of food hadn't decreased noticeably. "Luke is visiting with his brothers and sisters at Annie's. Josiah and Miriam are there, along with Emma and Thomas and Mark and the twins. They have a full house."

"And Luke didn't want his fraa and his

little ones with him?" Daed shook a toothpick from a small jar on the table and applied it diligently to his front teeth, then
dropped it on his plate. "You don't do your
visiting together?"

"There's blueberry, peach, and cherry fry
pies. Or, if you're in the mood, gingersnaps
or brownies." Mudder hopped up from her
chair and picked up Daed's plate. "There's
still strawberry-rhubarb pie from last night,
if you'd rather."

Daed shook his head. "I have chores to
do. Join me, boys?"

Mattie's husband Abe, who never spoke
unless spoken to, nodded and stood. The
brothers — Seth, Enos, and Robert — followed. Seconds later they were out the door.

"Well, that was quite a visit."

The look of pain on her mudder's face
made Bethel regret the sour remark the
second the words left her mouth. Her lined
face marred by a frown, Mudder picked up
the empty gravy bowl. After a second she
set it down again. "They'll be back for dessert and visiting after they do the chores.
Work first."

"Jah." Leah stabbed a pickle with her fork
and lifted it to her mouth. She chewed, a
strange look of satisfaction on her face. She
pulled the jar toward her and added more

to her plate, ignoring the potatoes, corn, and chicken, now cold. "Work first. Work second. Work third. That's our life here at the Graber farm."

"As it should be." Mudder handed Bethel a plate of brownies. "Eat. You look too thin."

Bethel took the plate but passed on the brownie. "Did you ever feel tired . . . or sad after you had a baby?"

A shoe smacked her ankle hard. Bethel suppressed a yelp. Mattie looked from Leah to Bethel. She nodded to Rosie. "Start washing the dishes. We'll be in to help in a minute. Girls, help Rosie."

The other girls followed while the boys ran for the door. They'd find plenty to do in the barn. Enos's wife grabbed the chicken platter and the empty bowl that had held potatoes. Robert and Seth's fraas began to pick up the plates. "Y'all visit. We'll oversee the girls in the kitchen."

Finally, only Leah, Bethel, and Mattie remained with Mudder.

"You certainly know how to clear a room," Mudder crossed her arms and shot Bethel a stern look. "What are you trying to say?"

"She's trying to say I'm having a baby and I don't want it." Leah stabbed another pickle. "Are there more pickles?"

■ ■ ■ ■

The brisket tasted like straw in Luke's mouth. He chewed and chewed, yet the lump still hurt his throat when he finally forced himself to swallow. He dropped his fork on his plate and eyed the door. He needed air like a man who'd worked in the fields all day needed a long, cool draught of water.

"Don't you like the brisket?" Annie fussed over the fresh basket of sweet rolls she'd carried from the kitchen. His sister baked better than any Plain woman he knew and that was saying a lot, considering Plain women baked from the time they were toddlers. Leah was a close second. Anger surged through him. He tried to focus on his sister and this visit. This longed-for visit. She looked at him, perplexed. "I baked it all day, just like you like it, then I finished it off on the grill so it would have that nice crispy outside."

"It's real good, real good."

Luke couldn't meet her eyes. She knew something was wrong. Everyone in the room did. A fraa didn't simply take off like that without saying a word. What ailed the woman? Why did he feel like he'd done something to cause this? He hadn't done anything except be a husband and a father and a provider and a spiritual leader. Everything a man was called to do, he had done.

"I made your favorite for dessert — pineapple upside-down cake." Her face crinkled with concern, Annie looked toward Isaac, the man Luke suspected she would marry someday soon. "Isaac sampled it right out of the oven. He said it smelled so good, he couldn't wait until supper."

Isaac grinned and patted his flat stomach. "I sample all her cooking. Just to make sure it's done right."

Miriam and Josiah smiled. Everyone smiled. Luke forced his mouth to follow suit. "Sounds good."

Thomas slid his plate away from him. "That was a mighty fine meal. I expect I'll have to wait until later for dessert when I have a little more room. Luke, would you take a look at Annie's horse? She says his front left shoe is loose or it has a rock in it or something. He's favoring it."

"I'll do it." Josiah stood. "Being I'm the town blacksmith now and Luke hasn't done any shoeing in years."

"No, let me do it." Luke put all his big-brother authority into the words. "I need a breath of fresh air and your sister has cake, which I know you could never pass up."

His expression confused, Josiah dropped back into his chair. He picked up his fork and looked around as if seeking his cake.

Luke thrust back his chair and rose, thanking the good Lord for Thomas. Anything to get out of this room. It wasn't fair to Annie or Miriam or the rest of the folks who'd been looking forward to this visit. Leah was spoiling it for everyone. How could she be so selfish? Again, the anger burned hot and he tried to tap it down. She hadn't been herself in a long while.

Outside, he breathed the crisp night air greedily. He strode toward the corral.

"Slow down. That horse ain't going nowhere." His friend's deep bass rumbled behind him. "You're running off like a pack of wild hogs is chasing after you."

"Only my thoughts."

Thomas caught up with one long stride. "Where's Leah?"

"She left."

"Go get her."

"Is that best?"

"She's your fraa."

"I'm thinking she's changed her mind about that."

Thomas paused at the corral gate, his big hands on the metal railing. He didn't speak

360

right away; he simply stared at the tree line in the distance. The silence stretched. Luke wanted his friend to say something, anything, that would tell him what he should do.

"Nee. Not Leah. Even if she wanted to do that, she never would."

"That doesn't make me feel better."

"It's not about you."

"I know."

"What are you waiting for, then?"

For her to choose to come back. For her to want to come back. It had only been a few hours, but his small, simple world had fractured. The farming landscape had tilted so far to one side he might never be able to straighten it. "She left."

"The folks in our community chose you to be a leader."

"And you."

"God chose you to be bishop."

"What does that have to do with Leah?"

"Running away is her cry for help. Help her. You're not only her husband, you're her spiritual leader. The community looks to you to set the example."

"Truth is . . ." Luke cleared his throat. Thomas might be the one person in the world he could tell, besides Leah. His fraa who had run away. "Truth is I don't feel like a leader."

Thomas raised his face to the setting sun. His features were set in stern lines that reminded Luke of his father. "It doesn't matter how you feel. You are. You were chosen."

"She wants to come back here to Bliss Creek. She doesn't want me to be bishop. She wants the life that we had back before my parents died. I can't give her any of those things."

"Sounds like what she really wants is her husband's attention."

"So it's my fault." The anger surged again. Anger did him no good. He squashed it back. "What is it that I'm doing wrong? Tell me that so I can fix it."

"It's not about laying blame. It's about sewing up a wound so it can heal."

Everything Thomas said rang true. Still, the thought of confronting Leah made Luke's stomach twist in knots. He liked their life. He liked the house and the farm in New Hope. He'd even, truth be told, become accustomed to the idea of being bishop. Why couldn't she be happy?

"Stop twisting in the wind like an old shirt on a clothesline and go. I'll tell Annie. The boys are helping gather wood for the fireplace. It gets mighty cold after dark these days."

Thomas could be a pain sometimes.

"Fine. I'll go."

"Godspeed."

Luke trudged into the barn and saddled a horse. Not long after he was riding up the dirt road to the Graber house. Half a dozen buggies dotted the yard. Plenty of visiting going on here. He pulled up on the reins and took a steadying breath. Now that he'd arrived, he couldn't remember the speech he'd practiced on the road.

"That you, Luke?"

The voice of Leah's daed came from the shadows on the porch. In his introspection, Luke hadn't noticed the big hulk of a man sprawled in a hickory rocker. The low rumble with that touch of demand in it sent a shiver up his spine, just as it had when he'd first started courting Leah. Uriah's stare always seemed to go right through Luke. He could never tell if the man approved or disapproved. Not even after Luke married his oldest daughter. The man had limestone for a face.

"It's me."

"It's about time. Get on up here and sit a bit."

Luke did as he was told.

363

"What's wrong with you?"

"What's wrong with me?"

"Your fraa's in there fixing to spend the night with three of your kinner."

"Jah."

"So, again, I ask, what's wrong with you?"

"I came to get her." He offered that fact in hopes that it would appease, but knowing Uriah as he did, Luke knew better. "She's been under the weather and homesick. I figured a little time to visit with her mudder would help."

"We'll visit plenty at the wedding and on Thanksgiving."

"Jah."

"I raised those girls right."

"I know."

"If she's running away from being a fraa, you best set her straight."

"Jah."

"I done my part. Do yours."

Luke clamped his mouth shut. He'd heard the stories from Leah about how she'd been raised. Uriah was short on affection and long on discipline. He clung to the Ordnung. Luke had no problem with that, but Uriah was one of those people who didn't know how to mix a love of rules with a love of people and find the right combination.

"Don't get me wrong." Uriah shifted and

the rocking chair squeaked under his big body. "I know she ain't an easy woman to put up with. Always been real headstrong."

"There's where you're wrong." Luke couldn't believe the words had escaped him. "Begging your pardon. I found her easy to put up with for ten years."

"All right, then. It takes a certain kind of man to control a fraa the likes of her."

"Truth be told, I don't know what's wrong."

"Nothing a firm hand won't fix."

"Jah."

"I heard tell you're the bishop of the new district."

"Jah."

"Never heard of a bishop who had fraa troubles."

Neither had Luke. He'd never heard of many marriage problems, not in Bliss Creek anyway. "She's been under the weather. She'll be fine."

"If need be, I'll send her back to you."

"You'd put her out of your home?"

"She's a grown woman with a husband and children. She knows her place. And it's not here."

Luke prayed it wouldn't come to that. "I best get in there and talk to her."

Even as he stomped across the porch to

the door, he felt Uriah's disapproving stare bore into his back.

Bethel stopped, wet bowl clutched in a soapy hand. Luke stood in the doorway, his bulky frame filling it, blocking the light from the other room. Her brother-in-law looked as if he'd rather be standing in any other kitchen in the country. She dipped the bowl into the rinse water, gave it a good swish, and handed it to Mattie. "Luke, you missed supper, but we have lots of dessert left. Mudder made fry pies and gingersnaps."

"There's plenty. Cherry pie too." Mudder slid the plates into the water, making a healthy splash. "And *kaffi,* if you have a hankering for it."

"Where's my fraa?" Luke's voice cracked a little. He cleared his throat. "Uriah said she was here."

"She didn't feel good." Bethel wiped at her itchy nose with the back of her wet hand. She felt hot and sweaty, even in November, and too tired to pick her words with care. "She went to bed."

"She didn't help with the cleaning up?" Surprise mixed with concern on his face. He looked worn around the edges, like a sturdy wagon beaten down by long, hard use. "What was she thinking?"

"She was under the weather."

"We talked about staying at our house — Annie's house." His gaze encompassed Bethel's brothers' fraas. They looked as if they were curious and trying not to show it. They weren't succeeding. "She went off without . . . she didn't say . . . Where are the twins and Jebediah?"

The other women in the room all seemed to be looking at Bethel, waiting. She shouldn't have to tell Luke. He knew. He and Leah had talked. They'd talked and then they'd stopped talking. She'd endured the silent meals and the morose looks for weeks now.

Leah was his fraa. Leah was her sister.

She wiped her hands again, needlessly.

"Tell her to come down now." His voice deepened into a hoarse command. "And she should bring the kinner with her."

Bethel couldn't stand in the way of a man seeking his fraa. It wasn't done. But the bone weariness and the great sadness that had mingled on Leah's face kept Bethel from doing as he directed.

"Now."

"Hold on." Mudder stepped between Bethel and Luke. "Give her a good night's sleep. I'll care for the babies so she can rest. They're already asleep. Why wake them?

Leah will feel different at the other end of a good night's sleep."

"I want to take her back now." He crossed his thick arms over his chest. "She's my fraa. Uriah agrees. She must come with me now."

"She's sick." Bethel blurted it out before Mudder could acquiesce. "I . . . Luke, I talked to the doctor where I go for therapy. She says there's a name for what Leah has. It's called postpartum depression."

Her mudder's shocked intake of breath echoed in the silent room. Mattie stood with a plate half submerged in the dishwater. Enos's fraa dropped a fork. It clattered on the counter. She grabbed it and two more fell to the floor. Seth and Robert's fraas dived to pick them up at the same time and bumped heads. Their simultaneous *ouches* were muffled by their hands over their mouths.

"You talked to a doctor about my fraa?" Luke's skin darkened to an almost purple crimson. "Without my say-so?"

"I'm sorry." She hugged her arms to her chest, feeling as if the floor was shifting under her feet. She'd been right to talk to Doctor Jasmine. She cared about her sister. She wanted her to get better. "She's so unhappy. Even for Leah, it's not normal."

"She needs time to get used to the new

place. That's all."

"My therapist says she needs medication. To help her with the moods. Otherwise . . ."

"Otherwise what?' Luke took off his hat and ran his fingers over the brim. "She'll run away from home? She has babies to tend to, a house, a husband."

"It's not something she can help. It's her body. It's physical." A shiver ran through her and her hands felt clammy with the embarrassment of this conversation. "Medicine will help. Otherwise, after the baby comes, she could —"

"She could what? She's a mother. She has five children already. She knows what's expected."

Nothing Bethel said would change the determined look on Luke's face. She realized now he could never understand. This was too far outside his world, where women had babies every day and thanked God for the blessing. She didn't dare tell him what the doctor had said about women with this condition hurting themselves or even their babies. That didn't happen in his world. It wasn't possible. "It's not her fault."

"I want her down here."

"She's already asleep." Mudder looked up at Luke with a stern stare. "Give her tonight.

369

A good night's sleep and she'll be right as rain."

Luke shook his head, looking like a big bear coming out of a long winter's sleep. Confused. Irritated. Not sure where he was. "Tomorrow, then. Uriah agrees with me."

"Uriah is a man." Mudder said the words with such soft deference it took Bethel a moment to realize she was disagreeing with her husband. She never openly disagreed. Never in all the years Bethel had watched them as man and wife. "He doesn't understand."

"Understand what?" It was apparent Luke didn't understand anymore than Daed. "She's my fraa."

"When Leah was fourteen she took over running this house. She thought I would die and she would be left mother to all her brothers and sisters."

"But you didn't die."

Mudder smiled, the same luminous smile Bethel saw on her face every time she talked about those dark days when she'd had cancer, been declared cancer-free, and then had it return for a second vicious attack. "Nee, I lived. But some people are marked early with the hard facts of this life. Leah took care of Mattie and Bethel as if they were her own. A little mother bird she was.

370

She stopped laughing after the first bout. She stopped smiling after the second."

The smile had disappeared, replaced with a painful regret that Bethel didn't want to see on her mother's face. She didn't know why God had allowed these trials for her family, but she did know they'd come through to the other side stronger than ever.

Mudder trudged closer to Luke, close enough to touch him, but she didn't. Bethel couldn't see her face any longer, but the set of her shoulders reflected an earnest desire to speak her piece. "She stopped smiling until you came into her life. You made her smile again."

Luke's face crumpled. His breath sounded loud and ragged. His Adam's apple bobbed. "Tomorrow then. Tomorrow, she comes back to Annie's after the wedding." Reluctance etched his face with new lines. The words were law. And he had the right. Leah was his fraa. "We'll come for a visit on Thanksgiving."

He slapped his hat back on his head and stalked out the back door, his work boots making a disapproving *smack-smack* on the linoleum.

Bethel exhaled and leaned into her crutches. She hadn't realized she'd been holding her breath. She lowered her head and closed her eyes for a second. Purple dots danced inside her eyelids. Lightheaded, she opened them and tightened her grip on the crutches.

"It's all right, schweschder." Mattie slipped closer, a bowl in her hand. "If need be, I'll take her home with me."

"What about Abe?"

"He never has much to say about anything." Her smile said she didn't mind. "He's a good man. As long as I put food on the table, keep his pants washed, and clean his house, he will let me take care of Leah until she's better and then send her on home."

"Luke is right." Mudder sank into a chair. "She's his fraa."

"She needs to get better or she'll be no help to him." Bethel wanted to tell her mother more, but again, fear held her hostage. Mudder had borne six children. She wouldn't understand. "Mattie's right. She just needs time."

Mudder nodded, but her eyes were filled with concern. "Uriah will expect her to go home."

"Daed will stay out of it once it's out of his house." Mattie shrugged. "All he wants is peace and quiet."

Mattie was right. Her daed wanted nothing of these conflicts. He wanted an orderly home. A quiet home. Children should do their chores and mind their elders. Fraas should do their chores and mind their husbands. People should mind their own business and follow God. All the rules laid out nice and neat. Bethel swung around on her crutches and headed back to her chores. Sometimes life didn't follow a lovely, orderly path. That she'd learned the hard way. She suspected God wasn't through with this lesson yet.

CHAPTER 30

Luke shifted on the hard wood of the bench in the last row in the Daugherty living room. Despite his best intentions, he'd been one of the last to arrive for the wedding ceremony. Too many folks in his house — Annie's house now. His back ached, as did his behind. A chilly breeze wafted through the open windows, mingling the scent of wet earth with the aromas of roast duck, chicken, and cake. He leaned into the breeze. Despite the cool, winterish day outside, the air in Helen's living room had turned warm and moist with the people who had gathered to witness her marriage to Gabriel Gless.

His long sermon ended, Micah Kelp opened the German Bible and began reading from the first chapters of Genesis. The words were bees buzzing Luke's ears, reminding him of his own marriage ceremony. Had it really been ten years ago? Leah, dressed in beautiful blue, had answered the questions with a voice so soft he could hardly hear her, but her gaze had been firmly fastened on him and she'd never once hesitated.

Afterward she'd sat on his left side at their table, their witnesses and the wedding party spread out in the Shirack house, eating in shifts, the young, single men vying for the attention of the young, single women across the table from them. She'd laughed and eaten and enjoyed the singing of the hymns and watching the younger folks play the singing games. Later, she'd come willingly to the room they shared in her parents' home for the first few weeks of their married life.

Micah's voice calling Gabriel and Helen to the front of the room forced Luke from the bittersweet memories. They came, Thomas, Tobias, Annie, and Emma trailing behind them as their witnesses. Helen was smiling up at Gabriel, her round face and short, stout figure so different from his tall, angular one. They looked as if they were in a hurry. In a hurry to start their new lives together. Luke remembered that feeling. He wanted it back. He hazarded a look across the room. Leah sat squeezed between Bethel to her left and Mattie to her right. Her sisters each had a twin on their lap while Leah held Jebediah, who squirmed and giggled now and then. She seemed engrossed in providing him with bits of cookie to keep him quiet. Her gaze lifted at that second and met his. Her expression broke his heart. His mouth opened, but no sound came out. Jebediah squealed. Her gaze dropped, she shushed the child, and the moment fled.

The questions began. Gabriel's deep bass mingled with Helen's high, excited voice that reminded Luke of a bird twittering over a nest full of chicks.

"Do you also promise your wedded wife, before the Lord and His church, that you will nevermore depart from her, but will care for her and cherish her, if bodily sickness comes to her, or in any circumstance which a Christian husband is responsible to care for, until the dear God will again separate you from each other?"

The words swept over Luke. He hadn't hesitated to say yes to that question ten years ago. Never had he imagined a sickness, whether of mind or body, as Bethel had argued the night before, that would make his fraa not want to have children with him. Was he, as a Christian husband, responsible to care for Leah under these circumstances?

Yes. The child she carried belonged to him. Her sickness, whatever it was called, involved him as her husband and father of her children. *Gott, how can this be? Deliver her from this ailment. Deliver me.*

He ripped his gaze from his clasped hands and watched as Micah guided Helen's plump fingers to Gabriel's mammoth, callused hand. They clasped and Micah laid his own hand over those of the newly wedded couple. "So then I may say with Raguel the God of Abraham, the God of Isaac, and the God of Jacob be with you and help you together and fulfill His blessing abundantly upon you, through Jesus Christ. Amen."

Luke whispered amen, feeling that he himself had spoken those vows again. He was blanketed with peace and the knowledge that he had signed up for this when he chose Leah as his fraa. Leah would be his fraa until the day he died. Together, they would weather this storm.

He loved Leah. Nothing would change that.

Luke shot from his seat and squeezed through the crowd, angling for his fraa. She'd already allowed herself to be swept away in the crowd of women who would help serve the food and wash the dishes and set the tables for the shifts of people waiting to eat.

She didn't wait for him. Why? Why did she flee? He couldn't fathom it. Even with all Bethel's babbling about baby depression and medicine and Englisch doctors, he couldn't see it. His fraa had always been a good mother. She wanted children as much as he did. They had been of one mind in this for ten years. The more the merrier, as his own daed had said many times. He dodged Josiah and Mark, shaking his head when they spoke to him and plowing forward through the mass of women scattering to the kitchen and men who'd moved outside for a breath of fresh air before the serious visiting began.

He would catch Leah in the kitchen and insist she go outside with him to have a discussion in private. Anywhere out of earshot of the massive Gless and Daugherty clans and all the friends who had joined them from as far away as Gabriel's home state of Indiana. Anxious to have the conversation, he lengthened his stride.

"Luke, wait!"

The deep voice of Micah Kelp stopped him in his tracks. Burying a sigh, he spun around to face the bishop. "All went smoothly."

"It did." Micah lumbered toward Luke, his wife Susannah immediately behind him. "I just got word from my cousin that Elijah left a message on the phone. Silas needs to go home. I imagine you'll want to go with him."

"We planned to stay through Thanksgiving." Luke tried to digest Micah's words. They'd only just arrived. "Is someone hurt? Is Elijah sick?"

"Nee, nee, but Silas's barn and chicken house burned to the ground last night. They saved the horses and one of the buggies. Everything else is gone."

Luke rubbed the spot that throbbed on his forehead. "Vandals? Was anyone hurt?"

"Not vandals. No people hurt. Martin was burning some stumps out by the corral and the fire got away from him. They tried to put it out, but by the time the volunteer fire department arrived, it had spread."

"We had better get back then."

"I'll find Silas. You round up your kinfolk."

His heart hammering, Luke strode into the kitchen. Leah would not be happy to return to New Hope early, but she would understand the emergency. They had to go home. Even if she didn't understand, she would go. No more of this silliness. Silas and his fraa needed their help. A barn rais-

379

ing. Replacement of the lost livestock. Starting over.

Again.

Jebediah on her hip, Leah stood arranging cookies on a platter that shared the table with three kinds of cake. As if sensing his presence, she looked up. Her eyes filled with tears and her gaze dropped. Her mouth quivered. For a split second he wanted to cover her lips with his own mouth. Somehow connect with her. Make her understand how hard he wanted to make whatever ailed her right.

"Come outside."

Silent, she jerked her head toward the other women, busy preparing food, chattering, and laughing.

"Now." He leaned toward her, keeping his voice low. "We must talk."

His chubby hands waving, Jebediah gurgled and chirped, "Daed, Daed, Daed."

"I need to help here." Her tone defensive, Leah shifted the boy to her other hip. "It's expected."

"Silas's barn burned down last night. The chicken house too. His livestock is gone."

Leah's hands stopped moving. She stared up at him. Comprehension stole over her features and her face crumpled. Jebediah began to fuss as if her grip hurt. He waved chubby arms, his fingers wet with slobber. "Daed, Daed."

"Come here, son." Leah gave him up without argument. Luke took his son into his arms. The boy's warm weight against his chest steadied him. "Come outside, Leah."

She shook her head. With hands that trembled, she lifted the platter. "I have to help."

"We have to talk."

"We came for Thanksgiving. I'm staying for Thanksgiving."

"We talk outside, not here."

"I'm not going back to Missouri!" she shouted. "I'm not going."

The chatter in the room ceased. The women froze. The drone of men talking outside filtered through open windows. Jebediah opened his mouth and wailed.

It was all Luke could do to keep from joining him. Shamed to his very core, he stalked out the back door and stomped down the steps. He paused in the brilliant sunlight. Squinting, he tried to see his way. He needed to get the children together. Get Bethel. They had to pack up. The van driver — he needed the van driver. He tried to catch his breath, but it stuck in his throat.

Jebediah patted his face with wet, plump fingers. "Daed, Daed, Daed."

"Son." A sob, unbidden, lodged in his chest. He'd forgotten for a second that he held his son in his arms. "Jebediah."

"Nee, not Jebediah." Leah scuttled down the steps, her momentum hurling her toward Luke, arms outstretched. Luke put out a hand to catch her. She stopped just beyond his reach. "He stays with me. The twins must stay as well. The boys go with you."

"You'd tear our family apart?" His world spun at a dizzying speed that made nausea rise in his throat. "You'd keep the babies from their father?"

"Our family is torn. It's broken." A sob made the words almost intelligible. "It's my fault, not yours. There's something wrong with me."

On that they agreed. He gritted his teeth to keep from shouting at her. He'd never raised his voice to her in all these years. "We need to go now. Get the boys and the twins. I'll meet you at the buggy."

He marched toward the long rows of buggies lined up beyond the corral where the horses munched on hay stanchions in amiable silence. People waved and hollered greetings, but he kept moving. Puzzled faces watched him go.

"Stop, stop!" Leah gasped when they

reached the buggy he'd borrowed from the Shiracks. "Give me the baby."

"You're acting strange. How do I know you'll care for him?"

"I'll have help." She tugged at Jebediah. The baby crowed in delight as if they played a game. A game of who keeps the baby. "Mudder and Mattie and their girls. My brothers' fraas."

"Your daed says you're to come back with me."

"Mattie says I can stay with her."

Blood was thicker than water. He'd always thought that a good thing. Until now. Now, Leah had choices. She had people to fall back on. It shouldn't be this way. They should honor the vows. Separation would not be tolerated. Micah would send her home. He should speak to Micah. Or Deacon Altman.

"Give him to me." Leah tugged again. "Give him to me, Luke. He needs his mudder."

Tired of the game, Jebediah began to cry. "Mudder, Mudder!"

"You can't have it both ways. You aren't fit to be his mudder. Or you are. Which is it?"

"I need time." She gazed up at him, strands of her shiny brown hair escaping her kapp on her forehead, her eyes huge in a white face with pinpricks of red in her cheeks. "Try to understand. Give me time. Don't go to the bishop. Give me time."

"Did you not hear the vows spoken just now? Those are our vows. Nothing changes that. Until death, we are united before God." He looked down at the sobbing boy in his arms. Despite everything in him that screamed to hold onto his son, he handed Jebediah to Leah. Doing so was his commitment to her and their family. It said he trusted her, as he always had trusted her to be mudder to their children. "I'm going back to Missouri to help our friends rebuild their barn. I expect you to come back too. I'm leaving in two hours. I'll see you back at Annie's."

She didn't nod. She didn't even acknowledge his words. She whirled and stumbled toward the house, Jebediah wailing at the top of his small lungs.

Only sheer determination kept Luke from the doing the same.

CHAPTER 31

Bethel squeezed William's shoulder. He looked up at her, his small face forlorn. Glancing at Luke, who stared out the window as he had done the entire time since the van pulled away from the Shirack farm and onto the road for the long trip back to New Hope, she put her arm around the boy's shoulders. To her surprise, he leaned against her. With his walnut-colored hair and round face, he was a miniature of his father. And just as troubled.

"Where's Mudder?" he whispered, raising his head to peek around her at his father. Luke's stony gaze remained on the world whizzing past them. "Why didn't she come back with us?"

The boy didn't frame the question as *why didn't she come home with us*. It wasn't home yet to him. Or to any of them. Least of all Leah.

William and Joseph had taken turns asking this question throughout the trip. Luke ignored them. Bethel knew why. He couldn't talk about it without revealing his anger or hurt, neither of which he wanted to show his sons. His world crashed around his feet, but he didn't want the boys to know. She respected that, even as she saw the hurt and bewilderment in their faces.

"She's coming later." Bethel leaned close to him, hoping her voice didn't carry over the rumble of the engine to her brother-in-law's ears. She prayed her words were true. "She wanted to stay for a longer visit and your daed needs to get back. There's been a fire . . ."

She didn't finish the thought. She need not justify to the children their father's actions or their mother's. They were children, after all.

"You'll need to take care of the house."

Luke's voice sounded hoarse, as if from lack of use. It took Bethel a second to absorb his meaning. Of course, she would take care of the house and the children until Leah came home. She'd assumed as much. "Jah."

"The boys will work with me when they're not at school."

"Jah." She didn't know what else to say.

"I'm sorry to impose."

386

"I'm Leah's sister. Family." He wasn't thinking straight or he would see this. "I'm glad to help."

"I'll ask Silas to send Ida to help you."

Silas's sister-in-law Ida was a widow. Her children were grown so she lived with her brother-in-law and helped her sister. "That's not necessary. I —"

"We can't stay in the house, just us."

His meaning struck her. "I don't . . . of course, I mean . . ." Her stutter only served to increase her embarrassment. "We could . . ."

"And you need to help Deborah at the school. You'll have your hands full."

She nodded. "You also. Luke, I'm sorry —"

"We're here."

Luke snatched his hat from the seat and plunked it on his head for punctuation. End of conversation.

The van rolled to a stop in front of the house. She was almost afraid to look. What if it had that awful orange paint on it again? They'd only been gone two days, but somehow she feared they would have to start over yet again. A quick gander proved her fears groundless. Neat and clean, just as they'd left it.

Luke shoved the door open and vaulted

from the van.

Bethel managed to slide out on her own. Good thing, since Luke made no move to help her down. Without a word, he strode into the house. He didn't even look back to make sure the boys followed. Using the van to prop herself up, she struggled through the mud to the back and flung open the doors. William, his small face as miserable and uncertain as it had been throughout the trip, climbed into the back and handed her the crutches. Joseph grabbed a bag almost as big as he and dragged it toward the house.

"You're here."

Elijah stood in the yard.

"And you're a sight for sore eyes." She blurted the words without giving them time to ping-pong around inside her head. "I mean —"

"You too. Come with me." He grinned and nodded toward the barn. "I have a surprise for you."

"A surprise?" The boys spoke in unison. William jumped from the van and Joseph dropped the bag's handle. "We want to see."

"Nee." Elijah shook his finger at them. "Take in the bags and get unpacked. You're big boys. Your daed needs your help."

He clapped both hands together. "Get.

Chop-chop!"

They got.

Bethel laughed for the first time since leaving the house. "You're good with children." Her own words surprised her yet again. "I guess . . . I hadn't noticed that."

"There's a lot you haven't noticed." His smile fled for a second and then reappeared. "Right now, you need to come to the barn."

"You heard about Leah?" She hopped forward on the crutches. They sank in the mud, making a *slug-slug* sound when she pulled them out, forcing her to work twice as hard for each step. "How?"

"Emma called the phone shack and left a message on the machine. She figured we should know, be ready to help."

"But you need the help. The barn . . . the chicken house."

"We'll help each other." He turned and walked backward. He made flapping motions with one hand. It didn't seem fair. He could walk backward and flap his arm around and she could barely move forward in a straight line. "Come on, you're getting behind."

"For a reason." She couldn't keep the aggravation from her voice. "What's the hurry?"

"I want to show you something. You'll like

it." He looked like a boy anxious to open presents on his birthday. "Hurry up, slow poke."

"Slow poke?" She hurtled herself forward. "I'm the fastest crutchwoman in the west."

"Right!" He shoved the barn door open. "Get in here, crutchwoman."

Inside, the cool darkness blinded her momentarily. She blinked and sniffed. Hay and manure and feed. Comforting, homey smells. "What? Is there a batch of new kittens? I've seen a couple of cats running around here since we arrived."

"No, no, it's not kittens." He shook his head in mock disgust, then pointed toward the stall at the end of the row. "Over there."

She swung forward. "What is it? Oh, Elijah." She stopped, overwhelmed by the sight. "How . . . where . . . I mean —"

"You're speechless." He smacked the stall door open. "My work here is done."

Bethel swung into the stall and surveyed its contents. A stationary bicycle, second-hand from the looks of it, and a treadmill took up the back half. "Is this about feeling guilty?"

"Guilty about what?"

"You know what. Telling Luke about Shawn."

"*Ach,* no." He shook his head so hard his

390

hat flopped back. He righted it. "This is about . . . in a way, I guess it's all the same thing. I did what I had to do, what I thought was right. I know therapy once a week isn't enough. I want you to get better because . . . well, I just want you to get better so I thought if you couldn't go into town for the sessions, this was the next best thing."

He ran down, looking so embarrassed Bethel felt the need to rescue him. "It's . . . they're beautiful." If one could call workout equipment beautiful. She leaned on her crutches and stroked the bike handles that stood straight up. "What about the electricity?"

"I rigged the treadmill to run on a propane generator. I even vented it out the back of the barn."

"And Luke? Does he know?"

"I spoke to him before y'all left. It's a good thing I went into town and picked them up right away. I didn't know you'd be back so quick."

"Neither did we." She stuck the red knob into the proper notch on the treadmill's dashboard. It lit up with places for distance and calories burned and pulse. "How did you find them? And how much did they cost?"

"It's not polite to ask how much a gift costs."

"A gift? Nee, it's too much."

"A gift is a gift, period."

They'd see about that. "Where did you find them?"

"Diana Doolittle's junk store."

"I don't think she would call it a junk store." Bethel thought about that first day they'd driven into New Hope and met Diana Doolittle. So much had happened since then. "I can't believe she sells exercise equipment."

"She sells everything. She has a whole warehouse full of stuff she sells on consignment for people who don't want it anymore. She has lots of exercise equipment. She says Englisch folks buy them, thinking they'll lose weight as a New Year's resolution, but they get tired of messing with it by February and by April they're using them to hang clothes on."

Elijah's voice trailed away. He stared at her, but she had a feeling he was seeing something else. He entered the stall and strode toward her until he was so close she could smell his earthy scent. Woodsy. "Do you like them?"

Again, like the little boy on a birthday, this time wanting to make sure his gift was appreciated.

"Jah."

"Try them out."

"Nee." She backed away. "I can't."

"Why not?"

"Not in front of you." She stumbled over the words. "Not in these . . . in this dress."

"*Ach,* silly me." He smacked his forehead with the flat of his palm. "Right."

"But I will, later."

"Gut."

The silence stretched. He rubbed a hand across his chin, then crossed his arms over his chest. One boot kicked at straw on the ground. Bethel wanted to tell him to stop. He reminded her of her scholars when they didn't know the answer to her question. Instead of fessing up, they studied the wooden floorboards as if they would tell them the sum of twelve times nine.

Maybe she could make it easier for him, whatever it was. "Danki."

He looked up then, the sharp angles of his sculpted face hidden in the shadows cast by the loft overhead. "Can I ask you a question?"

"I don't know. Is it . . . will it be . . . seemly?"

He kicked at the straw some more. "I don't know what else to do, so I guess I'm taking a chance that it is. Seemly."

"Then go ahead."

"Do you like me? Even a little?"

So many emotions welled up inside Bethel, she found it hard to capture even one. They were like minnows in the pond, darting in all directions, daring her to take them prisoner for use as bait on a summer night of fishing. She didn't dare tell him. She couldn't bear to tell herself. "Why?"

"You're answering a question with a question?"

"Jah."

His gaze pinned her against the stall. "I'm not certain of much these days. Except that I seemed to have missed the time where I was supposed to find the woman I would share my life with and start a family with."

"What about Viola?" Bethel closed her eyes. He asked her a simple question and she turned it around and used it as a weapon against him. "Sorry. Don't answer that."

"If you knew me at all, you wouldn't ask that question." He backed away. "I hope the equipment helps you get off the crutches. Then you can get on with your life."

The rest of that thought echoed around them. *Without me.*

"Don't go." She tried to move toward him.

Her crutches slipped on the hay. She wavered, then righted herself. "I didn't mean it. I'm just . . . We haven't . . . you haven't even tried to court me. We don't know each other. You drive me to town and bring me home. You give me a wonderful gift. What happened to the flashlight?"

He continued to back toward the door. He truly had a gift for walking backward. "I don't know."

"So I'm not the only one who has fears."

"Nee."

"Then don't blame me for asking an obvious question."

"I like Viola."

Her heart hiccupped in such a painful manner, Bethel nearly doubled over. "Then what are you doing here?"

"There are a million reasons why Viola and I would be more suited for each other."

"Starting with the fact that she has two good legs."

"Starting with the fact that she speaks her mind. She has her own life and she's content to wait for God to direct her. The problem is she says I'm already taken."

"She says you're already taken?"

"Jah."

"By whom."

"According to Viola, you."

"She doesn't know you or me."

The lines around his mouth were white. "If we're going to talk about Viola, maybe we should bring Shawn along too."

"Nee."

"I know he was here." His boot kicked harder at the straw. "The night before you left."

"How do you know?"

"Luke told me before y'all left the next morning."

"Why would he do that?" Embarrassment coursed through her. Luke had talked to Elijah about her? "It's private."

"To give me a kick in the seat of the pants, I figure."

"Luke was matchmaking?" The thought startled her beyond measure. "That's a crazy thought. Luke wouldn't do such a thing."

"I wouldn't call it that. I think he was more wanting to make sure you didn't make a choice that would be bad for you."

"And bad for him as bishop."

"That's uncalled for and you know it." Elijah's voice, the edges rough, deepened with anger. "Your brother-in-law is a good family man trying hard to be the leader of his family and this community."

"I know."

He moved until he could lean against the stall, but his gaze never left her face. "So what about Leah? What happened?"

Bethel thanked God for the change of subject. Something in his face told her they weren't done with the first topic, but he seemed to need the same breather she did. Leaving out most of the painful details, she told him about Leah's behavior.

"Luke tried to get her to come back. We all did. Maybe if we'd been able to stay for Thanksgiving . . ." She stopped. She didn't want to make Elijah feel guilty that they'd rushed home to help his brother rebuild his barn and sheds. "Anyway, she wouldn't come."

"It sounds like Leah had her mind made up. Days or weeks, she wasn't coming back here."

"With our family around her and time to rest before the new . . . for a while will help her. She'll be back."

"She's expecting?" His ears turned red.

She dropped her gaze to the ground. "Jah."

"They've been so blessed." His voice, filled with a strange plaintiveness, trailed away. Silence echoed through the barn. A shaft of light from the loft fell on his face. Bits of hay and dust floated in the light.

"They've been blessed."

"They have." She started the treadmill on its lowest speed and began to move her feet. Each step cost her. Why wouldn't her feet lift when she asked them to do it? Commanded them. Cajoled them. Nothing but slow, dragging steps. "But sometimes that's hard to see when you're in the middle of something. You lose sight of the important things."

"You're doing it. You're walking." Elijah sounded so pleased with himself, as if he'd personally moved her feet. In a way, he had. "You're walking."

"I am." As long as she held on. If she let go, down she went. "Sort of."

"You never answered my question."

Here they were, back at the beginning again. She longed to be able to hop down from the treadmill and run from the barn on her own two feet. Run far and fast. "Why are we talking about this?"

"Because I won't make the drive to Webster County if I know you will come outside when I shine the light in your window."

"So you have a backup plan?" Did Viola know she was the backup plan? "It must be nice to have choices."

"You would know. Is Shawn coming back out or are you meeting him after a session?"

398

"You know I wouldn't do that."

"And you know I'm not the kind of man who would do such a thing either."

"I don't know anything for certain. Except that I can't be a wife to anyone in this condition. I'm not even sure I can . . . I can . . . be a proper wife . . . a mudder."

His mouth dropped open. After a second he closed it. "So that's what this has been all about? You're afraid."

"I'm not afraid. I don't want to sell anyone a bill for damaged goods."

"You're impossible."

"I am who I am." She gripped the treadmill, swallowed a lump in her throat the size of a volleyball, and hit the button, upping the speed. Her legs answered the challenge and her feet moved faster. "Broken, but still standing."

"Good for you." Elijah turned and strode to the door. He pushed it open and glanced back. "The woman who becomes my fraa won't be afraid to lean on me when she needs help."

Then he was gone.

CHAPTER 32

Bethel let her crutches lean against the kitchen wall. Balancing herself, she grabbed hot pads, opened the oven door, and removed the last of the pumpkin pies from the oven. The heat rose and brought a shine to her face, but she didn't mind. The nip in the air and overcast skies outside felt like more snow couldn't be far off. Winter, it seemed, wasn't much different in Missouri than in Kansas. Nor was Thanksgiving. The scent of cinnamon and nutmeg baked into fresh pumpkin made her mouth water and sent her mind reeling back to the days when she, Mudder, Leah, and Mattie had made dozens of pies for the Graber family gathering. She would miss that enormous mass of hugs and smiles and endless streaming conversations as they visited and caught up on all the year's events. She straightened and set the pie next to two apple pies, a pecan pie, and the shoofly pie, her favorite.

If it hadn't been for the fire, they'd be in Bliss Creek right now, praying and sharing their blessings with her family and Luke's family.

Be thankful. She scolded herself silently, but with vigor. *I'm sorry, Gott. I'm so blessed.*

The men had spent the good part of the last two days cleaning up the debris from the fire. To her endless relief, the work kept Elijah busy and away from the farm. She hadn't seen him since he presented her with the exercise equipment. She hadn't used it either. Too much work to do. They all still had much to do, but everyone would pause on this day to give thanks. As they should every day. *This is the day the Lord has made. Rejoice and be glad in it.* Her mother's favorite verse. She had recited it every day before she went to her cancer treatments.

"Are you ready?" Luke stuck his head in the doorway. "The boys are in the front room."

Bethel wiped her hands on a towel and followed him. The two boys looked small and lonely perched on the couch. A house once noisy with two toddlers and a baby had grown silent. She settled into a rocker and waited for Luke to do the same.

"We'll pray." He bowed his head without waiting to see if the boys did the same.

The silence stretched and stretched. Bethel did her best to concentrate on their many blessings. Finally, Luke cleared his throat. Bethel raised her head. The boys drooped against the couch, William with his face set in a gloomy frown and Joseph a little teary-eyed.

"You first, William." Luke leaned forward, elbows on his knees. "What are you thankful for?"

William picked at a scab on the back of his hand. He wiggled and then kicked at the coffee table with his scuffed shoe.

"Well? It shouldn't be that hard."

"I'm thankful . . . I'm thankful for the new kittens I saw in the shed yesterday." He sniffed and wiped at his nose with his sleeve. "I'm thankful for Aunt Bethel's green bean casserole."

Bethel sneaked him a grateful smile. The corners of his mouth lifted, but it was a dismal attempt to return the smile.

"What about you, Joseph?"

Joseph crossed his skinny arms over his chest and glowered at his daed. "I don't see why we're doing this when Mudder isn't here and Esther and Martha aren't here and Jebediah isn't here and we're not going to see Groossmami or Groossdaadi. We were supposed to get to stay —"

"Whoa!" Luke's tone cut like a well honed butcher knife. "We'll not be complaining on this day, of all days. We don't always get what we want, but we still have plenty to be thankful for."

He was truly right, but Bethel could see both sides of the coin. She too wanted the family to be all together for the holidays. That's what holidays meant, especially for Plain folks who had few opportunities, what with farming and livestock, to visit for an entire day.

"Let me give it a try." She smiled at Joseph. "Then you can go. I'm thankful for both you boys and how you help me hang the clothes on the line and mow and do extra chores because you know it's hard for me to be on my feet.

"I'm thankful for this new house and how warm and snug it is. I'm thankful for your daed and all his hard work in getting the farm ready so in the spring we can plant the vegetable garden and the flowers and he can plant the fields. I'm thankful for the cows that give us milk and the chickens that give us eggs and the pigs that will one day be ham and bacon and sausage on our plates. I'm thankful to God for the blessings He gives us that we cannot earn and don't deserve."

She stopped. No one spoke for several seconds. Finally, Luke blessed her with a grateful smile. "Amen."

"Okay, okay, my turn," Joseph, suddenly eager, popped off the sofa and flung his hands out. "I'm thankful for the fire in the fireplace and the rugs on the floor that keep it from being so cold in here. I'm especially thankful for the turkey Daed shot yesterday that we're taking to Silas's to roast. And for the pies we're taking too. And the rolls Susannah makes that melt like butter in my mouth."

"Jah, jah. Enough with the food." Luke laughed, the first time Bethel had heard him do so since their return from Bliss Creek. "Get your coats on. It's time to go. Don't forget your gloves and your stocking caps and scarves. It's cold out there and the wind is enough to cut you into two pieces."

Bethel shuffled to the hooks on the wall next to the front door and snagged her heavy coat. The boys pounded up the stairs where they'd apparently left theirs.

"I appreciate your help." Luke slid into his coat and donned a pair of thick gloves. "I know it hasn't been easy."

"We're fine." Bethel put all the warmth into the words she could muster. "We are fine and we will be fine. We'll have even more to be thankful for when Leah comes back."

His mouth tightened at the mention of his fraa's name. "I'll hitch the buggy and pull around to the front steps. No sense in you struggling against that wind."

"The boys can help carry the pies."

It wasn't much later that they were stumbling from the carriage, their hands and faces half frozen, and scurrying into the Christners' house. Silas met them at the door with a giggling nephew under one arm and a giggling niece under the other. "Glad you could make it. Come on in. I'm treating these little hooligans to rides while the womenfolk make a mess in the kitchen. I'm sure they could use all the help they can get, Bethel."

He turned and chucked both children over his shoulders. They squealed with delight as he carried them away. Bethel laughed and motioned for the boys to carry the pies and the turkey, plucked and ready for roasting, into the kitchen. There she found a dozen or more members of the Christner family squeezed into the room, laughing and carrying on like schoolgirls as they stirred, fried, boiled, and baked a mountain of food. The mingled savory aromas of gravy and stuffing and casseroles dizzied her. Her mouth watered and her stomach growled.

"Bethel, so glad you could come." Katie separated herself from the mass of feminine forms and offered a quick hug. Her apron was stained with cranberry juice and her face was damp with perspiration. "Those pies look lovely. Boys, set them on the side table there and skedaddle. The rest of the kinner are playing games upstairs. It has to be colder than cold up there, but it's so crowded downstairs, they didn't have room to spread out."

The boys didn't have to be told twice. They skedaddled.

"How can I help?" Bethel eyed the array of pots and pans on the stove. "Do you have room to roast another turkey?"

"We'll cook it while we're eating and have it for leftovers tonight." Katie grinned and wiped flour from her cheek. "You can never have too much fowl for this group."

"We do like our turkey," Ida chimed in. She looked rested after taking the previous evening off to come home and be with their visiting family. "And pumpkin pie. Yours look delicious."

"You can help set the table if you like." Katie pointed at a stack of plates on the counter. "I think I counted sixteen adults and twenty-eight children."

"Oh, good, I like even numbers." Bethel let Ida carry the plates with silverware stacked on top into the middle rooms where sliding partitions had been removed to make the dining and living room one big space. Perfect for prayer services and holidays. "Are the napkins already on the table?"

"Indeed they are." Ida bustled about, leaving Bethel to straighten up the silverware next to the thick, white china plates. "*Ach,* I'm short a couple of plates. I'll be right back."

While Ida went in search of more plates, Bethel busied herself arranging the cutlery.

"They look straight to me."

She didn't want to raise her head, but after a moment of hesitation she knew would not be lost on Elijah, she did. She'd known he'd be there, but somehow had managed to not think about it. No point in anticipating it or worrying about it. Luke had accepted this invitation and she knew none of them wanted to be sitting at home thinking about the distance separating them from the rest of their family. Silas probably felt some responsibility for that, it being his barn and all, but the invitation had been extended with the greatest of humility.

"I like the table to look nice," she said finally. She met his gaze head-on. He wasn't smiling. "Don't you?"

"I'm more interested in how the food tastes." He gripped the back of a chair with both hands and tilted his head, his gaze inquiring. "How's the therapy?"

"We've had so much work . . ." She straightened a knife and fork and then moved to the first of the children's tables. "I haven't had time to use the equipment . . . but I will. Soon."

"Tuesday, you go back to therapy in town."

"If you can drive me." She went back to the silverware. "If you have time."

"You don't mind me driving?" A fine veneer of sarcasm covered the words. She was sure of it. "I know how much you like to stand on your own two feet."

"No need to be snippy. I appreciate your help."

"You really want to pretend the words we spoke in the barn didn't happen?"

"I haven't thought about them one way or the other." She stopped. Number one, her words sounded mean. Number two, they were a lie. "I'm sorry."

"No reason. You're just being honest."

"No, I'm not. I'm not a mean person. I don't know why you bring out the worst in me."

"I'll get out of your way so you won't have that problem."

"Wait." She leaned against the table with both hands. "It's been hard without Leah. Luke will be happy to have you back at the farm when the holiday ends and the barn is rebuilt. So will I."

He shook his head, his lips puckered as if he'd bitten into a sour granny apple. "Okay." He sighed, the exaggerated sigh of a boy in a man's body. "Have it your way. I could eat a bear, how about you?"

"Jah, me too."

"Would you like to go for a sleigh ride after we eat?"

"A ride?" She thought of the icy wind that took her breath on the ride from their farm and the ache in her fingers that gradually disappeared as they went numb from the cold. But she didn't dare turn down his peace offering, did she? "Maybe. Lots of dishes to wash."

"After the dishes. Come on, fresh air will be good after stuffing ourselves." His lopsided smile begged her to give him a chance. "I fixed up the sleigh. It'll be fun and warm, I promise. Lots of blankets, a warm stone wrapped in a towel for your feet and another one for your hands. You'll see."

"Okay."

"Okay."

After that Bethel forgot about her growling stomach and watering mouth. The meal was wonderful, the company good, yet she couldn't remember what anything tasted like. Every time she looked across the table to the men's side, Elijah was looking back at her.

It took almost two hours to wash the dishes and clean the kitchen, but the time passed quickly in the steady chatter of Katie's sisters and her nieces and her sisters-in-law, all come to visit from Wisconsin. As soon as she felt the work was done and the plans laid for supper, Bethel slipped away through the living room and past the men gathered around the fireplace discussing the calendar for planting in the spring — how soon was too soon and what if they had a late frost — and the children playing a variety of games. The peace of it washed over her and her stomach settled. In Bliss Creek they'd be doing the same and the thought steadied her further. Families blessed with the bountiful.

She peeked through the curtain. Sure enough, Elijah was driving up the road in a sleek sleigh pulled by Silas's new Morgan. She grabbed her coat and scarf from the hook.

"Where are you going?" Luke called from the rocker where he sat, his long legs stretched out so far his big boots nearly touched the fireplace hearth. "It's colder than an icebox out there."

"I need a bit of fresh air." She did. The heat of the kitchen and the mass of women scurrying to and fro had left her feeling damp and sweaty. "I won't be gone long."

She slipped through the door before he could question her more, but not before she heard the words *fool woman* catch on the cold wind and whip out ahead of her.

The gray woolen scarf wrapped around Elijah's face reminded Bethel of pictures she'd seen of a mummy in the *National Geographic* magazines in the library. Only his red nose and blue eyes showed. Without a word, he helped her into the sleigh. After arranging an enormous fur robe over her, he shouted *giddy-up* and snapped the reins. They took off with a jerk that turned into a smooth glide over the glistening piles of snow.

"What do you think?" His breath made white puffs of smoke when he spoke. "Nice, eh?"

"Nice."

She tightened her scarf around her ears and burrowed deeper under the robe. The cold froze her nose and cheeks. Her throat and lungs burned with each breath.

For a while, they didn't speak. She enjoyed the sparkles of light on the cascades of snow that tumbled alongside the road. Bare tree branches dipped and bowed in the wind, causing shadows to dance across the barren landscape. The sun began to warm her face a little even in the brisk breeze made by their forward movement.

"Beautiful day, isn't it?"

"Beautiful. And cold."

"What's a little nip in the air? I like it." His scarf muffled his words, making her lean toward him to try to hear. "Makes me think of Christmas coming and the New Year."

"We've only just celebrated Thanksgiving. Aren't you getting ahead of yourself?"

He laughed. "I like to move along." He snapped the reins again and they picked up speed. The trees zipped past. "I like to get to the good parts."

"The good parts?"

"Making gifts for the nieces and nephews, watching their faces when they rip off the paper. I'm carving farm animals for Hannah and Lydia. If I have time, I might make a barn to put them in."

"I didn't know you were a carver."

"Lots of things you don't know about me."

412

Bethel didn't doubt that. Curiosity got the better of her. "Like what?"

"I can whistle every hymn in the Ausband."

"Are you allowed to do that?"

"I never heard any rules in the Ordnung about whistling." His tone was wounded. "My lips are not a musical instrument."

She laughed. "I want to hear one."

He pulled down the scarf so she could see his elaborate preparations. Much exercising of his lips and wrinkling of his nose before he launched into a soft, slow rendition of "Lord God, We Cry to You."

She clapped her mittens together. "Another, another!"

"Sorry, my lips are chapped and cracking and my throat is dry from the cold air. My technique is much better in the spring."

"A rain check, then."

"A rain check. I promise."

A promise for the spring. He held both reins in one hand and reached toward her. For a second she thought he would touch her face. Instead he tugged at the robe and pulled it up almost to her chin. "I don't want you catching a chill out here."

"I'm plenty warm."

His smile added to that warmth. She forced her gaze to the pines that lined the clearing. They smelled clean and fresh. She wanted a bough to put on the fireplace mantel to remind her of this day.

She cast about for a new topic of conversation. "Did you ever want to play a musical instrument?"

"I did play one." He didn't sound the least bit sorry or embarrassed at this infraction. "More than one."

"When?" She tried not to sound shocked. They'd all broken a rule now and again. The point was to not do it again. "Why?"

"During my rumspringa I asked an Englisch friend to show me how to play a guitar."

"Did you like it?"

"Jah. Not enough to leave my family and faith over it, but some. I learned to play 'Amazing Grace' and 'Jesus Loves Me' and 'Farmer in the Dale.' "

She giggled. That was the point of running around, after all, to scratch those itches and be done with them. "What was the other instrument?"

He chuckled. "A harmonica. It was harder than the guitar to play. I never quite got the hang of it."

Who knew? She ruminated on that fact for a few minutes. She hadn't done much exploring during her rumspringa. Her daed kept them close to home, and after what her mudder had been through, she hadn't wanted to worry them.

"Your turn. Did you break any rules?"

He made it sound like a foregone conclusion that she had not.

"Of course. That's part of figuring out whether we can live with them, isn't it?"

"So?"

She dug through her memories, casting aside all the ones she'd thought about breaking but hadn't. "I tried lipstick."

"Lipstick?" He chortled. "A regular rebel, you are."

"Vanity is a terrible, sinful thing."

He sobered. "You're right, but you aren't vain. What did you think of this lipstick? What color was it?"

"Berry mauve." What a silly name. It had looked sort of purple-pink to her. "My Englisch friend Jenny said it complemented my skin. But it got on my teeth and it felt greasy."

"Not your cup of tea. Good thing, huh?"

Indeed. A simple lesson learned. Her lips were the color God intended.

"How are you getting by at the house?' He started across an open expanse of pasture. The Morgan picked up speed and it felt as if they were skimming across water, so smooth did the sleigh ride. "Katie says the boys are well behaved and helpful."

"Jah. It worries me a little."

"That they're good boys?"

She clutched the warming stone to her, searching for words. "They seem worried. I think they think if they're bad, Luke will leave them too."

"Leah didn't leave them."

"She stayed behind and kept the little ones with her while allowing Luke to take the boys. What does that say to the boys?"

"I hadn't thought of it that way."

"They're trying to be grown up for their daed." She gazed across the pasture, searching for familiar landmarks. Everything looked so different blanketed by snow. "They don't want to be trouble to him."

"She'll come back soon."

"I pray so."

"Me too." He turned the sleigh in a wide arc. They hit a drift and the sleigh rocked, then righted itself. "Gott knows what He's doing."

"What about you? Are you happy?"

"That's a strange question." He pulled up on the reins and the sleigh slowed. "I have my family and I work with my brother and your brother-in-law. In the spring we'll plant and in the summer we'll reap."

"I know. I know. I meant . . . are you content?"

He didn't answer for so long, she thought he might not. She couldn't imagine anyone else to whom she would have posed such a question. Elijah, like her, hadn't married in the expected time. For different reasons, he found himself, like her, living with relatives and helping them raise their families rather than raising his own. He didn't show any signs of minding. Maybe she was the only one who fought off feelings that made her feel like a spoiled child questioning God's plan for her.

"I work hard at being content."

"Me too."

"But the fact that you're here in this sleigh with me gives me hope."

"Hope?" A flush of warmth that had nothing to do with the robe or the warming stones coursed through her. "Hope of what?"

"That I don't always have to be content with being an *onkel*. I could maybe one day be a daed."

"Elijah."

"Don't start with the reasons against that. Start with the hope that there could be more."

"I want to, but —"

"No buts. God is bigger than we are. With God all things are possible."

"We don't know what God's plan is. What if His plan is for you to have children and not for me?"

"You're right. We don't know what God's plan is. That's why it's called faith."

She swallowed words of misgiving.

"Do you like me, Bethel?"

"That's beside the point."

"Do you like me?"

"It's not enough."

"Answer my question. I need an answer."

"I do."

"What is that?" His gaze, so intent and so unavoidable, at that moment shifted beyond her. He frowned. "Is that a truck?"

She swiveled to follow his pointing finger. "It looks like the back end of a truck."

"That it's in a ditch isn't a good sign."

"I wonder if there's someone in it."

Bethel grabbed the side of the sleigh as Elijah made a sudden turn and headed toward the ditch along the road that led to the Shirack farm. In a matter of minutes they slid to a stop a few yards from the shiny red pickup. The *tick, tick* sound of a warm engine told her it hadn't been there long.

"Stay here." Elijah leaped from the sleigh. "There's a man on the driver's side."

Bethel could see that. She followed suit and wrestled her crutches from the back seat. Not that they would help much in three feet of snow. Fortunately, the hard-packed crust held and she managed to hobble her way toward the truck.

"What are you doing? I said stay in the sleigh."

She didn't let Elijah's pique stop her. The wind took her breath away. She banged on the window. Slowly, the glass came down.

"Darlin', how do you like my new wheels?" The gravel in Shawn's voice sounded even rougher than usual. The smell of something like gunpowder wafted from the truck. A huge rubber balloon deflated over the steering wheel. Blood trickled from a gash over his forehead. "I came to take you for a ride."

CHAPTER 33

Trying not to look at Shawn, Bethel tugged on the truck door. The bank of snow kept it from budging. His expression unreadable, Elijah reached in front of her, applied force, and jerked it open. Still avoiding his gaze, she leaned in to inspect Shawn. The *schtinkich* of cigarette smoke wafted out. The rubber bag that had exploded from the steering wheel covered Shawn from the waist down. His glassy-eyed face was white except for the blood on his forehead and under his nose. "Are you hurt?"

"It's just a scratch, sweetheart." He grinned up at her. The slur in his words reminded her of the night he'd visited her at the farm. "Although I think the airbag broke my nose and maybe a couple of fingers. Ain't that a hoot? It's supposed to protect you and it smacks you around big time."

"Don't call me sweetheart." Embarrassment washed over her in a drowning wave. Elijah stood on one shore, Shawn on the other, Bethel in the river, the water over her head. "Do you hurt anywhere?"

"I can't feel my legs." He guffawed. "Oh, right, I couldn't feel them before I slid off the road into a ditch."

Elijah stuck his hands on his hips and shook his head. "How can you be driving?"

"These days us guys can do a lot we couldn't do before." Pride mixed with belligerence in the words. "I drive with my hands."

"Too bad you didn't do a better job."

"Now's not the time." Aware of Elijah's questioning gaze, Bethel steadied herself against the truck's door and forced herself to look at him. "We need to get him to the hospital."

"Can we move him ourselves, do you think?"

"Don't talk about me like I'm not here." The slur worsened, causing Bethel's concern to grow. Shawn wiped at his nose and the back of his glove stained red. "Just use that horse to pull my truck out of the ditch and we can take that ride, darlin'."

"You're hurt. You need a doctor." Bethel surveyed the crumpled front end of the truck. "I don't know anything about cars, but it doesn't seem likely your truck can be driven."

"It don't start. I already tried. Must've busted something in the engine."

Engine came out *jin-gin.*

"He's been drinking." Elijah's tone sounded carefully neutral. "That's why he's in a ditch."

"The road was icy," Shawn protested, the slur growing. "Nothing to do with the holiday cheer my mom served with the turkey and stuffing. It just helped the food go down."

"Should we try to get him into the sleigh?" Bethel considered whether Elijah could carry the other man to the sleigh. Could they drive it into town? It didn't seem likely. The roads had all been cleared of snow. "Or you could go to the phone shack and call for an ambulance."

"Best make the call." Elijah held out a hand. "You'll fall in the snow. Let me help you. Come on."

"We can't leave him here alone."

"You can't stay here." The steely determination in Elijah's voice matched his grim countenance. "Don't just stand there. We need to call for help."

The upbringing instilled in her by her father made Bethel take one step toward the sleigh. The part of her that couldn't bear to see someone hurt pulled her back. "We can't leave him by himself. We need to put him in the sleigh and try to drive it to town." Even with the soft pleading tone of her voice, she knew she was treading on thin ice arguing with Elijah. "Or the shack is right down the road. You won't be gone more than twenty minutes."

The emotions warring on his face made Bethel want to look away. What's more, they made her want to demand he trust her. Elijah must have seen something of this in her face, as well. "Come here."

"Elijah."

"Now."

She teetered on her crutches until they were out of earshot of the truck. "Are you sure you'll be all right?"

"He's hurt."

"I know. You're right not to want to leave an injured man by the road, but I want to make sure you . . . if there's a problem . . ."

"There won't be a problem. Shawn's a good person at heart."

"He's been drinking."

"I know, but I've spent time in a therapy group with him. We talk about many things in that group. A person's values become clear."

His indecision played across his face.

"Go. He's hurt."

Elijah turned and stalked across the pasture, returning a few seconds later with the robe. "Get in."

"What?'

"Get in the other side. You can't stand out here in the cold and he's probably in shock. You need to cover up. Both of you."

"Still here," Shawn crowed. "My legs may be shot, but my hearing's good."

"Hush up." Bethel got into the truck. Her palms damp despite the cold, she slid onto the passenger seat and took the robe. "Hurry back."

Elijah nodded, his face grim. "You can count on that."

The minutes ticked past, each one slower than the last. Shawn's head lolled against the seat. Bethel tapped his shoulder with one hesitant finger. "Don't go to sleep. Stay awake."

"You read that in a book?"

"My mudder taught me about first aid. My brothers were always dinging themselves on the farm machinery or falling off a ladder and such. We like to doctor our own if we can."

"You know, I didn't mean no harm."

"I know."

"Your boyfriend thinks I'm a menace."

"No, he doesn't." For the first time, Bethel didn't deny the boyfriend label. Elijah was more than a friend. "He's worried."

"Then he thinks I'm competition."

"He doesn't think anything."

"He's right."

"We're going to sit here and be quiet."

He shifted and groaned through chattering teeth.

"What's wrong?" Bethel swiveled in the seat. Despite the cold, Shawn's white face had a patina of sweat. "Where does it hurt?"

"My chest hurts a little."

He leaned his head back and closed his eyes.

"Shawn."

"Light a cigarette for me."

"No."

"Come on, give a guy a break. I really need a cigarette right now."

"It's bad for you and it stinks. I'm not opening the windows. It's too cold."

"Then hold my hand."

"Shawn."

"You want me to stay awake? Give me a cigarette or hold my hand."

The cigarette would be more proper. The letter of the law versus the spirit. Bethel couldn't see how God would think it right

425

for her to choose something bad for another person in order to save herself from embarrassment or possible censure. She eyed the extended hand with its bent fingers. A friend in need holding out a hand for comfort. Taking a deep breath, she took his into hers. His fingers were icy. "You need more robe."

"Body heat would be better."

She recoiled and dropped his hand so fast it might have been a skillet straight from an open flame.

"I didn't mean it that way. I'm not a jerk." He drew a ragged breath. "I mean it would keep us warm."

"The robe is the best I can do."

"Better than nothing."

His eyes closed again.

She took his hand. "Stay awake."

"I'm pretending it's warm, and we're at the beach." His eyelids fluttered and then closed again. "You're wearing your sweats because I know you don't own a bathing suit."

"I do, but I wouldn't wear it on the beach."

"Or with me."

"Or any man."

"It's a strange world you live in, Bethel Graber."

"A godly world."

"God made your body."

"Keep going and I'm getting out of this truck."

"Sorry. You don't have to be so prickly."

"You don't have to try so hard to rile me."

"But you make it so easy."

Sirens in the distance sounded more joyful to Bethel than the singing of birds.

"Bethel!" Elijah's voice preceded him by only a few steps. In the side mirror she saw his precipitous flight across the pasture. The worry on his face caused something hard and cold in her core to dissolve. "I'm coming for you."

He halted at the door, his gaze fixed on her hands covering Shawn's. She let go, but it was too late. Elijah's concern fled, replaced by a blank stare. His lips a thin, tight line, he jerked open her door. "Wait in the sleigh."

"I didn't want him to go to sleep. His hands were cold so I warmed them up."

"Get in the sleigh."

She slipped from the truck and stood in Elijah's shadow. Before she could try to right his perception of the situation, flashing blue and red lights pulsated across the snow. A sheriff's car screeched to a stop at the top of the embankment. Sheriff McCormack tumbled out the door before it came to a complete stop, it seemed. He was in full uniform, making her wonder if he'd spent any time with his family on this Thanksgiving holiday. Surely there wasn't so much crime in New Hope as to make it necessary for him to work.

Toothpick clenched between his teeth, he slipped and slid his way down the embankment. He halted and extracted the toothpick, which he deposited in his coat pocket. "The ambulance is right behind me. You folks should stand out of the way."

Elijah jerked his head toward the sleigh. "Go, Bethel."

"It's your son, Sheriff. It's Shawn." Bethel couldn't see how to soften those words. She wanted him to know before he reached the truck. "I don't think he's hurt too bad."

The fear that flitted across his features lasted only a second, but long enough for Bethel to see it. Then it faded behind stone. "What was that fool doing out here? Who was driving?"

He didn't know his son drove now. "He was."

"It's not my son, then." The sheriff brushed past them and approached the driver's side. Confusion written across his craggy face, he leaned into the window. "You idiot, what do you think you're doing?

428

Since when do you drive? And why would you do it when the roads are covered with ice and more snow on the way any minute?"

"Happy Thanksgiving to you too." The strain in Shawn's voice was apparent despite his attempt at lightness. Both broke Bethel's heart. "If I'd known wrecking a truck would get you to come see me, I'd have done it in front of the house. That way Mom could see you on the holiday too. I sure could use a cigarette."

"I gave up smoking." His face the color of radishes, Sheriff McCormack gripped the door frame. "Where does it hurt, son?"

"Don't call me *son*. It doesn't hurt. I'm fine. Just get me out of here." Shawn coughed, a hacking, dry sound. "You quit smoking. Your timing always did stink. I guess you're a better man than I am in every way."

"Shut up." The sheriff looked around as if he wanted to yell at someone. Seeing only Elijah and Bethel, he slapped his mouth shut, his jaw bulging.

The EMTs arrived then, chugging down the embankment with a stretcher between them.

"Hurry up," McCormack yelled. "Before hypothermia sets in."

"It hasn't been that long —"

"Stop jabbering, Gill, and get to work on him."

His expression annoyed, the first EMT brushed past them, carrying a black duffel bag. "Hold your horses, Sheriff. We're coming as fast as we can."

"It's my boy. He's hurt."

"Let's go." This time Elijah grabbed Bethel's arm and propelled her up the slope. "We're only in the way here."

"I just want to make sure he's —"

"You can check on him when you go in for your session." He stared straight ahead, his grip like a vise around her arm. "I think it's time for Ida to start taking you. I have too much work to keep driving into town all the time."

"You're being silly."

"Don't worry. It'll be the last time I act anything but polite around you."

Chapter 34

Luke turned on the pole lantern, adjusted the light, and sat down at the table where Leah's letter lay, facedown where he'd left it that morning. He'd found it in the mailbox along with a stack of letters from Annie, Miriam, his Aenti Lottie, the boy's *Young Companion* magazine, and the latest edition of the *Budget.* The women's letters had been full of chatty news about the goings-on in Bliss Creek, all about the Englisch farmers being offered more than a thousand dollars an acre for mineral rights on their farms. And now some company wanted to pay them to put giant wind turbines on their land for wind power. Some of their Englisch neighbors were getting rich and set for their retirements. It all seemed like something very far removed from him. Another life. Except that life now included his fraa.

Leah's letter was filled with tidbits about

Mattie's girls playing with the twins and teaching them new words. Jebediah took two steps on Wednesday and then sat down and clapped for himself. A tooth coming in on his front lower gum caused him to be cranky and wake up during the night. Mattie's girls made all the pies and bread for Thanksgiving. Everyone had gathered together for a good visit. Everyone but Luke, Bethel, and the boys. They had been missed. The family had missed them, she said.

The letter didn't say anything about coming home. It didn't say anything about regretting the decision to stay. It didn't apologize for embarrassing him in front of their family and friends. It didn't apologize for hurting him. It didn't even acknowledge that she might have.

He stared at the flames flickering in the fireplace. He should put more wood on it. The chill in the air invaded his limbs despite the crackling fire. At the end of the letter, Leah had written one line that gave him hope. Three words. Not the words he would've chosen. But still words that imbued him with the hope that he still had a chance at the life he thought they had together.

I miss you.

With slow deliberation, he reached for the

clean piece of paper lying next to Leah's letter. He picked up the pencil already sharpened to a fine point with his knife.

Dear Leah,

He closed his eyes and tried to imagine the words spilling out onto the page, just as he'd been doing all day long as he helped Silas and his boys clear the debris that had been the Christner barn. Tomorrow they would buy the wood and supplies needed for the raising. A load of folks from Webster County would come up next week. The foundation needed to be ready and the supplies laid in. If the weather held. All day he'd worked, his shirt soaked with sweat despite the icy northern wind, his face grimy with soot, his hands blackened, the muscles in his back and legs screaming with fatigue, and still, he'd written this letter in his head. He would tell her he prayed without ceasing that she would feel better, be better, be well.

"What are you doing, Daed?"

Luke jumped at the sound of Joseph's voice. The pencil made a jagged line on the paper and the point snapped. He loosened his grip and breathed. "I'm writing a letter to your mudder."

Joseph climbed into the chair across from Luke. He grabbed a piece of paper and selected a colored pencil from the cup of pens and pencils in the middle of the table. "I want to write to Mudder too." He crinkled his upturned nose, making his freckles wiggle. "I want to tell her about the wolf I saw on the hill yesterday. Teacher was scared, but I wasn't."

Biting his lower lip, he began to print in large block letters with no hesitation. "I'm gonna tell her I helped you and Silas take the stuff from the barn to the dump. And I drove the wagon from our house to Silas's." He grinned. "She'll be glad I'm making myself useful. That's what she always says, to make myself useful."

"That she does." Luke could hear Leah's voice, firm but laced with affection when she talked to her boys. He watched Joseph's face as he concentrated on making the *m* and the *u* and *d* in *Mudder.* He scrunched up his whole face with the effort to make each letter legible. *Dear Mudder.* Leah had written of everyday things because she couldn't put on paper the things that needed to be said. Still, she'd written. She wanted to communicate with him. For now, that had to be enough. It was all she could give him, so he would accept it for the gift it was.

He selected another pencil and stared

down at his blank paper. He'd never been good with writing words. He could still hear his teacher's words ringing in his ears when he didn't turn in his English essays on time. *It's not that hard. Just write down what's in your mind.* She was wrong. The words in his head did not come out at the ends of his fingers. They milled around, all jumbled together like a bunch of cattle spooked by a bobcat.

Dear Leah,

"I'm gonna get William." Joseph dropped his pencil and slid from the chair. "He should write Mudder too, don't you think?"

"He should."

"We can draw pictures too, to go with our letters." His toothy grin widened. "We can send her a package. That way she won't miss anything. You can draw something too, Daed, if you want to."

"Okay, son. You go get William." He cleared his throat and studied his blank piece of paper. "I'll be right here, working on my letter."

Joseph trotted away, a boy on a mission.

Dear Leah,
We're doing all right. The boys miss you. They don't understand why you're there and we're here, but they're doing all

435

right. They're hard workers, as you know. They're doing real well at school. Teacher says they're doing good with learning English and their sums. Joseph drove the wagon today. William ate too much of Bethel's spaghetti last night and threw it all up before bedtime. Serves him right for being such a piglet.

He dropped the pencil. It rolled across the table and fell to the floor with a tiny pinging sound. *Come home. This is home, Leah. Home is with me.* Her face danced in his head. He remembered the way she'd looked the day they moved into their first house together. Her smile so wide, it reached the corners of her face. He tried to remember the last time he'd seen that smile. Years. Maybe Bethel was right. Maybe this baby depression thing was real. How could that be? His fraa didn't want babies? Babies made her sad? *Gott, how could that be?*

Gritting his teeth, he slapped his hands to his face. His breath came in short, hard rasps. He tried to breathe through it, but his chest hurt as if he'd taken a terrible blow to his ribcage. *Gott, help me. Help me. Please help me. I don't understand.*

"Luke?"

Bethel.

He dropped his hands from his face, swiped his cheek on his sleeve, and leaned over to retrieve the pencil. "I thought you were going to bed early tonight. If you're going to help Deborah at school tomorrow, you'll need a good night's sleep."

She swung into the room, her crutches clacking against the wooden floor. "I am. The kitchen is clean. I just wanted to say goodnight."

"Goodnight."

"Is there something I can do?"

"You're cooking the meals, cleaning the house, doing the laundry, making sure my boys are clean and neat for school. I'd say you're doing enough."

"I meant for you." Her cheeks reddened and she turned toward the fireplace. "I meant if you needed to talk, I could make some hot chocolate."

"Nee." It would be wrong to confide in his sister-in-law. To talk of personal things to his wife's sister. He hesitated. There was something he needed to tell her. She wouldn't like it, but Elijah's report about their encounter with Shawn McCormack made it necessary. "Where's Ida?"

"She went upstairs to her room." Bethel's expression darkened. She must've seen something in his face. "She'll make sure

William and Joseph get to bed before she turns in."

"She'll take you to the therapy session on Thursday."

She stiffened. "I know."

"I considered not letting you return."

"I see." Her voice was barely a whisper now, but he saw the consternation in her eyes. "Elijah told you."

"He did." Luke laid the pencil down. His first talk with a member of his community and it had to be his sister-in-law. "I'm talking to you as your bishop as well as your brother-in-law. Your father has entrusted your keeping to me. Your Lord has appointed me as your spiritual leader. I take both responsibilities to heart."

"I know."

"Sometimes an action can seem very small, minor, without consequences." Like letting a mother hold her child, not realizing the father wouldn't see the child again for months. "I don't want to forbid you to go to the sessions. Your improvement is slow, but sure, and I know what it means to you."

"Jah."

"Tread carefully. Your eternal life in Jesus Christ is more important than whether you walk freely again."

"Jah." Again the barest of whispers. "I know."

"Do you?"

"I do."

"Keep to the Ordnung and you never have to worry."

"I only wanted to give him comfort."

"That comfort could be misconstrued, especially by a young man so in need of comfort that goes beyond physical pain."

"How do you know that?"

"I have eyes and ears. I listen." Even if he had been blind and deaf to his own wife's misery. "At least I try."

She turned to go, then hesitated. "You're a good father and a good husband."

"I'm not so sure that's true."

"It is. Don't let what's happened take that certainty from you."

His throat closed. He swallowed, but didn't dare speak again. He nodded.

"I'm sorry, Luke."

"I know." He picked up the pencil and turned it over and over between his fingers. "But you're doing better and you'll keep getting better."

"I mean about Leah. I should've tried harder to get her to come home."

"You tried. I tried. Everyone tried." He shook his head and forced a smile. "She'll come home. The boys are writing her letters. Joseph went to get William. They're coloring pictures. When you go into town, you can mail them."

"She'll like that." Her voice was so soft he could barely hear her. "Goodnight, then."

"Goodnight."

When the sound of her crutches on the floor had receded down the hallway to her bedroom, he reread the words he'd written. They said everything but what he meant to say. He wanted his fraa back. Not so she could cook and clean and raise their kinner. He wanted her, warm and solid, next to him in his bed. He wanted her sitting across the table from him at breakfast. He wanted her scolding him for tracking mud into the kitchen and shooing him away from the pie cooling on the windowsill. He wanted to sneak up behind her and plant a kiss on her long, white neck while she stirred batter for a cake with a wooden spoon, which she would proceed to wave at him, threatening to spatter him with the bowl's contents. He wanted her standing in the doorway on Saturday night with a clean towel in her hand, telling him in no uncertain terms to get in there and take his bath. Like he was a little boy who hadn't learned to clean behind his ears.

He wanted her to fill up all the cracks in his life where she'd always been for him. Like no other person. His fraa.

Come home. The boys miss you.

I miss you.

Luke

The words in his head would not be forced into obedience on the page. He folded the piece of paper in thirds just as Joseph raced into the room, William behind him. "Walk, don't run in the house." The words came automatically. They sounded like Leah. The boys slammed to a halt, running into each other, all arms and legs like colts frolicking in the corral. "And be quiet. Aenti Bethel has gone to bed early. It'll be time for all of us to turn in soon, so write the letters quickly."

"But we have to color our pictures first." William looked up at him with those solemn, owlish brown eyes. It was as if Leah looked up at him. "Aren't you going to color a picture too? Joseph said you were going to color."

"I will." He settled back into his chair. "What shall I draw?"

"Mudder will like anything you draw." Joseph held out a fat green crayon. "She likes everything you do."

The ache in Luke's throat spread to his

441

chest. Was this what a heart attack felt like? Like a propane tank sitting on his chest, ready to explode in a fireball? Joseph looked up at him, his face expectant. "Draw grass. Then you can have the blue for the sky. Mudder likes the grass and the sky. She told me so when she was hanging the pants on the clothesline and I was mowing. She said they're the same everywhere, no matter where you go. God made them that way so we'd know He's always with us no matter where we are."

Luke accepted his son's offering. His small face content, Joseph wiggled up onto his knees so he could reach across the table and rummage through the box of crayons, lining them up in blues and greens, yellows and oranges and reds. Nice and neat, the way Leah would've wanted them. Luke swallowed his pain. Leah could be looking at the sun hanging on the horizon in a blue Kansas sky right now. The same sun, the same sky. The ache in his throat eased. The pain in his chest subsided.

He began to draw, outlining the frame of the two-story house and then adding the windows and the porch on one side and a chimney on the top. It had been years since he'd drawn anything, let alone colored with crayons. He felt like a little boy again. Peace stole over him as he listened to Joseph and William discuss what color the kittens were in the litter they'd found in the back of the barn.

"That's our house, isn't it, Daed?" William propped himself up with both hands on the table and craned his head to examine Luke's drawing. "You've drawn our family and our new house. You did a nice picture."

"Mudder will like that a lot," Joseph added. He held up his drawing. "Look, I've drawn the same thing."

Indeed, he had. Not as neatly, but still discernibly a house. Crowing, William held up his drawing. Another picture of their home.

"But you need to color the grass and the sky, remember?" Joseph tilted his head and touched the paper with one finger. "And you forgot the sun. It's the same everywhere too."

With a sudden rush of hope, warm and sweet as hot cocoa on an icy winter day, Luke added the sun in broad yellow, orange, and red strokes that filled the sky over his family — all of them, wherever they were.

Taking a long, shuddering breath, Bethel turned up the flame in the kerosene lamp with shaking fingers. Shadows danced across the wall in her bedroom. Ashamed of the tears that threatened, she straightened and ran the back of her hand over her cheek. Elijah had spoken with Luke. Obviously. Shame weighed her down. Nothing could be done about it. Done was done. Elijah hadn't been to the house since Thanksgiving and she couldn't go gallivanting across the pastures to hunt him down. It wasn't done. And he didn't deserve it. He'd taken a harmless gesture and turned it into a grievous violation of an unwritten rule — she wasn't even sure which one. He'd taken a lovely sleigh ride and tossed it aside over what had followed. An accident. A man by the side of the road who needed their help. She'd offered her help from the heart. Her heart said she was called to help. Just as he'd gone to the phone shack, she'd stayed behind and offered Shawn McCormack her company and her comfort.

Gott, did I go too far?

She stood in the center of the room and waited. No answer. She squeezed her eyes shut and listened. The chill in the air greeted her with the certain sense that she was expected to come up with these answers on her own. Hadn't her parents brought her up right?

Stewing over it wouldn't help. She needed

to think of someone other than herself. Like William and Joseph. They needed their mother.

Ignoring the painful ache that radiated from her heart to her head, she rummaged through the top drawer of the small dresser in the corner. It held her scant personal possessions. A nub of a pencil, the eraser completely gone, and a piece of plain stationery in hand, she curled up on the bed, using an old copy of a Burpee seed catalogue as a sort of portable desk.

Dear Leah,
Luke and the boys are out in the front room writing letters to you. I think they're planning to color some pictures too. I know you'll like them. They're such good boys — all three of them! I wanted to tell you again how sorry I am if I spoke out of turn. I want you to know that I only meant to help. I care for you and Luke and the kinner. That's why I did it. I wanted you to feel better. I wanted you to be happy about the baby. As happy as Luke is. You might not like this, but I had to do it. I spoke with the doctor again. She says if you come back and come to see her, she will help you. She will help you have the

baby and get some medicine to help your mood. She says that with the medicine, along with the right amount of sleep, good foods, and a bit of walking alone — no children hanging on your apron — you'll be right as rain. You'll be able to smile again. I know you want that. I know Luke wants it. He misses you so much. We all do. Please consider it. If this is too much, then talk to Emma. She knows about these things.

I never told you this, but I love you for taking care of me when I was little and Mudder was sick. Thank you for being there when Daed was cranky and yelled at us. You always took the brunt of everything and you never once complained. Thank you for helping me get through that awful time when I was little and I thought Mudder would die and leave us all alone with Daed. Now let me help you.

Love,
Bethel

CHAPTER 35

Despite the sunshine beaming down on her, Bethel shivered in the cold winter air. The crowd squeezed in closer to the auctioneer's parked wagon in front of the schoolhouse. The horses, still harnessed to the wagon, stamped their feet and whinnied. She understood Luke's desire to have the auction right now, but winter weather didn't lend itself to a big crowd. Despite her boots and thick wool socks, her feet were frozen and she couldn't feel her fingers. She tried not to think about it, instead listening to the cadence of Nathan Bontrager's booming voice as he coaxed the price for the old tractor up another fifty dollars. Luke had been so pleased Nathan had been willing to make the trek from La Plata to serve as the auctioneer after Diana Doolittle's husband declined. Nathan had the voice and he kept things moving like a cowboy herding cattle. An Englischer from Bolivar wanted the tractor badly. The price shot up another hundred dollars. Bethel wanted to clap, but she kept her glee to herself. The proceeds from the auction would pay for Deborah's salary, additional desks, chairs, a new set of encyclopedias, textbooks, and supplies for the school.

"The quilts sure are pretty." Viola Byler slipped in next to Bethel. She had a package under one arm and a soft pretzel slathered in mustard in her gloved hand. "Did you help make any of them?"

"I worked on two of them. The Broken Starburst and the Turkey Tracks." Bethel kept her tone friendly. Viola had done nothing to her. She seemed nice enough and it wasn't her fault Bethel suffered jealousy pangs. It was an ugly — if human — thing to see that in herself. *Gott, forgive me for the sin of jealousy.* "But Katie Christner is the real quilter in our community. She shows the rest of us how to do it. What did you buy?"

"A set of embroidered hankies for my Englisch friend in Seymour. She's a teacher at the Englisch school. It's her birthday." Viola took a dainty bit of the pretzel, chewed, and swallowed. She had a dab of mustard on her upper lip. "They have the days of the week on them and each one has

448

a different flower in one corner. Too fancy for us, but perfect for her."

"Edna Daugherty made those. She has a lovely stitch, doesn't she?" Bethel offered Viola a paper napkin she'd picked up with her own snack of sugar-dipped doughnut holes.

Viola took the napkin, but she didn't seem to know she needed to use it. "I'm more of a knitter myself."

"My sister knits." Bethel's gaze caught Elijah's approach. Of course, anytime Viola appeared in the vicinity he came out of the woodwork. A perfectly unfair thought. Bethel brushed it away. "Baby blankets mostly."

Elijah dodged two Englisch ladies weighing the pros and cons of a handcrafted oak dresser and matching armoire. Silas's handiwork. A big smile on his face, Elijah waved as he threaded his way toward them. "You made it."

Bethel started to respond and then realized he was talking to Viola, whose smile turned all dimples at his approach. "I wouldn't miss it for the world. My daed let me tag along."

"Did you see the maple cradle I told you about?"

They'd been discussing cradles? Bethel's

skin prickled at the thought. She forced her mouth shut and waited for him to acknowledge her presence.

"I saw it. It's perfect." Viola popped the remainder of her pretzel in her mouth and chewed. She still had that spot of mustard on her lip. "My sister will need a second cradle before the end of the year."

"Did you bid on it . . . ?" Elijah's voice trailed away. "You have a dab of mustard . . ."

To Bethel's surprise, he dabbed away the mustard with a napkin gripped between gloved fingers. His face turned beet red. "Sorry, you had some mustard —"

"Don't be sorry." Viola grinned up at him. "Thanks to you I won't go around all day with mustard all over my face."

Her knowing look encompassed Bethel, who felt her own face color. She should have said something. It was small of her not to do so. And it put Elijah in the position of feeling obligated to do something. And embarrassed them all. Even tiny decisions had repercussions. Small acts and smaller omissions.

"Bethel! There you are. We knew you'd be here."

The gravelly voice was a momentary interruption that Bethel welcomed, although she knew it belonged to someone Elijah wouldn't want to see. Far from it. More kerosene on the flames.

Wrapped in a black down jacket and black ski cap, Shawn rolled across the bumpy ground in front of the schoolhouse, his chair tilting and bucking on the rutted earth. Mark and Crystal followed in a small procession of wheelchairs. Following them was Doctor Jasmine, whose hair had been freed from its customary braids and her work clothes exchanged for jeans and a corduroy jacket over a thick turtleneck sweater. She looked more like a teenager on a field trip than a therapist.

Bethel couldn't have been more surprised if the town of Bliss Creek had come to Missouri for the sale. "What are all of you doing here?"

"Yes, what are they doing here?" Elijah directed the question to Bethel, the first time he'd spoken directly to her since Thanksgiving.

"We came to support the sale." Shawn didn't seem the least bit perturbed by the pitiful welcome. His bruises had faded some and he no longer wore a bandage over the cut on his forehead. "We heard it was a fund-raiser for the school, and we wanted to buy Christmas presents or something."

"I heard I might be able to get a nice quilt for my grandmother." Doctor Jasmine's smile widened. "She used to make quilts herself, but her fingers aren't nimble enough anymore."

"Yeah, I heard my mom and dad talking about the sale," Mark added. "They said there'd probably be some good bargains. You make good quilts and furniture, they were saying. Too bad you're so . . ."

"So what?" Elijah's tone turned cool. He cleared his throat. "I'm not sure what you mean."

"Backward," Mark finished. "I know that's lame. But they don't know any better. When they get to know y'all, they'll think differently."

"Kind of like you guys were when Bethel first came to therapy." Shawn pulled his chair closer to Bethel. "Kind of ignorant, huh?"

"Hey, I'm not ignorant. I learn."

"Okay, boys, okay." Bethel held up her hands. "We all learn. That's the nice thing about it. We can all learn and do better."

"I don't know." Elijah's frown spread into an all-out scowl. "You don't seem to have learned anything at all."

He stalked away, leaving her standing there with Viola, who looked as if she didn't know whether to follow him or melt into the scenery.

"He sure has a burr under his saddle," said Shawn. "Or is he just a sourpuss in general?"

"He wasn't a sourpuss when he went to get help for you on Thanksgiving," Bethel pointed out, not sure why she was defending Elijah. He did have a burr under his saddle. "He went out of his way to help."

"I know, I know." Shawn had the good grace to look abashed. "And I never thanked him."

"No thanks are needed. He'd do the same for anyone in need."

"But he is very nice." Viola's gaze seemed riveted to the spot where Elijah had stood. After a second, she swiveled toward Bethel. "It looks to me like he has heartburn."

"Heartburn?" Whatever made the woman say such a thing? She obviously didn't know Elijah that well. He had a cast-iron stomach. "How can you tell?"

"It's obvious his heart hurts." The other woman's face had turned wistful. "I'd rather think it's something he ate than someone who hurt him."

With that extraordinary statement, she strolled away, package tucked under her arm.

"What was that all about?" Doctor Jasmine asked in her therapy voice. It seemed the sessions went on, even in the great outdoors. "Is she friend or foe?"

"I don't know." Resolute, Bethel turned to her little therapy group. "But what I do know is I'm glad you came. Thank you."

"Our parents may be old and stuck in their ways, but not us." Mark sucked on his oxygen. "We're way cooler than they are."

"No kidding. They're totally clueless," Crystal added. "My parents still think you guys are bigamists."

"And let little girls get married." Mark sucked in more air. "I tried to tell them."

"Keep trying." Shawn had a satisfied look on his face. No doubt he had enjoyed Elijah's sudden exit. Bethel hoped not. She hoped he was a better man than that. "Change is hard."

"Look who's talking." Doctor Jasmine patted his shoulder. "Have you adjusted to the changes in your life? No more drinking and driving."

"Nope, I learned my lesson. Cross my heart. Now, I'm gonna bid on a horse." He jolted the chair away from them. "How's that for change?"

They all laughed. Bethel didn't tell him no horses were for sale at the auction. He'd figure it out soon enough.

"I'm serious."

"You have a place to keep a horse?" Sheriff McCormack squeezed between two wheelchairs and stopped next to Doctor Jasmine, his hands stuck in the pockets of his shiny navy jacket with its gold insignia. "You have money to pay for feed and hay and a vet?"

"I'll figure it out." Shawn's bravado turned to a mumble.

"That's what I thought." The sheriff turned to Bethel. "Who do I talk to about those outhouses?"

"About the outhouses?" The girls' and boys' outhouses on either side of the schoolhouse were marked and open to whoever needed them. Her face went hot. "They're right there, Sheriff."

"I know. I see them. What I want to know is if they're constructed with cement tanks to hold the waste."

"The waste." By now her skin burned so hot, she might burst into flames. "I'm sorry?"

"You have to have a permit, and you need to contract with a certified, inspected company to haul off the waste."

"I . . . I'm . . . I don't . . ." She had no idea what he was talking about. "We use the waste as fertilizer."

The sheriff made a *tsk-tsk* sound. "Like I said, who do I talk to about the outhouses?"

Bethel tried to hide her flinch. Poor Luke. As if he didn't have enough on his plate.

"Sheriff, it's good to see you here." Luke strode toward them, a friendly smile firmly fixed on his face as if he wasn't the least bit surprised to see this particular Englischer at their sale.

"I doubt that." The sheriff stalked past his son's wheelchair and into Luke's path. "Let's talk outhouses."

The sheriff kept talking, but Luke had stopped listening. On top of everything else, this man wanted him to close the outhouses at the school and buy the services of a company that would bring out portable bathrooms. He'd never heard of such a thing.

"You understand these are the rules?" The sheriff stared at him with a perplexed look on his face. "Everyone has to follow the rules. Even folks like you."

Luke realized the other man was waiting for a response. "I understand."

He didn't, but what else could he say? He wouldn't pick a fight with the town over outhouses. Rules were rules. They would

456

figure out a way to make it work.

"Mr. Shirack. Mr. Shirack. There you are!"

He turned to see Diana Doolittle trotting in their direction, her plump red face wreathed by the brightest, pinkest scarf he'd ever seen. She wore a pink down jacket that added bulk to her already plump body and pink polka-dotted rain boots. Looking uncertain, Doo, the boy who'd spray painted the barn, dragged his feet behind her. They'd come to the auction. Luke turned that startling revelation over in his mind. They'd come to the school fund-raiser.

"Diana." Not knowing what else to do, he shook the hand she proffered. "You're here."

She nodded at the sheriff, but didn't shake his hand. "I am. Of course. I wouldn't miss this auction for anything. I want one of those gorgeous quilts." She nudged the bony arm of her son. "This is my boy. John Doolittle. But then I suspect you know that."

He nodded. Something about this loud, bright woman made him tongue-tied. He hadn't been tongue-tied since he was a teenager taking Leah for a ride in his buggy after a singing. The memory made his chest clinch and hold, as if frozen mid-beat. He sucked in cold air and tried to focus.

"Does Bob know you're here?" Sheriff McCormack had a pinched look on his face

457

liked he'd smelled a skunk. "Who's minding the store?"

"Not that it's any of your beeswax, Virgil, but my sister Julie Ann is working today and Bob is over in St. Joe looking at a new truck." She sniffed. "I don't need his permission to attend an auction. I'm a grown woman and an entrepreneur. I'm just here looking for goods I can sell in my store."

The sheriff looked mighty put out at her response. He opened his mouth but then shut it as if he'd figured this was an argument he couldn't win. Luke suspected he was right.

"Doo's the one who suggested we come." Diana put her arm around Doo's waist and squeezed. The boy turned beet red and squirmed from her grasp. "He said you all are good folks. He wouldn't say how he knows that, but I'm thinking there's something he's not telling me."

Luke raised his eyebrows and his shoulders, but kept his mouth shut. He nodded at Doo and the boy nodded back, his long hair flopping in his face.

"That's what I thought." Diana shook her head. "Whatever it is, I apologize. I do that a lot for this boy, but what can I say. He takes after his dad."

"Ma!"

"Hush. Go buy me a dozen fry pies." She extracted a wad of bills from her too-tight jeans, peeled off a twenty, and handed it to her son. "And a cup of hot chocolate. Now — what are *you* doing here?" She turned her bright gaze on Sheriff McCormack, whose face turned the same color as her son's. "I don't imagine you're in the market for a new quilt or an old combine. I'm betting you're stirring up trouble for these good folks. I bet old Sam sent you to bug them about some stupid regulation he made up when he was mayor."

"Just doing my job."

"Somebody break the law here?" She sniffed with disdain. "Maybe it was my husband who sent you out here. Him and Sam are thick as thieves and about as smart."

"Now, Di, don't *you* be sticking your nose where it don't belong."

"Me?" She thumped her chest with the palm of her hand, her eyes wide in exaggerated surprise. "Like I would ever do a thing like that."

The sheriff grunted and turned to Luke. "Remember what I said about the outhouses."

"I will."

With that Sheriff McCormack took his

leave without saying goodbye.

"Good riddance," Diana said after he was out of earshot. "That man has the social skills of an orangutan."

"I reckon he's just doing what he thinks is best for his town."

"What's best for this town is to keep our minds and our hearts open." To Luke's utter amazement, she patted his arm. "We claim to be good Christians. We should act like it, don't you think?"

"I do."

She smiled. "So, the first order of business is to buy myself one of those quilts. Point me in the right direction."

Feeling better than he had in weeks, Luke did as he was told.

CHAPTER 36

Her breath making little white puffy clouds
in front of her, Bethel whipped along the
path to the school. Even with the crutches
under her arms she made good time. She
felt good. She felt useful. At her insistence,
Ida had dropped her at the beginning of the
path that led from their farm road to the
school so she could walk the last part of the
way, just as she always had in the past. A
few days of sunshine had melted most of
the latest snowfall, but this morning the air
wafted crisp and cold around her ears. An
overnight freeze made the brown stubble of
grass crunch under her feet. She ignored
the stench of the blue port-a-potties, one
on each side of the outhouses, with their
yellow caution tape drawn across the en-
trances. Luke had tried to get an exception
for their outhouses, but the health department inspector wouldn't budge. Next step
was some board of variances. Luke's expres-

sion when he explained this hadn't boded well. Nevertheless, nothing would spoil her mood today. Not when she would be at the front of the classroom for at least part of it. As Deborah's helper, of course, but it still gave her a sense of purpose that had been missing from her life.

"Teacher, teacher, you're back!" Eli Brennaman straightened from the tree where he leaned, a baseball in one gloved hand. The boy loved his baseball, even in winter. The other boys who were crowded around him all turned to look at her. "Where's Deborah? Isn't she going to be our teacher anymore?"

The muscles in Bethel's lower back spasmed. She suppressed a wince and slowed. "Isn't she here?"

"She's usually here when we get here. She starts the fire so the room will be warm," Eli's sister Rebecca chimed in from where she sat on the front step. "She likes to clean the room too, even though she cleans it before she leaves in the afternoon. She's says a clean room helps us learn."

"I'm sure she's just running a little behind today." Bethel breathed a prayer she was right. She hadn't prepared lessons, thinking she would be following Deborah's lead. "Did you boys bring in wood? It's chilly this morning. We might get some more snow before the end of the day."

"We did," the boys chorused. "Lots of wood."

"And we started the fire," Rebecca added. "And put away the lunches."

"Very good. Then I'll go inside and make sure everything is ready."

And hope Deborah showed up.

"Bethel, Bethel, wait."

She paused on the small porch and turned. Deborah's brother Enos Daugherty halted his horse, reins pulled tight. This didn't look good. Why was Enos here and not Deborah? Her empty stomach tightened. Silly as it seemed, she'd been too nervous to eat breakfast. *"Gudemariye."*

"Gudemariye. Mudder sent me to tell you Deborah is sick. She's running a fever. She can't come."

"All right." Bethel nodded with what she hoped looked like complete calm. Her pounding pulse made her feel lightheaded. "Tell her I hope she feels better."

"She said to tell you she's sorry and she'll be better tomorrow and to start with their sums. They'll know what to do."

"We'll figure it out. Tell her not to worry."

Bethel turned and slipped through the door before he could see the look of fear on her face. She'd done this many times. Today would be no different. She would teach. They would learn.

Inside she opened the door on the stove and shoved in more wood. The familiar scent calmed her. Dusting off her hands, she propped herself on her crutches and surveyed the room. Neat as a pin, she could say that of Deborah. And she'd written the assignments for each grade on the chalkboard before she left the previous day. *Wunderbaar.* Bethel took a long breath and pulled the bell rope. Its loud clanging made her jump despite herself. *Calm. Be calm.*

The students filed in, chattering and laughing, the boys pushing a little. Bethel rang the small bell on Deborah's desk and the noise subsided. They took their seats in rows by grade, girls on one side, boys on the other, expectant looks on their faces. So far, so good.

"I'll read from Ephesians." Her voice didn't quiver and she remembered her English perfectly. Again, so far, so good. "Whose turn is it to choose the songs?"

"Mine and Elizabeth's," Rebecca sang out. "Deborah marked the pages yesterday."

"Deborah is reading Psalms," Mary objected. "Three verses each day until the end."

"That's fine, but I'm here today." Bethel knew it was important to be firm. A new teacher had to take charge or all would be lost. "When Deborah comes back, she can pick up where she left off."

After that, it was easy. They settled into the old, familiar rhythm. The Lord's Prayer. Hymns. Then algebra first. Then oral reading, first graders struggling with their English, one word at a time. Their noses wrinkled, lips pursed as they tried to form the unfamiliar words, while the older children exchanged their sums and checked them. Recess passed quickly with a game of hide and seek, and then it was on to writing the alphabet for the little ones and writing essays for the older ones. Before Bethel knew it lunchtime had rolled around. They rushed to warm their meals on the stove and eat, shoveling the food in so fast she feared some of the boys would choke. Lunch meant playtime — almost an hour compared to the fifteen minutes mid-morning.

They raced out the door and the baseball game began immediately in spite of the slush and mud from the melted snow. Eli led the charge and the girls took sides in the outfield — the meadow.

"Come on, teacher, play with us, play with

465

us!" Martha begged. "You can be the catcher. Deborah likes being the catcher."

Bethel leaned on her crutches. How she longed to swing a bat again. "I'll watch. You play."

Eli got the first hit, a solid line drive that sent the ball into the pasture where Martha chased it, giggling the whole time. He raced all the way to third base — a flat rock. His buddy Reuben took a turn next. He was a big boy, taller than Eli and heavier, and good at games like this. Mimicking Eli, he took a ferocious swing — and got a tiny piece of the ball. Whether from excitement or overexertion, he let go of the bat as he bolted toward first base. The old fashioned wooden bat sailed much further than the ball, right down the baseline, right at Eli. It smacked him head-on in the face. Down he went, flat on his back.

It took a second for Bethel's mind to process the scene. Eli down. Not moving. No one moving for a long, exaggerated second. Time ticked by.

"Eli!" Rebecca called, breaking the stunned silence. "Eli, are you all right?"

Her cry jolted Bethel into action. She struggled across the muddy, uneven ground. Her crutches sank into the mud. Thomas's Eli. Her charge. She needed to get to him.

Her legs wouldn't cooperate. She had to get to him. "Eli? Eli!"

"I didn't mean to do it." Reuben cut across the pitcher's mound toward third base, leaving her far behind. "My gloves are slick."

"What do we do, teacher?" Rebecca raised a white, scared face to her. "We need to help him."

Bethel's crutches hit a low spot in the ground, and she stumbled. Her legs folded under her. She hit the ground. She raised herself up and struggled to her feet again. *One step, two steps, three steps.* She sank to the ground next Eli. "It's okay. Let me get a look at him." His eyes were closed. A red patch tattooed his forehead. "We need to get him into town."

"I'll take our buggy to the phone shack," Hannah offered. "I know how to make a call. My mudder showed me."

Bethel tried to think. The girl was eleven, old enough to take on this responsibility. Did they dare wait or should they take Eli into town in the buggy? "Reuben, get your buggy. We need to take him to town." She turned to the other children. "Sarah, you're in charge of banking the fire. School is dismissed. Gather your things and go home. Rebecca, run home and tell your daed what's happened."

"I want to go to the hospital with you."

"Nee. Eli will need your daed and Emma when he wakes up." She pointed at Elam Christner. "You go with her. Hurry, run!"

They took off across the pasture, feet flying under them.

Bethel prayed as the older boys picked up Eli and settled him into the back of the buggy. She prayed as they helped her into the front seat. She prayed as Reuben picked up the reins and yelled *giddy-up!*

She had wanted to teach. With teaching came the responsibility of keeping each child safe every day. *Gott, don't let me fail.*

Elijah surveyed the emergency room. Englischers — some coughing, some slumped in their chairs, little ones crying — occupied most of the seats in the room, but it still only took him a second to find Bethel in her long, blue dress stained with mud. His sore heart jolted at the sight of her. He told it to behave. It didn't listen. She sat huddled in a chair, her kapp-covered head down, her hands smoothing her apron over and over. Reuben sat in the chair next to her, snoring. Teeth gritted, he strode toward them, thinking she would look up at his footsteps. She didn't. She looked so forlorn. Leave it to her to feel guilty about a simple accident. He wanted to wipe that look from her face. He wanted to see her smile, even if only for a second. Try as he might, he couldn't stay angry at this stubborn woman. She would be the death of him.

"Bethel, are you all right?"

Finally, she raised her head. "You?"

"Jah, me. When Luke heard what happened, he asked me to come get you so Reuben could go home." He patted Reuben's shoulder. The boy awoke with a start. "Head on home. Your daed will be wanting you for chores."

Reuben yawned and stretched and went on his way with a barely audible goodbye.

Elijah turned to Bethel. He squatted so he could talk to her at eye level. "You look done in. How's Eli?"

"I don't know." She straightened and looked around. "Thomas and Emma went in to see him as soon as they arrived. They haven't come back."

"I'm sure they're sitting with him until the doctors let him go home."

"It's my fault." She gripped a hankie in both hands, her knuckles white. "I should've —"

"Should've what?" He knew it. She would pick at herself over an accident she couldn't have prevented, short of keeping the children inside at their desks all day long. He rocked on his heels and stood. "They're kinner. They play games. They get knocked around. We did when we were their ages. Why would it be your fault?"

"It's my responsibility to make sure they're safe."

"He got hit by a bat. You brought him here. Seems to me you did all the right things."

Her eyes bright with unshed tears, she peered up at him. "You think so?"

"I know so."

She looked beyond him and stood. "There's Thomas."

Elijah turned in time to see Thomas push through the double doors and stride toward them. He smiled. A good sign.

"Well?" Bethel pushed past Elijah. "How is he? What did they say?"

"He'll be fine." Thomas's relief billowed from him, enveloping Elijah. "Doctor says he has a mild concussion. He wants to keep him here overnight for observation. He'll be home in time to see you at school tomorrow for at least part of the day, I reckon."

"School?" Bethel's gaze faltered. "I'm sure Deborah will be back tomorrow."

"Eli said to tell you he'll see you tomorrow." Thomas spoke with more force, his deep voice firm. "You fall off a horse, the next thing you do is get back on and ride."

"He's right," Elijah added. "You know he is."

She sighed. "You don't blame me, Thomas?"

"I'm thankful you were there to help him."

She nodded, but she didn't look convinced.

"I'd better take you by the school on the way home." Elijah whipped his arm out in a flourish as if to say *after you.* "You'll want to write the assignments on the board for tomorrow."

Her face broke into a smile — finally. "I guess you're right. I wouldn't want my scholars to get behind."

"No, I sure wouldn't want that either."

Given, he'd always been behind in his assignments. He figured Bethel remembered that too. Her smile said she did. "Thomas, tell Emma if she needs anything —"

"She knows." Thomas smiled. "Now go, teacher."

She went. Elijah followed, feeling as if they'd made progress in some small measure. One step at a time. With Bethel, it might always be one step at a time. But that might be better than nothing at all.

CHAPTER 37

Bethel planted her feet in front of the hearth, lifted the pine bough, and laid it on the fireplace mantel. The scent wafted around her. She inhaled and smiled. It smelled like Christmas. Despite everything, she couldn't help but revel in the thought. The birth of Christ. A season of renewal. She wouldn't dwell on all the ways this season would be different from Christmases of the past. Being so far from the rest of her family. Leah's refusal to return to New Hope. Living in this house with her brother-in-law and her nephews. Not being up to the task of running a classroom by herself. She liked being Deborah's aide. She did. Really. She didn't mind that every chore was a battle. That meant she appreciated the victories all the more.

She eyed the chair where she'd intentionally laid her crutches. Since Eli's injury at the school, Luke had begun insisting she practice walking on her own and that she use the equipment Elijah had given her. He wanted to make sure she could help the kinner if needed. She wanted to be able to help the kinner here at home too. What if one of them were hurt? What if Ida or Luke weren't around?

Gritting her teeth, Bethel struck out across the room. *One step, two steps, three steps.* Arms thrust out to aid in her balance, she felt as if she straddled a narrow bridge high over a canyon. She bit her lower lip in concentration.

"Aenti, Aenti!" William blasted through the front door, scarf flying behind him, snow and mud from his boots marring her clean floor. "We need more blankets. Elijah says we need blankets."

Bethel teetered. Her arms flapped. A big bird, that's what she looked like. Down she went into the chair. At least she hadn't fallen. She grinned in triumph. "I did it!"

"Did what?" William looked confused. "You fell in a chair."

"I walked."

"Aenti, we need blankets!" Joseph barreled into the front room behind his brother. "Elijah says Cinnamon is having her foal."

She pulled herself from the chair and balanced on her feet again. This was indeed exciting news. "In December?"

"Yep. Come look!" Joseph grabbed her hand. "Come on, Aenti. Cinnamon's having a baby!"

Her nephews' grinning faces looked up at her. They wanted to share their excitement with her. It was a gift. God had given her the gift of her nephews. She tried hard every day to deserve it. She loved the idea of a new foal. They were so cute and sweet, all legs, stumbling around as they followed their mamas. But she had responsibilities here in the house. "I have chili on the stove and cinnamon rolls in the oven. Your daed will be in from repairing the chicken coop and he'll be starving."

"He ran out of bailing wire and went into town."

Leaving her with Elijah.

"Come on." Joseph tugged on her arm. She swayed. He let go. "Whoops! I'll get your crutches."

"Yeah, come on," William said in his best wheedling tone. "You don't want to miss this."

She wasn't a coward. Besides, Elijah had been nothing but polite and downright sweet since that day at the hospital. He seemed to be waiting for something. She couldn't be sure what.

474

"Get the extra blankets in the cedar chest in your room. Not the quilts, though. And don't be tracking mud up those stairs." She grabbed her crutches and hopped toward the kitchen. "I should be able to take the cinnamon rolls from the oven now and I'll turn the stove off. We can reheat the chili after the foal gets here."

Shedding their boots without sitting down, the boys accomplished the task in less than a minute and a half. She donned her coat and the boys were back into their boots in no time. "Come on, Aenti, come on!"

They flew out the door, blankets flapping behind them.

She shoved through the door and heaved herself down the steps. Elijah stood in the corral, his hand on Cinnamon's bridle. Even at a distance, she could hear his cooing, his breathing coming in white puffs. The man had a deft touch with horses.

"I thought the babies came in the spring," she called as she drew closer. "Is it coming early?"

"Most come in the spring, but not all of them." Elijah ran a hand across the horse's back. She dipped her head and whinnied, a nervous, high-pitched sound. "She needs to be inside."

"Will the foal die if it's born when it's cold?"

"Foals have kind of a fuzz that insulates them. As long as we keep it dry and out of the wind, it'll be all right." Elijah urged the horse toward the barn. "William, run ahead and put down a thick blanket of hay in the last stall. Joseph, you stuff some rags into the cracks along the wall. We don't want a draft in there."

Inside, Cinnamon, oblivious to her rapt audience, pranced about in the stall for several minutes, then sank to her knees. She rolled to one side, then stood again. Once again she sank to the ground. Seconds later, the long, knobby knees of a foal made an appearance. Bethel gasped. William and Joseph joined her in a chorus of exuberant surprise and excitement.

Elijah joined Bethel at the railing. "You've never seen a foal born before?"

"Nee." She hesitated, aware of the boys, who had crawled up on the railing to sit and watch, their expressions enthralled. "Is it all right if I stay, do you think?"

"It's amazing." His voice softened. "The birth of one of God's creatures is a miraculous thing. It reminds us of the beauty of God's plan and His infinite care in creating this world."

He sounded as awed as she felt.

Cinnamon whinnied and tossed her head. She tried to rise, then sank back.

"Looks like she needs a little help." Donning rubber gloves, Elijah approached the horse. He spoke a steady stream of soft nothings as he gently tugged on the long legs. The baby's head, cloaked in the birth bag, appeared. A few seconds later the rust-colored filly slid into the world in one big *whoosh*. Bethel imagined most women would like to have their babies so quickly. The filly's spindly legs and slim head rested on the hay for a bit while Elijah helped Cinnamon finish up the job. Then he cleaned out the baby's mouth and removed the birth bag so she could wiggle free.

"A beauty. What a beauty," Elijah whispered as he worked. "You done good, Cinnamon. Old Wally will be a proud papa."

Cinnamon must've agreed. She snorted, stood, and began to clean her baby.

"That a girl, good mama."

The foal tried to stand, her long, almost white legs stuck out in four directions. She wobbled and went down in an awkward pile of bones. The second time she teetered, lost her balance, and rolled over, legs flung in all directions. The boys chortled and flapped their hats in extreme amusement. Bethel couldn't help but join them.

A stubborn little critter, the foal gave it all her might and the third time managed to stay up. Covered with bits and pieces of hay, she dipped her dainty neck and tossed her head. Her legs were spread so far out she looked like a tent with the poles too far apart. She didn't seem to have any idea how to pull them in.

"She's doing fine. She's a strong one." Elijah tugged off the gloves and leaned on the stall gate. His big hands, fingers clasped, hung over the edge. Bethel had to force her gaze from those hands, so strong, to his face. He looked satisfied. Content. "She'll be running all over the pasture in no time. Luke will be pleased."

"I'm glad I was able to see it.'

"I knew you'd like it."

The significance of his words registered. "You sent the boys to get me, didn't you?"

He tilted his head toward her, his voice low, the words between the two of them. "I figured you were there when we had to put down Ned. You should see the other side of the coin."

"Danki."

The foal was trotting around the stall in perfect step with Cinnamon as if she'd been doing it her whole life. All fifteen minutes of it. "That day in the barn, I acted like a spoiled child who didn't get his way."

"More like a jealous beau."

She held her breath, waiting for his reaction.

His eyebrows went up. So did the corners of his mouth. "Maybe."

"Maybe, but you made up for it by coming to the hospital to get me. We're fine."

"Are you sure?"

"Jah."

Cinnamon's foal would start a new life today. Bethel breathed a silent prayer that she and Elijah might also have a new start.

How many new starts would God give them before they managed to get things right? Bethel didn't ask that question aloud either. The God of second chances never gave up on His children.

Elijah's hand stole across the space between them and rested on hers. She forgot how to breathe. His fingers were warm and his grip solid. His gaze came up and met hers. "I need to know something."

"I already told you I like you," she whispered, acutely aware of her nephews clowning around on the railing a few yards away. Her heart slammed against her chest so hard she couldn't breathe. Every nerve in her fingers pulsed at his touch. "I'm . . . I think I really do . . . like you, I mean." She sounded twelve. Not like a grown woman who knew her own mind. "I do. Like you."

"Good. I'm glad we cleared that up." He took a step closer. "It's one thing to like me. That's good. It's fine. But do you imagine a future where you might do more than that?"

She wanted to say yes. She wanted to blurt it out. Catch her dream and reel it in before it slipped away in a cold, winter wind. "I try."

"You try. Is it that difficult?" His voice hardened and his hand began to withdraw.

She caught at his fingers. "I don't want you to be disappointed." "Me?"

"I may never be the woman I was before the storm. I may never be the woman who taught school on her own again."

"I didn't even know that woman." The boys looked up at the angry disappointment in Elijah's voice. He smiled at them and softened his tone. "I know you and I like you fine with the crutches, without the crutches. It doesn't matter to me. Can't you get that through your thick head?"

"You are the sweet talker, aren't you?"

"You aggravate me to no end."

What had Emma said about Thomas aggravating her until she finally married him?

"Then what do you want with me?"

"I want everything."

"Then you'll be patient with me."

He gritted his teeth, a pulse beating in his jaw. After a few seconds, he sighed. "I'm not getting any younger."

"You only act like it." She wasn't getting any younger either, so why was she arguing with him? Because something about him told her if she ever gave in there was no going back. The look on his face, the feel of his hands on her waist. He indeed wanted it all, and that scared her. What if she didn't have all to give? "Like a child who can't wait for his supper."

"Supper." He groaned. "You think this is like supper. It's like birthday and Christmas bundled together and thrown so far into the future, I can't see how they'll ever get here. I'm not getting any younger and neither are you. We're not teenagers still going to singings and trotting around on buggy rides late at night."

"Hush."

Too late. This time William hopped from his perch and trotted toward them. Bethel let go of Elijah's hand. He took a step away, but she still felt his presence invading her space, the warmth of his skin against her fingers. His glare told her the conversation hadn't ended to his satisfaction. "Are you all right, Elijah?"

Elijah rumpled the boy's walnut-colored hair. "Where's your hat? Best find it and then go carry some firewood into the house. A real blizzard is expected to kick up tomorrow. By evening, we won't be able to find the wood stack."

William scampered toward the door. Joseph followed suit. They were two peas in a pod. Bethel tugged on her gloves and prepared to do the same.

"Where are you going?"

"To finish the chili."

He grabbed her arm and swung her around so she faced him. Her crutches fell to the ground, but she stood on her own. Before she could fathom his intention, he bent his head and his lips brushed against hers. It was the merest of kisses for the briefest fraction of a second, but the look on his face spoke of an intent that could not be mistaken.

His gaze locked on hers with a ferocity that made her shiver. Within the good-natured youngest son who gave up so much to care for his parents lived a man of deep emotion. "You're scared, aren't you?"

"You're not?" Her voice trembled. Her first kiss. Over before she had a chance to reciprocate or even know how to feel about it. "I'm not afraid to admit it, either. Marriage ties two people together for the rest of their lives. There is no going back. No room for a mistake. I'd be silly not to be afraid. Aren't you?"

"Is this about Shawn McCormack?" His hand dropped from her arm, but she could still feel his touch. "If you have doubts because of an Englischer, then you're right. This goes no farther."

He read her too well. Her fascination with Shawn McCormack could only serve to hurt him. She couldn't let that happen. "Come to supper?"

He frowned and jerked on his gloves with more force than necessary. "I don't think —"

"Chili, sourdough bread, cinnamon rolls. You like my cinnamon rolls. You know you do."

"I do." He rolled his eyes and sighed a gusty sigh. "But I like you more. I will come to supper."

Gut. She liked him too. Was it enough? How did a woman know when it was enough?

"I kissed you." His glance dropped to the dirt floor, then made its way back to her face. "I meant no disrespect. I should have

483

contained myself. It's just you provoke me — not that you are at fault. I'm the one at fault."

"I felt no disrespect."

Far from it. The brief touch of his lips on hers told her something about Elijah that she needed time to absorb. That he saw her as someone he wanted to kiss, that he liked to kiss, told her something she needed and longed to know. He found her . . . she sought a word not part of her vocabulary. Despite her weak legs and her crutches and her disabled body, he saw something when he looked at her that made him want to kiss her. She wasn't ugly to him. To a Plain man who wanted a fraa and children, she might be enough for him.

He raised both hands in the air, fingers stretched out, his face questioning. "That's all you have to say about it?"

"I'd like to do it again sometime." The words burst from her before she could stop them. Her cheeks burned. "Not to be forward. I mean someday if all goes well."

His face went red as a tomato. "I'm glad," he stuttered. She'd never heard him stutter before. "I mean, we're not done talking."

"I know. Give me time. What I need is time." It did her heart good to know he was as nervous as she was. "We're not done with a lot of things, getting to know each other better being at the top of list."

His expression eased and he nodded. "I like the sound of that."

So did she. If she could keep the doubts and the fears and the uncertainty at bay long enough, she might learn how to think of herself as worthy of the love and companionship of a man who wanted her at his side. A man who kissed her and told her with the look in his eyes that he longed to do it again.

Elijah inhaled the cold air and let the frigid north wind blow away the heat of the barn and his embarrassment every time he thought of his actions. What had possessed him to kiss Bethel? He'd never thought of himself as a man who let himself get carried away by his emotions. He smacked a log against the wall with more force than necessary to remove the snow and slapped it in the hollow of his arm. *Gott, forgive me.* He scooped up a half dozen more pieces of wood. Bethel aggravated him until he couldn't think straight. That's what happened.

Nee. He couldn't blame his actions on her. She didn't deserve that. He turned and bent his head against the wind and tromped across the porch.

"What's the matter with you?" Silas swept snow from the porch with a vigorous motion that served to shove the piles under the railing and onto the ground with great efficiency. "You've been a grouse ever since you returned home. Katie's thinking about dosing you with some medicine. Thinks you're coming down with the flu or something."

"I'm fine. Just tired."

"It doesn't matter how tired you are; you always have a story to tell the kinner when you come home at the end of the day. You always play a game with them or help them with something. Tonight you barely opened your mouth."

Elijah avoided his brother's gaze. He saw too much. He was more than an older brother now; he was a minister. A leader of the community. A wise man. Elijah bit his chapped lower lip and considered. "I did something I shouldn't have done."

Silas's bushy eyebrows leapt up. He leaned the broom against the wall and opened the door for Elijah. Elijah stomped snow from his boots and eased past his brother. Once inside, he dumped the wood into the box next to the fireplace. He turned to his brother, waiting.

Taking his sweet time, Silas tugged off one

boot and then the other on the rug by the door. He set them in a neat row next to a dozen others in varying sizes. All black, all well used. Finally he straightened. "Are you going to tell me what you did?"

"Nee. It involves someone else. It's of a private nature."

"Ah."

"Don't *ah* me."

"Did you break a rule of the Ordnung?" His stern tone said he expected a simple, straightforward answer.

Elijah considered. He hadn't thought of it in quite that light, more concerned for Bethel's reaction. "It didn't go that far."

"But you were afraid it might."

"Nee. I would never. Nor would . . ." He let his voice trail away, not wanting to reveal more. It was a private matter, when it was all said and done.

Silas grinned as he hung his coat on the hook and went to stand in front of the fire. "A word of advice from an old married man?"

"I'll take anything I can get."

"Stop making it so hard."

"What?"

"Trust the way you feel and do it right and proper."

"What if I make a mistake?"

"I've watched you grow up, little bruder." Silas stretched his hands toward the fire. The flames illuminated the wrinkles just starting to form around his eyes and mouth. He looked a lot like the daed Elijah remembered from his younger years, before age and ill health took his vigor. "You're a good man with a good head on your shoulders. You spent years taking care of Mudder and Daed. Somehow in the course of that, you lost your faith in your ability to do anything else. Let nature take its course and get on with your life."

"That's not true. I know I can do this. It's what I want. It's all I think about."

"Then ask her."

"You don't know —"

"It's written all over your face every time you look at her and think she isn't looking at you."

"She's not sure she wants it."

"You're afraid she'll say no?"

"Jah."

"She won't."

"How do you know?"

"Because I've seen the way she looks at you when she thinks you're not looking at her."

Elijah snorted, but somehow he felt a little less cranky. He added wood to the fire and picked up the poker to rearrange the logs.

"I'm subdividing the land. I'm giving you the seventy-five acres north of the creek."

Elijah froze at the words, so unexpected. He felt rather than saw his brother move to stand behind him. He stared at the flames, leaping and dancing as if for the joy of the Lord. He couldn't have spoken if his life depended on it.

"You're welcome," Silas chuckled, that deep rumble in his chest that again reminded Elijah of Daed. "In the spring, we can start building your house up on that knoll that overlooks the river."

"I'm . . . I don't . . . Silas, what about your boys? I —"

"I'll work that out with them when the time comes. What you did for our parents . . . You gave them comfort and care for the last days of their lives. You're a good man. Any woman with a brain would be happy to have you."

Elijah managed a nod.

"So ask her."

Again, all he could do was nod.

Silas laughed and clapped him on the shoulder. "Enough of this talking. I need a cup of kaffi to take the chill off these old bones. How about you?"

Elijah managed to stumble after Silas to

the kitchen. If he ever got his tongue under control, he'd thank him. And then he'd do as he was told.

Ask her.

CHAPTER 38

Luke watched as the boys played checkers on the rug in front of the fireplace. Their faces were red from laughing over some silliness Eli had told them. He sprawled on the sofa, egging them on from afar. Neither of Luke's boys had asked about their mudder since yesterday before their prayers on Christmas morning. Visiting with Emma and Thomas and their kinner on the second day of Christmas had been good medicine for the quiet stillness of their own home on this holiday. A blessing. He stretched his boots toward the fire and closed his eyes for a second, hoping he could forget the empty chairs at the table. The absences.

"Did you eat too much, bruder?"

He lifted one eyelid to see Emma plop down in the rocking chair next to him. She had a sleeping baby on her shoulder. From the looks of her, it seemed possible another one was on the way. She hadn't said and he wouldn't ask.

"If it's a nap you want, feel free to use Eli's room. He's going hunting with the Daugherty boys and Silas in a few minutes. Thomas is conked out in our room."

"Nee, I'm fine. Just resting my eyes."

"I'm sorry Leah's not here to celebrate with us."

Leave it to his sister to get right to the heart of the matter. "Are you really?"

"That's an unkind thing to say." She continued to rub the baby's back with a gentle hand, but she frowned. "Our families are meant to be together when we celebrate the birth of Jesus."

"You never liked her."

"I can't lie. She makes it hard." Emma began to rock. The chair creaked on the wooden floor, a sing-song noise. It reminded him of their mudder and the hours she'd spent rocking their twin sisters, born years after Mark, two little surprises. "But I've been thinking it's likely it's not her fault."

Luke knew as much as anyone how difficult Leah could be. He also knew how loyal she was, how dutiful, how loving a mother she was. Had been. Always. "What do you mean?"

"Do you remember how Catherine acted after Mudder and Daed died?"

"How could I forget? That business with Melvin and the wedding and all the tears and silliness."

"Not silliness." Her tone was dry and stern. For a second, Luke heard their Aenti Louise in her voice. "She had a sickness. A sickness of the mind. The doctor told us as much. You didn't believe it then and you still don't believe it now, despite everything that happened."

"No, not really." He didn't like excuses for bad behavior. Their parents' deaths had been hard for them all, but God chose to take them. They went home that day after their buggy collided with a truck on a wet stretch of highway. "The rest of us got through it fine."

"We weren't fine. Not really. But we managed to get through it. Each person is different."

"I know. Some are stronger than others."

"Sickness of the mind is not a weakness anymore than sickness of the body." Her tone turned soft, soothing, as if directed at the baby in her arms. "It's arrogance on our part to think otherwise."

"Arrogance on my part you mean." He simply wanted a quiet, peaceful day of visiting. "Who are you to judge?"

"You are my brother whom I love." She

493

smiled for the first time. "I know we don't go around saying such things, but there are days, like today, when I am so thankful for what I have and for my family members, I can't contain myself. I'm sorry if it makes you uncomfortable."

Luke shifted in his chair. He gripped his hands in his lap, wishing he had a piece of wood to carve or a *Budget* to read. Wishing this conversation would end. He stood. "I need some air."

"Our minds can play tricks on us. Make us think terrible things. There are sicknesses that we can't control." She glanced at the boys. They were arguing over a move, oblivious to the adult conversation going on around them. "From what I understand, sometimes the cause is physical and medicine is needed to fix it. To fix the person's mind."

His legs weak beneath him, he sat. "What are you saying?"

"Medicine helped Catherine. She stopped being depressed. She became herself."

"She became an Englischer."

"I know. I don't understand that either, but she stopped crying. She stopped being so sad. She stopped wanting to die."

"She wanted to die?"

"Jah. She was so sad she wanted to die."

494

The agony of his frustration burned through him so fiercely, he feared he wouldn't be able to swallow the lump in his throat. It would suffocate him and he would fall at his sister's feet. "I don't understand." The words were a hoarse whisper in a voice he didn't recognize as his own. "Wasn't that enough? Weren't the deaths of Daed and Mudder enough? Now this?"

How dare he question God's plan aloud? He couldn't help himself. He raised his head and met his sister's gaze. "Haven't we suffered enough?"

She rose and laid the baby in the playpen in the corner. When she returned she sat next to him on the couch instead of the chair. "Do you remember Deacon Altman's sermon about the thorn in Paul's side?"

"I didn't sleep through his sermon, whatever you might think."

She chuckled, the sympathy in her face enough to undo him. He looked away.

"Three times he asked God to take it away. But God said His grace was sufficient."

"For His power is made perfect in weakness."

She nodded. "You *were* listening."

"You sound so much like Aenti Louise." He swallowed. That lump just kept coming back. He cleared his throat. "She was a wise woman."

"Bethel told me the same thing not long ago. It's strange — or maybe not so strange — that we find the wisdom of a particular scripture applied so often in our daily lives. We only have to pay attention." Emma relaxed against the chair, her expression serene. "Stop being so proud and go bring your fraa home."

His entire body stiffened. "Who are you to tell me what to do?"

"Were you really listening to what God said to Paul? Leah is afflicted and you're her husband. She needs you." Her somber gaze pierced him. "Do you love your fraa?"

"That's personal." She was sounding more and more like Aenti Louise. Maybe it wasn't such a compliment. He didn't like it. Not one bit. "Not your business."

"You're my bruder. It hurts me to see you in pain."

"I'm not —"

"Don't let pride keep you from doing what you need to do."

"And what is that?"

"You need to bring your fraa home."

"I can't make her come home."

"Tell her you'll take her to see a doctor. You'll take her yourself. You'll get her help."

"I can't —"

"Do you want to spend the New Year the way you're spending Christmas?"

The lump in his throat had grown to the size of an overripe watermelon. When he was sure he could get the word out, he opened his mouth. "Nee."

"Then go. I'll help Bethel. We'll keep an eye on your boys. Go bring your fraa home."

He stood. Unable to speak, he nodded. She nodded back. "Happy Christmas, Luke."

It would be when he had his family back together again. "Happy Christmas."

CHAPTER 39

Luke leaned into the van window and waved goodbye to the driver. He wasn't Michael, but he was a pleasant enough fellow who didn't expect a lot of conversation. Luke appreciated that. He'd spent most of the drive from New Hope to Bliss Creek alternating between prayer and the rehearsal of his speech in his head. He turned and faced Mattie and Abel Kurtz's neat, white, two-story house. The bitterly cold air burned his throat. His breath came in white puffs. Smoke wafted from a chimney and the familiar smell of wood burning calmed him. He went up the steps and stamped his feet to clear the snow clinging to his boots. Before he could knock, the door opened. Leah's sister Mattie smiled up at him.

"It's about time." She backed away from the door. "Come on in. It's cold out there and you're letting the heat out."

Heaving a quick breath, he did as he was told.

"Leah's upstairs putting Jebediah down for a nap." She motioned toward the sofa as she trotted toward a playpen. She picked up a squalling baby and tucked her on her hip. The baby's cries subsided. "Have a seat. I'll get her."

"How is she?" He didn't recognize his own voice. It sounded so tentative, so unsure. He cleared his throat. "Tell me how she is first."

Mattie wrinkled her nose as if thinking hard. The baby babbled something and Mattie patted her back absently. With her blue eyes and dark hair, her looks made her the most striking of the three sisters, but she never stood out, choosing to be the most self-effacing as well. She had an even keel that Luke found refreshing. "She has good days and bad days. I know she misses you something awful."

He tried not to jump on the words. "Me or the boys?"

"Of course she misses the boys, but she pines for you."

"Pines for me." He repeated the words. They sounded strange spoken aloud. He couldn't imagine Leah saying them. "Did she say so?"

"Not in so many words, but she talks about you all the time."

"She does?"

"You sound so surprised." The baby burped. Mattie grabbed a dishtowel from the coffee table and wiped spit-up from the baby's chin and on her own dress. Her placid expression didn't change. "Leah thinks of no one else but you and the children."

"She left me. She left us." The simple truth.

"Only because she's ashamed, and she's sure she's failed you as a fraa. She doesn't think you'll forgive her for that."

He had forgiven her, hadn't he? Or he would as soon as she made it right and came home. "I —"

Mattie held up a hand. "Tell her. Not me."

She ran up the stairs with a step so light she didn't make a sound. Luke sat on the edge of the sofa, hands on his knees, gripping so tight his fingers hurt. He tried to loosen them, but to no avail. He practiced breathing. His chest hurt. His lips were cracked and dry. He licked them and they burned. He studied the room, trying to find something to occupy his mind besides the thoughts that galloped about, worrying him, agitating him, shaming him. He'd prayed and now he had to accept God's will for himself and for his family. Come what may. He took a steadying breath and let it out. Come what may. *Gott?*

Minutes ticked by. Would she not come down and face him? He'd traveled all this way. Nausea made his stomach flip over. He stood and went to the fireplace to warm his hands. Perspiration beaded on his forehead and tickled as it ran down his temple. He wiped it away with the back of his hand. How could he be warm and cold at the same time?

"Luke."

He forced himself to turn from the hearth and face her. She stood at the bottom of the staircase, her face wan, brown eyes huge in her thin face. She'd lost weight, making the slight swell of her belly all the more noticeable. For once, she didn't look tired. Only sad and tentative and uncertain and angry and rebellious, all jumbled into a stew of emotion that overwhelmed Luke.

He wanted to take a step back, but he found himself pinned against the fireplace, flames leaping hot behind him, her emotions searing in front of him. The words of his speech flew from his head, leaving a curious blank space like all memory had been wiped away. Everything he'd learned

501

in school, everything Emma had said to him in her living room, everything he knew to be true. He drew a long, painful breath. "Leah."

She took two tentative steps so that she stood on the edge of the large braided rug that covered most of the wooden floor. She halted as if an invisible barrier kept her from crossing over and reaching him. "You came."

"Happy Christmas."

"Did you come all this way to wish me a happy day?"

"Nee."

She twisted her fingers together in front of her. Color had crept into her cheeks. "I got your letters."

"I received yours."

"The drawings were nice. I hung them on the wall in my room — the room I sleep in." She looked around, tilted her head as if to see behind him. "Where are the boys?"

"At home with Bethel."

The light in her face banked. "Do you want some kaffi or hot tea? I think we have some hot tea."

He couldn't take this. "I'd like to see Jebediah and the twins."

"They're napping. You can see them at supper if you stay. For now, we could . . ."

"Talk?"

"Jah. Why did you come?"

"You're my fraa." And because he loved her and missed her and wanted her in his bed at night and across from him at the table each morning at breakfast and each night at supper. Because she was the mother of his children and his best friend. "You're my fraa."

"Jah. But I haven't . . . I'm not . . . I'm not a good fraa."

Luke moved away from the fire and covered the space between them. He wanted to run. He wanted to grab her and shake her and make her see. He wanted to kiss her.

He stopped within arm's reach. "You are a good fraa."

She shook her head. Tears glistened in her eyes, but they didn't fall. "Don't lie. You have never lied. Don't start now."

Luke took off his hat and examined the brim. He tossed it on the rocking chair. He didn't have a clue. How did they bridge the cavernous gap that had grown between them in the last few months, maybe even years without him realizing it? How could he have not seen? How could he have not noticed her pain? She was the woman he'd vowed to share the rest of his life with and he hadn't even noticed her agony. She didn't need to make this right. He did. He opened his mouth. "I love you. That's the truth. That's not a lie."

Her head bowed and the tears begin to fall. Luke couldn't stand it. Every tear ripped away another piece of his heart. He couldn't stand to see her so sad. He couldn't stand to see her so alone. He had done this to her by being absent in his own home. He'd failed as a husband. He hadn't taken care of her. He'd left her to fend for herself in her despair. Remorse wrapped itself around his heart. He covered the space between them in one long stride.

"Stop. Don't." He jerked her against his chest in a rough embrace. He could feel her bones, knobby and sharp in her thinness and the swell of her belly. "I'll do whatever it takes to get you better. I'll go with you to the doctor. We'll figure it out. Everything will be better."

She sagged against him, tears coming in hot, ugly hiccupping sobs. He tightened his hold. "I've got you. Don't worry. I've got you."

She lifted her tearstained face. He lowered his head and did what he'd come to do. He kissed his fraa like a man reclaiming his life after a long, dark absence. She didn't resist. Her thin arms came up and encircled his

504

neck. He picked her up and hugged her to his chest tightly so she would understand. He would not let her go again. He would find her whenever she went into those dark places where she felt alone and sad and afraid. That's what a husband did. He'd forgotten that for a time, but he wouldn't let it happen again. Never again.

She pulled away. "I'm sorry."

"Me too."

"Forgive me?"

"Jah. Forgive me?"

"Jah."

"We'll see the doctor?"

"We'll see the doctor." He set her back on her feet and then put both hands on her stomach. He hunched down until his forehead touched hers. "We'll take care of this baby as a family."

Her hands smoothed his head with a touch so soft it felt like a feather brushing against him. He swallowed shameful tears. Her hands moved to his cheeks and lifted his head. "Let's go home, then. I want the whole family to be together on New Year's Day."

Luke couldn't wait for that New Year and its promise of a new beginning. "Let's go home, then."

But first, he kissed her again.

CHAPTER 40

Smiling, Bethel lowered herself from the buggy, her mittens sticky and wet with half melted snow. She waved her thanks to Ida, who returned the smile and waved back, blithely unaware of Bethel's frustration with her. Thanks to the older woman's staid approach to buggy driving, Bethel was too late to have a physical therapy session before group. She would barely make it to the group session. It didn't matter. Nothing would upset Bethel today. Not since she'd listened to Luke's voice recorded on the machine in the phone shack. Leah had decided to come home. They would be home on New Year's Eve. They would start the New Year together. Luke and Leah and the entire family would get that new start. Bethel turned to grab her crutches from the backseat. Her shoes slipped and she wavered, arms flung wide, and managed to right herself. Freezing rain mixed with snow overnight had made every exposed surface, from roads to sidewalks to porch steps, dangerously slick. The temperature continued to drop, with more snow in the forecast. Common sense dictated a slow pace, even if it tried her patience all the way into tomorrow.

Hanging onto the buggy with one hand, she grabbed a crutch and stuck it under her arm. Luke and Leah would get their new start, but what about her? What about Elijah? Every time she thought of Elijah's hand on her arm and his lips on her mouth, her heart fluttered like the wings of a hummingbird. As much as she might want to find her way back to another kiss, she knew it was best to avoid temptation. At least until they figured out where they stood and where they were going. She should be thankful for Ida. Without her, Bethel would be stuck at home, not here with her group for the last time before the New Year.

She struggled against a brutal northern wind that flung flakes like icy darts in her eyes and mouth where they melted against her warm skin. Her shoes slipped and slid on the slick, ice-covered sidewalk. "See you in a few hours," she called to Ida. The wind whipped the words into the air while Bethel tugged a package in a plastic bag from the backseat. "Take care on the icy roads."

"I'll be back in plenty of time." Ida was off to enjoy a nice visit with Tobias's fraa and her sister visiting from Ohio. The Daugherty farm was closer to town and Ida enjoyed using this outing as an excuse to make the rounds. Bethel would be lucky if Silas's sister remembered to return by lunchtime to pick her up. "Have a good time."

Ida obviously didn't understand what Bethel did on these trips to the rehab clinic. Using her crutches to tap her way to the door, which caught in the wind and smacked on the wall when she opened it, Bethel entered the building with a sigh of relief. She unwound her doubled-up scarf from her head, removed her wool bonnet, and straightened her kapp. Her fingers and toes ached and she couldn't feel her nose. The warm, dry air that whooshed from overhead vents seemed almost miraculous.

"If you're worrying about missing your PT session, don't." Georgia looked up from paperwork at the receptionist desk and favored Bethel with a smile. "Doctor Karen is trying to get in from a trip to St. Joe. She called and said they're shutting down the highways. She's trying to find a back road."

Bethel considered this as she laid her

package on an end table, propped her crutches against a wall, and shimmied out of her coat. She then rearranged everything in order to make the trek down the hall. "She might be better off staying where she is."

"Can't tell that woman a thing," Georgia chuckled. "When she heard her chickedees were making their way in, she became all the more determined."

Relieved that she wouldn't have to change clothes — heat or no heat, it was a chilly prospect in this weather — Bethel headed toward the group session room. Most of the chairs were still empty. Crystal grinned at her and waved while Mark tossed a *howdy* in her direction. She returned the greetings and settled into her chair, her present for Elaine in a plain white box on her lap. She'd given the group a polite no to the Christmas party planned by Doctor Jasmine, but she wanted to honor the custom of gift giving. They drew names and kept it a secret so no one knew who was getting whom a gift. In deference — Bethel suspected — to Bethel's faith and customs, Doctor Jasmine had refrained from calling it a Secret Santa gift exchange, although the others had been less circumspect.

Bethel hoped her embroidered dresser

scarf would be pleasing to Elaine. With the start of the New Year, she might not get to come anymore. Leah would need her. The news that her sister had agreed to return home filled her with relief every time she thought of it. Tomorrow they'd all be together again as a family. Bethel wiggled in her chair. She would miss seeing her group. Truth be told, with the exercise equipment, she probably couldn't justify coming here, especially with the cost. She still couldn't walk unaided and it seemed she might have to accept she never would. Doctor Karen refused to give up hope, but Bethel saw the look on her face when she studied the charts after the therapy sessions. This would be the thorn in her flesh. Like Paul. Her affliction.

As if on cue for that thought, Shawn rolled into the room, a package wrapped in bright red paper and a gold bow perched on his lap. His grin stretched across his face. He'd never mentioned his accident on Thanksgiving Day, but he still went out of his way to cross her path at every turn. She nearly tripped over him some days. His practice now was to tell her a joke every time he saw her because, he said, he liked to hear her laugh.

"Knock, knock." He pulled his chair in

next to hers, forcing Crystal to back up and adjust so their wheels didn't bang together.

"Shawn."

"You're supposed to say *Who's there?*"

"Who's the present for?" Hers looked rather drab next to his. Flashy draws attention, she reminded herself. "Didn't you go to the party?"

"Knock, knock."

"Who's there?" Crystal interceded.

"Not you." Shawn glared for a second, then gave in. "Your turn after Bethel's."

He turned to Bethel again. "Knock, knock."

"Who's there?" It couldn't hurt to humor him.

"Doris."

"Doris who?"

"Doris locked, that's why I'm knocking."

A chorus of groans filled the room. Bethel permitted herself a small giggle. He'd worked so hard, he deserved it.

"Here. This is for you." He shoved the box toward her and leaned back in his chair, a pleased look on his face. "Open it."

"Why did you —"

"I drew your name, silly."

"Actually, he bribed me to let him have your name," Crystal corrected. "I ended up with Ed. Soldier boy owes me rides wherever

511

I need them for the next six weeks."

"Hey, that was our little secret."

"Your little secret, you mean. I never agreed."

"Okay, okay." Bethel accepted the gift and set it on top of hers. "Don't bicker, children."

"I'm not a child." Shawn pretended to bristle. "I'm a grown man giving a grown woman a present."

Bethel wavered. She should give it back if he was suggesting what she thought he was suggesting.

"Just open it. I promise it's nothing bad or whatever . . . *inappropriate,* like Doctor Jasmine is always saying. I'm capable of filtering and making good choices."

Bethel hadn't seen many of those good choices, but she believed in the innate goodness of people. "Thank you for the gift."

"Open it. Open it!"

Crystal and Mark joined in the chorus. Seeing that she had no choice, Bethel picked at the tape and carefully removed the ribbon, trying to save the paper so it could be used again.

"Rip it off. Come on!"

"This is my present to open as I see fit, isn't it?"

He rolled his eyes and nodded. "Whatever."

A moment later she lifted a heavy hardback book from its nest in white tissue paper. The cover had a beautiful color photo of horses galloping across an open pasture.

"It's a book of pictures." Shawn leaned over and tapped the cover. "Pictures of Kansas. Of wheat fields and farmhouses and, you know, landscapes."

She smoothed her hand over the cover and opened to the first page. A pretty photo of sunflowers running rampant alongside a dirt road that wound its way off the page.

"It's beautiful."

"I know you folks don't take photos and there aren't any pictures of people in there. I know you don't like those graven images." He grinned, pleased at his own wisdom. "But I figured since you don't have any pictures from back home, this would give you a way to remember what it looks like."

She wanted to laugh at the way he said it, as if he was trying very hard not to express his disagreement over the graven images idea, but she was touched at how much thought he'd given to his gift. "It's so very nice of you to have thought of this." She turned the page to a sweeping vista of rows and rows of cornstalks backlit by a sun sinking on the horizon. "I will treasure it."

"Good." He turned and gave Crystal a high five followed by a fist bump. "Told you so."

Crystal returned the gesture. "You so nailed it, dude."

"I wonder where Doctor Karen is." Mark sucked in air, making his machine burble. "I'm supposed to go to PT after group."

"All of us are in that boat." Crystal shrugged. "Except Miss Conservative over here who does her therapy at the crack of dawn so no one will see her."

All gazes turned on Bethel. Before she could share what Georgia had told her, Doctor Jasmine bustled into the room, her usually smiling face creased with worry. "I don't think the rest will make it today. I've been listening to the radio in the PT room. That storm they've been talking about — it hit early. They're shutting down the highways all over the state. Doctor Karen was driving in from St. Joe. I don't think she can get through."

"So we should blow off the session and head home?" Crystal sounded disappointed. Apparently she liked PT more than she let on. "We won't be coming back until next year."

"Next year is only two days away," Shawn

514

pointed out. "You can live without PT that long, can't you?"

"Be nice, Shawn." Doctor Jasmine set the portable radio on an empty chair and fiddled with some knobs. "Holidays are especially hard for a lot of folks."

"Did they teach you that in touchy-feeling school?" His mocking tone took the sting out of the words. "Should we have a group hug now?"

"Don't tempt me." Doctor Jasmine turned up the volume on the weather report. "From what I heard, the snow is coming down so hard now and the wind is so bad, it's a whiteout."

"A whiteout?" Bethel wasn't familiar with term. "Like a blizzard."

"In other words, you can't see your hand in front of your face out there." Shawn settled back in his chair. "I guess we'll be hanging out together until it passes."

Bethel chewed her lip. She hoped Ida stayed put at the Daugherties. Even with the battery-operated heater, a buggy ride in the winter was cold enough without blizzard conditions. And the older woman wasn't familiar enough with the roads to find her way in low visibility. *Gott, keep her where she is.* Even if that meant Bethel stayed here at the clinic with Shawn. And the others.

What was the worst that could happen? They could make hot chocolate in the break room and have some of the snacks the staff made sure were kept handy for the people after their hard work in the PT room. She would consider it a simple, extended, last session.

"We'll be fine," Doctor Jasmine said as if in agreement with Bethel's unspoken thoughts. "Who wants hot chocolate?"

"I do —"

The room went dark.

Elijah sopped up the last of the savory brown gravy with a ragged chunk of bread. He stuck it in his mouth fast, but the gravy still dripped down his fingers and onto the tablecloth. He looked up to see Katie shaking her head. She handed him a fresh napkin.

"Some example you set."

"It's mighty good gravy. Lots of beef flavor." He grinned. "Besides, cold weather makes me extra hungry. And this pot roast was extra good." He elbowed William, who sat next to him at the Christner table. "Besides, we worked up a powerful hunger throwing snowballs and skating before the snow picked up. Didn't we?"

516

William nodded, but didn't talk. His mouth was full of mashed potatoes.

"Weren't Ida and Bethel supposed to be here to eat with us?" Joseph didn't have a handle on manners the way his brother William did. His words were muffled by a mouthful of beets. "She said she would bring us some elephant ears from the bakery."

Elijah considered. He'd taken a few hours after the daily chores to carouse with the kinner at the pond and had lost track of the time. Ida and Bethel were to come here after the trip into town so they could pick up the boys and take them home after the noon meal. Then he'd get back to mending tack in the barn. "It's probably taking them a little longer because of the snow."

He dropped his napkin next to his plate and stood. Something in Silas's gaze made him follow his brother into the kitchen, leaving the boys to chatter with their cousins. "What is it?"

Silas nodded toward the window over the sink. "Look out there."

Elijah moved to join him. He couldn't see anything. Just white. After all the chatter and laughter at the table, the kitchen seemed quiet. The house creaked and groaned. Wind whistled through the eaves.

Pellets of snow pinged against the window's glass. "The storm came early."

"Yep. A blizzard."

"On top of the sleet we had overnight. The roads are a mess out there, I imagine. Ida and Bethel should be here by now."

"Maybe they stayed in town once they saw how bad the storm was getting." Silas's expression didn't match his optimistic words. "Surely they knew better than to start for home."

"What if they thought they could beat the storm and took off before it got really bad?"

"Then why aren't they here?"

"It would be slow going." Elijah didn't want to think about just how slow the going would be. Best to think positive. And pray. "They'll be here in time."

"Right. They'll be here in time."

An hour later, his head tired from so much praying, Elijah paced the floor in front of the fireplace, trying to decide how much longer the trip would take in these conditions.

Silas sat reading his Bible, his wire-rimmed bifocals perched on the tip of his nose. "Stop pacing. I'm trying to get into the right frame of mind for the prayer service Sunday."

"What if they got lost?" He did as his

518

brother commanded, but his mind continued to wrestle with worry no matter how hard he insisted that Bethel and Ida were in God's capable hands. "The roads are icy. What if they slid off and are stuck in the ditch?"

"What if they're in town, waiting for the storm to pass?"

"If they're in trouble and we wait too long, they'll freeze to death out there." Saying the words aloud made it all the worse. "We need to look for them."

Silas closed the Bible and laid it gently on the end table. "If we go out there, we may end up lost or in a ditch as well."

"That's a chance I'm willing to take. I'm going." Elijah marched to the door and snagged his coat from the hook.

"Then I'm going with you." Silas removed his glasses and stood. "I don't need you getting lost out there too."

"No, you go to the phone shack and see if you can get through to the sheriff's office. Maybe he knows something. Or he can use one of those snow pushers and go look for them."

"Are you taking the buggy or going on horseback?"

Elijah considered. "Better the buggy for some shelter from the wind and snow."

"Best wear your long johns."

It took another half hour to don their warmest clothes and then string a guide rope from the house to the barn. Silas gave Katie strict instructions to keep everyone in the house, but he strung a rope from the house to the woodshed in case they were gone so long more firewood was needed. Katie heated the warming stones in the oven and wrapped them in towels for both men to stick under their feet on the floor boards. They threw blankets on the seats for added warmth and said their goodbyes.

"Take this." Katie handed them each a tall thermos. "Hot kaffi."

She looked as if she might say more but instead opened the door. The wind nearly took it from its hinges. They trekked through and together managed to slam it shut. Bent against the fury of the storm, Elijah trudged down the porch steps. He looked back and saw Katie peering though the window, her worry evident in her face. He waved. She waved back and disappeared from view.

Silas took off for the Shirack farm while Elijah headed the other direction. In addition to the battery-operated lights, he'd stuck flashlights in the front of the buggy in hopes oncoming traffic wouldn't veer into him. He was so swathed in woolen scarves and coats he could barely raise his arms to snap the reins. It only took him a few minutes to realize his preparations did little to insulate him from the piercing wind. Snow crusted on the scarves around his mouth and eyes, his lips turned icy, then numb. He could only imagine how Ida and Bethel were faring if they'd ventured out into this whirling mass of furious snow. They weren't prepared for such an on-slaught of wind. The thought propelled him past the stop sign and onto the highway.

He peered to the left and to the right, seeking some sign of life. If they were out here on the side of the road, he would never see them. "Bethel? Bethel! Ida!" He shouted the names, but the wind whipped the words away and lifted them uselessly into the gray sky. They wouldn't hear him but he couldn't give up. "Bethel! Ida!"

Nothing. Only howling wind and his own ragged, painful breathing. He struggled to see some landmark that would tell him where he was, trying to figure out how far he'd come. The snow obscured the surface, but he was sure he was still on the highway. He should be at the turn that would take him into town by now. He could no longer feel his feet, the heat of the warming stone long gone.

If Ida and Bethel were out here, they were freezing to death. He couldn't let that happen. He had to help his sister-in-law and the woman he loved.

After a second he remembered to shut his mouth, wet with frozen flakes that burned his lips and tongue with cold. He replayed the thought in his head. The woman he loved. He did love Bethel. He didn't care about her legs or whether she could bear children. He loved her.

He had to find her. He had to tell her. "Giddy-up, giddy-up, girl, let's go. We have to find them!"

He doubted even Daisy could hear his voice, but the horse would feel the pressure of the bit in her mouth and the halter on her long head and the reins on her back. They were connected by touch and feel. Could the horse feel his desperation? They picked up speed. Maybe she could.

Where was the flashing yellow light that signaled the last turn before town? He couldn't see it. He couldn't see anything. The day had turned to night. He snapped the reins and urged Daisy forward. *There.* The yellow light flashed, encouraging him on, telling him he hadn't strayed from the path. He was getting close. He had no idea if there were oncoming cars turning onto the highway at the intersection. He couldn't see beyond Daisy's nose.

With a breathed prayer for their safety, he made the turn. The wind buffeted the buggy. The wheels slid. The buggy rocked. Elijah tugged on the reins, fighting to regain control.

They skidded to the right, then the left. By then he had no idea where the right lane was. He could be in the center of the road. He prayed there were no oncoming cars.

Daisy reared her head and whinnied. They were moving too fast. Elijah pulled harder on the reins. The buggy bucked and whipped back and forth, back and forth. The horse screamed.

The buggy slid down and down. They were going down.

The buggy tipped and rolled. Rolled and rolled.

Elijah dropped the reins and grabbed for the arm railing, but it was gone. He sailed free for a few seconds as he breathed a prayer. *Lord, don't let this happen to Ida and Bethel. Please Lord, protect them and keep them safe.*

Something hard smacked him in the forehead. The pain radiated swift and fierce. And then gone in a blessed nothingness.

He couldn't feel his hands or his feet. Maybe that was a good thing. Compared to the agonizing sledgehammer pounding in his head, numbness could be counted as a blessing.

Elijah tried to open his eyes. They seemed to be crusted shut. If his fingers would cooperate, he would wipe at them. He raised arms that weighed a hundred pounds each.

His fingers swiped at his face and missed. He tried again. Connected. Snow.

He brushed the best he could. Flakes flew. His fingers touched his forehead.

Bad. Bad move.

He wanted to curl up with the pain of it, but he couldn't move. A wheel held his legs to the ground. Where was the horse? He peered between the spokes. He couldn't see through the blowing snow. He couldn't hear anything above the howling wind.

"Ach. Ach. Ach." The syllables rang weak and hoarse in his ears. He had to do better. "Get yourself up and get moving. Now. If you have to walk, walk."

His voice reverberated in his ears. It sounded hollow. He managed to raise his head and look up. The bed of the buggy loomed over him. The aching cold beneath him, threatening to suck all the warmth from his body, would be a bed of snow. A bed where he could close his eyes and sleep.

The thought came naturally. Drowsiness assailed him. To close his eyes and sleep would be a blessing. No more pain. No more thought.

His body started, muscles tight in spasms. Nee. He couldn't stay here. He had to get up. He had to find Bethel.

"Bethel." His voice gained strength. "I'm coming."

He strained to lift himself. Something warm trickled down his forehead. He raised his hand again. His glove came away stained red. The pain bloomed so fierce his stomach clenched with nausea. Ignoring it, he shoved hard on the wheel. The buggy shimmied and then lurched to one side. *Breathe. Breathe.* He rolled and scrambled to his knees. More jagged, fierce pain, this time in the leg that had been pinned under the wheel. He couldn't stand on it. *"Ach."*

He sank back to the snowy bed, welcoming its softness under his bruised body. He breathed in and out, in and out. He'd rest another minute or two, then try again. The cold didn't seem so cold anymore. Maybe the storm had ended. Maybe now it would start to warm up.

Don't sleep. Don't sleep. Bethel. Don't sleep.

The minutes ticked by, banging inside his head. The pain waned, dissipating in a blessed numbness that could only mean he would soon freeze to death. *Gott, if this is the way I'm to go, so be it. Please keep Bethel and Ida safe. Watch over them. Please watch over them.*

He mumbled the prayer again and again, making every word count as if it might be his last.

"Elijah Christner? Mr. Christner!"

The gruff tone of a man used to being answered when he called pierced the thick wooliness that had wrapped itself around Elijah's brain, thicker with each passing second. "Mr. Christner!"

He raised his head. "Here. Here!"

The sheriff tromped through the snow in boots up to his knees, the beam of a flashlight crowding Elijah. He tried to move, but found his legs no longer responded to his commands. "Sheriff."

"You look frozen to death." Sheriff Mc-Cormack knelt beside him. "Let's get you up and out of here."

"We have to find Bethel. Bethel and Ida. They're out here."

The sheriff stuck his hands under Elijah's

526

arms and dragged him to his feet. Elijah tried to cooperate. Pain swirled around him in a nauseating pulse. "Bethel."

"Yeah, we'll get to Bethel, but you first."

"Bethel. She's out here."

"You're delirious. No one's out here. I've spent the last hour combing these roads. You're it."

"Bethel!"

"Okay. Okay, buddy. We'll find Bethel."

Hearing those words, Elijah sank into a welcome oblivion.

CHAPTER 41

Bethel breathed on the glass in the clinic's front door and rubbed a circle with her fingers. The glass felt icy to the touch. The whiteness outside the rehab clinic might as well have been darkness. She couldn't see a thing. Inside the clinic, it was almost as dark. Georgia had disappeared into the interior, where it was warmer, leaving Bethel in charge of the front door. Still, she knew full well no one would be arriving in this blizzard. She tugged the blanket that Jasmine had laid across her shoulders tighter. Even with her coat, shawl, and the blanket, she still felt a chill as the heat continued to seep from the airy rooms with high ceilings and dozens of windows. Unlike the hospital, the building had no backup generator. Jasmine said hospital administrators hadn't deemed it necessary because it wasn't a twenty-four hour facility with critical care patients.

"Maybe we could try to get to the hospital. It would be warm there and there's a cafeteria, hot coffee, and beds to sleep in."

Bethel turned from the window to find Shawn wheeling down the hallway, a battery-operated lantern dangling from his bent fingers. He set it on the coffee table in the reception area.

"I told Jasmine I'd lead the way. She tried to call them to see if they could send an ambulance or something to get us, but the phone is down here and her cell phone has no bars. What good is a cell phone if you can't use it in an emergency?"

"It's at least six blocks from here. We'd have to walk and I'm afraid we'd get lost. I'm not sure it's smart to go anywhere." Bethel didn't know anything about bars on a phone, but she assumed no bars was a bad thing from Shawn's frustrated tone. She hobbled toward the table, the light from the lantern drawing her as if she might gather warmth from it. "Anyway, a storm like this can't last long, can it?"

Shawn shrugged. "I've never seen anything like this and I've lived here all my life."

"We had some bad storms in Kansas, but I don't remember anything this bad." She cast her memories back to the days when her mudder used to send the boys for piles

529

of wood for the kitchen stove and the fireplace. They'd gather round and make popcorn and cocoa in big pots on the stove. Good memories. Not like the ones they were making in a cold, drafty building. "I always liked winter nights when we were all together by the fire. Daed read his Bible and Mudder sewed and we played games."

"Yeah, you were used to not having electricity. You geared up for it." Shawn contemplated the lantern. "The bedrooms must've been mighty cold."

"That's why we stayed downstairs, together, by the fire." She placed the good memories back in that special place she kept them, in front of the more difficult ones from the years of Mudder's sickness and Daed's silent withdrawal into his work of keeping food on the table and a roof over their heads. "We didn't go upstairs until the last minute and then we took hot water bottles for our feet and burrowed under tons of blankets and quilts. Once we got warm, it was quite toasty."

"How many brothers and sisters do you have?"

"Three brothers. Two sisters. All older."

"Wow." His expression turned wistful. "I'm an only child."

Which explained some things. "That's

hard for me to imagine."

"It has its good points and bad."

"Like what?"

"Like you never have to share your candy and you get all the presents at Christmas, but it also means they put all their hopes and dreams on your shoulders and expect you to do whatever it is they wanted to do and didn't accomplish."

She considered. Plain families with one child were unusual, but it did happen. It didn't matter. They all wished the same for their children, that they be baptized into the Amish faith and live their lives with their families and community. Simple expectations. But there were some who couldn't meet them, drawn as they were into a world different from their own. "Your daed loves you."

Shawn gave her a lopsided grin. "I know."

"Not everyone gets to have that. I have good friends whose parents both died in a buggy accident, leaving them to raise their little brothers and sisters."

"That stinks."

"Their parents are with God."

"Does that make them feel better?"

"Yes, it does. They still miss them, but they take comfort in God's plan for them."

Shawn stared up at her. "What's God's

plan for you?"

"There's no way for me to know that. I only know He has one."

"And it doesn't include me."

Bethel searched her heart. She examined her feelings, all jumbled up for so long. They milled around in her head, and then righted themselves into straight, even lines.

"It's okay. That long pause says it all." He tugged on the chair's wheels and turned away.

"You'll always be my friend."

He stopped, his back to her. After a few seconds he wheeled around. His smile, if forlorn, still qualified as a smile. "As much as an Amish girl can have a guy like me for a friend, right? I'll take it. I'd be a fool not to want your friendship."

They stared at each other. "Doctor Jasmine's raiding the snack horde Doctor Karen keeps in her office and apparently there's protein bars and nasty healthy stuff in the storeroom." His tone sounded determinedly cheerful. "I knew I should've eaten breakfast this morning. I was in such a hurry to get here to see . . ."

His voice trailed away.

"How are the others doing?" Determined to move the conversation away from dangerous grounds, she smiled at him. "Do we have enough blankets?"

He nodded, his somber eyes unblinking and so knowing. "They're fine. Crystal's cranky, but she's always cranky. Elaine is worried about her kids. She can't get any reception on her cell phone. Neither can I, for that matter. And Ed is napping. He says it's nothing to get excited about."

"At his age, he is the voice of experience." Bethel picked up the lantern. "We should stay together."

"Huddle together for warmth, you mean?" His expression brightened at the thought. "I like the way you think."

"That's not what I meant at all and you know it. I only meant for moral support —"

"I knew what you meant." He wheeled closer. "I just want you to know I've stayed away from the booze and pills since Thanksgiving Day. No more drowning my sorrows."

"Good. That's good."

"I like to give you a hard time and I like talking to you, but I would never do anything to you know, to get you into trouble."

"Do you understand why we can't date?" She stumbled for words he would understand. "Like boyfriend and girlfriend."

"I do. And I don't want to ruin any chance of us being friends by being stupid."

"You're not stupid."

"And you're too nice to ever put me in my place the way you should. I'm thinking that gets you into trouble with your family and I don't want that."

An emotion Bethel couldn't identify touched her. Relief. A tinge of sadness. Yes, she felt sad. She would concede that. But also a sense that they had moved to a place where they could really be friends, as much as was possible for a Plain woman and an Englisch man.

"*Gut.* That's *gut.* We can be friends, and then maybe other folks in New Hope will think more kindly of us too."

"We all like you." Crystal rolled down the hallway to the foyer, moving faster than she should, as usual. Georgia followed, wearing a long green coat that made her look like a big cucumber. "I told my parents I think you're really cool. All you bonnet folks."

"Me too." Mark rolled right behind Georgia, like a parade. "I'm sorry I acted like a jerk when you first got here."

"You didn't act like a jerk."

"Yes, I did. I said stupid stuff."

"Maybe a little."

An awkward silence ensued. Georgia patted Crystal's shoulder and started toward her desk. "Look at you guys. Doctor Jasmine will be so proud. Your support group thing is really working."

"I'm still calling you darlin', Bethel. I don't care what anyone says," Shawn broke in with his usual bravado. "And I'm inviting your family to come to a barbecue at my house one of these days."

Bethel laughed. "Now wouldn't that be interesting? I think —"

The double doors swung open and Sheriff McCormack stumbled in, dragging with him Elijah. His head lolled to one side, eyes shut. "I need some help here." He gasped for breath. "He's half frozen to death."

CHAPTER 42

Bethel dropped her crutches on the clinic's tile floor. Sheriff McCormack disappeared from her sight. Her gaze honed in on Elijah's still, white face and his limp body. She launched herself toward him. He couldn't be gone. He couldn't be. They hadn't begun yet. They didn't have their new start. "Elijah! Elijah, please!"

"He's not dead, just hypothermic." Sheriff McCormack's gruff voice penetrated her fear. "And he may have a broken leg. I didn't take the time to find out."

Bethel grabbed Elijah's free arm and helped the sheriff ease him to the floor. With a grunt he dropped to one knee, unfurled his scarf, balled it up, and stuck it under Elijah's head. "He may have some frostbite. He definitely took a blow to the head — probably when the buggy went cup over teakettle into the drainage ditch. We need blankets. We need to warm him up."

Bethel tugged a wet glove from Elijah's hand and gripped it between her own warm ones as Georgia whipped around the counter and scurried down the hallway. Elijah's eyelids fluttered and then closed again. His skin looked white and waxy. A nasty red and purple lump swelled on his forehead. He groaned and mumbled something she couldn't understand. She glared up at Sheriff McCormack. "Why didn't you take him to the hospital?"

"Because I got here first and because he insisted from the second I pulled him from under the buggy that he needed to find you. He seemed to think you were dying or something." Sheriff McCormack sneezed into the crook of his arm. He wiped his face on the sleeve of his coat. "I couldn't see anything through the windshield. Nothing. There could've been a semi in the intersection and I wouldn't have known until I hit it. Plus he kept saying your name over and over again. I tried to talk to him and he mumbled something about the clinic. The guy who called me —"

"Someone called you?"

Sheriff McCormack looked beyond her. He didn't answer. She swiveled to follow his gaze. Shawn stared at the sheriff. Neither spoke.

"Sheriff, please."

Sheriff McCormack shoved his hood back, revealing a stocking hat pulled down over his hair almost to his eyebrows. "I got a call from Silas Christner."

"Silas called you?"

"Do you want me to tell the story or do you want to keep interrupting?"

"Tell us."

"He called and said his brother Elijah had gone to look for you and his sister-in-law Ida. They were worried because you hadn't come home yet, and they were afraid you'd started out from town and gotten caught in the storm."

Elijah had put himself in danger in order to find her. To rescue her. It was so like Elijah to come galloping to her rescue, even if she didn't need it. Because he cared. He cared for her enough to risk everything. "I was here the whole time." She swallowed back tears at the thought. He'd risked his life for her and she'd been safe and warm. She breathed through the ache in her throat. "I'm sure Ida stayed with the Daugherties."

"I told him you didn't seem stupid enough to do something like that. They apparently don't give you enough credit. You're smarter than this here idiot —"

"He's not an idiot. I'm sure he was just
—"

Elijah groaned again. His arms flailed. Bethel caught his other hand and hung on. "It's all right. We'll get you warmed up in no time. I'm here."

He thrashed about, his free hand nearly connecting with her cheek. "Bethel. I need to find Bethel."

"It's okay, I'm here. You found me. It's okay."

"She's out there. She's cold. So cold." His entire body convulsed in shivers. "I can't find her. She'll die out there before I have a chance to tell her I love her."

Bethel stopped, her hand suspended in air. Everything came to a halt around her. She heard someone say something, but the words were far away, in a distance place. She leaned over Elijah, rubbing his hand. "What did you say?"

"He's delirious," said Sheriff McCormack. "It happens with hypothermia. He's got all the symptoms — shivering, confusion, slurred speech, fumbling hands."

Elijah had said he loved her. Delirious? "It's okay. I'm here, Elijah. The sheriff found me. I'm not going to die. I'm right here."

His hands fumbled until they found hers.

His eyes opened. "Is it you?"

"It's me."

His eyes closed again and he sank back to the floor. "Thank You, Gott, thank You."

She ripped her blanket from her shoulders and laid it over him, tucking it up under his chin. "Elijah, stay awake. Stay awake." Her heart pounded with the fear that she might lose him before she'd ever really had him. She scrambled to her feet, swaying without her crutches. "We need to get him into the back rooms. It's warmer there. I'm sure Doctor Jasmine has medical supplies —"

"The break room is the warmest room in the building." Doctor Jasmine bustled down the hallway ahead of Georgia. "I have extra blankets. We can run some tepid water and stick his feet in it. I wish we had some way to heat coffee or hot chocolate."

"I have the thermos of coffee I brought with me this morning in the car." Sheriff McCormack struggled to his feet, his knees cracking, and pulled his hood back over his head. "I have a little Coleman stove in the trunk too."

"Always prepared." Shawn's tone didn't make it sound like a compliment. "That's my pops."

"Some things a guy can't prepare for." Sheriff McCormack's jaw jutted out.

"Sometimes it takes a guy a bit to adjust to some things. You know, to figure out it's something he can't fix."

"Yeah. Well."

"What are we talking about?" Mark asked, his face bewildered.

"Nothing. Let's get him back to the back and I'll go for the thermos."

"What about his leg?" Bethel took the crutches Doctor Jasmine thrust at her. "Should we splint it before we move him?"

"How do you know about this stuff?" Shawn didn't look surprised, only curious. "You were a teacher."

"We do a lot of our own doctoring. My brothers had plenty of broken bones. Life on the farm, and all."

Doctor Jasmine squatted and examined Elijah's leg with quick efficiency. "It's his ankle. I can't tell much without an X-ray. Right now, it's most important to get him warm and to do that, we need to move him."

"We'll get him." Sheriff McCormack directed his statement to Bethel. "You lead the way."

In a strange procession, the folks in the wheelchairs led the way with the lanterns. Bethel followed on her crutches, and Elijah came next, propped between Doctor Jasmine and Sheriff McCormack.

In the break room, Doctor Jasmine pulled open one of several cots she'd found in the storage room along with boxes of granola bars, energy drinks, bottled water, and dozens of packages of peanut butter crackers. "Put him here," she directed. "I've got plenty of blankets. I wish we had heat packs, but we'll have to make do."

She brushed Elijah's hair from his forehead and studied the massive, angry red knot. "Didn't break the skin. He'll have a doozy of a headache." Next, she examined his hands. His fingers were the same waxy white as his face. "Bethel, get his boots."

"Pardon me?" Bethel gripped her hands in front of her, uncertain. "What do you mean?"

"Get with the program, girl. Take his boots off. We have to see if he has frostbite." Doctor Jasmine looked up, her face full of concern. "Sheriff, how long do you think he was out there?"

Bethel took a deep breath. Never in her wildest imagination had she pictured herself removing a piece of clothing, not even shoes, from a man.

"Bethel, do you want me to do it?" Crystal put her hand, with its rings on every finger and tiny butterfly tattoos flitting across the back, on the weather-beaten leather boot, wet with melting snow. "You don't look so good."

"No, no, I can do it." She would help Elijah just as he always helped her. "I should do it. He's my . . ."

"Give her some room, why don't you?" Shawn wheeled back. "Come on, everybody. Doctor Jasmine knows what she's doing and he's Bethel's friend."

Bethel tugged at the boot on his good leg. It was wet and cold and muddy. She couldn't get it off. She tugged harder. Elijah's leg jerked and his foot kicked. She held on tight and pulled hard, nearly going down in a heap when it came off in one abrupt slide.

"His socks, too." Doctor Jasmine's tone made it an order. "They need to come off."

Bethel swallowed hard and peeled away two pairs of black socks with their darned stitches on both heels. Katie took good care of her brother-in-law. Just as Bethel would from now on.

Doctor Jasmine examined his feet, which looked white and vulnerable sticking out from his black pants. They shouldn't see him like this. They shouldn't look at his bare feet. She moved so she stood between him and Crystal and the others.

"I don't think he has frostbite. The wool

socks and heavy boots were enough." Jasmine replaced the socks. "I'll use an ace bandage on the ankle until we get some help. How long do you think he was out there, Sheriff?"

"I have no idea. I found his buggy overturned in the drainage ditch just past the last turnoff north of town." Sheriff McCormack slapped his gloves back on. "I had to let the horse go. I didn't want to waste time getting this fellow into town. I'm hoping he found his way home."

Bethel hoped so too, for the animal's sake, but also for the Christners. They'd already lost one since moving to New Hope.

"How long after you got the call?" Doctor Jasmine persisted.

"Maybe an hour and a half. It was slow going out there. I was afraid to go more than a few miles an hour for fear I'd hit something that I couldn't see or start sliding around on the ice and end up in a ditch." The sheriff shifted on his wet boots. "I'll get the thermos. Could I have a second with you, Miss Bethel?"

Surprised, Bethel wavered. She didn't want to leave Elijah. "I can't —"

"Just one second. Please."

Trying to ignore the curious looks on everyone's faces — except Shawn, who looked suspicious and a little mad — she hobbled to the hallway. Sheriff McCormack shifted from one foot to the other. He removed the stocking cap and clutched it in his hands. His hair stood up all over his head in ruffled tuffs like weeds in an overgrown field.

"What is it, Sheriff? I don't want to leave Elijah right now." She didn't want to be rude either. This man held a lot of power in New Hope. She wanted him on their side. "We need the hot coffee from the thermos and your travel stove."

"I'll get right to that, ma'am. First, I wanted you to give a message to your brother. Luke is your brother, right?".

"Brother-in-law."

"Yeah, well, tell him I'm sorry." The sheriff shifted from foot to foot, his boots making squelching sounds on the tile. "Real sorry."

"Sorry? You don't have anything to be sorry for."

"Sure I do. I never tried to make y'all feel welcome." He wadded the stocking cap into a ball and stuck it into the pocket of his enormous down jacket. "More than that, I tried to run you off."

"We don't hold that against you. We figure it takes time to get used to new people."

"It does, but there's no call for ugliness.

Not when y'all been nothing but pleasant. You been nice to my boy, nicer than I have been, and your brother-in-law took it upon himself to be good to the Doolittle boy and his friends."

"You knew about that?"

"I'm the sheriff. I get paid to keep my ear to the ground. After everything the kids around here have done to y'all, Luke showed them kindness. It takes a certain kind of person to do that."

"We believe in forgiveness."

"That's some serious forgiveness." Wistfulness stole across his craggy, wind-whipped face. "I'd like to get me some of that."

"You mean from Shawn."

"Yeah, Shawn." He ducked his head. "And his mother."

"He's here now." Sometimes what was right in front of a person's face had to be seen from another perspective. "He wants to talk to you. I know he does."

"I don't know. There's a lot of water under the bridge. A lot of stupid words."

"He's not going anywhere. He can't. Maybe this storm, this blizzard, happened for a reason." God's plan. God's hand moving over them. Not just Shawn and his father, but Elijah and her. Could that be? She needed to get to Elijah. She needed to

546

tell him how she felt. "It's a good time to back him in a corner and tell him what's on your mind."

"You think?"

For everyone involved. "I do."

"Bethel. Bethel!" Elijah's hoarse groan startled them both. "Bethel!"

"I have to go." Elijah needed her. He needed her. "Get the thermos, please."

Her heart banging in her chest, she fumbled with her crutches with shaking hands. One fell to the floor. The sheriff swooped down and grabbed it before she could. "Thank you," he said. "For being so forgiving."

"That's what we do. It's the right thing to do." She took the crutch and struggled back to the door. "I have to go. Elijah, I'm right here. I'm right here."

The group clustered at the foot of the cot parted so she could get through. She dropped the crutches and knelt next to him. "I'm right here."

His eyelids fluttered, then opened. "There you are. I thought I'd lost you."

"I'm right here and I'm not leaving you. Not for anything. Not for anyone." She tucked his icy hand in hers and began to rub. "You found me. You don't have to worry anymore."

His fingers clutched at hers. "Marry me."
Silence.

"Everybody out." Doctor Jasmine stood and pointed to the door. "Everybody but Bethel."

Bethel waited, mouth open, as the others filed from the room. Shawn gave her a diffident smile as he went out the door, the last to leave. She tried to smile back, but her lips were frozen.

Doctor Jasmine piled another blanket on Elijah. "I think there's a pillow in Doctor Karen's office. She naps on her couch sometimes. I'll be right back. Stay close to him."

No problem there. She would never let go of Elijah's hand. Certain her face was as red as the petals of the Christmas poinsettias on the break room table, Bethel managed a nod.

She waited until Doctor Jasmine left the room. "Elijah? Can you hear me?"

"Will you marry me?"

"Open your eyes and look at me."

One eyelid popped open. Then the other. His eyes were bloodshot, the blue bright against the red. "You know, if I had a beard my chin would be a lot warmer."

A giggle burbled up inside her. "You're delirious."

548

His body convulsed with shivers. "I can't get warm."

"I know. Jasmine says it will take a while for your body to warm up."

"The parts I can feel hurt." He gasped. The shivering intensified. "Why can't I feel my fingers and my feet? That's bad, isn't it?"

"Jasmine says we caught it in time. The feeling will come back. We need to keep you warm and put your feet in tepid water. It'll prickle for a while, but you'll mend." She wanted more than anything to wrap her arms around him, to warm him. She didn't have that right, not yet. "I'm sorry this happened. You should've stayed at the farm."

"I couldn't stand the thought of you . . ." He closed his eyes. His breathing grew more ragged. "This could've been you."

"And Ida."

He coughed. "And Ida. Do you think she's all right? I couldn't get to her either." He struggled to sit up. "We need to look for her."

"Ida didn't come for me because she knew better. She stayed where she was. You don't give the women in your life enough credit." She pushed him back on the cot. "You need to rest."

"I want an answer to my question first."

It hadn't been a question. It had been a command. Born of disorientation and delirium. "You're delirious."

"With love."

"That's the silliest thing I've ever heard you say." And there had been plenty in the last several months. She tried her best to make light of it. Her heart needed to stop beating so quickly. It might burst from her chest otherwise. "An Englischer I might expect that from, but a Plain man?"

"I love you and I want you to marry me." He paused, his breathing harsh. "Silas is giving me seventy-five acres on the other side of the creek. I've already picked the spot where we'll build our house."

The words rained down on her, washing away doubts and fears and uncertainties. He wanted to build a house with her. He wanted to build a life with her. She ached to say yes. Still, she had to make sure he understood what he was getting. Was he willing to risk being tied to a woman in her condition? "I don't think I'm getting any better. I can stand, but I can't walk. Even after months of therapy. And I know you want children."

His eyes stayed open this time. His gaze fastened on her face as his hand clutched hers. "Take it on faith. Take it all on faith.

That's what I plan to do."

He was willing to risk it all. How could she not do the same? "I will marry you."

A whoop went up in the hallway. Clapping rang out, along with pounding on the wall. "Wahoo! Yeah!" Her friends' voices joined in a chorus that filled the room.

They had an audience, it seemed — one that didn't mind letting them know the entire conversation had been heard.

"Eavesdroppers!" Bethel smiled down at Elijah. "Hush up out there!"

Elijah tugged her toward him. "I want to make sure you don't change your mind."

She leaned down until their noses nearly touched. His eyes were so blue and so intent. They closed and he tugged her down until the gap closed. Their lips touched, and this time he didn't pull away. His lips were cold. She touched his cheeks with her hands, trying to warm him. His fingers covered hers. The kiss deepened, full of promise. When she finally pulled away, he smiled up at her. "I'm feeling warmer. How about you?"

"Elijah!"

"I hear the patient is feeling better." Doctor Jasmine marched into the room, a pillow tucked under one arm. Behind her, Crystal's head bobbed around the corner.

"The guys want to know if they can come in for a second. They want to congratulate you."

"Yes."

Bethel started to remove her hand from Elijah's, but his grip tightened, refusing to let her go.

A Coleman stove in her lap, Crystal led the procession. Elaine brought up the rear, Ed leaning on her arm.

"We just wanted to say congrats." Crystal set the stove on the table. "We'll throw you a shower and invite the whole town. Everyone in New Hope will want to come. You're the best, Bethel. You're so nice to us, even when we weren't nice to you. So congrats and all."

"Yeah, what she said." Mark chimed in. "Way to go. We want to come to the wedding."

"Yeah, can we come to the wedding?"

They had no idea what they were asking. Bethel warmed at their enthusiasm and their kindness. "You might not want to sit through three hours of German, but for sure, you're invited to the food and fun afterwards."

"Cool," Crystal and Mark chorused.

"Congratulations," Elaine said, her tone prim, after the raucous noise of her fellow patients died down. She held out a thermos. "Sheriff McCormack asked me to give it to you."

"Where did he go?" Bethel tilted her head, trying to see around Elaine. "Where's Shawn?"

"In the group therapy room." Mark shot a fist in the air and pumped it like the winner of a race. "He and his dad are talking. His dad pushed his chair right into the room and shut the door."

"Hallelujah!" Doctor Jasmine trotted over to give Mark a fist bump. "Best news ever, second to the pending nuptials here."

"Best news ever," Bethel repeated. Shawn would get his new start too. She squeezed Elijah's hand. "All in God's time."

"Amen." He squeezed back. His hand began to warm in hers. "Amen."

EPILOGUE

Bethel clasped her hands in her lap and waited. She didn't look to her left, knowing that Elijah sat on the other side of the Shiracks' front room, flanked by his brothers. If she looked at him, she might not be able to contain the desire to struggle to her feet and tell Luke to hurry up. She wanted to be married to Elijah now. Despite the crush of people squeezed into Luke and Leah's house, she felt no nerves, only a sort of breathless anticipation. Her wedding day had dawned clear and cold, the air crisp and light and full of promise. Someone had opened a window to allow the cool air to dissipate the warmth of so many people crammed into the house. The aroma of roasted chicken and stuffing and gravy mingled with the cakes and breads that awaited them after the service. The smells reminded her of the many, many weddings she attended over the years, always thinking her day would come. When it hadn't, she had struggled to accept Gott's will for her. Now, to her utter surprise, the day had arrived.

Her wedding day. The thought still confounded her, delighted her, and raised her up.

The decision to allow Elijah and her to marry in February had been met with delight by their families. Loads of folks from Bliss Creek had arrived the previous day. Her parents, Mattie and Abel, her brothers and their fraas, Annie and Isaac, Helen and Gabriel, Josiah and Miriam and all the others. They would have to eat in shifts. With no fields to plant or gardens to tend in the dead of winter, Luke, Thomas, and Silas had seen no reason to make them wait almost an entire year until the more traditional wedding season. No new snow had followed in the last few weeks so the roads were clear. The visit that had been curtailed at Thanksgiving would be recouped now, in February.

For all this, she was deeply grateful. Elijah didn't want to wait and neither did she. She wanted to begin her life as Elijah's fraa before another day passed. As husband and wife, they would build their new home together in the spring. The promise of this new beginning made it hard for her to sit still. She wanted to run to it now. Though still burdened by her crutches, she would run. Embrace it now. Embrace him now. She breathed and tried to focus on Luke's sermon, on pace to last a good two and a half hours.

Unable to contain herself, she sneaked a glance at Leah, who sat next to her, Jebediah on her lap. She looked the picture of the happy mother and wife. The sessions with the doctor in Jefferson City were helping. Each day a little rounder with the baby she carried, Leah didn't talk about her illness or the treatment, but she looked like a woman at peace. She smiled at Bethel and leaned closer. "Nervous?" She kept her voice a whisper.

"Nee." Bethel put a hand to her mouth to shield the whispered words from the others around them. "Not as nervous as Luke was about conducting his first wedding."

They exchanged smiles. Luke had paced the floor for hours the previous evening, deep in thought, but this morning the delivery of the long sermon based on the first verses of Genesis had been made without faltering.

"Elijah and Bethel, come forward."

Despite herself, she started at the sound

of her name. Leah stood and handed Jebediah to Mattie. Bethel was relieved to have her older sister as her witness. It made the walk to the front of the room easier knowing Leah followed. Her legs trembled now, when they had been sure and steady when she'd walked into the room hours earlier. Her mouth felt dry and her throat closed, making it hard to swallow. All gazes were on her as she pulled herself forward on her loathsome crutches. How she longed to throw them away and march to her destiny with a firm, determined stride. Instead her legs dragged behind as they always did. In seconds she would vow to be Elijah's wife, to care for him and cherish him and nevermore depart from him. Would he do the same for her? Should he be yoked with her until God separated them?

Gott's timing. Gott's plan. He would not forsake her now.

Her breathing ragged, she stumbled to a stop in front of Luke. Elijah had reached the front first, with Silas right behind him. His gaze met hers, his eyes full of an emotion guarded there for her only. Caught in the welling of love she saw there, she found she couldn't look away. She saw there in those blue eyes his love for her and his need for her. Without saying a word he'd already promised her to never leave her, to care for her, and to cherish her. If bodily sickness came to her, he would be there. As he was now, in this moment, taking her as his fraa, with a body that wouldn't obey her commands, but a heart full of the desire to be everything to him that a fraa should be.

He would be her helper.

And she would be his.

Luke's voice penetrated and the fog lifted. His face somber and his voice steady, he asked the questions and she answered them, but the vows between Elijah and her had already been made. The answers came easily.

The corners of his mouth tugging up in a suggestion of a smile, Luke took her hand and placed it in Elijah's. Her husband's hands were warm, his clasp firm. Their gazes held and Luke placed his big, callused hand over theirs.

"So then I may say with Raguel the God of Abraham, the God of Isaac, and the God of Jacob be with you and help you together and fulfill His blessing abundantly upon you, through Jesus Christ. Amen."

Elijah's hand tightened on hers. His face broke into a broad grin.

"Amen."

She grinned back. "Amen."

Bethel and Elijah faced their friends and family as one. Each made whole by the other. Bethel let the crutches fall to the floor and stepped into the circle made by her husband's arm. He would hold her up and she him.

"Amen."

DISCUSSION QUESTIONS

1. Bethel Graber believes she needs to be healed of her back injury in order to be a proper wife and mother, so she prays to God that her affliction be healed. She prays, she goes to physical therapy, she does everything she can to get better . . . and yet her disability remains. Have you ever prayed for a healing you didn't receive? How did you feel about it? Why do you think God sometimes gives us an answer that is different from the one we wanted?

2. Elijah Christner spent years helping his parents through illnesses late in their lives. Most people would see that as admirable. Bethel doesn't want Elijah's help. She sees it as pity and her disability as a weakness. Is her attitude fair? How do we as a society see people with disabilities? What does God's decision not to heal her disability

teach her about her attitude toward herself, marriage, and Elijah?

3. How is Bethel's attitude toward Shawn and his disability different from her attitude toward her own disability? Why do you think that is?

4. If you were in Bethel's shoes, would you have made the same choice when it came to Elijah and Shawn? What qualities did you admire in each man? Did they have any qualities that would make them undesirable as life mates? Do you agree with Bethel's decision to make the choice based on her faith and community rather than her feelings about Shawn?

5. Leah's family and friends chalk up her behavior to her personality. Do you ever judge people's actions without delving deeper to see what might be going on in their lives to cause that behavior? How might Leah's situation have been different if family members or friends had spoken to her sooner?

6. Leah is caught between postpartum depression, which prevents her from being a happy mother and wife, and the expectations of her husband, family, and faith.

Have you ever experienced a situation where what you feel is different from what you believe your faith demands? How did you react?

7. What role do you think Luke played in Leah's predicament? How could he have handled the situation differently within the confines of his faith and upbringing?

8. Leah doesn't tell Luke how she is feeling or even that she is expecting a child again. Luke doesn't ask her if something is wrong. He doesn't tell her how he's feeling about her behavior. What are the consequences of their lack of communication? What steps should a husband and wife take to ensure they are communicating about important events in their lives and the feelings that go with those events?

9. In Romans 12:12 Paul says God told him to be "joyful in hope, patient in affliction, faithful in prayer." How difficult is it for you to be patient when you have an illness or other problem that needs healing? What can you do to become more joyful in this process of learning to trust God's plan for you? Do you sometimes pray and expect God to take care of things ASAP? How

do you feel when he doesn't?

10. In 2 Corinthians 12:9, Paul reports that God told him his grace is sufficient and his power is made perfect in weakness. Do you find it difficult to accept weakness in yourself? What can we do to see ourselves through God's eyes and not the world's?

ABOUT THE AUTHOR

Kelly Irvin is a Kansas native and has been writing professionally for 30 years. She and her husband, Tim, make their home in Texas. They have two children, three cats, and a tankful of fish. A public relations professional, Kelly is also the author of two romantic suspense novels and writes short stories in her spare time. To learn more about her work, visit www.kellyirvin.com.

To learn more about books by Kelly Irvin or to read sample chapters, log, on to our website: www.harvesthousepublishers.com